HERE AND NOW AND THEN

MIKE CHEN

mira

mira

ISBN-13: 978-0-7783-0898-0

Here and Now and Then

Copyright © 2019 by Mike Chen

For questions and comments about the quality of this book, please contact us at CustomerService@Harlequin.com.

BookClubbish.com

Printed in U.S.A.

Praise for *Here and Now and Then*

"Clever, thrilling and full of heart, it is an instant sci-fi classic."
—*Hypable.com*

"In this heartfelt and thrilling debut, Chen revitalizes the trope of the absent and unavailable father... Chen's concept is unique, and [his characters'] agony is deeply moving. Quick pacing, complex characters, and a fascinating premise make this an unforgettable debut."
—*Publishers Weekly*, starred review

"This gripping, fast-paced time-travel thriller is also a warm, moving story of a man pulled between two lives and families. With plenty of humor and suspense, Chen has crafted an original and captivating story."
—*Shelf Awareness*, starred review

"Chen carefully balances heart, humor, and precise world building to bring alive an emotional and genre-bending story."
—*Booklist*

"[An] enjoyable venture into time travel.... Although Chen's novel is set in a futuristic world, it is ultimately about the bond between a father and his daughter. While Kin's dilemma is one that readers will never face, they will be drawn in by the human questions at its heart."
—*BookPage*

"At its core, Chen's book is really about the prides and perils of parenthood, and I'm certain that's what I'll always remember about it.... The plot twists and turns in speedy, page-flipping style, defying me each time I thought I knew what was coming. But even more than these delightfully surprising turns, the novel's strength lies in Kin's actions as he tries to save [his daughter,] Miranda."
—*NPR*

"A compelling, sensitive, innovative story... A glorious read that filled my heart and kept me turning pages, all the way to its poignant and satisfying conclusion."
—*20somethingreads.com*

Look for Mike Chen's next novel,
A BEGINNING AT THE END,
available soon from MIRA Books.

For Amelia

HERE AND NOW AND THEN

PROLOGUE

No pulse beat beneath the skin.

Kin concentrated, waiting for the familiar *thump* to barely register with his senses. Not his heartbeat, but something equally important: a Temporal Corruption Bureau retrieval beacon, one fine-tuned to his specific biometrics.

After twenty-eight assignments over eight years, the implanted beacon's soft pulse usually faded into the background, another subtlety of time travel that was simply part of the job. Like one's own heartbeat, it was one of those things that went unnoticed until it vanished. Now it was gone.

And with it, his return ticket to 2142.

Kin unwrapped the bandage, ignoring the burning pain through his abdomen as he tore the fabric off. His fingers found the dried green edge of binding gel and peeled the adhesion away from the gunshot's entry point beneath his ribs. He carefully collected any dried gel fragments in a motel towel to be burned later—even in his roughest shape, he always adhered to timeline corruption protocols. No need for nosy 1996 janitorial staff to find future medical tech, even after usage.

The bright LED numbers on the wood-trim clock radio across the motel room showed that eight hours and four minutes had passed since his encounter. He could still feel the factory rooftop gravel digging into the back of his neck while wrestling his target, a time-traveling merc who'd been hired to delay a senator's husband, causing her to miss a vote on a seemingly benign banking regulation that would actually have decades of negative consequences. They'd engaged, his arms and legs locking hers in a vise hold before she managed to grab a brick fragment and smash his kneecap.

Now his fingers gripped the bathroom sink's rim and he steadied himself, his left knee refusing to carry much weight.

A brick to the knee and a boot to the ribs. Then a gunshot, not from a plasma discharger but an era-appropriate semiautomatic pistol.

The target's smirk still burned in his memory, the slightest of smiles visible through thin moonlight. For a flash, he'd wondered why she found their encounter amusing, but when the gun's barrel slid down from his forehead to the implanted retrieval beacon, he knew.

Stranding him, it seemed, was a crueler twist than murder.

Kin cursed himself for letting her get the better of him, for trusting his gut instead of the endless intel notes provided by the TCB.

She'd let her guard down a few seconds later, which was the only opening he needed, adrenaline powering a takedown. The sickening crunch of a snapped neck brought on both relief and self-loathing, typical rushes that came with TCB Protocol Eight Ninety-Six:

In case of life-threatening resistance, field agents are authorized to eliminate the target in lieu of apprehension.

Mission accomplished. Now what?

Kin racked his brain, searching through memories of processes, protocols, and training, anything that might give some insight into what happened when the beacon went offline. But the endless list of technical specifications and failsafe details offered little comfort, things field agents memorized for no good reason, really.

Except there *was* a good reason: the beacon never went offline. It couldn't. Not while he was alive.

Assess and execute, he told himself. Processes, lists, mental visualization, his mind's eye sorted it all using years of agent training. Kin's hand pressed firmly against the wound, waiting for the slightest of tremors to register across his palm. Blood oozed out, bright red slipping between his dark brown fingers and running down his shirtless side. One drop hit the bathroom tile of the motel room safe house, then another and another. "Temporal Crimes field agent I-D-R-one-five, code E-six, interface active." The activation phrase given at the end of every mission.

Two minutes passed, a hundred and twenty frozen moments.

Kin waited, then repeated the activation phrase. One second ticked by, then another and a third. Everything after became a blur; he stared, eyes squinting, awaiting the holographic projection with tactile interface, what *always* appeared when he said the activation phrase.

He could *see* the holo now: the blue-and-orange semitransparent lines with a simple input/output display floating a few inches from his face. He could feel the tactile *thump* response of the virtual keyboard while entering in mission status codes and confirmation thumbprint signature.

But only in his head. No holo interface, no ability for end-of-mission transmission to the Mission Control war room.

Kin grabbed a small black rectangle from his first-aid kit. "Vital measurement scan," he said, and a hologram of letters and numbers floated in front of him, broadcasting his body temperature (slightly elevated due to injury), heart rate (same), hydration level (dehydrated), respiratory rate (normal), and blood pressure (steady). All of that should have coordinated with the beacon to confirm his identity and fuel its thermal-generated power source.

A thin black stick popped out of the device with a quick hydraulic hiss. He gripped the plasma scalpel, palm wrapped around the cylinder so tight that his hand throbbed. Two inches above the gunshot wound. Then a diagonal line about eight inches down, held at a slight angle inward.

In theory, if the beacon had even a flicker of power coursing through it, removing it would fire an emergency retrieval signal to a Mission Control tracking system in 2142 as its final shutdown act, a trigger upon exposure to raw air.

Kin ignited the scalpel, the stench of burning flesh harsher than the gradual burn into his skin.

But if the beacon was totally dead, he'd have a gaping wound on top of his existing injuries. Not ideal conditions for patching up ad hoc surgery, especially with a lack of basic medical supplies.

The scalpel retracted its thin beam of heat.

Towel. Water. Pressure. Binding gel. For now, he bandaged the wound while considering the next logical step. Two more days in 1996 until the end of his two-week mission span, two more days in 2142 before Mission Control scanned for a retrieval signal. Normally, he appreciated the TCB's strict scheduling, a one-for-one policy that prevented field agents from appearing to age at an accelerated rate. Now that just meant two more days of asking what-ifs.

When the TCB failed to detect a signal from his beacon, common sense dictated they'd pick him up and bring him home. Even without the beacon's geopositioning, access to all of the digital records in human history made this easy.

That had to be it. They wouldn't leave him here.

Would they?

His wound bound and cleaned, Kin sank his naked back against the bathroom wall. He slid down and let out a breath, an oppressive weight collapsing down on his chest.

A new option appeared in his mind, the only one left: stay calm, wait, and see.

An unknown future. The thought gripped every muscle in his body. Kin's groan echoed off the thin, dirty walls of the motel bathroom, and though this room had harsh lighting, his eye caught something behind the toilet. Despite the burn in his side and stinging in his knees, Kin reached, gut cramping from the wound, and he slid the object into view while fighting off the slight tremble taking over his hand.

A penny.

A quiet laugh fought past the pain spidering throughout his battered body, past the fears he didn't want to acknowledge. The most worthless piece of physical currency in 1996. Or a sign of something else.

He grasped the coin, his fingers curled into a fist, pressing so hard the edges dug into his skin. A calm came over him, his breath returning to normal and his heartbeat slowing to a regular rhythm. It had to be something, this one little sign of his past—or his future, depending on perspective.

Hope. Of course. What else would a penny be to him?

CHAPTER 1

K in Stewart used to be a time-traveling secret agent.
Eighteen years ago, give or take a few months. At least that's what his instincts told him. But even now, he wasn't sure where he was or what just happened, let alone *who* he was supposed to be.

His eyes opened.

Lights. Light, and a hard pavement. Aching in his knees. Cold on his cheek, his ear.

A car horn.

Then voices. Two female voices, muffled but gradually coming through, one distinctly younger than the other, speaking at urgent clips.

"Kin? Kin! Are you okay?" the older one said.

"Should I call nine-one-one?" the younger one said, panic wrapping each word.

"Come on, come on, get up. Can you hear me?"

"What about a doctor?"

The world blinked into focus. He closed his eyes, took in several breaths, then pushed himself to remember.

Something must have knocked him out. Cold fingers touched his face, and agent instincts immediately kicked in.

From the way the fingers felt, he calculated the angle of the hand. His peripheral vision picked up two kneeling silhouettes—they were behind him. He was on the floor, facedown. Prone. He had to get to safety. But where?

His hand flew up, pushing the fingers away, and he rolled a full circle, shoulders to back to shoulders again until propping himself on his knees, arms in a defensive position.

Two terrified faces stared back at him. Around them, sparkles in his vision flashed and tracked with his eye movement.

Heather, still in office attire with her long red hair hanging down, one arm extended and hand open. His wife.

Miranda, standing slightly behind her in her high school soccer uniform, concern tinting her wide eyes. His daughter.

And the blind spots, like fireworks everywhere he looked, another symptom that arrived shortly after a blackout.

His mind registered Miranda's fear. Heather's concern. He'd had another fainting spell and he needed to reassure them, even though his wobbly frame barely stood. He projected a smile, not a huge one, but one grounded in warmth, a father and husband offering comfort through a single expression despite the tornado whirling inside him.

"I'm okay, guys. I'm okay. I just…" The dull aches in his knees lit into a sudden burning, causing him to buckle ever so slightly. The pounding in his temples thumped to its own rhythm. Daylight from the open garage door blinded with an overwhelming intensity, and the rumble of Heather's idling car filled his ears. "I must have just tripped."

Miranda leaned over to her mom. "I think we should call a doctor," she said. "This is the third time this month."

Her voice was low, but Kin still heard it. He had to put them at ease, especially his daughter. "It's fine. I promise, let me get my bearings. See?" He straightened past the aches and muscle spasms firing up and down his body. "I'm good."

"Miranda, I know you have to go. I'll help Dad out."

"Okay." The fourteen-year-old reached into the car and grabbed a backpack and gym bag before approaching. "I hope you're okay, Dad."

"I am. I'm fine, sweetie." He put his arm out, and she half leaned into his attempted hug. "I'll get started on dinner soon. Lasagna tonight. My own recipe. Adding a layer of quinoa for texture." The sentence finished, prompting details to flood his mind. Years of training and missions had informed his mental muscle memory to scan every scene and identify all variables, so much so that he couldn't shake it during the simpler tasks of cooking and garage cleanup. He visualized the recipe, steps and ingredients superimposing in his mind's eye, along with projected cook times and the bubbling cheese of a perfect lasagna, something he hoped worthy of TV's *Home Chef Challenge*—if he ever got the nerve to audition.

Kin looked at Heather, who offered her usual smirk and subtle eyeroll whenever he prattled on about recipes, and Miranda, who shot a worried glance back at him while rolling her bike out of the garage.

Now all that training was used for family mode—and he wouldn't have it any other way.

"Wait—the four questions."

Whatever concern Miranda had seemed to slip away, a crinkled brow arriving instead. Kin fired off the first of the four questions asked whenever she went out. "Where are you going?"

"Tanya's. To work on our programming project." The answer arrived with slanted lips and weight shifting back and forth. He'd happily take irked teen disrespect over a worried daughter at this point.

"Who's going to be there?"

"Just Tanya. And Tanya's parents."

"When will you be home?"

"Seven-ish. It's—" Miranda glanced at the wall clock "—three forty right now. So in time to try your lasagna."

"In case of emergency—"

"You can call to check on me. I'll have my phone. Good?"

"All right. Don't forget, it's first-Monday-of-the-month TV night."

Miranda turned with barely a nod. She glanced at her parents, forming the inscrutable mask that appeared more and more these days. Heather beamed out a smile at their daughter before looking his way, the anxious creases returning. "I'll pull the car in," Heather said. Kin nodded, still rubbing his head, and Heather went back to the idling sedan. As the car rolled forward, a crunch echoed in the space, and something fired out from beneath the tire.

Kin tried to focus, examining where the sound originated and the possible debris trajectory only to catch a sudden flicker of blue light and a high-pitched burst of sound. Perhaps some post-blackout symptoms lingered.

Heather opened the car door, but stopped half a step out. "Oh no," she whispered loud enough for him to hear. A dour line formed across her mouth and she picked up a ping-pong-sized chrome sphere off the garage floor. "Not this. You were looking at this thing again?"

A Temporal Corruption Bureau retrieval beacon. Mostly

smooth outer chrome shell with bits of technological cuts and grooves in it, along with one gaping bullet hole. (Heather once called it a cross between a Death Star and a Borg sphere; he took her word for it rather than look it up.) Voice activated, holographic interface. Once implanted into his body, right beneath his rib cage.

Those details remained while other facts disappeared. Maybe because he bore the self-surgery scars to prove it.

Pain stung the side of his head, in and out like a sewing needle.

Kin remembered now. Some ten, fifteen minutes ago, he'd pulled it out from his toolbox beneath a stack of wrenches and stared at it, trying to will memories into existence.

"It's like when I first met you. The headaches and forgetting. Things were good for so long. Why is this back? Why is it getting worse?"

Kin wanted to tell the truth: when they first met, memories of 2142 and the TCB were still disappearing. His brain eventually reached an equilibrium between his past and present around the same time their relationship blossomed. After that, symptoms appeared only when forcing memories.

Until recently.

"Six months ago..." he started. He needed to say *something*. Revert to the long-standing cover story of an ex-military life and ongoing PTSD? Or finally reveal that it felt like his few remaining agent memories were fading to the same black hole that swallowed up his memory of whoever he was prior to meeting her? That staring at the beacon was an attempt to trigger proof that he wasn't going mad?

That would sound totally insane. Especially to an already-worried wife. His focus turned to the dead beacon in his hand, its futuristic alloy surviving a bullet from years ago and now apparently Heather's car.

"Come back to me, Kin. Family is here. Metal thingy is there. What is it about this?" Heather's voice was soft. "I've found you passed out three times with it. You're obsessed."

"It's only some old work equipment." He set the beacon down on an adjacent shelf. "I was seeing if I could fix it."

"It can't be a coincidence. Please get rid of it. Throw it away." Out of nowhere, she winced, eyes tightening and teeth biting into her bottom lip, hand at her temple. He reached over to her, but she turned away. "I'm fine. It's just been a long day and I still have calls to make." Heather was an attorney, a career that brought her pride and stress in equal measure.

"Hey, you're the one telling *me* to go to the doctor."

"Seriously, I'm fine. Other than all these client briefs I have to review." Her serious expression broke into a wry grin, putting a different kind of weight on his mind. She took his free hand, her pale fingers contrasting against his. "Look at us. Bickering about who goes to the doctor first for headaches. Like an old married couple."

"Give us the senior discount, already, huh?"

"Well, I think these—" Heather touched his face, pointing at the creases around his mouth "—and this," she said, stroking the flecks of gray in his hair and tapping his glasses, "make you look distinguished."

"You, too," he said, his tone light.

"You're supposed to say I don't look a day over twenty-five," Heather replied with a laugh. "Don't blame *that* on the headaches." She gave him a playful shove, though the change in balance brought his hands to his head. "Sorry. Sorry, sorry."

"It's okay. It's okay, really." Kin stood, wiping the oncoming sweat off his forehead before his wife could notice. "I'll be fine."

"Please. Get rid of that thing. Look," she said, her tone dropping into serious territory, "your headaches, your memory lapses. They scare me. Miranda is worried sick. Finding you like this doesn't make things better." She took his hand. "You need to get help."

"I'm fine. I had a CAT scan years ago. There's nothing wrong."

"You're not hearing me. We can't live like this. It's weighing on Miranda. She's clamming up. Get help. Maybe it's anxiety or something. Something about this—" she grabbed the beacon "—is giving you panic attacks. I don't know why. Maybe it's subconscious. Reminds you of the orphanage. Or the special forces. PTSD, it's common for ex-soldiers wounded in combat."

Heather's pleas meant that Kin's cover story still stood, even now. He just didn't know if that was a good or bad thing anymore. "I don't want to talk about that. Those were bad years."

"That's *why* you need to talk about them. I mean, what happens if you fainted again and smacked your head on something and died? I'd have to learn to cook and I'm not about to start that at thirty-eight." She laughed, pulling him in, her long arms wrapped around him, drawing him toward her tall frame. "There's no stigma to PTSD these days. It's very real. You can get help."

PTSD. How could he possibly explain to a doctor that his brain suffered from residual time-travel fragments, not PTSD? "So says the tax attorney?"

"I've been Googling it between meetings."

Kin looked at the beacon, his eyes tracing the scored ridges exposing the device's core. "One more incident and I'll go. Okay?"

"Oh, Kin," she said, blowing out a sigh. They remained

in their embrace, only she deflated, sinking into him, her sharp chin digging into his shoulder. "Why are you fighting me on this? It's gotten worse each month."

"I'm not fighting. I got it covered."

He said it with the conviction of epiphany, of a step so obvious that he couldn't believe he'd ever missed it. Of all the planning and processing, lists, and visualizations, how did this option never surface before?

Let the past go.

"But you're right. If there's still a problem, I'll see someone."

Heather must have sensed the change, the unconscious knowing that only came with years of marriage. Her forehead pushed against his, their noses touching. "You are one stubborn bastard," she said, affection wrapping the words, "and I love you for it."

"Thought you loved me for my cooking."

"You found me out." She topped off their embrace with a kiss before stepping back and glancing at the empty driveway. "I'm gonna work on a brief until dinner. No more metal thing. Okay?" Heather disappeared into the house, footsteps echoing through the garage walls as she went upstairs, followed by the *thump-thump-thump* of a dog rushing behind her. He stood in silence, his eyes slowly turning back to the damaged future tech.

It wasn't worth it anymore. Not when it scared his family.

Kin didn't even know why he held on to the scrap. Maybe his subconscious sought hard evidence of his prior life. Or perhaps his stories about the orphanage and special forces and the cross-country trek were reality and the TCB was the fantasy. That would explain why he couldn't remember parents, friends, girlfriend, anything specific from his supposed future life.

Either way, it didn't matter. Kin grabbed the beacon, marched out the side door to the large black garbage bin, and dunked it in.

There was no future. There was only the present.

Kin returned to the garage, though he paused when something in the driveway caught his eye.

A deliveryman. Complete in work boots, brown shorts and shirt, tablet in his hands. Young, maybe midtwenties. Yet no package. No truck. Only a small backpack.

And a stare. A wide-eyed stare usually reserved for disbelief.

Wasn't the driveway empty seconds ago?

"Can I help you?"

The man continued looking at him, and though they locked eyes, an irresistible urge drew Kin's focus away, forcing him to avert his gaze. Probably residual mental shrapnel from the beacon. "You looking for an address?"

The deliveryman started and stopped several times, only fractions of sound coming through before he looked down at the tablet. "I gotta start dinner," Kin said, "so, if you don't need anything, I'm going to close up."

The man hesitated, then shook his head. "Sorry, my mistake," he said in a crisp English accent before walking off.

The garage door rolled down, dwindling sunlight bouncing off Heather's car's side mirror and catching a weathered penny taped up above his workbench, something he'd carried with him since he could remember. The mere sight of it draped calm over him despite the afternoon chaos. He marched over and without thinking, he kissed his fingers and planted them on the penny, his lucky penny, the action so reflexive he barely remembered it.

He considered one last look at the beacon, one final visit with the future. The gesture seemed moot, especially since he had a new lasagna recipe to try. He might even use it for a *Home Chef Challenge* audition.

After all the trouble caused by his old life across eighteen years, saying goodbye came with a sigh of relief. With the past behind him, anything was possible.

CHAPTER 2

Kin remained silent.

He would have said something if he could have, but the mother/daughter battle unfolding in front of him rendered him speechless.

A few minutes before they'd called Miranda down to dinner, Heather pulled him aside and said she knew a way to get her to open up, to lighten the mood after the afternoon. "Stop overthinking things and just serve. I'll handle the rest." He obliged, unsure of what to expect.

They ate at half his speed, all while Heather and Miranda debated, voices growing louder and hands getting more animated. Heather occasionally went out with her so-called "geek friends" for movie nights. Was this what they discussed?

"And Janeway *crashes the ship*," Miranda said complete with hand gestures, "to restore the timeline. You can't top that."

"It's good. It's up there, I agree. But I'm sorry," she said. "In terms of self-sacrifice, you're never going to top Spock. 'The needs of the many outweigh the needs of the few.' That is science fiction at its best. That list I read today agrees with me."

"Oh, come on. They write those things so people like us argue over it."

"It's working, right?" Heather finally resumed eating the lasagna, her fork clinking against the plate. "Tell you what. Tonight we watch *Star Trek II* for First Monday. Tomorrow, we'll watch those *Voyager* episodes. Bonus family viewing." Heather gave Kin a knowing look, her lawyer's strategy plotted out from the first word to the final punchline of squeezing in some family time with Miranda. "And then we'll revisit the argument."

Miranda gave a mock groan that turned into a laugh, and both mother and daughter turned to him. "What do you think?" Heather asked.

"Dad fell asleep the last time we watched *Star Trek II*."

For most of her life, Miranda had been a daddy's girl, tagging along with a soccer ball in tow or sitting with him during early morning Premier League matches broadcast straight from England. But in the past two years or so, there'd been a gradual shift, like all the sci-fi seeds Heather planted long ago suddenly sprouted. Now she and her mother spoke in a vocabulary he couldn't even understand. A twinge of jealousy surfaced, enough for him to needle his way into the conversation despite knowing better. "You know, I've recorded the Arsenal/Tottenham match. I bet Miranda would much rather watch that. Am I right or am I right?" Kin looked at his daughter, though rather than seeing the expected nod of approval, her eyes darted back and forth between her parents. "Miranda?"

Tension filled the dining room table, something far too palpable for a simple TV debate. Heather's brow wrinkled with a concern heavier than it should have been.

"Actually, I had a suggestion." Miranda quietly offered.

"Remember, this week's match is huge. Arsenal can take over first—"

"I was going to say we try *Doctor Who*. I know Mom will like it." Her eyes dropped to her plate, aimed directly at the small piece of remaining garlic bread. "You might, too, Dad."

"I don't think I'll ever get—"

Heather's voice came with a quiet persuasion, eyes staying solely on their daughter despite speaking to him. "Maybe we should try Miranda's suggestion."

Miranda continued looking down. Even Bamford, who'd been snoring away in her dog bed, seemed to go quiet. Heather's phone began vibrating violently on the table, an insistent buzz that caused the flatware to dance against the dishes. "It's the firm," she said, looking at the small screen. "I gotta take this. But *Doctor Who* sounds good. I keep hearing about it." Heather's voice gradually disappeared as she made her way to the home office upstairs, her tone shifting into an efficient professionalism that seemed at odds with the woman who was just debating *Star Trek* as a means of family bonding.

"Dad, this show. It's about…" Miranda's warbled voice trailed off and Kin noticed her taking short, quick breaths. "It's about *time travel*."

Miranda's mention prompted a different physical response from his usual time-fragment headaches, not quite the usual pounding temples, but a tight chest and tighter jaw.

What was she implying?

"I'm, uh…" The very fact that Miranda brought up time travel in such a direct and pointed way left Kin speechless.

Miranda glanced down the hall, then finally returned her dad's look. "Dad." Miranda paused. "I have a confession to make. I hope you're not mad."

Anger was the last thing on Kin's mind. Fear stood out, reminiscent of his early days here, constantly looking over his shoulder, wondering if the TCB would come and rescue him—or if he might be considered a temporal fugitive himself for breaking the agency's noninterference protocol. The exact protocol remained muddy, but it was definitely bad for anyone to know about the secret agency's existence—in this era or 2142. "I'm not mad." He set his chopsticks on the plate. "I'm glad you're being honest with me."

Miranda nodded, though she continued looking away. "Mom doesn't know this but I found your notebook. The one in your workbench. I was looking for a screwdriver the other day. You know how you're so weird about your tools?" Weird must have been teen speak for practical, since his tools were arranged by function, size, and frequency of use. Like how he arranged his cooking utensils, his work desk, his sock drawer, all of it felt instinctual, part of the very core of his being. "I noticed one drawer was messy, junk just thrown in there. I looked at it for a laugh but then I noticed a notebook in there."

It took several seconds for Kin to realize—to remember—what Miranda was talking about.

The notebook. His journal.

The epiphany caused a jabbing pain against his skull, forcing him to steady himself.

He'd completely forgotten it, how he'd pulled it out some six months ago, studying it in the garage to restore lost details. He'd fought off the oncoming headaches, desperate to mine specifics of his missing past.

It didn't work, as if his body didn't want him to remember. Then sometime during the last few weeks, that moment also evaporated from his brain. Until now.

A flush burned Kin's cheeks; ironically, his mind went full agent mode, visualizations of response options.

Including a new one, one he hadn't considered in any conversation over the last eighteen years: tell her the truth.

Before he picked, Miranda spoke. "I thought you should know I liked it." The color drained from her face, a grayish tan rather than the usual light brown. "I mean, I never knew you wrote science fiction. You don't watch any of our shows."

Science fiction. She thought the journal was filled with tales, like her *Doctor Who* or Heather's *Star Trek* shows. Yet they weren't fiction, they were details of a very real future: case histories, equipment specs, protocols, any facts he possibly recalled in a mad scramble to document things before his brain erased them. That ink had dried about sixteen years ago, shortly before he'd met Heather.

After he'd met her, searching for lost memories seemed as important as old tools in a junk drawer.

Kin's whole body relaxed, from his shoulders down to his toes. "Ah, that." More options came up, ways to spin the tale without going much deeper. "I took a class shortly before I met Mom. I don't know if you'd call a bunch of notes 'writing.' I wasn't very good at it. I didn't even tell her about it."

"Your details, they were so specific. Like you were there, seeing it all." Miranda's uncertainty turned into a broad grin. "It was awesome. 'Temporal Corruption Bureau.' Scaling boots for climbing buildings. Plasma dischargers. Branches around the world. Weird sciency stuff about how time travel works. 'Sphere of influence,' 'tentpole events,' how did you even come up with all that? It's like the world-building stuff my teacher was talking about. 'First you code something fun, then you build a world around it to make people care.'" Her eyes narrowed as she turned away to look out the window. "You should write more."

Kin's mind zeroed in on one option, the only option in this case: change the subject as fast as possible. "I don't know. I did that a long time ago. I barely remember it. Wasn't really my thing. I took up cooking instead."

"No, I mean you should *write* more." She faced him, seriousness carved in that seemed decades older than her fourteen years. "I was excited when I found it. I thought you might have found a new way to, you know, express yourself. Because you should write more."

"Cooking is much—"

"To help your PTSD." Miranda's eyes lingered, bringing an extra weight to her words before she looked down again. "They say that writing is therapeutic for healing trauma."

Her words stopped him cold. This wasn't about a cool fictional time-travel world. The fear from earlier, her concern over the headaches and fainting, this was Miranda's way to turn anxiety into hope. He wished he could hold her the way he did when she was a newborn, when a swaddle wrap and father's arms were enough to soothe her.

"Who says that?"

"Google." Miranda continued to look away. "I searched for it."

"You and Mom both, huh?" Kin reached over and squeezed his daughter's shoulder, his voice low. "You shouldn't concern yourself with those types of things."

"I'm fourteen. I know how the world works. I can tell, your symptoms are getting worse."

"I'll be fine."

"I worry about you." Miranda's hand landed on top of his. "The blackouts, the memory stuff. It's, like, all gotten worse in the past few months. Bad things happen when you don't treat PTSD. I mean, what would we do if something happened to you? Have you tasted Mom's cooking?"

"Mom worries about the cooking part, too." They both laughed, though Kin blinked back a sudden rush of tears. He was pretty sure Miranda did, too.

"I mean, what bad stuff could have caused all this?"

"I know I don't talk about my past much." His admission came with a heavy sigh.

"You never do. I always thought it was 'I could tell you but I'd have to kill you' stuff. But I really think you need to get it out of your system. In real life or in fiction. Or talk to someone. Like, a therapist." Her lips trembled, the next few words barely making it out. "Or, you know, me."

The fake specifics were cemented into his mind, repeated so many times that he practically believed them. The false Social Security number and identity that he'd paid for so many years ago probably even registered as official. Even if the details came from fiction, they were fact now. That was all that mattered.

"Maybe sometime we can go get some dessert and...try. You and me."

When was the last time she'd opened up like this? Had she ever?

Or maybe he'd never noticed before. His whole life since getting stranded in 1996 was spent protecting himself from the past. But here, in this moment with Miranda, he'd let his guard down in a foreign, almost unnatural way.

It was great.

"Listen." Kin turned to his daughter, meeting her eye to eye. "I made a promise to Mom and I'm making it to you, too—the dizzy spells, the fainting, all that stuff, it will stop. I know it's gotten worse. Trust me when I say that I also know—" he hesitated, picturing the beacon buried safely away in the garbage can "—where a lot of this comes from."

He left out the part about not knowing why some memories remained headache-free while others crippled him, why some headaches were worse than others, why some involved nausea and others just beat his skull into submission. It didn't matter. In the end, it all held him back from what really counted.

"Traveling through time to capture bad guys?" Miranda said with a laugh.

"Yeah," Kin scoffed, "that's it. I used work for the Temporal Corruption Bureau." Though the words came out brightly, the very statement caused a spark up and down his spine, punctuated with the smallest twinge of a headache.

Kin vowed to himself that this was the last time he'd ever waste a breath or thought on the TCB again.

"It's behind me. For good." He had more important things to focus on. "Now, can you promise me something?"

"What's that?"

"Don't tell anyone about the journal. Especially Mom. It's embarrassing enough as it is. She didn't even know I took the class."

Kin held his hand out, and Miranda slapped him five like they used to when he was teaching her basics of soccer years ago. "Deal." She stood up, plate in hand, though she stopped halfway to the sink. Her mouth fell open and she angled her neck, looking out the window. "Dad?" The softness left her voice, replaced by urgency. "Someone's in the backyard."

Kin stood up and peered through the glass. Though dusk stole some visibility, Miranda was right: the silhouette of a man moved across the yard. Long-dormant instincts to target and pursue flickered to life, fusing with a relentless urge to protect his family. The man stayed close to the fence, and it took Kin only a second to realize that it was the mystery deliveryman from earlier.

CHAPTER 3

Adrenaline coursed through Kin, reactivating a spectrum of reflexes. While his mind didn't remember the specifics of 2142 or the TCB, his body retained muscle memory despite cumulative impact of age and injuries.

Knees bent. Head down. Arms tucked. Left foot. Right foot.

He crouch-walked around the front yard, gently placing one foot after another to minimize sound, his knees burning against the pressure.

Before he went outside, he'd told Miranda to not worry, go work on her project. He'd said it confidently too; given all the PTSD talk, the last thing he needed was for her or Heather to think he'd become paranoid to boot. With each step, the creeping caution melted away into an excitement, like popcorn exploding inside a bag.

He'd slipped out the front door to avoid detection, then locked it behind him. As he'd moved to the side yard and up to the gate, everything felt natural, his eyes darting corner to corner, searching for anything of note. The gate pushed open, Kin guiding it back against the post softly to avoid its usual creaky hinges. He took one step in, then another, then another until he hit the corner and peeked.

It *was* the man from before. The deliveryman, the one with the British accent and no package or truck. He stood next to the garbage can while looking at his tablet.

Intimidate. Approach. Observe. Wait. Surprise. Each had its merits, and in a few seconds, Kin whittled down the pros and cons. The options continued playing out, though a new one arrived: get inside, call the police, and lock the doors.

But the element of surprise won out. If he was going to get the jump on this guy, now was the time. The man began muttering to himself, and as he did, Kin took his first step out, angle of approach visualized in his mind. The man shook his head, then spoke inaudibly again. Suddenly, an orange glow materialized, a semitranslucent brightness floating in front of him.

Blood drained from Kin's face, his stomach a nest of butterflies trying to escape. His hand reached for the house to steady himself, the oncoming disorientation causing him to try twice before he succeeded.

Was that...?

Even in the purple hues of dusk, Kin saw the distinct outline of a holographic interface, and once the image registered in his mind, a stinging pain drilled into his temple, causing him to fall to his knees.

The man turned around and they locked eyes.

The urge to pass out rose and fell, crashing like waves against the beach. Kin's temples pounded, and he steadied himself with his palm planted flat into concrete.

The man approached, the holo dissolving away. He held his hand out as he took cautious steps forward. Kin urged his body to fight, to move and protect his family against this intruder, yet nothing worked. The very sight of the holo petrified him, the pain in his head throttling his ability to even think.

The man stopped, his scuffed work boots mere inches from Kin. He knelt and looked Kin square in the eye. "Agent Stewart?"

Agent? The last time someone called him that was, well, he couldn't remember. He absolutely couldn't remember. Those details evaporated from his mind years ago.

Kin tried to respond. No words managed to make it out.

"My god, Kin. What happened to you?"

The face. The voice. Even the man's posture as he knelt. It all seemed so familiar, an old photo album with the details blurred out. The more Kin looked, the worse the headache got, pressure mercilessly jackhammering his temples. "TCB?" he managed to eke out before all his limbs went numb.

"Looks like we're a little late," the man said. Kin's entire body froze, from his curled toes to his unblinking eyes. The man reached into his back pocket and pulled out a chrome tube. The tube's tip retracted with a hiss, revealing a short needle. "There's something I need to do."

"Dad?"

Miranda's question lingered as Kin's faculties returned. Unlike earlier, he didn't have to peel himself off the floor. Instead, he stood in the backyard, though he wasn't sure for how long.

The final rays of sunlight disappeared beyond the skyline of their suburban San Francisco neighborhood, leaving wisps of purple and pink among the gradually darkening orange. It'd been brighter just moments ago. Hadn't it?

He came out here. He saw the deliveryman. Something about him petrified all of Kin's senses. A headache, too. And a syringe.

And then a whirlwind of images, like he'd pounded the strongest coffee of all time, then chased it with an energy drink.

But where was the man now? He'd called him "Agent Stewart," hadn't he? He'd said something when he pulled out the syringe, or at least Kin thought so.

"Dad? Are you having another...problem?"

Kin blinked and turned to find Miranda in a tentative posture. Behind her, Bamford, their brindle greyhound stood, her ears alert like butterfly wings.

Bamford wasn't barking at any invading strangers. Miranda wasn't scared or hurt.

The man was TCB. He had to be. The holo interface, the chrome syringe. For what purpose?

Kin weighed his options and decided on calm. No need to worry Miranda. If they came to hurt him or his family, they would have already done it. He scanned the backyard again; no trace of the mystery man or anything out of the ordinary.

"No. No, not at all. I'm fine. I promise. Look," he said, pointing at the melting colors in the sky. "Just enjoying the view." Miranda lined up next to him, her lanky body leaning into his.

"It's pretty."

"Sometimes we take these things for granted."

"Yeah," she said quietly before turning to him. "Though,

my science teacher says that nice sunsets are because of pollution. Chemicals in the air."

"Well," Kin said as Bamford came up, her long nose demanding scratches with a nudge, "it still looks nice."

"Everything cool with the delivery guy?"

"Yeah. The delivery guy." Kin pulled specifics from his memory. The details were alive, vibrant; he could see the man's face now, from his sandy hair and fair complexion to the crook of his Roman nose. He could even hear the inflection of his accent. "He was told to put a package in the Sladens' backyard and couldn't get their gate open, so he tried it from our yard. That's all."

The memories didn't give him a headache.

That should have been a good thing. Instead, more questions rattled through his mind, and he told himself to *not* look confused in front of Miranda—especially since Heather just made her way out. "Am I missing something here?" she asked, a playful lilt back in her voice.

"A sunset."

"California sunsets." Heather came up behind Miranda, planting her hands on her daughter's shoulders. "It's because of pollution, you know."

Miranda shot a grin Kin's way.

"I'm done with work for tonight," Heather said. "Promise. So, time travelers?"

"Be right there. How about starting some popcorn?"

"Microwaves. *My* specialty," Heather said with a grin. Miranda grunted an affirmative, then turned around, her flip-flops making the noise they were named after. Heather and Bammy followed her in, the dog's nails clacking against the pavement.

Kin went the opposite direction, farther down the backyard to the garbage can where the man had been lurking about earlier. He lifted the lid and looked down.

The beacon was gone.

Kin reached in, pulling out plastic bag by plastic bag until the large bin was empty. A quick survey of the backyard showed no other signs of tampering. No patio chairs were moved, no plants were knocked over, even the ceramic turtle in the corner still sat in its place, a six-month ring of algae forming on the pavement around it. Nothing amiss but the vanished beacon.

Kin's back pocket buzzed, and he pulled out his phone to read the text that appeared. Except this message wasn't the office complaining about another hack to the Gold Free Games server.

It came from an unknown number.

9:30 AM at the Noble Mott Cafe. We need to talk.

He hadn't imagined things. This was real.

TCB had arrived from 2142.

CHAPTER 4

"You made it." The man reached over for a handshake.

Kin almost *didn't*. The night before had been a blur of staring at the ceiling waiting for some further sign of the TCB, followed by strange, too-real dreams of a mysterious woman silhouetted against the backdrop of a futuristic cityscape, something straight out of Heather's movie collection. After that, he'd spent all morning debating whether to show up for this clandestine meeting, while dodging questions from Heather about what was bothering him. Rather than go to work, he'd driven to a park two blocks away from Noble Mott Café and sat.

Ignore the text. Go to the meeting. Confront the man. Sneak up on him and knock him out. Lure him out for interrogation. Play along and act happy to see him.

Run. Pack up Heather, Miranda, and Bamford and run like hell.

The ultimate choice seemed logical: meet the man, find out what he wanted, then reassess. Then execute. And keep his emotions at bay. This required clarity.

Kin approached the café and then the table, keeping his arms at his side while he studied the man. Gone was the delivery uniform, the disguise of choice in residential areas, replaced by gray pants and a black jacket—standard-issue casual clothing for mission events in public places, a look that blended in easily during nearly any modern era.

He knew that. Where did he pick up that detail? And why wasn't his head pounding him into submission at remembering it?

"Okay, then," the man said, pulling his hand back. "Guess we're gonna have to work back up to that. Sorry about disappearing on you last night. I heard someone coming so I got out of there. Sit down." Processing the coffee shop interior, Kin noted four other people, three customers scattered along chairs and couches and one person behind the counter. All of them remained out of earshot, which probably was a good thing, what with the whole timeline corruption thing. If they overheard, would this man get a demerit on his record? "Agent visualization method, huh?"

Was it that obvious? Kin thought he still had all his agent skills, but time must have worn away his ability to be subtle. "I'm not sure what you're talking about."

"Right, the whole 'silently darting eyes' is actually you contemplating life, huh?" He laughed. "You field agents think you're so clever. 'Assess and execute,'" he said, his fingers forming quotes in the air. "You know what I love about era twenty-one-A?" He held up his paper coffee cup, a little dribble forming a dark brown trail down the side. "The coffee. So much better here. I only wish they wouldn't look at me strange when I asked for honey in it."

Coffee with honey. Heather hated the aroma of Kin pouring honey into his coffee. She wouldn't like cafés in the future. "So, you *are* TCB."

"And we're eighteen years late." The man's downturned mouth and low-pulled shoulders gave off an air of regret. Kin didn't need to be an active secret agent to figure that out. "Look at me. Really concentrate." The man pointed to his face. "You know this. It's just gotta wake up."

The details were the same as last night in the yard. And something new...

Markus. His name was Markus. Markus...something. A retriever agent.

Kin winced, almost out of reflex. He expected his temples to be pounding. Instead, no sudden tension took over, no stinging on the side of his head. He sat back in his chair, the ease of the memory causing a creeping anxiety. "Your name is Markus. People like you arrive when the mission ends. You verify the result and bring the time-jump accelerator to take us home."

"Good. No headache?"

"No."

"Anything to note since last night? More headaches, fewer headaches, dizzy spells?"

"I had a dream last night. It was vivid. Real. But distant." Flashes came back to him, details of the dream suddenly snapping into his mind's eye. A woman he didn't recognize, her random words played back—was that an English accent? Her face came into focus, round cheeks and expressive eyes and dark brown hair. Applause surrounded them, but from who? The way she looked at him with such certainty in her eyes—but why?

And a feeling. Of what specifically, he couldn't tell, but something tangible was there.

"REM sensitivity due to hyperactivity in the cerebral cortex. Side effect of this," Markus said, reaching into his bag on the floor. "Can you tell me what this is?"

Markus held up a thin chrome tube between his thumb and forefinger. The same thing he pulled out last night.

A metabolizer injection.

"Metabolizers. The injection slows the body's metabolism rate, reducing cell decay and extending the human life span to an average of…" Numbers flew through his mind, the details just out of reach. "Two hundred? Something like that. Annual long-form treatments starting at age eighteen. TCB agents get additional boosters to protect themselves against the body's reaction to time travel. Time-jumping without the additional boosters create a destabilizing effect on a cellular level." The words spilled out of Kin's mouth, an encyclopedia rattling off details without any filter. Another memory flashed through his mind, not of injections, but rather the page in his journal with notes on this. "That's why you look so young and I look the way I do." Markus nodded at the observation. "There was some more technical stuff behind it. I think I never learned it."

"Excellent. Yes, vivid dreams are part of the body's acclimation process to metabolizers. Your body's starting fresh. Memories will start to return. Can't say which ones or when, or even why some disappeared and some didn't. They have a theory about it, like why you may be missing some personal details."

Kin's eyebrow raised reflexively. "Try *all* personal details."

"All. Really?" Markus's complexion shifted, as did his balance in his seat. His mouth pursed and he looked everywhere in the room except at the person sitting across from him. "Well, if I knew what was happening in your brain, I'd be a rich doctor, not the guy who gives you a ride back to the future."

"You gave that injection to me. Last night."

"I did. And I'm sorry about the whole natural aging thing. You probably reverted to that about a year after you landed. Oh, and—" Markus reached into his bag again "—I did my job," he said, producing the missing beacon. "Except I usually retrieve the beacon by bringing the person home. Guess you could say it's an out-of-body experience." Markus's laughter at his own joke quickly stopped when Kin didn't react. "Anyway, that's a first. Congratulations, Kin, you'll be part of official training material from now on."

Benign details started to trickle back—facts, professional tidbits, bits and pieces that could have been taken from a dossier. Nothing about whether or not they were friends, though judging by Markus's polite-but-neutral demeanor, Kin figured not.

"Listen, I can't tell you anything. You have to awaken the memories yourself through exposure. Without metabolizers to support it, the human brain can't sustain two time periods. It buries the information, focusing only one era. Forcing it causes the headaches. Force it too much and it incapacitates you, creates seizures. Give the metabolizer some time. We should review any mission specifics you can remember. Think about it. I'm getting a pastry. You want anything?"

Kin refused to mention his weakness for chocolate chip cookies. Markus took the hint, then walked the long way around the coffee shop, keeping measured distance from anyone sitting at a table or a barista cleaning a spill. It reignited little tidbits of agent protocols—walk out of the path of others, only get in line when there's no one else around, avoid foot traffic as much as possible. All these rules, all designed to dance around being inserted into another time and minimize corruption on the job.

He buried his head in his hands for what seemed like minutes, partially to stem the oncoming torrent of awakening facts and figures and partially to squelch the panic that arrived when he thought about explaining this all to Heather.

"I got this for you," Markus said, putting a chocolate chip cookie in a folded napkin on the table.

Lucky guess.

"So, the target? Our political interloper?" Markus bit into his muffin with a satisfied *mmm*.

"Eliminated. Can't remember much."

"The beacon?"

"Damaged. The target shot me—shot the beacon while inside my body. I didn't have metabolizers to boost the healing process. It got infected. I felt its parts whenever I moved. It was remove it or let it take me down."

"The bullet must have hit the transmitter before emergency power sent the final ping. One-in-a-million shot. You had it removed? Black market doctor?"

"No. I cut it out of myself."

Kin couldn't tell if Markus's unblinking eyes meant he was horrified or impressed. Perhaps both.

"I broke into an animal hospital and stole anesthetic, painkillers, morphine, antibiotics, stitches, that sort of thing. Medicine in this era still requires external support. And then I sat down and did it. Half an inch beneath the skin, in the fatty tissue below the left rib cage. When I realized the TCB wasn't coming, I had to. Same reason I dismantled my equipment and got a job." Kin leaned back in his seat, trying not to show surprise at the vividness of his recall. "The beacon's dead. How did you locate it? How did you find me?"

"In my time, it's been two weeks since you left. Standard

detection span for your two-week mission. I came to work, activated the beacon sensor, and got a ping at this geotemporal location. Detected yesterday afternoon at sixteen forty-one. Right geography, wrong year, but we have to go to the point of detection. It's pretty beat-up, so something must have jarred one last transmission out of it."

Sixteen forty-one. Four forty-one in the afternoon. The garage. Heather's car. There was a flash and a high-pitched noise.

He'd dismissed it as headache fragments.

The car's impact must have mashed a circuit closed for a split second, just long enough to fire off a signal before becoming disabled again. "What if it never transmitted? If it stayed dead?"

"There are no instances of MIA agents since the subcutaneous beacon was introduced in 2122. Trust me, I looked last night. One hundred percent recovery rate. Emergency power, fail-safes, that sort of thing, even if the agent was killed. Before that, when it was an external device, the protocol for nontransmission was to send the retriever and a backup agent to the end-of-mission date and scout for anomalous activity, then bring the agent home."

"You mean if you didn't detect a signal from last night—"

"I would have showed up at the end of your mission span. Two weeks after you arrived in 1996. But because of the beacon signal, I had to come now, not then. We have our rules to follow."

"But...you know now. You know I've been stuck for eighteen years. Why not just jump back to 1996 and grab me?"

"That'd grandfather the mission. And you know how the TCB hates grandfathers. Besides, Paradox Prevention agents are really weird people." Grandfathers. It took a few seconds for Kin to grasp what he meant—a grandfather paradox. If the

TCB rescued him before Miranda, before Heather, arriving eighteen years ago with the knowledge they had now, that would have aborted the beacon ping sent from Kin's garage. This meant a theoretical chain reaction, preventing Markus from ever arriving, thus never discovering the information with the 1996 rescue information in the first place. They'd create a grandfather paradox, possibly undoing the space-time continuum and sending them all into oblivion. Or something like that; Kin never knew if that was merely bureaucratic obfuscation to keep mission planners and agents in line. "So, you'll have to answer for getting a job in this era. They'll run their temporal scans to check for any timeline deltas. As long as your presence hasn't killed presidents or toppled governments, you'll hopefully only get a stern lecture, debrief and full medical scan after the jump."

Mission details. Even with the metabolizer surfacing memories, getting together a debriefing would be difficult—

The jump?

Markus must have read the sudden change in his face. "I reported the situation after last night's encounter," he said, his words slowing down, "then waited for the metabolizer to kick in. Mission Control and the assistant director debated how to handle this. The AD decided to give you today to close out your affairs, remove your temporal footprint. Quit your job, give notice to your landlord. You should inform people that you're moving. Unexplained disappearances create more problems. Our Logistics team will also hack some records for final cleanup."

"Landlord?"

"Of the house you're renting. I assume, what, you've got the basement apartment of that family's home? Property ownership is a timeline corruption, obviously. You know the rules."

Kin's teeth gritted, grinding against each other. They didn't know. *Tell the truth. Lie. Avoid the question.* What would cause the least damage?

The truth was too important to lose out.

"I own it," he said at a deliberate pace, "with my wife. Heather." Markus's expression changed, the slight smirk he'd had all this time falling into slanted lips and wide eyes. "We live there with our daughter. Miranda."

No words came between them, only the surrounding din of coffee cups and espresso steamers. Seconds passed, possibly minutes, the whole time Markus remaining exactly still until finally breaking the silence.

"That's, um." His fingers rubbed his temples, though he probably suffered from a different type of headache than Kin's usual ones. "That's a problem."

"You left me here for *eighteen years*. What was I supposed to do? Stay isolated forever?"

"Yes."

"No person could do that."

"Those are the rules we signed up for. Protocol Eleven Twenty-Three. Besides, what about P—" Markus stopped short. A frown marked his face, and despite the youthful appearance of his metabolizer-enhanced body, his eyes showed a seriousness that betrayed his true age. "I have to update Mission Control," he said after several seconds. He pulled out a tablet—the same tablet from yesterday, as far as Kin could tell—and began tapping away at the lit screen. "I'm sending an email."

Kin scoffed. "Email is ancient history in 2142."

"Right. Sorry. Figure of speech. Keeping up the era-specific terminology, you know?" The thin line between Markus's lips twisted, forming an uneven crack that zigged and zagged. His eyes shot downward, drawn to the wood table rather than the person sitting across it. "This situation needs further input."

Each word burrowed deep down into Kin, pushing so far inside that drawing air felt like willpower of the highest order. He stared straight ahead, nothing else existing except for a clear understanding of the TCB's capabilities.

"Elimination," he finally said through gritted teeth. "You're talking about elimination."

"Not necessarily."

A flush came to Kin's cheeks, burning with such warmth that it radiated to his palms as he rubbed his face. "But it's on the table, isn't it?" He stared at Markus, a new list of options zooming through his mind, all of them offering the most drastic of responses.

"We're not assassins. We're a security agency. We have protocol."

"Can you guarantee their safety?"

"I—" Markus hesitated, then stared straight out the window. "I will try my best." The word *best* never felt so empty. Kin's fingers drummed across his thigh, and he scanned the coffee shop again for any notable changes since he sat down. "This discussion might take a while. My advice? Stay away from your family. It's safer that way for now. I can't promise anything. Knowing Mission Control, they'll probably hammer on noninterference." He blew out a sigh, then tapped his tablet—a standard iPad. This one, though, was probably brought back to 2142 and commissioned by Resources for use in era-appropriate missions. "I'll find you when I know more."

The gravity of Markus's words set in, launching Kin's pulse into a breathless rhythm. His feet welded to the floor, flat, and his neck tensed, as if a string pulled everything taut. "You can't make me stay away from them."

For the first time since they'd met, Markus matched Kin's steely ire. "Tell me about your job. What you do."

Kin gave a matter-of-fact answer, although he didn't know why it mattered. "I manage network security for Gold Free Games. Free-to-play MMO games, 'build your empire' or 'raise your farm' type of stuff…" He stopped when it became clear that the Research department didn't brief retrievers on the era's gaming fads. "Deal with a lot of hackers. I reverse engineer a lot to see how they covered up their tracks and—"

"No, see, that's where you're wrong. You're a Temporal Crimes field agent for the TCB. You don't manage networks. You don't reverse engineer anything. Not anymore. You abide by Protocol Eleven Twenty-Three. *That* is your job. Stay away from everything else—all of it—until I contact you. I will do what I can to keep your family safe." He returned to the tablet, eyes narrowing as he stared at the screen. "Don't forget your cookie."

Kin watched Markus for several seconds before blurting out the first thing that came to mind. "At least give me one bit of my past. Something, anything."

"Okay. Fair enough." Markus bit into his muffin, chewing in contemplation. "Do you remember your name?"

"Kin Stewart. Kin Luther Stewart."

"No. Your first name is Quinoa. When you were born, the trend was food-inspired names. You've always hated it, which is why you've always insisted on going by Kin."

The very mention of the fact prompted a familiar sting to the side of Kin's head, not nearly as bad as before, but enough to demonstrate what Markus meant about being told information. "That's funny," Kin finally said, his voice reduced to a dry gravel. "Quinoa was a big part of my recipe last night."

"You cook? Oh. That's…" The harsh creases of Markus's expression lightened, almost forming a smile before returning to its serious default. "That's interesting. And you kept your name."

"At first, it was to give the TCB something to track me by." The vibrancy of the memory surprised Kin, and those facts didn't seem to exist a mere day ago. "It just stuck. You meet people, become part of their lives. It's not like you can change your name without people noticing."

Markus huffed out a breath, a sullen air taking over his demeanor. He opened his mouth, lips hovering without anything coming out until he straightened up and shot out a few quick words. "Regardless, you should get moving."

Kin stood up, playing out the scenarios in his mind. *Negotiate. Bribe. Lead him outside to incapacitate him or—eliminate.* Was he even capable of doing that?

All the different possibilities, the various ways he might be able to work with the TCB, ran through his mind. But his gut told him something different.

Those options, those assumed that the TCB was even willing to negotiate, listen. Any guarantees he felt were merely speculation, conjecture based on half-filled memories and nostalgia.

No, keeping his family safe meant taking matters into his own hands, not even giving the TCB the opportunity to do or say anything.

He needed to move quickly. Time was not on his side.

"What do you think will happen?"

"I don't know. They will have to decide."

They. Markus said it so casually, like it was just another mission, just another decision.

This wasn't. This was his family. This was his decision.

A paranoia surfaced, bringing anxiety and suspicion with everything he saw. If Markus blended in, who else might be here? How else could they monitor a whole family of time-line corruptions?

Kin walked out of the coffee shop, his pace picking up with each step. At this point, there was only one way to stay ahead of the TCB: run.

CHAPTER 5

Kin had seen this before. Or at least something extremely close.

All day, small things triggered memories. The way the shadow of a mailbox cast a slanted form similar to a skycar on a landing sequence. The way a TV's reflection on glass appeared to float like a holo news display. The way a helicopter's distant *whip-whip-whip* sound mirrored the first ten seconds of atmotube launch. Thanks to the metabolizer Markus had given him, pieces were being returned to the unfinished puzzle of Kin's mind.

On the bed now sat a duffel bag, zipped open, the bare necessities thrown in: phone, chargers, bottles of water, passports, protein bars. The sight of it jarred a memory, an evening from seventeen years ago—a bridge between his life in 2142 and the one he'd built with Heather.

The memory unfolded.

He'd been stranded for about a year. His memories of 2142 had been mere fragments sprinkled around his tiny Berkeley studio space, all parts of a frameless puzzle, pieces yearning to lock in but without any connective tissue. And he had only a few minutes to tear it all down.

He'd thrown the duffel on the bed, arms and legs moving at a frantic pace. His eyes scanned the room, identifying any hint of the future needing to be cleared away. Not the bits of his IT job he'd brought home, his pager and clear-blue plastic Zip drive sitting between a roll of Ethernet cable, but his true job. They had been the only way to hold on to his past, the things he documented in obsessive detail when he realized several weeks prior that his memories were disappearing. But any particular trace or fragment—timeline charts scribbled on pinned sheets of paper, remaining pieces of equipment, the damaged beacon—it all had to be hidden, preserved, safe from plain sight. Twenty minutes counted down to scrub the place clean of that future.

How else could he appear normal to the lanky redhead that he'd dated over the past two months?

In the dingy apartment, Kin held the damaged beacon, fingers tracing over the jagged edge where the bullet pierced it. Dried bits of blood remained visible across the chaotic ridges, the color oxidized to a harsh brown. When Heather had come into his tech support station in the east campus computer lab, flirting came naturally, easily. He never thought the UC Berkeley volleyball player would eventually visit the place hiding the remaining fragments of his other life, all the bits and pieces that rationalized his growing memory gaps.

The beacon got shoved into the bag, followed by a journal showing the wear of everyday writing and reviewing.

The journal, the one that Miranda would find some sixteen years later. Kin had picked it up, flipping the paper pages, his handwritten details of the future and the TCB scrawled feverishly up and down, left and right, front page and back, paragraphs and paragraphs with crude inked sketches and numbers bordering and running alongside the text. He stopped at the last written page, and even now, his metabolizer-enhanced brain visualized the words in his memory so specifically:

History of time travel: the time-jump accelerator was created in 2097 as a top secret collaboration between the US, Australia, and Japan. The first object sent through time was a pen, sent a week earlier to a predetermined location with a sequestered scientist to prevent any grandfather paradoxes. This experiment was repeated with larger objects and eventually mammals. The first human to travel through time was Albert Beckett, the scientist who cracked the calculations necessary to create a dampening field that enabled particle acceleration at lower energy levels. In November 2098, the United Nations formed the Temporal Corruption Bureau as an independent overseer of time-travel technology and temporal security, with its existence only on a need-to-know basis within the intelligence community.

As he stared at the duffel bag, waiting for Heather to arrive, his gut filled with a sickening discomfort. Page after page he flipped, looking at notes and details written mere days before, yet nothing registered as familiar. Over the course of a year, those memories fragmented and scattered, seemingly stored now in the impenetrable puzzle box of his own mind.

And of all the things he'd written down in recent weeks, not a single line about his personal history. His life had been so exactly erased that he didn't even realize it.

He'd started the journal too late.

Kin sat on the edge of the bed, staring at the pages, a headache going from light gallop to full rumble against his temples. Eyes forced open, he refused to give in to the headache. On the tip of his tongue, the edge of his mind, something started to poke through. Not a name or a face or anything concrete, though his mind raced with one repeated thought.

The lucky penny. The penny, just a penny, over and over and over.

But what did it mean?

Then Heather knocked. Early. Or maybe he'd lost track of time.

He looked up, his mind and body returning to equilibrium. In his hands sat his past, or at least pieces of it, clues and hints and facts without context, all painting an out-of-focus picture of who he used to be, something tangible over the horizon if he fought for it hard enough. He could hold on to all that. Or he could let Heather in, put history into the archives for another time.

Another knock at the door. The journal, the bag, the equipment. Headaches. Mystery. Frustration.

Or the woman at the door.

Kin looked back and forth, weighing the two for seconds that felt like hours before Heather broke the silence. "Kin," the voice came through, "I'm a little early. Sorry about that. Should I come back in a few?"

Kin stuffed the journal into the bag and put it in the corner. It could wait.

"So I finally get to see your secret lair," Heather had said when he opened the door. He motioned her in, and she stepped inside, taking in the sparse living of his home. She set her purse down, the top half of a magazine sticking out, its cover featuring the re-release of a 1970s sci-fi movie—the same one that got his coworkers all worked up. He took her coat and their evening began.

One thing led to another and to another that night, and they'd wound up missing their dinner reservations, wrapped around each other in his uncomfortable twin bed. The next morning, he awoke to the sound of cabinets opening and closing.

"Sorry," Heather said, clothed only in underwear and a T-shirt, "didn't meant to slam it so loud."

Kin had snapped awake, becoming fully alert to the fact that Heather might have accidentally stumbled upon some trace of the TCB, maybe even opened the bag. He sat up, adrenaline pumping in a different way than the last night. Heather held up a package of convenience store cupcakes. "Breakfast? Found this in a cabinet."

"You're okay with cupcakes for breakfast?"

"Dessert is the best way to start the day. Unless you're making magic out of the two apples in your fridge."

"I'm still learning to cook."

"Like I said—" she sauntered back over to the bed, manufactured baked goods in hand "—breakfast." While she'd struggled to open the plastic wrap, he glanced back to the duffel in the corner. It remained closed, untouched, still resting in the odd dented manner from the night before. When she'd looked around his place, Heather had seemed more interested in the small stack of VHS tapes sitting on the counter, at least until she realized they were recordings of Premier League soccer matches loaned out by the school's UEFA Fan Club. And this morning, her attention was on cupcakes.

"God, I'm terrible at opening these things. Do me a favor?" He pulled his eyes from the duffel to see Heather holding the cupcake package in his direction.

A single thought struck him with the impact of a gunshot to the gut. Did a missing past even matter anymore compared to human touch in the here and now?

Years later, the same duffel bag sat on the bed he shared with the same woman, now his wife, packed tightly because that missing past suddenly mattered on a level of life and death.

From downstairs, the sound of Bamford's collar began to jingle, soon followed by the opening and closing of the front door. "Kin?" Heather called out.

Sweaty palms. Trembling hands. How un-agent-like he felt when he needed it most. "Upstairs," he said before reminding himself to stay focused.

"What's the matter? Your text said it was an emergency." Rapid footsteps echoed up the stairs. "Is Miranda okay? I'm supposed to pick her up in a little while."

Kin turned and faced his wife, her wide eyes the opposite of his serious squint. "We need to go." A tremor made it into his words, and he hoped she didn't pick up on it.

Heather stayed frozen. She didn't even appear to breathe. "Go…where?"

"Somewhere. Anywhere. Help me pack. But pack light."

Heather put her hands up and began a slow walk toward him. "Let's think this through. You are literally telling us to—" she pointed at the duffel bag on the bed "—pack up and go? What about Miranda? And Bammy?"

In an instant, all of Kin's fears and feelings got shoved aside, compartmentalized. Lists visualized, options and potential travel scenarios flooding his mind, all keeping the emotions at bay. Adrenaline? Training? Survival? Perhaps a mix of all three. "We'll take them with us, of course. We'll pick up Miranda from school and—"

The floor squeaked with each of Heather's approaching steps. She got close, face-to-face, and her hands reached over and gently held his cheeks. "Hey. It's me. We're home now.

You're having another PTSD flare-up. It's okay. Let's sit down, we'll talk through this—"

He turned, his breath pushing out in a huff. They didn't have time to debate this. TCB agents could be anywhere: down the street, at Miranda's school. Maybe even hiding in their garage. Markus had been in their *backyard* last night.

Could he say that without sounding completely out of his mind? "I can explain. Not now, later. Everything—*everything*—will make sense. Everything you've ever wondered about me. After we make sure that we're far enough away—"

"Kin, it's getting worse."

"No, it's not. Heather, listen." From his peripheral vision, he sensed that Heather remained glued to her spot while he stared at the bed. "I know this sounds crazy. You have to trust me. We're in danger. We need to leave. Pack light. Get our family together. They could be right behind us. They could be watching now. I mean, they tracked me down and—"

The noise caused Kin to stop, though it wasn't a crash from an invading agent or a surprise visit from Markus. Instead, the gradual escalation of Heather's emotions, from a stifled sniffle to a full-blown cry.

She hardly ever cried. His tears flowed more often than hers did. She even told him he had a horrible crying face when he got emotional over Arsenal winning the FA Cup.

He was losing her. Fear, desperation, panic, all of those crept in and he resisted. *Not now.* For now he had to focus, get his family to safety. *Then* he could breathe.

Kin turned to her, and she straightened, tears streaming down her face. "Listen to yourself," she said, her finger pointing with every syllable. "Just *listen* to what you're saying. Kin, you need help. *Please* get help. You're scaring me—you scared Miranda, you're scaring her with your—"

The words bounced off him, sound going in his ears

though their meaning got lost shortly after. His goal, his only goal, was to convince her to run with him. "We talked, she gets it, I told her not to be worried—"

"You get dizzy spells. You pass out in the garage. You space out." Heather's voice had completed the transformation from cautious sympathy to desperation, and it got louder with each word. "You've been doing this since I met you, but it hasn't happened for years. Why now? Why the past six months? Why don't you go to the VA office and get help? You're a *veteran*, damn it, you took a bullet in your gut for them," she said, pointing to the spot where Kin cut out the beacon, "and now they have to help. They have to help you. They owe it to you. Just, please, listen to yourself."

"Heather," Kin said, eyes closed. The details of missions had started to come back. Initial scouting from afar. Identifying movement patterns, target sleep cycles, behavioral habits. Using intel from Mission Control to track them down in isolation before apprehending and/or executing. Meticulous. Relentless. Precise. That might all be happening now, only this time with his wife, his daughter as targets. Fear of losing Heather's trust poked at him, yet fear of the TCB finding them eclipsed that, taking the only spotlight that mattered. "I understand everything you're saying. I am *present*. You don't know what we're up against. I do. We need to go now. We have to get ahead of them."

"Who are they?" Heather roared, her voice louder than he'd ever heard. "Listen to yourself. *They*. Who are they? If this is so important, why can't you tell me?"

"I can't. Not right now. When I know we're safe, I can…" Kin hesitated for two, maybe three seconds, long enough for doubts to sneak in. His focus lost grip, its tenuous hold giving way to a barrage of questions. He'd had only one metabolizer injection. How long would it last? How long would his brain hold together, and how soon before the details started to wither away again? "I will write down everything I know and give it to you." His words rippled on their way out. "Because I may forget it."

"You're not making any sense." Heather buried her face in her hands. "Oh god, you're not making any sense. It's so much worse than before." Heather's posture began to droop in a way Kin had never seen before, as if something turned her bones to mush, and if they waited long enough, she might even collapse on the floor.

"We can talk about this later, we need—"

"Stop. Just stop." Heather grabbed his shoulder, her hand heavy though her fingers barely gripped him. "We can't live like this. Do you hear me? You. Need. Help."

This wasn't working. Kin tried to recall his options, his plan for convincing her, but nothing arrived. No ideas, no visualizations, nothing except a growing dull pain at the back of his skull. He started to massage his temples, though it wasn't from the familiar headaches. "Let's back up. Start over—"

"No. No starting over. You need to get help before you hurt yourself or you hurt us."

"I would never hurt you. Or Miranda. Come on, you can't believe that."

"Not on purpose. But what happens if you have a dizzy spell while you're on the road? If you think you see something, whatever it is, and you miss a red light? If you black out while taking Miranda somewhere? Could you live with that? Could I live with that? You need to get help. We can't continue this way." She winced, though Kin didn't know if that was from the situation or from her own headaches. Either way, her words began to sink in. He didn't need any of his agent training to piece together where this was leading. "You've been avoiding this for months. Get help, Kin. Now."

Heather took in a slow breath. Her hands quivered slightly, and she crossed her arms, either to hide that fact or perhaps to just support herself. "Please. Don't run away. Just do it."

Every single fiber of his being urged him to fight for her. Except he'd gotten them into this. Everything that was happening now, everything that could happen when the TCB found them—he'd started it all when he decided to break Protocol Eleven Twenty-Three and live a life in the past. When he returned Heather's smile in the computer lab all those years ago. And rather than throw himself in front of the time-traveling speeding bullet, he'd actually asked his wife to pack up her family and go, leaving everything behind to rush off to parts unknown, no promise of coming back or even a hint as to *why* they needed to go.

Of course Heather wouldn't follow. She was too smart, too sensible. He'd let blind hope win out over logic.

"You're right." He was more aware than he'd been for years thanks to the metabolizer. Markus said to stay away to keep them safe. At this point, being around him could only be dangerous. It was so simple. It was time to run.

Not them. Just himself.

"I should go."

"Thank god—"

"No, I mean, I should go." He was the former agent, not them. He was the one Markus came for, not them. He could protect them by simply staying away, at least until Markus resolved things. "Not just counseling. A live-in rehab center. For a few days, few weeks. Whatever it takes."

"What?" She wiped her eyes, her mascara now raccoon-like smudges. "You can't leave. Kin, we need you. We're a family. What will Miranda think?"

"She needs stability. I can't provide that right now. Let's think this through." Kin's throat was dry, the sound getting lost in the cracks in his voice. "The sooner I do this, the sooner things get back to normal for our family. I'll even look this afternoon. Maybe—" the possibilities for cover stories exploded in his mind "—they'll even admit me today."

"It's so sudden—"

"No, you're right. Every day that passes is a gamble. I can't risk it. We can't. I need help. And I can't hurt you or scare Miranda anymore. I won't." The epiphany left only one thing to say, but each word became an exercise in moving mountains. "I need to leave to protect you two."

Heather stared at him, her brown eyes locking in while the rest of her face danced from emotion to emotion across minutes. He visualized her practical mind processing the ideas, the rational justifications working with her attorney's logic until reason settled in. She finally nodded, despite the sudden heaviness that slowed the slightest of her moves.

"You're right."

"It'll be over before you know it. I promise."

"You probably have a plan already, huh?"

"Always."

Her hands came up, palms rubbing her face until she looked at him again, the previous intensity fading into a resigned softness. "The needs of the many..." she said, words barely above a whisper.

"What's that, babe?"

Her long fingers swept through her hair. "'The needs of the many outweigh the needs of the few.' Spock says it. In *Star Trek II*."

Kin's heart pounded, his chest a bubble about to burst, not because of anxiety but from seventeen-some years of shared life. Of course she would quote *Star Trek* to him in a moment like this. "I love you, Heather Stewart. Never, ever, ever change."

"And I love you." Heather's small smile turned into a smaller laugh. "You and your stupid plans." Kin nodded, the uncertainty on his face carrying a different weight from what he actually felt. "Ever since I met you—" she pulled him in close, arms squeezing him so hard that he couldn't breathe "—I've felt like I sometimes come in second place to *something*. But we're in this together. Even if we're not physically together. This is for all of us. The needs of the many."

This is for all of us. Heather ripped the words directly out of Kin's mind. Except his thoughts were set against a different context, one that she couldn't possibly comprehend. "The needs of the many," he echoed quietly. Her body melted against his and he absorbed her through each of his senses, the arch of her back, the smell of her hair, the way her cheeks were the exact same height as his when they pressed together. He locked the details to specifics that he hoped didn't evaporate. He kissed her, a quiet gesture of pure devotion, and she returned it, the same warmth but with a passion that propelled them into something more. Their arms went from tender to urgent, a sudden franticness that only two people facing separation could know.

Though Kin knew that separation meant something completely different—this chasm spanned space and time.

As their hands clutched each other desperately, as Heather pressed her lips up and down his neck, as he tried to permanently carve her very essence into his memory, he reached over and pushed the duffel bag off the bed. Though TCB and Markus didn't give him a choice on leaving, for one final time—as he did sixteen years ago—he chose Heather over his past.

CHAPTER 6

At midnight, Kin allowed himself to indulge in music. He'd trailed Heather's car when she picked up Miranda. He called her shortly after, using a cover story that a PTSD rehab center in Marin had accepted him and he was leaving tonight, that he was already on the road to make their registration time despite her pleas to go as a family. He followed them home at a distance, parking in the dark under a tree, one block down. When the downstairs lights went out around eleven, he moved the car closer, the whole time his eyes trained on the Stewart house. His stomach grumbled from a lack of food, and his eyes fought a losing battle against fatigue. But nothing mattered more than keeping a quiet and steady watch for any potential TCB activity.

He focused on that all night long. It helped dam up the onslaught of other thoughts inside him.

Finally, after hours, he turned on the radio, reflexively wincing at the pounding drums and fuzzy guitars of Miranda's alt-rock station.

Except he didn't need to. Modern music usually triggered at least a sting in his temple, occasionally worse, as if the combination of rhythm and instruments brushed too close to popular music from 2142. He'd spent his current life listening to classical music, its strings and horns safely distanced from the future.

Nothing poked his head this time. The metabolizer's effects must have been spreading. Instead, he hit the preset to the classical station, not as avoidance, simply because he wanted to. The music crescendoed, an aria by Handel he recognized, and he gave himself a second to close his eyes when a knock came on the window.

It was Markus.

Kin glanced over to his house, squinting to detect anything unusual. No movement through the shrubs. No change in lights, doors, or drapes. No shadows traipsing across the fence.

The window opened while he turned down the radio. "Are you alone?" Kin asked.

"Yes. And you shouldn't have come here." Markus looked straight at the ground. "I guess it doesn't matter. Do you want to hear what the Washington folks decided?"

"Do I have a choice?"

Markus shrugged and leaned against the car frame. "Your family is safe. Despite the level of timeline corruption, our regional AD and the national oversight committee have elected to let them be. The only condition is that they can't have any knowledge of the future or the TCB. Zero contact."

"How generous."

"It is. Our whole agency is built around eliminating time-line corruption. You were never supposed to be here, but we can't do anything about that now." Markus looked up, meeting him eye to eye. "They're not heartless, Kin. These are people like you and me, and you've put them in an impossible situation."

"What's the plan? What's my 'exit strategy'? How do they expect to bring me back without anyone noticing?"

"You'll drive over the Golden Gate Bridge and meet me in Sausalito. Tonight." The explanation continued as if Markus read it off a sheet of paper.

Tonight. It stole all the air from Kin. But Markus kept going, words rolling out relentlessly.

"We'll ditch your car and take a separate vehicle up to the time-jump point. And we'll jump. It might be a rough ride with your body having been here for so long. A medical crew will be waiting for us. In this era, the Logistics team will ensure a clean handoff."

Markus described the situation so clinically that it took several seconds for its meaning to fully register. Once it did, a tingle ran across Kin's skin, from the top of his forehead all the way down to the tips of his toes.

"Define 'clean.'"

"I don't know the plan. That's not my job. But they'll do whatever it takes to minimize the timeline corruption for anyone you've ever interacted with." Markus's face hardened, like a schoolteacher scolding a rebellious teen. Did Kin have that face when he tried to talk to Miranda? "You can't ask for sympathy now. This is our job. You see that car driving down the street? That person's whole life is ahead of them. You come here and maybe pass her on her way out. She's only a few seconds off her original schedule as she waits for you to go by. Those few seconds mean she hits a stoplight, holding her up another few minutes. That propagates for-ward. What have you changed for her? Did she miss bump-ing into her future spouse? Maybe you rescued her from a car accident? Or maybe you caused the car accident that kills her. What gives you the right to alter her destiny that way?"

"Or maybe nothing happens. You're getting dramatic."

"Or maybe nothing. Maybe she's just a few minutes later getting home, she goes to bed at the same time and nothing changes. The psych team always tells us that people revert to their patterns. Thing is, we can't control what happens to them *while* they're returning to their habits. The vari-ables, we're here to control those. We can't undo the things that have happened because for every single thing undone, a hundred more get created. Our job is to eliminate time-line corruption."

"No, your job is apparently to destroy families."

"That's not fair. Kin, you *are* a timeline corruption. You knew better than to get involved. Who was your wife sup-posed to end up with? What doors did her relationship with you close in her life? In everyone else's?" Markus cleared his throat and straightened up, though he didn't look Kin in the eye. "And your daughter. She's the ultimate timeline corruption."

"She's a fourteen-year-old girl."

"Who shouldn't even exist. You've swapped out whatever life Heather should have had, whoever her natural children should have been, and replaced that with you and Miranda. Miranda's existence is a corruption in itself. And corruptions need to be addressed. That's what we do."

"So you want me to just disappear on them?"

"Yes. You signed up for this when you became an agent. You knew the rules then, you knew them when you got stuck here and you broke them. You may have changed, but the rules haven't. You break them again and the TCB has to course-correct the corruption." Markus leaned back and looked up, eyes tracking to the sky above. "Let's not let it get to that point." Suddenly all the weight that held Kin down wanted to escape, to unleash in defense of his daughter against Markus, against anyone who could possibly want to hurt her, against every weapon and threat from the future. "You must leave. To save them."

Just like that. Heather wouldn't have a husband.

Miranda wouldn't have a father. She wouldn't even get a chance to say goodbye to him, or ask him the four questions.

Silence seemed to be an appropriate reply, and after several seconds, Markus gave an uncomfortable shift in his posture. "It's ten past twelve. I'll meet you across the bridge at two."

"We're friends," Kin spit out, "in your time. We're friends, right?"

"You remembered?"

"No. Only wondering."

"Yes. We're friends." Markus shook his head. "I shouldn't have told you that."

"Why would you do this to a friend?"

A guttural sound came from behind Markus's clenched teeth. He shook his head again, then looked up at the black night sky. "Things will come back to you."

"What are you going to do now?"

Markus's professional demeanor cracked, and he shot Kin a smirk, like he expected him to know the answer. "What I always do when I visit this era. Get some fast food." He reached into his coat pocket, and pulled out a long, thin object.

Chopsticks.

So that *was* a future thing. "Heather always makes fun of my chopsticks. I figured it came from 2142. Couldn't totally remember."

"The doctors said that personal memories were the most likely things to disappear during your stay here. But everyday habits stick with you. Chopsticks. Coffee with honey. Arsenal. Like muscle memory. See? People revert to their patterns. I can't believe they use forks still, it's such a pain. Well," he said, holding up his chopsticks before turning away, "duty calls."

"That's timeline corruption," Kin called out as Markus began to walk away. He stopped and turned to face him. "That thing you said about slowing people down. You'll do the same thing ordering food. I should turn you in."

"Protocol Seven-Fifteen—era visitation. Walk on empty streets. Don't buy when there's a line. Don't sit in a crowded place. Execute with zero impact. Midnight is the perfect time for that." Markus's eyes lit up, flashing as if he forgot that lives hung in the balance for a moment before returning to reality. He glanced at his watch. "Two a.m., Kin. Then we leave. You can bring some keepsakes if you want." Kin continued glaring at his supposed friend until his silence was met with a short nod and a silent march.

The window closed, the sound of a single cello filling the space around him. He reached into his pocket and found his lucky penny, the coin that yesterday sat peacefully above his garage workbench, cellophane tape holding it in place.

For those few seconds, nothing else existed except him and the penny. His fingers wrapped around it, the edge of the coin digging into his palm, then he held it up to the moonlight, observing the spot of oxidation on Abraham Lincoln's hair, the etched 1978 by Lincoln's lapels, the scratch across the top half of the dull surface.

It was just a penny. Yet for now, it was the only thing he had in his world. Kin held it and took a breath.

CHAPTER 7

The academy taught new recruits about the theory of the multiverse, where each individual choice spawned off a new universe—an infinite number of universes, some wildly different from one another. All theoretical, of course, and even with 2142 technology, not even the brainiest of physics professors had the means to prove it. But now Kin wished he could rip a tear across space and time and hitch a ride to the one where his biggest concern was perfecting an audition dish for *Home Chef Challenge*.

In this universe, however, an hour remained before walking down the Sausalito waterfront, getting in a car with Markus, and heading to the time-jump point.

For now, he found a spot to stare out across the bay, city lights across the water watching him back. All the walls and defenses he'd built up around his emotions had collapsed, leaving a thick throat, a hollow chest and too many questions to answer.

He sat, bag of keepsakes at his feet, focusing on memories. Random flashes of the future kept poking through, though he'd pushed them aside, fought through them. This was *his* time and he refused to let it be anything other than the memories he chose:

The moment Miranda was born.

She was smaller than he thought she'd be. At seven pounds, two ounces, she didn't arrive underweight or sickly. Yet holding her little body, the sheer fragility of the universe sank in.

Though Kin had jumped through time, saved and taken lives, nothing had quite prepared him for it.

Heather had looked up at him and chuckled, her sweaty hair matted down after the last ninety minutes of pushing. "You look like you're afraid you'll break her," she said from behind the handheld camcorder.

"I am."

"Babies are pretty pliable. You'll see. They fall on their face and keep going. Unlike us adults. We're the fragile ones."

Heather had spoken with the advantage of having four younger siblings. Memories of whatever family Kin had prior to Heather were long gone, so the experience of holding a child, particularly within minutes of birth, was completely new to him.

Miranda coughed, then a gurgle turned into a sniffle turned into a cry. "Come here, little girl," Heather had said, and they swapped the video camera for the newborn.

In the days leading up to Miranda's arrival, Kin considered the first thing he'd say to her. That morning, with the sun barely creeping over the horizon, he went with his first choice. "Life lesson number one," he said, one eye shut and the other looking through the camera's viewfinder, "in soccer, don't follow the ball. Go where the ball is heading."

"Life lesson number two," Heather had countered. "Jean-Luc Picard is the best *Star Trek* captain there ever will be. Ever. But just in case you need to be like Dad sometimes—" Heather nodded to the suitcase in the corner "—look in the front pouch. There's something for her."

Kin paused the recording, unzipped the rolling luggage and reached in, his fingers touching something that felt like yarn. "It feels like…" he started before pulling it out and unfurling it.

"In case she needs to bond with her daddy. In between watching sci-fi."

As Kin held up the baby-sized scarf, the word *Arsenal* woven into its red-and-white stripes, he beamed at his wife, a smile so wide it almost hurt. In that moment, nothing could be more perfect. He went back over to the bed, gently draping it over Miranda as she wiggled in her mom's arms.

"Your daughter is beautiful," the nurse said, putting a stack of blankets on the counter before grabbing a clipboard behind the door. "Miranda Elizabeth Stewart. That's such a lovely name."

"We like to think so." Heather laughed, her voice carrying on a gentle bounce that Kin never heard before. "Wouldn't we? Yes, we would." She continued cooing at the crying newborn, a gesture equal parts affection and desperation and hope only found in terrified-but-enamored new parents. Kin collapsed into the chair next to the hospital bed, the allure of sleep suddenly tugging on his eyelids. He heard the nurse leave and the world blacked out for just a second when Heather's elbow poked him.

"Kin!" Heather half whispered, nudging him again. He

looked over to find her weary smile. "Look," she mouthed, nodding at the baby in her arms.

A quiet, sleeping baby.

"Her first nap." Heather's words were barely audible. "Can you put her in the bassinet?"

She passed their daughter with the same precision and care as Kin used, and it dawned on him that despite her experience with her younger siblings, the confidence she projected was all superficial. Heather, the woman who sometimes doubled as a runaway train of opinions and ideas, a quick wit with a dash of too-smart-for-her-own-good sass, was actually as nervous about parenting as he was.

Kin cradled Miranda in his arms, walking with soft steps over to the heated hospital bassinet. He stood by it and hesitated to put her down, an uncontrollable urge to shell his own body around her, to shield her against any possible harm the past, present, or future might bring to her. The urge came and went, and in its place came an understanding of her place in the world now, that setting her down didn't mean he wasn't still protecting her. He put the still-sleeping Miranda in the bassinet and fell onto the hard sofa chair next to Heather, who'd already closed her eyes. His fingers interlaced with hers while he watched Miranda.

The lights across the bay blurred through his tears. Maybe he should have never let his guard down. Maybe the TCB would have caught up with him regardless. The thoughts compiled in his mind, forming the list to end all lists, and he closed his eyes until he forcefully shut off the visualizing part of his brain, the agent-trained mind that structured things in plans and options.

Those skills wouldn't do him any good right now. His memories, his moments with Heather and Miranda, those gave him enough to get through the night.

He had an hour left. And though he was separated from his family by the water of the San Francisco Bay, he hoped they somehow heard his thoughts while he sat and remembered them.

CHAPTER 8

Failure.

The word repeated itself over and over during the hour-long drive from Sausalito to some deserted two-lane road that wound toward the hills by the Pacific Ocean. Even as Kin followed Markus on foot up the mountainside, through weeds and shrubbery and crumbling clumps of dirt, failure was all he felt since leaving his family behind.

He'd failed his family by sitting in that car with Markus, by following him step after step up to the jump point. The logic of his exit strategy dictated that he had no choice, that asking Heather and Miranda to accept a ridiculous truth *and* a life on the run was unfair to both of them. And that part was correct.

Except maybe that wasn't the only option, and that defined the failure that ate away while he made small talk with Markus. "What'd you decide to bring?" Markus asked after quizzing him about his life with Heather.

"Not much. My phone. A charger. Figure there's probably a way to convert the USB interface to keep my photos."

"They may even be able to convert them to three-dimensional holos." Markus spouted out the fact as if it were stock photography, not images of the family he'd abandoned.

"I have some photo prints, too. My lucky penny. My wallet. That's about it."

"Your lucky..." From the side, Kin glimpsed Markus's mouth form a wavy line, as if deeply digging for the right word. "Coin."

"It's my lucky penny."

"It must—" Markus cleared his throat before starting again. "It must be very important to you," he said at a slow deliberate cadence.

"Actually, I can't even remember how I got it. Not yet, anyway. It's been with me through a lot. Why do you care? It's just a penny."

"Only curious. What people consider keepsakes, that's all." Markus began rambling about a psychology course he'd taken in college while assessing his standard-issue time-jump equipment, but Kin tuned out. Other, more important things started bubbling up in his mind.

He'd failed his family by giving up and giving in. With Markus configuring the time-jump accelerator, precious seconds remained before they left.

There was still time to fight back.

"So," Kin said, striking up idle chatter while he weighed his options. "What happens with the car?"

"The car?" Markus remained focused on the equipment, unaware of Kin moving into position.

Should he run away? Knock him out?

Kill him?

"Yeah. Isn't leaving that a timeline corruption?"

"Nah," Markus said. A flash of light paused his internal debate. Kin's vision adjusted to the glowing burst, focusing on the small holographic screen floating above the metal sphere in Markus's hand. "The Logistics team handles that stuff. I asked how they did it once, they're all department secrets and everything." Markus tapped the holo, continuing to mutter to himself. As he leaned forward, his ramblings became clearer. "Set temporal coordinates. Damn it, Stu, why didn't you reset the gauges? I swear, no one pays attention." His fingers danced over it, scowl bouncing up and down as colors and messages cycled through. "Seriously, guys? Was that so hard? Am I the only one who follows the rules? There's a reason why we have protocol."

Markus continued to work while Kin had quietly moved an arm's length behind him. Knocking him out offered the best chance, the most flexibility. At least then he might have a moment to decide how to get back to his family.

Except he hadn't subdued anyone in a long, long time. His fingers and toes curled in anticipation, a nagging doubt eating away at him about his rusty agent skills despite cocking his hands and elbows in place.

"All right. Your turn," Markus said, the holo disappearing, leaving them with only the night sky. "Ready to travel through time?" He turned and, despite the darkness around them, caught Kin's eye, causing his own to go wide. "What are—"

Before he finished, Kin squeezed the consciousness out of Markus in textbook fashion, Markus's chin jammed against the crook of Kin's elbow, and while dust clouds blew up from Markus's kicking feet, Kin put pressure down on the carotid artery—or at least he tried. Rather than going limp, Markus gagged and struggled, firing his elbow into Kin's ribs.

"Kin!" he squeezed out. "Stop!" Dirt sprayed up as Markus fell to his knees. Something wasn't going as planned, or Kin didn't have the strength to do this anymore; rather than black out, Markus wriggled and fought to get words out. "We're friends. We're like family."

"You're wrong. A friend would never do what you're doing." Kin pushed his knee into Markus's back, causing him to give. "You're not my family."

"Puh…" Something must have started working, because Markus went limp despite continuing to squeeze his breath out. "Puh…"

"I don't belong there. I belong here. With my family."

"Pen…"

"*My* family. I need to be here for Miranda."

Beneath him, Markus shifted back and forth, sucking in barely enough air to get one final word through. "Penny."

The sound of thunder rattled through, though only in Kin's head, buckling his knees while he winced. His hands pressed up against his temples, trying to push the storm out.

Markus broke free from his grip and pushed away. "Penny," he said again. That *word*. All it took was one word for Kin's head to turn into a soup of noise and light. "Penny." One more time and Kin fell flat on his back, knees curled up in the fetal position, an invisible jackhammer attacking from the inside out.

He'd heard that word plenty of times in his life. Why did it matter when Markus said it?

Kin couldn't see Markus's expression, but he heard a hesitation between the battling din in his head. "I'm really sorry I had to do that to you. This will help."

Kin forced a single eye open, only to find Markus approaching him, syringe in hand. "Don't," he huffed. Brush flattened underneath as he rolled to his side, his legs fighting against something formless until a weight came crashing down on him and something pierced his neck.

The injection spread quickly, a cool burst that spidered outward and circulated. The last thing he remembered before blacking out was Markus muttering to himself again. "It really is lucky, isn't it?"

Kin's wrists burned when he opened his eyes. His vision adjusted to the night sky, and he took in even breaths while he watched the scene in front of him: Markus, kneeling and working on the main time-jump accelerator's settings. His own hands were bound to the accelerator's proxy handles with what appeared to be plain old rope, the rest of him waiting facedown in the dirt.

Proxy handles—the handles connected to the accelerator. The handles that agents gripped and hunkered over for safe transportation across time.

More memories returned. First details appeared when he looked at the equipment, then other stuff, things that didn't need visual or audio triggers, they emerged from the woodwork on their own.

"You've tied me up."

"Yeah. Sorry about that. And sorry about using the P-word." Markus stood up and closed the bag at his feet. "That was cheating. You weren't ready to hear that from a familiar voice."

"What does that mean? 'Penny.' It's just a damn coin. It's one cent."

Markus bit down on his lip and avoided eye contact. "I can't tell you. Those are the rules. You have to remember yourself. The brain's not meant to know two different eras.

The first metabolizer helped. This booster injection should speed things up. It, um, relieves the inflammation in your brain. Supposed to help you comprehend the different eras. You'll remember things. And not feel like vomiting when you do."

"Look," he said, "I'm taking mine now." He twisted the cap off, revealing a half-sized needle in a short metal frame. "No tricks. Completely safe." The syringe pressed against the side of his neck. Markus pressed the tip down, grimacing for a second before looking back up. "There. Done. For me, it's a precaution. For you, it'll turn things back on. I should warn you, though—it might hurt when that happens."

Kin rose to his knees, but all the gears of his body felt out of step, disconnected. A dull burn coursed through his shoulders when he tried to push himself up, only to collapse in the dirt again. "How long have I been out?"

"Ten, fifteen minutes? Something like that. You're probably sore, huh? The booster is working. Sorry about tying you up. I had to make sure you came back with me." Markus's brow wrinkled in tension. "Right, we should get moving."

The floating control panel disappeared with a few more taps from Markus. "Start-up sequence initiated," the accelerator's disembodied voice announced. "Launch in sixty seconds. Fifty-nine. Fifty-eight."

"Hold on." The ropes tore against Kin's skin while he struggled, achieving only a fish-out-of-water flounder with his unfeeling limbs. "I can't leave. Markus, you said you're my friend. Help me stay here. Help me find a way." Dirt plumes kicked up as Kin's toes dug into the ground, trying to get some form of traction. "Please. I can't leave my family. Not like this."

The words flew over and around Markus, doing everything except connecting with him. He hunched over his own handles, kneeling and curling into a ball.

The textbook pre-jump position. He knew that. Of course he did. How could he forget it?

"Forty-five. Forty-four."

"Kin, just wait," Markus said. "Wait until you start remembering what—"

A gong rang through Kin's head, his muscles going limp. His body collapsed down the few inches he'd managed to prop himself up, and the sound exploded again in his head, creating a screaming pressure that demanded a release somewhere, anywhere. His eyes shut in pain as rapid-fire images arrived.

A woman with brown hair and round cheeks standing over a stove. A cat with white paws and a raccoon-like mask. A man kicking a soccer ball. Cars floating in between buildings. A ring on a hand.

"It's starting, isn't it? Come on. Stay with me. We'll get through this."

"Thirty-seven," the hardware said. "Thirty-six."

Information flooded his mind, details lighting up as if the power came back online. Penny. Akasha. The view from their apartment. Markus—Penny's brother.

The ring he gave to Penny when he proposed.

"Thirty-one. Thirty seconds to launch."

Another sonic boom hit, this one leaving his entire face stinging harder than he'd ever been punched. He knew he let out cries of pain, but he couldn't hear them over the nonstop ringing in his ears. More images flew by, mixing with the other ones in a blender that somehow made sense of his life.

Miranda. Heather. Traffic. Bamford. Work.

Right when the noises in his head quieted, a jolt of electricity zapped through him, causing his neck to arch upward while every muscle spasmed. Penny reappeared a thousand times over, a collage of memories overlapping one another, mixing and matching details except for the lone constant of her face.

"Penny," he said, more to himself than anyone else. "How did I forget Penny?"

"You didn't. You held on to her, even when your memory disappeared. Your lucky Penny." Markus nodded at the accelerator and its audible countdown. "It's okay. Don't worry about it. Just hang on."

"Twenty. Nineteen."

He left Penny eighteen years ago on a routine assignment. And yet, after that night in Daly City, after giving up any hope of rescue, after settling in, finding a job, she evaporated from memory. No voice, no images, nothing.

She didn't even make it into his journal.

"The wedding," Kin said, fighting the burning in his limbs. "Did I miss the wedding?"

"No, it's next week."

Cooking. The cat rescue group. The restaurant she wanted to open. The business loan they were going to apply for. Their *life*.

How many years was Penny reduced to a symbol—a coin?

The disembodied machine voice continued. "Ten. Nine."

The future versus the past. He couldn't choose between his new life and his old life. Not now. Not like this. Miranda and Heather didn't deserve to be betrayed. Neither did Penny. He needed more time to stop and think this through.

"Stop the countdown. Markus, I remember Penny."

"Seven. Six."

"I can't. We're locked in."

"No, I need more time to figure this out." The pounding returned, a rhythmic tumble coming straight from the rapid thumping in his chest. "I can't. I need more time."

"Two. One. Initiating."

A high-pitched hum pierced the air, followed by a rumble that caused the loose dirt and small pebbles around him to dance. Another hum started low before ramping up in pitch and intensity.

"Markus. Markus, I need more time. I need more—"

Before the final words made it out, a flash of white bled out Kin's vision, followed by absolute darkness, darker than the night sky over the Northern California countryside.

CHAPTER 9

Kin opened his eyes, and while he saw the bright dots of stars in the sky above, they quickly turned to streaks, and an overwhelming dizziness spun him despite being flat on his back. His fingers reached out beside him, gripping dirt and dead grass.

"Heather?" he called out. "I think I hit my head or something."

"Hold on one second, Kin," a voice said before it mumbled something unintelligible—a man, not Heather. The world stopped tumbling over, and his vision stabilized enough that he could see the stars and the twinkling of the Bay Area sky-line below it. He took it in, and judging from the proximity to the Golden Gate Bridge in the distance, he figured they must have gone for a night hike out in the hills by Mount

Tamalpais or something. Until a giant beam of light wiped out all his sight.

The light came with a low hum and the rattling of an engine, and as his vision adjusted, he saw the silhouette around the light. A car.

A car floating in the sky.

"Holy shit—"

"Okay, here we go, buddy," the man's voice said again. "You're just a little messed up from the time jump." A pain stabbed into his neck, followed by a sudden rush of blood that seemed to shake his brain back to the on position.

"Transport Six Two, land and wait for us," the man said into his watch. "He's disoriented."

Kin tried to crane his neck and look around, but every part of his body froze. A familiar pounding attacked his temples, the beat eventually giving way to a single brutal pressure that squeezed from the inside out. "My head."

Even with his eyes shut, he sensed the bright light above, and the noise grew louder and louder, like it had been wired directly into his brain. "Okay. Okay. We got you." Hands grabbed his arms and legs, lifting him off the ground until they rested him on a cloud, or at least it felt that way. His eyes refused to open, and his hands searched under him, feeling metal or plastic. When did a stretcher feel so smooth traversing dirt and rocks? He might as well have been flying—or hovering.

Hovering. A flying car. A floating stretcher. The man's voice. Markus? Heather wasn't here. She was gone, dead for a century.

He was in the future.

The next time Kin opened his eyes, the world returned with a sharpness he hadn't felt in years. And it wasn't only his (better-but-not-quite-twenty-twenty) eyesight, but the dull ache that always burned in his knees seemed fainter. For a second, the only urge he felt was to scan the room, assess the situation and figure out an escape route.

His mind fired off faster and better than it had done in ages, and it wasn't from agent-trained techniques. He didn't have to ask where he was as he sat up in the hospital bed. He just needed to look next to him.

A small black disk sat on the bedside table with a floating holographic message ironically showing traditional handwriting. *This is from Penny* it displayed with Markus's name signed and dated underneath.

Penny.

The very name brought up an avalanche of, well, everything, soon counterweighted by the life he'd just left. According to the medical chart floating in front of him, he'd been under for two weeks at TCB's medical wing—two weeks of metabolizer-powered healing to his body and mind.

Kin checked the disk's date again. He'd missed the wedding. The holo message deactivated the instant he touched it, and he held it for the sheer sake of holding on to *something* tangible.

Life details suddenly returned with startling clarity and definitive pieces about his life finally fell into place. He'd joined the top secret TCB academy at age twenty-two, with his first mission a year later at the Toronto branch before transferring to San Francisco. That last mission, Kin had skimmed the intel instead of digesting the plan thoroughly. He'd trusted his gut, his ability to scan and visualize and decide, only to totally misjudge the target's ability to blend into crowds, which led to her pouncing on him just outside the safe house. And when those details started to fade after he'd been stranded, in their place came a lurking apprehension about instinct, along with an urge to craft detailed plans and stick with them. That, combined with his agent-bred organization and visualization skills, made him perfect for the IT field of 1996, where he was stuck.

At the time he was thirty-two years old, but he easily passed for twenty-three thanks to his metabolizers. Trapped in the past, he'd aged at a natural rate for eighteen years, but now his body would resume aging in the modern extended rate.

He'd just look far older than all of his friends and peers.

Suddenly, the door opened and Markus burst in.

"You're awake. Let's go."

Kin straightened up, stinging pains tapping a beat against his temples. "Good to see you, too, Markus." Markus *Fernandez*. The detail awoke, along with the fact that names no longer revealed anything about ethnicity, since generations of interracial partnerships from the twenty-first century onward had rendered them meaningless. His pale complexion and sandy hair matched his accent more than his surname.

"I'm serious. We have to go. I'll explain on the way." Still clad in standard operational gear rather than civilian clothes, Markus overrode the floating semitransparent bed controls. "Come on."

"Soccer match?" Beneath him, the bed adjusted, handles coming up under his arms and the base forming a floater chair that elevated out of the bed frame. The foot of the bed detached and sank, and Markus grabbed the handles that had popped out behind Kin.

"I wish. Agent Melete is missing in your time. Your old time. They think you might be able to help."

The word *missing* pumped adrenaline up and down Kin's body, like his mission work had never paused. Markus tilted and turned the floater chair, handling it with an ease that wasn't possible with wheelchairs from Kin's past life.

They dashed through hallways and up elevators, passing through rows of offices and stations, Markus providing background while huffing and puffing. On assignment in 1991, Agent Imogen Melete's beacon tracked her until it became static earlier in the day. The Timeline Monitoring team confirmed that the archival delta—the difference between archived timeline records and the current timeline—hadn't reset to status quo yet. At that point, the retriever lost contact, though Melete's beacon kept pinging. Yet neither confirmation nor retrieval signals arrived.

"Do you think she's alive?" Kin asked as they passed through one set of security doors.

"Her vitals are transmitting. We haven't received an emergency recall yet. But something's wrong. You know the area best. Maybe we're missing something. It's a long shot but..." Behind them, heavy sliding metal doors bolted shut, leading them to a set of bulletproof glass panels. They opened, and Kin took in a sight he hadn't encountered since his first academy tour. He hadn't bothered to—he was a field agent, after all. Why would planning and monitoring stations interest him when his job consisted of staying stealthy and on the move?

The Mission Control war room.

Three rings of workstations, holos of data and security feeds and scurrying people, all towering over him. In the middle floated a massive grid of information. The combination of images and texts made for a dizzying array of color, and it took Kin several seconds to parse out which department sat where among the rings. Security Overwatch, which monitored gravitational field shifts caused by temporal distortions. Timeline Monitoring, which tracked and pinged for discrepancies and specific timeline changes. Mission Oversight, which relayed information between retrievers and other internal teams. And about three dozen people from various other departments dashing back and forth creating a wall of cross-chatter.

To the right of the grid sat the Tentpole Protection Board, with its list of historical figures and events that had to remain continuously monitored for changes regardless of morality. To the left, a facial rendering of the mission target calibrated from security footage, along with a list of known vitals and relevant data—the merc had been hired by an undetermined party to execute a stock transaction. A large *2* displayed next to his face, indicating a sphere of influence level two: time corruption isolated to financial gain with some generational impact and zero time-evolved casualties.

Simply money in the bank.

Markus yelled, breaking Kin's thoughts. "We're here. Any luck?"

"Geolocation in Chinatown. She hasn't moved in eight hours. Coordinates are an alley between buildings, but retriever Sydney can't locate her." A man standing on a dais looked down on them, holos floating all around his head. "Thanks for coming, Agent Stewart, but I think you're too late." He spoke to the hovering projection of a man in a clean white shirt and a big desk. "Inform the AD we have a missing, possibly deceased agent. Send a flag to Civilian Integration—prepare death notification protocol just in case."

"Cover story?"

"Depends if we ever recover a body."

The discussion continued, the logistics of time-jumping a corpse while preserving its integrity—if they even managed to find it. Terms like *binding* and *shielding* and *collagen quality* flew behind him, all spit out with a clinical tone that made Kin's stomach churn. The topic turned to informing the family: "funeral stipend" and "counseling stipend" and "trauma recovery period resources."

Was that how they told Heather about losing her husband? Or Miranda about losing her father?

Was that how they were going to talk to Penny if he hadn't come back?

"Incoming message," called out a voice from the top tier.

Holographic text flew above, and Kin's restored eyesight read it with startling clarity.

From: Sydney, Catalin (Retriever): I can't explore too much because walking tours keep coming by despite the empty stores. But she's not here. The beacons are accurate within six inches and it's just pavement.

Empty stores? In Chinatown? Kin's Bay Area experience started a few years after 1991, yet the idea didn't sit right. He shut his eyes, agent mode taking over.

1991. Closed shops. Chinatown. Facts and figures visualized, pulled from books and newspaper clippings and clunky HTML web pages, all those early days spent in public libraries now filling in blanks with metabolizer-boosted cognition.

1991. Something about that year. Something about those buildings.

Something…underground.

"She's there," Kin finally said.

Markus turned to him. One by one, every set of eyes in the monitoring stage followed suit.

"She's there. 1991. The country's in a recession. Some of those mom-and-pop shops probably shut down, the restaurants and bars, too. California buildings don't usually have basements but those spaces were built decades earlier. Some doubled as speakeasies. Chinatown has some old tunnels and rooms underneath those shops. The coordinates are right." Kin looked at everyone staring at him. "Check beneath the surface."

"Pulling up building records," a woman one level up said. Blueprint holos flipped by in rapid succession. "There. There's a sealed tunnel that links several buildings in the neighborhood. Sending."

Kin and Markus watched as real-time messages flew back and forth in holo form, the team in 2142 firing off instructions and guidelines while Sydney provided updates over email. The room went silent, the only hum coming from the ventilation overhead.

"Retrieval ping detected," someone yelled overhead.

Above them, a new message appeared.

From: Sydney, Catalin (Retriever): I've got Agent Melete. She's dehydrated, injured, but alive. The target was found deceased next to her in this tunnel. I'll put a stop onto the target's stock purchase. Send Apprehension Squad to Neil Marin of Montpelier, Vermont, with charge of hiring a temporal merc for purposes of financial seeding.

"Archival delta eliminated," another voice said. "Timeline is clean. Let's get the good guys home and bring the bad guys in."

Chatter returned as the crew barked orders about dispatching the cleanup squad to Vermont, and Kin wondered if he should have chosen this path instead of hopping through time. Arresting the usually white-collar criminals behind time mercenaries might have been a safer career choice.

Except without time travel, Miranda would have never been born.

"Bank robbers," Markus said. "That's all they are these days. Everyone knows that it's too easy to get caught doing anything bigger. You remember those tales they told us in the academy? Epic adventures of saving President Bosworth in 2040? All we get are bloody thefts. At least your business with the senator that time made it to sphere level four." He looked almost wistfully at the Tentpole Protection Board and its column of bright green status quo indicators. "I've never seen that board change."

But he *could* see Miranda again, Kin was thinking, almost entirely oblivious to Markus's chatter. All he needed was an accelerator. The rest would work itself out. "Bank robbers. Sounds fun." Kin sat up straight, puffing his chest out. "You know, I feel a lot better. Metabolizers are patching up my knees. Pain free. Give me a week and I'll be ready for my next—"

"Easy there, champ," Markus said, his mood considerably lighter than just a few minutes ago. "I know you like all the action stuff. Thing is, your body doesn't agree with you. All that time without metabolizers. The report says that you've got one, maybe two time jumps left in you before time travel degrades your cells—and that's if you had extra boosters and stabilizers and a doctor by your side the whole time." He turned the floater chair around and began pushing Kin back to the hallway. "Pretty sure the TCB won't spare the resources for that. I think they have something in Research lined up for you. But at least you won't get shot at.

See?" He pointed at the lingering holographic text behind them at Mission Control. "Still a hero."

"I've never seen transmissions like that before."

"Need-to-know. Field agents don't, in case you're caught or interrogated." The grin on Markus's face beamed out, like he'd been bursting at the seams to reveal these secrets. "Are you saying you didn't like leaving notes at drop points? Bet you didn't know electronic signals are benign. But it's true, in and out of the accelerator at headquarters without disturbing the timeline. We can even download video from the past, though we can only send text in bursts back. Everyone in this room is need-to-know. That now includes you. So congratulations. No one will try to kill you *and* you won't get seizures. It's win-win."

"I can't..." A million different ideas flew through Kin's mind, lists upon plans upon options—nothing yielded a clear solution. He probably should have felt anger or guilt or disappointment, except too many emotions came and went for him to process it all. "You mean, I won't be in the field?"

"Doctor's orders," Markus said. "Or at least as best as I can understand it. They started using some technical neurobrain fancy terms. I tuned out."

"No time-jumping." Kin's eyes closed, weighted by the idea of the door to his previous life slamming shut.

"You, my friend, are getting a desk job. And you know the biggest problem with all of this?"

He didn't have to answer Markus's question. The problem came in the form of a century-wide gap with his family.

Markus gave a dramatic pause before breaking into a grin. "Desk work doesn't keep you in shape. And we need you for the weekly soccer matches. So don't be getting lazy on me."

Kin stayed silent the rest of the walk. Markus didn't seem

to notice. He was too busy talking about soccer, the words coming at such a fast clip that Kin wasn't sure if they were an intentional distraction or if Markus really pushed Miranda and Heather aside that easily.

As Markus continued, Kin told himself to give his friend the benefit of the doubt. For now.

CHAPTER 10

Three more days had passed, and since then Kin had talked with agency counselors about his feelings of loss, the Research department about his new desk job where he'd be providing insight similar to what he'd done for Mission Control, and staff doctors about his health considering the large gap in his metabolizer usage.

In the TCB's fifty-some year history, the longest an agent had been marooned prior to Kin's case was thirteen months—and that incident was decades old, prior to the subcutaneous beacon. They offered theories about why he went undetected for so long—a combination of causality from the beacon's activation in the garage and the incremental accumulation of his life leaving micro-traces of temporal footprints, not the detectable shock wave produced by jumping in and changing history in bursts. Doctors poked and prodded him, marveling at how his brain managed to *not* implode given the duration of his stay. Their theories about why Penny and his personal life completely disappeared ("Clearly, your brain protected itself from its most emotionally powerful discrepancies") didn't settle or comfort him, nor did their theory that the last six months of renewed headaches and dizzy spells was a result of his brain purging the final future memories, leading to either a single-era focus and/or a fatal aneurysm without metabolizer intervention. They even projected what would and wouldn't heal or regenerate—his knees would heal almost entirely, he wouldn't need glasses after another week or so, but he'd be stuck with the gray in his hair unless he dyed it or used 2142 semipermanent color treatments.

Department by department, each group picked his brain. Resources wanted to know exactly when flip phones gave way to smartphones. Research asked about tricks on searching through social media. Logistics had him troubleshoot their attempts at programming in popular twenty-one-A codes. For three straight days, all he did was talk about himself.

He didn't, however, talk to Penny. Didn't even activate the holo message. He *thought* about her a lot, in the way adults looked at high school photos to relive their past. Resurfaced memories all filled in the blanks about who she was and how they lived their life together, crafting a rich and vivid picture that failed to animate. He even realized that the dream he'd had right after Markus visited was their engagement party, metabolizer-boosted clarity broadcasting it all in startling resolution but without the feelings to bring it to life. Instead, the way they'd looked at each other that night remained only a dream fragment. In its place was a different persistence, a repeated question that wondered if that feeling could ever be real again—and if not, what exactly took its place?

The counselors offered a simple answer. "Don't forget your cover story and take it slow."

Markus was more blunt. "Play it."

Kin sat, clad in street clothes and discharge notification floating beside his hospital bed, staring at the black disk.

"If you don't play it then I will."

The more Kin reintegrated into this world, the more Heather and Miranda weighed on him, as if the mere act of activating a holographic message seemed like betrayal.

Or saying goodbye.

Same difference at this point.

"You're going to see her in an hour. You have to do it now."

Kin nodded, stifling the feeling in his gut. The device beeped and booped before a miniature Penny appeared.

"Hi, Kin," she said, her London accent matching his memory exactly. Her hand rose and dropped, fingers fluttering in an awkward wave, and one side of her mouth tipped upward, like it always did when she was nervous. Which wasn't always her modus operandi; at work, she directed servers and line cooks with a focus and a force that might have even impressed Heather.

The way she commanded a presence when in a kitchen, especially when the spotlight was on her, or the way she practiced her restaurant pitch for the loan application like a sales professional, her inner drive stuck out. It was like night and day compared to the woman projected before him now.

Unlike Heather, Penny's gumption drained when things got personal.

He waited for her next nervous tell, a repeated pushing of her brown hair behind her left ear—never the right.

The movement triggered a memory, one that brought a weary smile to his face. That same awkward wave, the upturned mouth, the hair behind the ear. Her cheeks burned as she walked in front of Kin, and it took him a second to realize that Penny—who knew nothing about soccer except for what she heard from Kin and brother—was wearing a Tottenham Hotspurs shirt. She'd strutted out, her posture a result of embarrassment more than nerves, stiff arms betraying the forced nature of her walk, and when she turned around, she couldn't stifle her laugh, the name BAMFORD across her back.

Logan Bamford. Tottenham's best player. Markus's *favorite* player, the one who prompted him to run around the room chanting "Bammy, Bammy, Bammy, Bammy, BamFORD!" whenever he scored. And he *always* scored against Arsenal, leading to nonstop curse words from Kin each time, and that night Markus somehow convinced his sister to wear that shirt.

Penny had the moxy to keep a catering service moving like clockwork and draw up plans to launch her own restaurant, but never enough to say no to her family.

Did Kin really name his dog after *Bamford*, of all people? Or was that another way of holding on to Penny? A surge of affection radiated, though tempered by a sinking feeling as he remembered the dopey brindle greyhound who once yelped in fear because of a dewclaw caught on a knitted blanket. He figured he'd better get used to this; with his mind now able to process both eras clearly and cleanly, his heart had to sort out the rest.

He snapped out of the memory and focused back on Penny's hologram. The sinking feeling disappeared; in its place came a rush he hadn't felt in quite some time.

"Markus told me what happened. You boys and your government institutions. He said you're recovering in their hospital. I don't think I'll ever understand why the Mars colonization project is so guarded that I can't even see you."

Mars colonization—the cover story for working in a secret time-traveling law enforcement agency. Kin told himself to definitely remember that detail until it became habit again.

Her third tell came, biting down on her bottom lip and her hazel eyes pointing to the upper left—a move that her brother occasionally used, too. "So, you missed walking down the aisle with me. Suppose I can forgive you for that one. Standing me up. Only once, though. Radiation blast is a suitable excuse. Besides, I need time to rewrite this business plan for the restaurant loan, so you know, silver lining."

Radiation. His own personal cover story.

Penny tilted her head up, standing tall in her red dress and black tights—he remembered now, he'd noticed fashion similar to his era with Heather, and she'd called it sixties mod. The only real difference was that modern fashion's textile pixels adjusted color to lighting and special occasions.

Even at a holographic six inches tall, the welling tears became clear as Penny shifted her weight, left to right, and then right to left, back and forth. "Markus says they've got you knocked out, that you'll be okay in a few days. Your burn scars will heal. He said you might look a little older and you need old-fashioned spectacles for a few weeks, but that makes you look, um, *distinguished*. So, it's sexy. You know, I was baking chocolate chip cookies for every day that you were gone, then I wound up with a hundred cookies, and Markus told me to hold off for a little bit." Her laugh was barely audible, though Penny's bright cheeks rose to counter the tears streaming down them. "I'm tough," she said, straightening up and throwing a mock bicep flex pose. "I'm tough, though. I know you'll pull through this. In the meantime, I made a list." She smiled, and Kin found himself beaming back at the projection. "My list is called 'seven reasons why I miss Kin.' One, a cat doesn't keep the bed as warm at night.

Two, I still haven't convinced you that real cooking is better than insta-meals."

"She doesn't know I cook now," Kin muttered, his furrowed brow catching Markus's eye.

"Three, Markus keeps asking me to watch soccer with him and I hate that and I do it anyway. Four, someone has to rein in your gut instincts. Five, Paw-cific Heights Cat Rescue is looking for kitten foster volunteers, and if you don't come back soon, I might give in and bring Akasha some friends. Six, we might get a better interest rate on the restaurant loan when we're legally married, so I kind of need you around. And seven..." Eyes closed, Penny sucked in a breath and held it for several seconds. "I love you. I love the soccer and insta-meals and how you can't wake up in the mornings and your awful Bombay punk music you play when you work out." Bombay *throwback* punk was the proper musical genre. Those bits of info returned at frightening speed. "I love all of it. Come home to me."

Kin took in the words, the depth and sincerity of them; he wanted his own feelings to match. But layers upon layers of memories—new and old—pulled him in every possible direction, making it impossible to get there.

A tiny clap came as Penny brought her hands together, fingers intertwining. "So. You can't see this, but Markus is waving at me to hurry up because I guess he has to leave. I don't know if you'll wake up tomorrow or a week from now, so I guess, just— I love you, and I'll see you soon."

Penny raised both hands, twittered them in a wave, and then disappeared. It took a few seconds to realize that the quick, irritating rhythmic beeping noise came from his heart monitor. Tears blurred Kin's view, and the room faded away, replaced with replays of the wedding he *did* have—with Heather. His thoughts jumped to the last six months: the dizzy spells, the fainting, the cover of PTSD for whatever the TCB's doctors would diagnose.

He should include his death in that. Because he was dead to his family.

"Did she get the cats?"

"I told her to hold off. But she goes in the mornings. Told me she's bottle-feeding kittens and finding ways to make them shit. 'Stimulate their digestion.'" Markus shook his head and laughed. "Can't imagine what Mum and Dad think about that. Bet she didn't even tell them."

"What happened with the loan?"

Another headshake. "Denied. Bank said that she needed a more unique angle for the restaurant, so she has to write a whole new business plan. She said she's going to wait until after you recover, but between you and me, pretty sure it's because she doesn't know how to give them what they want."

Kin elected to not intervene in the sibling tug-of-war between compassion and condescension that Penny and Markus often displayed. He turned to face the window.

For the first time since he'd awakened, Kin looked, really looked, at San Francisco. A few years ago, he bought Miranda a helicopter tour of the Bay Area; they'd circled from the suburban hills of the peninsula over the city itself up to Marin County and back, even under the Golden Gate Bridge. The view from the chopper seemed distant yet real, like every detail before him popped in all its grimy detail. Today, right there, with the atmotube passing by overhead, the Trinity Towers built on top of the Transamerica building and skycars forming a constant stream of little dashes and dots across the skyline, nothing seemed real. He still had to deal with it. "Now what?" he asked, turning back to Markus.

"Well—" Markus's voice took on a matter-of-fact tone "—you love her. Obviously. Lucky Penny. Learning to cook.

In your mind, she was there. I bet you even used some of her recipes. Remember that time she'd layered quinoa in lasagna just to rib you?"

Her recipe. Was that another time-travel fragment? "I don't know how *there* she was." He reached back, trying to recall all the details he could about Penny: the mango smell of her favorite perfume, the way she rubbed her feet together when she was half-asleep, the way she'd click her nails together while she tried to figure out a problem. They all seemed out of reach, a movie out of focus. "I was married to Heather. We had a life together. I need to get used to this era again before I get used to another person." His voice dropped, his head following suit into his hands. "Markus," he said. He knew what he wanted to say, though admitting it to such a close friend—Penny's brother—took all his willpower to get out. "I don't even know her anymore. Those are only memories. Heather and I were together much longer."

For all his sarcasm and quips, a solemn scowl brushed over Markus's face. "Think of it as a chance to start over. Everything you learned in the past eighteen years you can use now to avoid mistakes. If I had a chance to redo some things with Enoch, I sure would." He glanced at the clock display floating above the door. "I need to get going. Mission briefing in fifteen. Soccer Saturday? First match back, yeah?"

Of course Markus would bring it back to soccer. Penny deflected with self-deprecation when things got uncomfortable. Markus deflected with sport. He knew the Fernandez siblings better than they knew themselves.

And yet, emotions pressurized within Kin, boiling at the way Markus seemingly distilled Heather and Miranda down to an annoyance, like their fate was a scheduling conflict or a spilled drink. Words formed to run to the defense of Kin's family when he looked at his friend.

So many things to say. And there seemed to be no fit for them, not the right way. A simple nod was all it took to send Markus on his way and leave Kin alone with his thoughts.

Visualizations helped Kin recall not only the directions from the building lobby to his apartment but the exact steps and turns. Each movement echoed within his mind, from the feel of the elevator's linoleum to the drab carpet that lined the hallway. The two eras of his life overlapped for a flash, and as he got to the front door, he instinctively reached for his keys before remembering that mechanical locksets weren't a part of city life in this era. He laughed and straightened, standing about two feet in front of the door and looking up at the facial scanner. Right before he assumed the position, the door slid open.

"Kin!" Penny threw her arms around him. She squeezed him hard, and the scent of her hair—different from Heather's— caused him to pause. Of all the times he'd caught that aroma, none felt as permanent as this. "I was so worried."

He told himself to return the embrace, letting his bag drop to the floor and adjusting to the fact that Penny stood a good six inches shorter than Heather. "I'm fine. Really. I'm sorry I messed up the wedding."

"New rule in this house—no apologizing for freak radia- tion accidents," Penny said before planting a long kiss that said more than her words. Her fingers wrapped around his, leading him into the small apartment. "They told me to help you take it slow. So I wanted to surprise—" Penny's voice stopped and her grip on him weakened.

Kin looked up and around, taking in the place he used to call home. Furniture sat where he remembered it. The view out the window hadn't changed. Even the smell, the mix of recycled high-rise air and a hint Penny's mango-scented perfume, same as it ever was.

Despite the *exactness* of it all, everything before him displayed an imitation of life, not the real thing.

Meanwhile, Penny's eyes glistened over, and her mouth trembled, drooping before moving into a smile that her eyes betrayed. Would everyone react this way? And how many times would he have to spit out his cover story? "How bad is it?"

"It's fine," she said, her smile becoming brighter as her expression got dimmer.

"I look old."

"No, course not. Old is like my gran. White hair, jowls, age marks. Like, you know, a hundred and fifty or so. You look…" She stared down at the floor, and her fingers flexed in and out of fists. "You look distinguished. And, I love the spectacles. Very crown."

Crown. Though he'd been awake for a few days now, this was the first time he'd heard the era's slang. "I look old," he repeated before walking in and easing into what used to be his usual spot on the couch. The contours and padding of the couch felt like marbles instead of something familiar and comfortable. His weight shifted, trying to find a familiar groove.

"Of course not," she said, settling in next to him though beginning a rapid repetition of pushing her hair behind her ear. "I mean, naturalists don't take metabolizer treatments. Their thirties are our sixties. My cousin Cassie, the naturalist one who lives in Scotland? You've never met her. She's my age, and she looks great. You'd never even know. Well, except for a little bit of—" She stopped herself, shaking her head. "I'm doing it again, aren't I?"

One memory clicked—Penny's nervous rambling could be

her most annoying and most endearing habit. "Are you saying I look like I'm in my thirties or sixties?" he asked with a wry tone intended to lighten the mood—both of theirs.

"Look." Penny propped herself on her knees, one hand on his thigh for balance while the other gently caressed his shoulder. "Let me start over. Let's pretend I'm 'Penny the chef' rather than 'Penny the blathering fool.' I'm so happy that you're home and that you're safe. I'm sorry the accident happened to you, and I want to do anything possible to make you comfortable. Markus said you might be feeling weak or sore from the radiation blasts. You look fine, I promise." She smiled again, this time with a more genuine warmth. "You'll forget all about it next week when you and Markus argue about Arsenal and whoever."

"Thanks, babe." *Babe.* He knew he'd slipped as soon as the word escaped his lips—that was his term of endearment for Heather, not Penny.

"Babe? One near-death experience, and you're getting soft with cute names. What else do you have in store for me?"

A low scratching sound came from behind the couch, soon followed by a ball of black-and-white fur landing on top of it. Akasha's pink nose and white chin went into overdrive as she sniffed Kin. "Akasha," he said, holding out his fingers to scratch behind the collar of the cat Penny saved from an alley next to a hotel catering gig years ago. It was too bad any mention of Bammy was forbidden by the TCB; Penny would have appreciated how he and Heather worked with a rescue organization to adopt the greyhound from a racetrack.

The cat followed his movement and hissed before springing off and running back to the bedroom. "Maybe she doesn't like the smell of radiation blasts?" he asked with a forced chuckle.

Penny's left eyebrow arched up at the mention of radiation.

Another agent method came to mind, a simple defuse-and-deflect technique: change the subject. "We've only talked about me. How was your day? Is that…" Kin took a second to take in and decipher the aroma permeating the apartment. "Chicken fricassee?"

Penny's head tilted at an angle. "Did the coma turn you into a chef?"

"Ha. I wish." Kin's past and future collided in his head, reflexes from both fighting against each other. He shouldn't know a single thing about cooking other than how to open and activate insta-meals. "Lucky guess. Smelled familiar."

"You know chicken fricassee?"

Of course. Miranda called it his "famous Frenchy chicken." Had he somehow taken Penny's recipe along with him to the past?

"They gave it to me at the hospital yesterday. An insta-meal version. I recognized the name, the smell." Savory. Rich. Tender stewed meat. His last variation included caramelized onions for a hint of sweetness. "You made it on our first date, too."

Penny's eyes brightened. "And I thought that brain of yours only recalled Arsenal facts. I figured—" her voice softened as she continued "—it'd be a nice gesture for coming home. Though I wasn't sure you'd actually remember."

"It's been jogged a bit lately." That night was about a week after they'd first met at Markus's barbecue. Which also included a week of Markus telling him all the reasons why a TCB agent should *not* date his sister. He'd arrived early, not on purpose, but simply because he did. Her apartment—smaller, denser than their current shared space, with a litter of foster kittens mewling through the closed bathroom door—smelled just like it did now, a savory aroma that he now knew to be a mixture of herbs and chicken broth. She'd opened the door in full chef mode, her hair covered by a bandana and a not-that-clean apron draped on, and one look told him that she definitely didn't appreciate the early arrival. Instead, he'd played it off, acting like he wanted to learn about cooking when really, he just wanted to continue the conversation they'd had the week prior before Markus tried prying them apart.

It didn't take too long for her to figure out that he was helpless in the kitchen. And yet somehow, they'd managed to agree to a second date.

"Besides, how could I forget a master chef's creation?"

"See, you're buttering me up now," she said with a laugh. "I'm no master chef. I'm just Penny."

Just Penny. Her self-effacing catchall whenever someone complimented her, probably spawned from a childhood under the thumb of her overbearing parents. He'd referred to the lucky penny as "just a penny" countless times, and all this time, the phrase, the coin, and the woman were anything but. "I was actually thinking maybe you could show me how to cook," he said, searching for anything that might rebuild the bridge between them. "That is, if you're willing to teach me."

Penny's eyebrows lifted, her mouth dropping half-open. "Kin Stewart," she said after a pause, "one coma is all it takes for you to finally be interested in food."

"When you're in a hospital bed, there's a bit of time to think about stuff."

Penny motioned him over to the brighter kitchen, the colors of her dress subtly changing hues to match the light.

"So, what's going on here?" Kin asked. "For real. Not like our first date."

"Well, this is simmering right now. I just added red wine. And I'm about to mince some garlic." A tray formed out of the countertop next to garlic cloves, a dull gray cutting board materializing out of standard kitchen furniture. "Some chefs like the auto-mincer but it's too precise. Too perfect. There's no love in it. I prefer to still cut by hand." Penny put the cloves on the board, then started quickly chopping, her hands in textbook position.

Kin knew it. Not from a cooking show or an online video or a book. He knew it because he fought the urge to join in, do it himself, and model her perfect form. Instead, he forced himself to stand still. Though when Penny stepped back, one thing became clearer.

Her work was much neater than his.

All those years, was he just emulating what lingered in the depths of his memory?

"So, you mince and add." Penny grabbed chopsticks off the counter and used them to push the garlic in before stirring. "Sprinkle it in, give it a stir, and taste." The contact of fresh garlic and hot liquid released a warm, savory scent into the air. Penny held up a tasting spoon to him, her eyes glowing. "I don't know what you did with the old Kin but foodie Kin is sexy."

Heather had always given him grief about loving cooking *too* much, claiming he sometimes put in too much effort to be practical. He'd have to get used to getting encouragement for this. He tasted, letting the flavors percolate, his mind deciphering Penny's alchemy. "What about adding caramelized onions?" he said, the words coming out reflexively.

"Caramelized onions?" Her fingers pushed her hair over her left ear, once, then a second, then a third time.

"Yeah. I mean, it's just an idea." Kin nodded but averted his eyes. "I read a little bit on it while laid up."

"No, it's a fine suggestion. It's just that..." A flush came over Penny's cheeks, her shoulders tensing up until they blended into her neck. She blew out a sigh, eyes closed, and her posture reset.

He'd struck a nerve with her. Only one hit that hard.

"It's just that my dad suggested the same thing. Yesterday. Told me he was helping me with 'unique angles' for my restaurant idea."

"I'm sorry. I didn't mean to—"

"It's fine. Really." This time, it was Penny's turn to nod to thin air. "I refused to use it. Wouldn't even try it. It could have made the best damn chicken fricassee in history, but they just couldn't help themselves from trying to tweak my recipe. It wouldn't be mine anymore. But," Penny said, opening the storage slot in the wall for vegetables, "now it's different."

"How's that?"

"You suggested it. On your first night back after a radiation accident. So—" she held up a bright yellow onion "—it's not their change of my recipe. It's your first suggestion as a chef." Despite her smile, a film covered Penny's eyes, and she blinked rapidly, the unpeeled onion still in hand. Kin reached over and pulled her in, the familiarity of her fit igniting even more memories and feelings.

"Hey. Don't worry. I'm back." Kin pressed his lips against the top of Penny's head, a surge of affection rising out of nowhere—and a completely impossible gesture for the much taller Heather.

"I'd really like you to think about a new job," she said into his shoulder, her voice barely audible. "You know, if we decide to start a family someday, we need something safer. Something without radiation."

The word *family* caused him to stare straight up to the ceiling, unblinking. His body stiffened instinctively, images of Miranda and Heather coming to mind at the mention of family. He remembered now, he remembered vividly that he and Penny had talked about this in the weeks following a day out with Markus's son—in fact, he told her that he wanted to have kids soon, much sooner than this era's standard of waiting until fifty or so. She was the one who hesitated, so his empty response probably threw *her* off.

Of course she expected a different reaction from him. To her, that conversation was only weeks ago. For him it was in another lifetime.

"You know what? I'm sorry. I shouldn't bring that up right now. It's not the time or place. We have plenty of time to discuss it later," she said, her syllables slamming into one another as she pulled back. "So, caramelized onions. It's your suggestion. You should cut it. Like this."

The knife's weight felt familiar in his hand, a hefty, solid presence. But Kin reminded himself of where he was, *when* he was, who stood next to him, and altered his grip to a much poorer form. And as he cut, he purposefully chopped at odd angles, slow speeds, failing to get all the way through. The result was something that almost looked like when Heather tried cooking.

She never could keep up with him in the kitchen, and when Miranda was born, she gladly handed all culinary responsibility over to him. She'd sit at the counter, sometimes with glass of wine in hand and laptop open, sometimes coloring with Miranda or reading to her, but hardly ever touching a pot or pan again. And always offering to do the dishes afterward.

He could hear her laugh now. It echoed in his mind, worming its way into every thought, every breath.

He missed her. And she'd probably been dead for a hundred years or so by now.

Penny took the onion chunks from him, though she caught his long look. He offered a smile in return that faded fast, even when he tried to force it. For the first time since returning to the apartment, a heaviness sank his limbs, an unnatural stillness that made every gesture become more and more difficult.

"Aw, don't worry. You did fine." Penny gestured to the cutting board.

She tossed the onions into an adjacent frying pan and punched numbers into the floating holo burner controls. "And now we let them do their thing. Sauté until the heat brings out the natural sugars in them." She cozied up to him again, not with the urgency that came with concern, but a softness that only affection could draw out. They locked eyes, and though something about Penny's very presence draped a familiar calmness around him, everything about her remained out of focus.

Their first date. And his first day back. Penny still felt like a silhouette in his mind, as if someone had copied and pasted another person's instincts onto his body.

Perhaps the mystery of the present simply needed *more* of the past to fill in the blanks. On that first date, they'd kissed by the stove. In this moment, Kin leaned over and did the same thing. They remained in each other's arms until it was time to stir the onions.

The next morning, Kin had to remind himself to play dumb, at least when it came to cooking. And while he could whip up an impressive eggs Benedict, with a rich handmade hollandaise sauce atop perfectly poached eggs, he opted for a much more basic dish of buttered toast and sunny-side up eggs, all delivered to Penny in bed.

"Aren't you the injured one?" she said, wiping her eyes. Akasha jumped up onto the sheets, suddenly eager at the smell of the eggs. "You should be letting me cook."

"My job starts way before yours. Government hours, not chef's. Thought I'd try to return last night's favor."

Penny took the fork off the tray and gently stabbed the egg yolk, a pool of yellow oozing out, an impressed "mmm" coming from her. She blinked sleep out of her eyes, and the morning hour probably stole the real meaning of the gesture from her.

He'd done this years ago, not after their first date but about two weeks later following the first full night at her apartment. Back then, the drive to impress her ran so high that he'd spent the prior three days, along with twenty-six eggs, trying to teach himself how to make sunny-side up with runny yolk. This time, he only needed four—the two on Penny's plate, and the two he'd tossed out because his use of spices would have given him away. And like then, Penny offered a smile, one that seemed to marvel more at the gesture than the content.

"I wish I could stay but I need to get to work," he said, both years ago and now.

The reactions in return split directions: past Penny playfully pouted before thanking him while present Penny reached over for his hand, eyes bright and smile beaming, then said, "I love you."

But the idea hadn't worked. He'd have to try again. He'd expected a burst of nostalgia or a surge of affection or something *tangible* from dipping into their past once more. Instead, all he got were memories as pure data, facts and figures and images to be mined for information but devoid of emotion.

The counselors had told him that he may not feel an immediate return of deep love for Penny, not after a lifetime with Heather. But the gap between the quiet affection he felt and the deep adoration and love that *should* have been there stretched to an endless, impossible distance.

CHAPTER 11

During the next two weeks, things reached a kind of equilibrium with Penny, a cautious affection that felt like muscle memory following physical therapy. He'd done this before, living under a cover story. In private, he cooked himself lunch and listened to classical music. Around her, he acted inept in the kitchen and still played his supposed favorite bands in the skycar. On two occasions, he'd even tried more of his reenactment experiments, to varying degrees of success.

The rhythm of their daily lives became familiar again, even if that deeper connection remained elusive.

At Kin's Research job, Markus was right: all of the targets were glorified bank robbers. The TCB's tentpole protection plan kept history safely static and bland from ideologues and idealists, leaving only those ambitious enough to fill their wallets by hiring known temporal mercs and fugitives. Information requests came, but rarely with the urgency of the Sydney incident. Instead, Mission Control and Resources asked for information on people, places, and events, some specifying the exact minute and location and others requiring drawn-out reports mining social media and news archives to pinpoint potential temporary safe house locations. Each call focused on planning, not reacting.

It was, in the truest sense, a job.

Then a single message changed everything.

The message's subject line didn't register right away. *Using the research portal to view past websites* seemed benign at first, especially since he'd spent his days looking at archived versions of websites across the first quarter of the twenty-first century, or twenty-one-A as the TCB code-named Kin's old home. However, opening the message revealed a new horizon.

Now that you've got the basics of the job, it said, you'll also need to dig deeper from time to time. Our digital archives are large, but they can't beat the real thing. See the following instructions to access the digital-temporal portal (DTP) for live snapshots of the internet from your designated period.

Digital-temporal portal. A fancy way of saying viewing the web across time—not an archive, but the actual websites that Kin used. Markus had said something about how electronic signals traveled temporally without impacting the timeline, and now a new idea stared him in the face. A way to look into the past, as it was happening, to find his family.

A different kind of time travel—a path to reach Heather and Miranda.

He'd been aching to discover Heather's fate after he'd disappeared on them. She was the capable one, the practical one, the steady one; every fiber of his being knew that

Heather would weather the storm and come out of it. And if she landed on her feet, that meant Miranda was safe. Heather would battle tooth and nail to make sure it happened.

He just needed to see it for himself.

Kin's hands hovered over the physical keys—a special request he'd made because modern floating holo keyboards didn't feel quite right—forefinger waiting for the signals from his brain to execute pressing down on the letter *H*. They fumbled over the rest of the keys, nerves shooting up and down despite his confidence that Heather would emerge from this experience stronger, smarter, better. That's what she always did.

Though maybe the possibility of her happiness without him was the true root of his hesitation.

He shook his head, cursing to himself, then typed out the rest of her name.

But nothing came up. Not for *his* Heather Stewart, anyway. Kin tried all the different ways to identify her—job, alma mater, friends, even using *Star Trek* as a cross-reference—all across different years. He backed up the dates, year by year until something finally hit in early 2014, mere months after his departure.

Obituary: Heather Jodie Stewart (Rivers)—Heather Stewart, age 39, passed away peacefully yesterday from complications related to brain cancer at Oakland General Hospital. She is survived by her daughter Miranda Elizabeth Stewart.

Born in San Diego, Ms. Stewart was an enthusiastic and kind soul who loved the outdoors, animals, and science fiction. In high school, she was an all-American volleyball player and received a scholarship to UC Berkeley, where she eventually earned a BA in economics and graduated from their law program. She practiced tax law at the firm of Newman & Lambert until her final days. A memorial service will be held at *Oakland Memorial District and Cemetery*.

The words petrified Kin, leaving him staring at the text in front of him as it lost focus and meaning. He forced himself to read the words again, then a third and fourth time before getting stuck on the phrase, "passed away peacefully."

Her headaches. In the garage, she'd said it was just stress. She probably didn't want to worry him, not with his blackouts at the time and Miranda's growing disconnect. She took it all on herself rather than take the time to get it checked out.

The needs of the many. That's what she'd said.

No amount of metabolizers or 2142-era medical advances could have curbed the sickening pit growing in his stomach. He needed to cry, scream, disappear, all of it at once. But he couldn't. Not here, not at work. And not at home, not with Penny.

Everything had to be buried underneath the surface. He'd done it before. He'd do it again. Kin steadied himself, palms flat on the arms of his chair, his breath even. Minutes passed, some undetermined time that somehow allowed him to step back into reality—a reality where a tumor had been growing inside Heather's body while he'd simply disappeared. He looked again at the date, overcome with the sinking realization that Heather would have died whether he was by her side or not. The only difference was in who remained to watch over Miranda.

A wave of nausea returned as the final thought hammered home: a life where Miranda didn't have either parent during her fragile teenage years.

Kin's fingers flew over the keys. While Heather's name proved difficult to type, Miranda's came aboard with an urgency that shoved aside the tremble in his hands.

Through the DTP's timeline feature, he zeroed in on a date about two years after his departure, then opened a normal search engine window and punched in Miranda's name and her high school.

No varsity soccer results arrived. Or student projects or any other results of note. Tension gripped Kin, his shoulders tight and breath short as he submitted query after query, inching forward in time. Finally, the first result appeared just past Miranda's eighteenth birthday—not from the website of a university, but a legal document that used an odd formal diction:

```
Incident 2093959: STEWART, MIRANDA E (F) DOB
8/28/2000
Call Type: TRAFFIC VIOLATION, DUI, POSSESSION
(MARIJUANA)
Result: CITATION, APPREHENSION (RESISTED)
Location: University/Bryant
```

Kin double-checked the webpage title, his heart sinking as he read the words *Palo Alto Police Department Report Log*. He stared, reading and rereading the words without blinking, leaning forward to the edge of his chair.

He didn't recognize the world anymore. Not this world.

The DTP refreshed, as Kin skipped ahead further. This time, the first result was a photo. Though he knew the woman in it was Miranda, she appeared unrecognizable: sullen bags under her eyes, a damaged posture loaded on her shoulders, eyes glued to the floor. She wore an orange jumpsuit, and behind her, a court bailiff stood at attention. Kin's fingers reached out and penetrated the holographic photo caption, as if that would make the scenario go away.

Miranda Stewart, 24, of South San Francisco listens to Judge William Hornby. Stewart pleaded no contest to the DUI crash that killed two people on September 16, 2024.

He skimmed the rest of the article, words unable to form into coherent sentences. "Third offense" and "blood alcohol content" and "second-degree murder" and "vehicular manslaughter" told enough of the story, the phrases stirring a nausea and light-headedness that had nothing to do with metabolizers or memories.

He tried more searches in between, pulling up loads of social media posts and photos, each showcasing a life, a person, that he didn't recognize. Images and videos of dilated pupils and slurred speech, of unsavory types and terrible friends, of half-empty cocktail glasses and not enough clothes. Gone was the bright student who talked about programming projects and *Doctor Who*. In her place was someone who represented the total opposite of the values he and Heather had tried to instill. Where did all the lessons of a young lifetime go?

Except Kin knew. Half of them vanished without explanation. Half of them died of brain cancer.

Kin told himself to focus, shaking his head out of his stupor and performing one more search, this time right around Miranda's thirtieth birthday. The top result read: Why PTSD is a Family Issue.

The web page loaded up an essay by Miranda hosted on *Prison Voices Journal*, apparently an online magazine featuring articles written by convicts. His head already swirling, the paragraphs seemed a jumble of vowels and consonants, an incomprehensible wall representing a future that never should have happened. When it came to her final few sentences, Kin forced himself to read every single word, slowly and clearly.

My father's PTSD went untreated. It went beyond his fainting and dizzy spells, it cast a dark cloud over our family for six months before he left a farewell note and was gone. Anxiety built a wall between my parents during those months, and it drove fear into my sophomore year of high school. It bent our family to the limit, and when my mother passed away, all I did was ask myself "Why?" over and over—there was no one else to ask. If my father had received proper counseling, if he'd modeled the behavior of accepting help instead of putting it off and fighting it, maybe things would have been better for him—maybe my mother would have taken his lead and gotten her headaches checked out much earlier. At the very least, maybe I would have made smarter decisions. But treatment starts at the top and trickles all the way down. Anything less and the system has failed us.

This was all wrong. A clean handoff—that's what the TCB promised. How could anything "clean" create such a downward spiral?

The shocking numb began to wear off, replaced with an imagined horror show of what Miranda might have gone through after he left them. A farewell note—that was all they did? And the burden of burying her mother on top of that?

A torrent of emotions coursed through him. Anger. Frustration. Despair. Many wrong choices. Or perhaps just one wrong choice.

In the end, it all led to guilt. The unending gnaw of guilt. If Kin felt that, Miranda must have experienced it a hundred times over.

Cancer took Heather. He couldn't change that. But Miranda fell victim to the gaping wound left by her vanished father. He reread the paragraph, her cohesive and sensitive thoughts composed under the most dire of circumstances while in the worst of places. Somewhere beneath sixteen years of absent parents and bad choices stirred the soul of the daughter he used to know.

A few days ago, he'd spent his time wondering about his life with Penny, the ins and outs of his job, and just possibly finding a way to check in on his daughter. Now, much more was at stake than peace of mind. There had to be some way, any way to contact her, to nudge her back on the right path, to course-correct her destiny into who she was supposed to be.

The pounding in Kin's chest seemed more suitable to running five miles on his recovering knees. He clicked down on the keyboard and scrolled down while reminding himself to stay calm. Viewing the web across time—*in* time—meant that he could establish a webmail account and contact Miranda. He saw no reason why it couldn't technically work, though doing so broke every rule in the TCB's book.

But would they catch him?

It took a good few breaths to drain the nervous energy out and assess the technical specifics: the portal gave access to a virtual computer, one that ran an emulated version of the era's popular operating system: same applications, same speed, same web browsers, and even preloaded with standard office software. The only difference was that the virtual computer was merely modern software pretending to be an ancient system.

That, and the TCB's monitoring. The change in Miranda's life would be a subtle civilian shift, not a documented financial boon or governmental coup. And there would be no time jump associated with it, no temporal frequencies for the Security Overwatch group to detect and begin investigating.

That only left one thing. He loaded up the message about the DTP:

As our goal is to minimize corruption, that means communication with the past is prohibited. Gambling, message forums, email, and any other type of direct interaction is strictly forbidden. Your browser's history and data cache will be transmitted in real time to our IT staff for verification. Failure to comply will result in appropriate TCB management actions. Any abuse of the DTP for personal reasons or attempts to reverse engineer its technology will result in immediate termination, potential apprehension, and/or elimination. For more information, please reference section 9.2 of the TCB Research Handbook, revision 18C.2.

Reverse engineering. The term lingered in Kin's mind, connecting dots between his past and present. When he'd told Markus about his old job, he mentioned reverse engineering the hacker attack to determine how they infiltrated the servers without leaving any tracks.

That applied here, too.

The TCB's system was a mere emulation of computers from his era. All those hours spent reverse engineering hacker damage to the Gold Free Games servers, figuring out how they broke in and erased their digital breadcrumbs, suddenly became Kin's training ground for rescuing his daughter from a damaged life.

Reverse engineer. Remove his tracks. Leave no trace behind. He couldn't bring back her mother, but he could at least somehow guide her from the future.

Back in the café, Markus said that thinking about server hacks was no longer his job. But he was wrong. It was just the start—and quite possibly the only way to reset Miranda's destiny.

CHAPTER 12

It worked.

Or at least the technical part did. Over two days, he'd put aside everything else and focused on writing computer code that hadn't been used in more than a century. It wasn't a matter of life and death, but it was the closest thing. Thanks to the DTP, he accessed and tested the coding on IT sites from his old era—sites that easily doubled as "research" on era-specific tech trends should anyone ask—and the results proved interesting.

It seemed simple enough: the code allowed him to view whatever he wanted through the DTP browser while instantly rewriting the recorded history that the TCB's staff downloaded and reviewed.

Email was accessible. His tracks were covered. Consequences would be avoided.

His tests proved it.

Only four quick steps existed between him and Miranda: log in. Activate DTP. Run the scripts. Make contact.

That still didn't give him any guidelines for telling Miranda how to stop her downward spiral. He'd pondered other ways to try to rescue her from the brink; those all depended on influencing other people, counselors or lawyers or whoever. That potentially created a footprint of timeline corruption spread far too wide.

Direct contact was the safest, most stable way to help her. At worst, she'd consider it a cruel prank and nothing would change. At best, she might actually believe him.

Kin's cursor hovered on the webmail screen with his old account. If it didn't work, he supposed he'd know soon. He'd either be lectured or fired or perhaps worse.

He pondered this threshold when something jolted him out of his stupor. Some parts of the era returned with ease, yet others, like the communicators everyone wore, still seemed foreign. A light *thump* came from the small wristband on his arm, repeating at regular intervals. He reminded himself that he had to flick his wrist to activate it, then said "Caller." A disembodied voice told him directly in his ear that it was Penny on the line.

The clock showed that it was approaching four o'clock. Even when he was doing desk work, things seemed to time-jump—wasn't it just noon? Or did his afternoon of ignoring his duties to hack cause the minutes to feel like seconds? "Answer," he said, and the wristband broadcast a tiny beep that rattled the bones in his ears enough so that only he heard it. "Hi, Penny."

"Hiya. How's your day going?"

"Oh, you know." Kin leaned back in his chair, three tiered holo windows showing various peeks into twenty-one-A before him. "Business as usual."

"Right. Well, I wanted to see when you'd be coming home. I've been toying with a new recipe. If it's 'unique' enough, maybe this is the one to showcase in the business plan for the bank. Come home in time and I can give you another lesson."

"If it sucks, I can always make tacos," Kin said, the words blurting out before he realized that that was the running joke with Heather, not Penny. In fact, it probably came off as a complete jerk response to Penny. He made a mental note to not confuse inside jokes with significant others. "Sorry, that came out wrong. Poor attempt at humor."

"Tacos? Did you want Mexican soon? I can do that—"

"No, no," he spit out before she picked up on the fact that he said *he'd* make them. "Really, I'm just kidding. Stupid joke. Your idea sounds great." Kin glanced again at the floating holo screens, and the enormity of the past few days hit him with a sudden fatigue that melted over everything. An evening of cooking and dining with Penny *did* sound great, and maybe even necessary before he dived into saving Miranda from herself. "I'll leave here in about an hour. How about we eat a little after that?"

"Lemme see…" The sound of beeps and boops came through, probably from Penny checking her recipe and the fridge inventory. "Okay. Yeah. Around sixish."

"Sounds good. I'll see you in a few."

"Okay. Don't work too hard. I love you."

Penny still said "I love you" like nothing had happened. "Love you, too," he bit out, and he heard the offline beep signaling Penny's disconnection and his cue to sigh.

Kin told himself to focus on the remaining hour of work,

not uncomfortable "I love you" statements, not incurable cancers from the early twenty-first century and especially not the message that might change his daughter's life.

The beauty of time travel was that those types of things could wait until tomorrow.

His finger swiped his data list to move on to the next to-do item, yet his mind kept veering back to the webmail screen.

It was right there waiting for him. He could give it a test run or at least draft the email. A few minutes of that, and then he'd go home to Penny and give his mind a break.

He should at least start.

The DTP's date cycled through the days, months, and years until it showed the day after Heather died. That seemed to be the most appropriate time. Any earlier would rob Miranda of her final moments with her mother. Any later would be too late.

He'd listed and outlined, created and deleted drafts, kicked himself for getting too far ahead, then kicked himself for not planning it out enough. It took repeated stops and starts to get even the first few sentences out.

From: Kin Stewart (chefkstew@messagemail.com)
To: Miranda Stewart (mirawho@messagemail.com)
Subject: I'm here for you

First off, I am so incredibly sorry about what has happened to Mom and that you are suffering alone. I know it's been months since you last saw me but I didn't just leave you, I promise. I am back with my old special forces unit handling something top secret. Technically, I'm not supposed to be revealing this to anyone, but you're too important and you've been through too much. I need you to know that I'm still here for you. You are not alone.

I want to say more except I want to make sure that you believe me first. Two conditions: first, you can't tell anyone that I've contacted you. If my unit somehow detects our correspondence, then they'll throw me in the brig or worse. Second, even if you don't believe me, please still abide by #1. The danger is no lie. Just don't respond, act like nothing ever happened.

You'll need proof, I know. Here it is. The last meal I cooked for you was lasagna with quinoa. I told you about it right before you went to Tanya's to work on your programming project. And that night, you and Mom argued about Star Trek. I hope this counts.

Even if you don't believe me, I hope you'll listen to this one thing: I was too stubborn to get help for my issues these last few months. It affected you and Mom and I'm sorry about that. This is a weird and difficult time for you, so find some support, no matter what it is. It's okay to let people in.

Love, Dad

The cursor hovered over the save button. It waited for him, one simple action that would release his thoughts so he could focus on Penny for a night.

But then he moved it over to the send button, the impulse to do so pulling like history's strongest magnet. His daughter's fate rested in seemingly a single click, a mere flick of the finger. A thought crept in, an insidious doubt that he'd never considered: even if Miranda believed him, would she accept this version of their relationship—a relationship that came with a history of his own mistakes?

He'd come too far to let that stop him now. Though he'd told himself he was only drafting—not sending—the message, his teeth dug into his bottom lip hard enough that the metallic taste of blood caught him by surprise, and he told himself to do it already.

He clicked.

A confirmation message appeared and disappeared, and he immediately reloaded his in-box to the next day.

Nothing.

Kin refreshed the DTP for the day after. Still nothing. And again and again, successive weeks forward until he'd moved a year out.

Still nothing.

Did TCB block the activity? Maybe the script interfered with sending data? Maybe the DTP didn't allow for data upload?

But he'd tested it. And if TCB detected him, Security would be here by now. The only remaining option was the most logical one.

Miranda had refused to reply.

The reason why, though, was unclear. Disbelief. Anger. Hurt. Fear. Maybe all of the above. Maybe it didn't matter. Kin reloaded the *Prison Voices* article, reading it and rereading it until he was certain that nothing had yet changed. Time hadn't rippled forward because Miranda still spiraled downward.

Kin targeted the DTP for the day after the first email and began typing.

From: Kin Stewart (chefkstew@messagemail.com)
To: Miranda Stewart (mirawho@messagemail.com)
Subject: I'm going to keep trying

I can tell that you don't believe me. But I'm going to keep trying. I'll send you a message every day with a memory only I could know. If you want me to stop, just say so and I'll stop. But until then, I need to prove to you that it's me. I need you to know that I really am here, especially with Mom gone.

The first memory: when you were three, we got you your first tricycle. But when we put you on it, you refused to stay on the seat. Instead, you stood next to it and pulled it by the handlebars in a big circle in the driveway.

The hesitation from moments ago failed to materialize. Instead, Kin hit Send with a purpose, and clicked the refresh cycle with a methodical determination that matched any field mission or recipe. No response from Miranda. No difference in the journal.

No change.

Kin loaded up the next day and began typing his next memory.

Twenty-six memories were sent Miranda's way while Kin sat at his desk. Each was a simple passing of information that took only minutes to compose, a few sentences detailing specific memories from Kin's life in the past before he checked for responses and changes to the *Prison Voices* site.

On the twenty-seventh try, a response finally arrived.

From: Miranda Stewart (mirawho@messagemail.com)
To: Kin Stewart (chefkstew@messagemail.com)
Subject: RE: Memory 27

"I'm sorry to leave you just a note but I have to go away for a long time, maybe forever. I love you very much and I hope you both have long, wonderful lives."

If this really is you, then tell me when you left that note.

128

Actually, I don't care. I just want you to read that so you know how it feels to get it.

The joy of receiving a response disintegrated quickly with the sheer punch of Miranda's words. That note didn't come from him; it was the "clean handoff" Markus mentioned. He considered all the different ways he might apologize or explain away the situation, to mend the emotional laceration caused by the TCB's Logistics department. He sat, gnawing on his knuckles while whittling down his options.

In the end, he couldn't tell her the truth. But he could still be honest, then leave the rest to her. And if he was going to fail at this, being honest was the best way to go out.

From: Kin Stewart (chefkstew@messagemail.com)
To: Miranda Stewart (mirawho@messagemail.com)
Subject: RE: Memory 27

I can't reveal the whole circumstances behind that note, but just know that every word of it is real and I'm sorry that was the last you heard from me. I can't change what happened and I can't bring Mom back, no matter how much I want to. All I can do is be here for you now.

I won't push any further. But I'll keep checking this email if you need an ear. And I love you very much.

Much to Kin's surprise, a response arrived nearly immediately.

From: Miranda Stewart (mirawho@messagemail.com)
To: Kin Stewart (chefkstew@messagemail.com)
Subject: RE: Memory 27

I don't know if it's really you or not but I don't really care right now. I miss you. I miss Mom. And everything hurts.

The email tore at him, every single character in the short message carrying the sorrow and burden of an entire family. But it also bore something else, something that cancer and the distance of a century couldn't take away.

She'd reached out to him. The tiny electrical signals whizzing in and out of time carried more than just text. They brought a lifeline to his daughter, no matter how thin the strand.

Kin looked at the time stamp of the email, and it dawned on him that this was as close to real time as possible. The conundrum of emailing with someone who was, at present, dead and buried messed with his head, and the TCB medical staff had warned him that the occasional pressure headache may still surface, particularly when thinking about his old life. That didn't happen now, perhaps because this wasn't a memory. This was a live interaction.

He didn't dare check her future. Not yet. Too many variables were at play now that they were communicating, and Kin needed to help her stabilize before looking again to see if anything had changed. The gears still turned on her possible outcome, the chaos still churning across time. Simply talking to his daughter was now the most important mission he'd ever taken on.

The next few hours sped by. Six months of Miranda's life unfolding email by email over thirty messages. She started off hesitant, revealing only tidbits of her life, such as how Heather's mother had moved up from San Diego to stay with her or how she slept with Bamford on Heather's side of the bed every night for a month until the dog stopped whimpering at night—or how she finally took her dad's advice and spoke to a grief counselor for teens.

Around the third month, she even started mentioning normal teenage life again. Classes, friends, projects; the sorrow remained but no longer controlled her. She completed her school semester, finished junior varsity soccer season, came in at the top of her programming class, and even went to her first school dance.

In the middle of it all, she turned fifteen. Her birthday came and went, and all Kin could do was write her a message. Over the course of that afternoon, he experienced the complete range of parenthood emotions, so much so that when his wristband vibrated with calls, he didn't even notice until the fourth time the present tried to pull him out of the past.

As his forearm pulsed, Kin leaned back. The curve of his neck ached, and a stinging burn attacked his hips, and a quick look around told him why. Day had turned to dusk, and the screen's clock showed that four hours had passed since he last talked to Penny. "Penny. Hi."

"Kin, where have you been? I've been trying to reach you for ages."

"Right. Right. I'm sorry. Work went haywire, and I kind of…"

Penny sighed, a subtle deflation of disappointment that mimicked her mother's silent indignation. Not that he'd ever tell her that she did *anything* like her mother.

"I should have called," he said, straightening up. "I should have taken one minute to step away from stuff and let you know I'd be late. I'm really sorry."

Another short exhale came over the line, this time sounding like it returned to neutral rather than bearing the weight of frustration. "I'm the one who should apologize," she said. "Your doctor warned me about short-term memory loss for a bit. I'll choose to believe it's that and *not* that you've suddenly lost your interest in cooking." She let out a quick laugh, and he imagined her shaking her head, her brown hair swishing back and forth.

Something rang familiar about her reaction. Not her words, but maybe her tone, the quick way she dismissed the conflict and returned to status quo. More memories arrived, not just their own fights but her battles with her family. They all ended with her shrugging it off, like she was programmed to resolve things the same way Kin programmed code to erase his temporal-digital footprint.

How easy it was for humans to fall back into their patterns, wherever or whenever they were. Except, apparently, being in mad, passionate love. That part wasn't quite as simple.

Kin's usual response to Penny's rug-sweeping was a grunt of acknowledgment, a way to reset things. But right before it came out, a different option appeared, one that may have been impossible before life in 1996—Heather, Miranda, and everything in between—changed him.

"Don't be sorry. It's not your fault." Kin nodded. The gesture may have been invisible to Penny, though maybe the affirmation wasn't solely for her sake. "I'm heading out right now. We can still have a good night," he said, "I promise."

They said their goodbyes, and Kin closed out the holo window for webmail, though he remained seated for just one more task. His hand trembled as he punched in the exact DTP search specifics for Miranda's *Prison Voices Journal* essay. The results' status bar loaded at the bottom of the screen, inching from left to right, fractions of a second stretching into the formless anxiety of waiting while the algorithm searched 2030 for any evidence of Miranda in jail.

No results found.

Everything released, from the muscles in Kin's shoulders

to the air he'd been holding in to the fears that clouded his thoughts. Seconds later—and for the first time since returning to 2142—he let tears flow. They might have been for the daughter he'd just saved, or the wife he'd just lost, or the fiancée who remained oblivious to the war inside him.

Or maybe for all of them and none of them; simply because he needed to.

He stopped asking why. All he knew was that he didn't care if anyone at the office saw him this time. For once, his guard dropped, consequences be damned.

CHAPTER 13

The scene created a perfect opportunity, particularly the angle behind him—no evidence of skycars in the distance or subatmospheric buildings reaching beyond the naked eye. Only a field with soccer players, each dressed in a way that hadn't changed much over the past century or so.

It was too bad that this was all he could capture for Miranda. Not the way his restored knees propelled him down the field, not the way his mind visualized three shooting options and two passing lanes on the final play, not the way he propelled a ball several inches above the diving goalie's hands.

An empty field would have to suffice.

Kin reached into his bag for another time traveler: his now-archaic smartphone. His fingers located the power button near the top and pressed down, triggering a small glow from within the bag.

As the phone booted up, Kin untied his cleats. One quick shake shed all the tacked-on dirt and grass—the only real difference between those shoes and the ones Miranda wore. He grabbed the phone, put it in camera mode, and held it at arm's length before taking a picture of himself and the field behind him.

"I knew it!" Markus called out, jogging toward him. "I knew you still had it!"

Kin tossed the phone into his bag before Markus could catch him. Except it didn't quite go inside; it landed right to the side of the opening, the camera's lens flat against the bag, making the viewscreen pitch-black. "Oh, hey, Markus. Good game."

"Don't try to downplay this—"

"It's not what you think." Kin's breath turned into quick, short inhales, and tension wound his shoulders into tight knots. "I can explain."

"Not what I think? It's *exactly* what I thought."

"It's no big deal—"

"No big deal? Kin, we needed you *weeks* ago. I knew you still had it. We should be at the top of the TCB league, but without our best scorer, we're stuck in the middle. You know how much shit I get from the Operations people? I knew you didn't need that extra time. Is this what happens when you warm up to classical music? I need a new playlist." Markus tossed an arm around him, giving him a heavy shake with a laugh. "Sharpshooter. Right on target. *Boom.*" He continued on, doing a mock play-by-play on Kin's game-winning goal, and with each passing second, the tension evaporated. "That's why I wouldn't let Research take you. I don't care if you're working for them now—you're on our team."

"Hey," Kin said, forcing out a wry grin. "I had to play it safe. Health concerns."

"Play it safe? With aim like that, you don't play it safe. You…" The words, which had been rolling with a raucous momentum, halted as the grin suddenly left Markus's face. Creases appeared, first around his brow, and then framing his frown. Kin tracked his gaze down to the bag sitting on the grass.

The glowing smartphone screen. Icons of various apps that died long ago. A background photo of Miranda.

The camera must have timed out, defaulting to the phone's home screen. They stood in silence, ten or fifteen seconds passing before the screen dimmed to half brightness. It might as well have been months or years. "That's your phone," Markus finally said. "Your phone from twenty-one-A."

A single bead of sweat trickled down the side of Kin's face, and it had little to do with playing soccer for the past hour. "I can explain."

Markus grabbed it and swiped through the screens before it could lock out. "These are recent pictures on here. You've been using this."

"A few. It's not that big of a deal—"

"Why would you do this? You can't have past tech out here. You know this. What are you even going to do with…" Kin could practically see the wheels turning in Markus's head as he stared at the just-taken selfie. "Tell me you're not actually doing this."

"I'm not actually doing this," he said with half conviction.

"Don't bullshit me. You're sending these to Miranda, aren't you? You've figured out a way past the system."

No words came out as a response, though maybe Kin didn't need to say anything. His expression gave him away. His fingers began drumming at his side, and a new list of possibilities played out, all of them involving Markus freaking out. "Listen—"

"You know what happens if you get caught? It's not just you who'll be in trouble—they'll get to her, too. She's supposed to believe you're gone. This is reckless, beyond dangerous—"

"I'm not going to get caught," Kin said, a defiance in his tone that took even him by surprise, "because I've covered my tracks."

"You're gambling with your daughter's life because you 'covered your tracks'?"

Who was Markus to judge him on this? Markus was the *cause* of all this; he'd had a choice when he showed up on Kin's doorstep, and he chose to follow the company rules. Pressure squeezed Kin's teeth together, clenching his jaw so tight that he nearly couldn't get any words out. "Maybe you missed it in your file, but I happened to work in IT back in twenty-one-A." The words launched at a rapid clip, and soon his thoughts couldn't keep up. "I know PHP and Ruby and Python and JavaScript inside and out. You're telling me that our network people know dead programming languages from more than a hundred years ago? They ask *me* for help when they can't crack old code." The justifications—things that he told himself when this whole thing began—made more sense now than they ever did. This wasn't just the right thing to do by his daughter, this was *the* smart thing, the sensible thing, the good thing that righted the wrongs committed by fate. "There's no way they'll know. I've covered all possible bases."

Markus shook his head, a simple side-to-side motion that grew into a regular cadence of rhythmic disapproval. "This is stupid. And dangerous."

Markus's comments were probably meant to keep Kin and Miranda safe. All Kin saw was an affront to his family—a challenge, a gauntlet that pitted the present against the past, and he wouldn't stand for it. Not now. "Stupid? Her not having a father is stupid. I looked up what happened to her after you pulled me back here, and it's clear she needed me. Heather died months after I left. Did you know that? Things got worse and worse for Miranda until she killed two people while driving drunk. I don't care if it's timeline corruption, Miranda is innocent in all this. She deserves the life she was going to have, not *that*. And I've changed it. The arrests, the DUI, all of it—gone." Weeks and weeks of bubbling rage geysered out. The momentum practically lifted Kin off the ground, bringing him to his tiptoes and streaming past any discipline or filters to explode on the only person who knew the truth, the only person he could possibly target. "You did this. You took my family away from me. Now you tell me, if Benjamin was ripped away from you, wouldn't you do anything to stay in touch with him? If his life fell apart because he thought you had abandoned him, wouldn't you try to change that? I know you would. Any parent would. I *had* to." Exhausted, the surge died down, turning down his nerves from boiling to a mild simmer.

"I was doing my job, bringing you back," Markus said, his voice barely audible. He swallowed hard, and his forehead was etched into weary lines. "Our job. This is what we signed up for."

Another silence arrived; unlike earlier, this wasn't a standoff. "Look, you're right. If it was Benjamin, I…" Markus avoided Kin's eye, instead staring over Kin's shoulder to some alternative world where it was his son, not Miranda, who was the victim of this. "I would do anything to make sure he had a good life." By now the field was completely empty, the only noises coming from skycar engines throttling overhead and the occasional dog bark in the far distance. "It's still dangerous. You've gotta be careful."

"It's not, though. I've tested it. Remember back at the café, you asked me about what I did at work? I'm doing the same thing here." Kin launched into an explanation of early twenty-first century technology, one that clearly went over Markus's head. "As long as I run through my process, everything's fine. All they see is that a portal is being used, right? I'm in Research—that's my job. I stay here, I do my job, and I get to stay in touch with my daughter."

Emotions cycled across Markus's face, and Kin knew his friend well enough to imagine the inner monologue that went with each of them—probably focused on rules and how Kin broke them. Kin exhaled as Markus settled on a softer, more thoughtful expression. "How is she?" he asked, his voice tender enough to read Benjamin a bedtime story.

"It's been about a year and a half since I left. She misses Heather. I can tell. But she's come out of this stronger. She's a survivor." He arched an eyebrow up at Markus. "She just got her learner's permit. My little girl. Driving."

"A year and a half? You've only been back for a few weeks. Is this why…" Markus stepped forward, a suspicious look on his face. "Penny says you flip between being all nostalgic about things you two have done together, then shutting off cold for hours. She thinks it's the trauma recovery period. But it's not that, is it? You are literally bouncing between Penny and Miranda. People aren't supposed to have lives in two eras. You know that, right?"

Kin searched for an answer that satisfied all facets of Markus: the friend, the company man, and Penny's brother.

"Are you having doubts? Is that why the wedding hasn't been rescheduled?"

For the first time in weeks—months? Perhaps even

years?—Kin let himself be completely honest with someone else. "It feels like I'm getting to know her again. But something's missing. Something's different. She still assumes we've been together for the past four years. I'm trying to keep up and I can't. I've had a whole life since I last saw her. I had a family. Things are just different and I can't reconcile that."

Markus broke his normally studious, protective mold. "This is why I never wanted my sister to date a coworker," he said, his tone half-serious. "Time travel is bad for relationships."

"Says the happily married man."

"I follow the rules."

"I keep revisiting my past with Penny. Trying to relive our moments together on fast-forward. It's helped me remember her, but I can't manage to remember *us*. The information is all there, but the feelings… All the research and analyzing in the world hasn't solved that."

"The rules would solve that. There's a reason why you're not supposed to have lives in two eras."

"I'm not getting headaches—"

"I'm not talking about headaches. Staying late at the office to communicate—illegally, I might add—with your secret daughter—also illegal—is not helping. Is. Not. Helping. We aren't meant to be pulled from two time periods at once. Emotions can't go in two directions."

Markus built a blunt wall of Rules with a capital *R*. But Kin was far too deep to turn back now. "What do you want me to do? Give up on Miranda? She's already lost her dad once."

"You're hurting her, too. Can't you see that? Do the math. From your perspective, you get a new email every time you refresh your screen. But from her perspective, she's getting your email, going on with her life for a day or two, then responding to you. You're experiencing seconds while entire days are passing for her. Think about it—if you answer four emails a day from her, that's only one day for you, but, what, a week, two weeks for her?"

In this case, Markus's attention to detail made sense. If Kin kept this up, her life could pass her by without him even realizing it.

Time travel indeed.

"Her life isn't a novel that you can sit down and read in one sitting," Markus continued. "Every time you email her, every time you read her replies, your time with her grows shorter. And every time you work late, Penny knows. She knows something's up. Because you won't talk about it—because you *can't* talk about it. And you know her, she'll never tell you it's irritating her, but it is. You have to rein this in. For Miranda. For Penny. Bloody hell, for yourself, man."

In Kin's exuberance over communicating with his daughter, these facts had never occurred to him. Her messages had become his daily habit, the thing that drove him to go to the office. Penny asked him why he seemed so preoccupied at times, but his mind pressurized with thoughts and lessons and nuggets of wisdom to pass on to Miranda—things he should have been saying and doing all along.

Still, Markus was right. On most days, the emails spanned a few weeks of her life. At this rate, she'd age fifty years in one passing year for him. Then he'd lose her forever. "Any ideas?"

"Go in real time. If a week passes in her era, let a week pass for you before writing back. Like how we schedule missions to prevent aging conflicts. You can't unsee her life. And you owe it to Penny to be more present."

He'd been home for weeks now, and yet every step forward was then met with another late night at the office, running back to Miranda and his old life rather than give Penny his all. No amount of reflecting on their past would fix that.

A week for a week.

The words sank in while they silently walked back to the main TCB building. They stepped past the sliding glass doors and looked up at the ocular scanner. A disembodied voice greeted them by name, and the security doors in front of them unlocked. "That's what I would do. Theoretically. If it was Benjamin I was trying to reach."

They stepped out in unison, and Markus pulled him aside before parting ways. "Listen. Don't screw this up. You do, and you lose everything—your career, your daughter, Penny. Be careful."

The floor clicked and clacked as the spikes of his cleats hit the tile. Kin walked down the narrow hallway of offices until he got to his desk.

An urge crept up from his gut, one to log in and read Miranda's next message.

Except he didn't. Markus was right about this, and Kin reminded himself that he nearly lost his daughter once; he didn't need to repeat that so quickly again.

Rather than log in, Kin continued down the hallway toward the department showers, his cleats echoing with each step. He told himself that his desperation for Miranda had to be tamped down if he wanted to hold on to her, especially since she'd moved far past the acute trauma of losing her mother. For now, Penny was where his focus should be.

CHAPTER 14

A dinner party.

Not just a few friends over for drinks and laughs, but a full-blown party with cocktails, appetizers, and a large guest list. Kin had suggested it. He'd had to.

Nothing else was working. Each time Kin tried to re-create a moment from their past, flashes of empathy and affection arrived, but nothing captured the same burning desire he'd felt for her in his dream. With each progressive attempt, the question of why—or perhaps why not—loomed larger in his mind.

While he'd managed to get his connection to Miranda under control—a comfortable once-per-week relationship that provided stability to his days—every time he looked at Penny, all he saw was the gaping hole he wasn't fulfilling.

He'd traded his guilt over Miranda for guilt over Penny.

And if this party didn't trigger those feelings that should have been there, maybe nothing would. After all, it mirrored their last big event—but this time, there would be no engagement to announce.

For Penny, that moment was just a little more than a year ago. But for Kin, it was a lifetime, an entirely separate wedding and relationship had come in between then and now. That night had been a celebration, with toast after toast in their honor, every time he'd looked at Penny his chest felt ready to burst. When Markus held everyone's attention, delivering a speech about all the ways Kin and Penny were *so* different and yet they still worked, they'd stood, hands folded together, the world seemingly before them.

So much of tonight echoed that day. The guest list was the same. The apartment looked and sounded the same. But *he* had changed, and the only one who knew just how much was Markus.

Penny grabbed his hand when the first guests arrived. "Nervous?" she asked.

He turned to face her, and though she was just trying to reassure him, her own anxious tells surfaced behind her smile and nod. "Looks like I should be the one asking that."

"I just want this to go smoothly."

"Your dinner parties are legendary. Everyone loves them."

"That's not what I mean." Her hand squeezed his, the tips of her nails pressing into his skin. "For you. You haven't seen these people since the accident. I just want you to be comfortable." She faced him, her eyes bright and wide. "I just want you to be happy."

"Me, too." Kin leaned in, planting a polite kiss on Penny's lips.

"Okay then," Penny said, sucking in a big breath, and Kin reminded himself to smile, too. His stomach had fluttered all afternoon at the weight of the evening.

And he hadn't even considered seeing so-called friends again.

"Open front door." The apartment's door beeped in acknowledgment and slid open. "Come on in," he said, motioning in the couple as he surveyed them.

Padma. An old coworker of Penny's. Wide smile to go with blank eyes—forced stare. Threw her arms out for a hug after a sharp inhale.

Her boyfriend, Devin. Ten years or so older than Padma. In prime shape, triathlete, though some marked wrinkles from too much sun exposure. He hugged, too, after he spent a split second too long studying Kin.

Kin reminded himself to expect this and turn agent mode *off*. He spouted out a practiced laugh when Padma said, "I don't know what Penny was talking about. You don't look different at all. Actually, you should have kept the spectacles. Retro crown, you know?"

"Appreciate it," he said, taking their coats, "but you can be honest. I won't be offended."

"Hey," Devin said with a gentle tone that was probably meant to be comforting, "as long as you're healthy. That's all that matters. Now, what smells so good?"

Devin and Padma returned to their normal voices when they greeted Penny, comments about great smells and brilliant recipes thrown around. The door chimed again; it slid open, revealing more people, including Markus hovering in the back.

Exaggerated greetings filled the space, hugs and soft pats on the back coming with a delicacy that made Kin wonder if they all worried that a hard hug might snap him in half. Markus avoided all this, instead offering a simple nod, his expression demonstrating a different type of sympathy. More familiar faces arrived and moved on to either the drink table or Penny's appetizers.

Penny and her brother exchanged quick greeting pecks.

"Sorry," Markus said, "Benjamin's sick. Enoch's on kid duty tonight." He looked around, neck craning as he surveyed the room. "Mum and Dad haven't stormed in yet?"

Penny stood up straight, mouth twisted like she chewed the inside of her cheek. "They're not coming."

"They canceled?"

"I didn't invite them. This is my thing, not theirs. You know what they'd do. Nitpick. Backhanded compliments. This party is for both of us," she said, nodding at Kin, "and I'm not going to let them turn it into something about *them*."

"Penny," Markus's voice took on a serious tone that Kin rarely encountered. "They will give you more grief for not inviting them. I'll call them now, they'll come over, just ignore whatever they say—"

"No. They're not coming."

"I'm just trying to protect you. I know how they get—this is the path of least resistance. Let me call them."

"They're not coming. End of story. Now, do you need a drink before I serve?" Before she let her brother answer, Penny spun on her heel and headed to the drink table.

Markus let out a heavy sigh before turning to Kin. "And how are you holding up?"

"Just watching Penny," Kin said, observing Penny command the growing guests and her kitchen, floating between both while never losing a step. "She's in her element."

"See?" Markus gave him a light punch in the shoulder. "That's what I keep telling her. She never listens to me."

"What's that?"

"That this is her thing. Why try to open a restaurant? The instability, it's absurd. She just got promoted, she gets to plan the menu for the catering gigs, and she can come home and throw her dinner parties. *This* is her element, not taking risks. Restaurants all seem to close in six months, anyway. I don't know why she doesn't listen to me, I'm trying to save her grief. And you, for that matter." As Markus spoke, his tone shifted, a strange brew of both protection and condescension fighting for space in his words. "You know I'm right."

Kin's instinct to defend Penny landed, despite his conflict within. "She's the best cook I know. Better than me."

"Yeah, but to have a successful restaurant? Mum and Dad didn't win all those awards simply because they were good. You can't just be *good*. It's like the bank people said—you need something unique. Something no one else can do. Let me guess—she still hasn't made a new business plan because she hasn't figured that part out yet." Markus shook his head. "My sister. Always got her head a few feet from reality." Applause echoed from the kitchen, and from their vantage point, Kin could see Penny's arms moving as she explained the recipe. A year or so ago, she'd grabbed everyone's attention with "we have an announcement to make." Now, she simply gestured to the stay-warm containers on the counter as he made his way to her side.

Their eyes met, and though he felt the pull of her look, nothing stirred in him like in his dream, and the disappointment of that caused his mind to wander toward his daughter. Thinking about Miranda was the only way to put aside his problems with Penny.

Perhaps that was the right choice for him. Kin's thoughts dwelled on the past—and Miranda's future-past—while Penny served her dish.

An hour later, Kin stood at the eye of a hurricane of people, each wanting to know how he was for a brief moment before going on about their own lives.

Patrick, the professional musician with two different bartending jobs.

Coriander, the serial dater who complained about being single at forty-two despite fifty being the average age of marriage.

Oswin, who decided to veer off into a political rant about how everything was corrupt.

Padma and Devin gushing about Penny's recipe. Zoe passive-aggressively reminding people that she was the youngest—but brightest—biochemist in her lab. Sophie spinning a long story about why Ace was her childhood nickname. Fareeha griping about her trouble with new hair-length freezing technology.

Noise upon noise.

"So glad you're feeling better. Have you heard our new drummer play yet? She's fantastic. Like Mozart and Bowie and a marching band rolled into one. We'll put you on the guest list."

"The length freezing worked but they cut it too short. Now I have this hair for the next year until it wears off."

"Joseph Marleau. Clearly the best all-around player in the league. His shot accuracy is unmatched. Did you see the match last night?"

More silverware banging against glasses. More yelling fueled by alcohol. More random clapping and random laughter.

More smiling and nodding on his part.

"And really, what do people expect these days?"

"I swear, some people never learn."

"Have you seen it? It is *crown!*"

The onslaught of people who *should* have made him feel welcome, comfortable, even happy all caused his inner barriers to build higher and stronger. He closed his eyes as Oswin said something about needing another drink before wandering off.

Kin saw nothing, the beautiful void of shut eyes. But his mind continued churning, processing every little thing picked by his ears.

The complaints. The stress. The emotion. It burned against his sensibilities, so much so that all Kin wanted to do was say that life had more important things to complain about, sparking a memory, one that prompted both nostalgia and a sinking realization.

Autumn 1998. The deck at Heather's family home in San Diego. A few months before their wedding. Invitations sat on the table in front of them, every card in the stack featuring a misprint that swapped two vowels in the hotel's name. The brick-sized phone handset, metal antenna fully extended, burned off battery heat after an hour back and forth with the printing company, a conversation that ultimately led nowhere except a vigorous bitching session over a plate of chocolate chip cookies. Heather's father, Don, walked by, his arms crossed in frank gruffness—a family trait that served his daughter's career well. His presence paused things, and as he pushed up his glasses, his salt-and-pepper eyebrows rose, and he said in a dry tone, "Before long, you'll be married. And you'll find that you've outgrown the concerns of your old life. Like wedding planning."

Back then, Heather told him to ignore her dad, that he probably just wanted them off the phone so he could go online and check his email. But the line always stuck with him, even years on and a century later.

Life with Heather and Miranda was simple, beautifully routine. They went to work. Miranda went to school. Their excitement started and ended with themselves—because it was family. Because that was what mattered. But now, standing among people that he'd once called peers, friends, colleagues, the people he'd shared triumphs and failures with before life with Heather, reality looked him square in the face.

Maybe it wasn't age. Or being a parent. Or traveling through time and dealing with criminals. Maybe Don was right.

Maybe he'd just finally outgrown his old life.

And maybe that included Penny. It made the next choice easy.

The most important role in his life right now was being a father. The thought repeated itself, tugging at him and urging him to leave the party *right now* and go check in on Miranda. He caught Penny by the arm, blurted that he had to go to the office, and headed to the door before she could reply, before Markus could stop him.

The elevator beeped with a single push and a verbal command for the ground floor, and, with that, tension melted off his shoulders.

The things that preoccupied the rest of the world in 2142 simply didn't matter to him anymore. He passed the drenched flower stand on his way to the adjacent parking garage, rain blending into his eyes with the stew of emotions inside him. He entered his skycar and navigated through the launch pipe, escaping into the air, the heavy winds tilting him left and right. Inside, raindrops still dripped off his nose and ears while maneuvering to the TCB parking level on the seventy-fourth floor immersed in Scarlatti's *Sonata in B Minor*.

Log in. Activate DTP. Run the scripts. Contact Miranda— even if it broke his new once-a-week real-time pattern.

From: Miranda Stewart (mirawho@messagemail.com)
To: Kin Stewart (chefkstew@messagemail.com)
Subject: So many tests

It's finally done. So many standardized tests for college, I can't even think straight anymore. But it's weird, doing tests and essays that, like, determine where I go to school, what I'll do. Sometimes I wonder if all of those hours of studying even mean anything in the long run.

Now that that's over with, Grandma said we should maybe tour a few colleges soon. Tanya's mom has her reading up on majors and minors. Seems like so much to deal with already.

Better than taking tests, though, right? :)

Miranda—looking at colleges already? It made sense, given her age and everything, yet a giant weight bore down on Kin's chest, causing viselike tightness. Was Heather's mom going through catalogs with her, looking at websites and videos of campuses? Or did she do that with Tanya and her other friends? Either way, it wouldn't be him.

Kin settled in, thoughts of Penny and the party dissolving away. He typed out a reply, trying to remember whatever he could pull from countless web articles he and Heather had bookmarked for this very thing, from eating healthy in dorms to applying for sports scholarships. Anything and everything he could recall with a metabolizer-enhanced memory wound up there, all accompanied by a constant nagging voice reminding him that he wouldn't be there to advise her in person.

The message fired off, and the impulse to read the response overwhelmed all of his senses. The *need* to parent her became as vital as the oxygen in the air.

From: Miranda Stewart (mirawho@messagemail.com)
To: Kin Stewart (chefkstew@messagemail.com)
Subject: RE: So many tests

You're too funny. Are you copying and pasting articles from a college prep guide? Don't worry, it's not like I'm deciding tomorrow. Grandpa has his opinions, of course. "I went to Berkeley, your mom went to Berkeley, you should, too." Guess I'm gonna hear that for a year, huh?

Halfway through his reply, his wrist vibrated with Penny on the line. "Everything okay there?" she asked. "We're almost ready for dessert."

"Oh. Right. Sorry about that. Work stuff. I, um, only have a few more things to take care of."

"Okay. Well, don't work too hard, okay?" In the background, noise from the party filtered through the line. "I used those spices from the Mars colony. I got it right. I think you'll really like it."

The Mars spices. She'd been researching her dessert recipe for weeks. Too much, and it made you drowsy for days. Too little, and it created flu-like symptoms. Just right, though, was the latest culinary trend without the nasty side effects. He'd been quite curious about how their blend of sweet and savory might work like salted chocolate, like the best chocolate chip cookies, though he couldn't tell Penny that.

He glanced down at his half-written message to Miranda. Dessert. The party was almost over. He could still go back for the end.

Despite what he felt—or didn't feel—he owed it to Penny on her big night.

"Be done soon," he said. "I'll finish up."

The line beeped off, and with it, the guests and music

and desserts disappeared, his focus back on his daughter. He finished replying, then initiated the shutdown process, all while telling himself—*forcing* himself—not to look at the reloaded screen.

Except one quick peek couldn't hurt, could it?

From: Miranda Stewart (mirawho@messagemail.com)
To: Kin Stewart (chefkstew@messagemail.com)
Subject: Brace Yourself

I have news for you, and I've been avoiding saying it for a few weeks. But, it's like one of those things that you can't avoid anymore. So, assuming you are you and I haven't been writing to a robot this whole time, I'll just say it. Okay? Here goes.

I have a boyfriend. I guess. We never, like, set official terms. But we like each other. Before you jump on a plane and kill him, let me tell you about him, okay?

His name is Alister, he's one year older than me, and I met him at our school's anime club. We're going to go to the big sci-fi convention this Saturday. His mom is helping us make costumes for it. We're doing this instead of going to the school dance.

That doesn't sound too bad, right? I know you warned me about boys and staying out and stuff, so I'll just say that Grandma met him and she approves. I already gave her the answers to the four questions, but here they are again for your sake.

Where am I going? Bay Area Space Con in San Francisco.

Who's going to be there? About 2,000 fellow geeks. Tanya is going to the dance instead. I can't believe her.

When will I be home? Convention closes at 9. We will probably get a bite after and that's it, I promise.

In case of emergency: I'll have my phone with me. And it's a very public, very crowded place.

So, are you all right? Please don't freak out. Because I'm a little freaked out about how I feel, too.

Good question. Was he all right? A number of thoughts pummeled through his mind, but not the ones he expected. Rather than obsessing about Miranda's security and safety, all he could think about was Heather.

She should have been around for this. *They* should have been freaking out together, as a family unit: Kin with his overthinking, Heather with her enthusiastic practicality, and Miranda with all of the emotions that stemmed from being sixteen and discovering her feelings. That was taken from them and so much more: Miranda's final high school soccer game, her graduation, moving to her college dorm. They wouldn't be together when Miranda got married. Or when she had her first child. Other people would take their place.

Was this how it was always going to be, projecting a life that never was wrapped in a gnawing, deafening guilt?

Kin typed his reply, the words chosen with a care that made every letter seem like fine craftsmanship.

From: Kin Stewart (chefkstew@messagemail.com)
To: Miranda Stewart (mirawho@messagemail.com)
Subject: RE: Brace Yourself

You sound excited. I hope you two have fun together and remember to just be safe. If you say he's nice and he treats you well and Grandma approves, who am I to judge?

Kin hesitated, wondering if the next thing would be okay to say. But in the end, he knew it to be true, which made it worth mentioning.

I know if Mom were still with us, she'd be excited for you, too. So enjoy it.

In this case, email turned out to be a fortunate twist since he probably couldn't have managed to speak those words aloud without breaking down. Miranda's reply, though, came with a steady thoughtfulness that seemed impossible when he first discovered Heather's passing all those weeks ago.

From: Miranda Stewart (mirawho@messagemail.com)
To: Kin Stewart (chefkstew@messagemail.com)
Subject: RE: Brace Yourself

I miss Mom. I wish she was here to meet him. They could argue about sci-fi together. It's not fair, you know? Don't get me wrong, I'm happy with what we have but nothing is the same without her.

Sometimes I feel like I can't move forward with things. Because it's not right that life is happening without her. But I keep telling myself that she would want us to change and move forward. She'd say an awesome quote and it'd make it all right.

So I'm nervous because of how I feel. But I'm also nervous because it's like this big life thing without Mom and I wonder how can it really be me without her. But then I remember that we're all different people all through our lives, but that's okay, as long as you remember all the people you used to be.

The maturity in Miranda's message felt impossible for her age, so much so that Kin checked the time stamps to make sure he didn't mistakenly email a much older, much wiser version of his daughter. Yet it came from her teenage brain, and a surge of pride radiated through his chest. That's a really good attitude, he wrote, and I think if you can keep up that kind of approach, you're pretty much set for the rest of your life. I'm so proud of you. Mom is, too, I know it.

Her reply came back in an instant.

From: Miranda Stewart (mirawho@messagemail.com)
To: Kin Stewart (chefkstew@messagemail.com)
Subject: RE: Brace Yourself

I wish I could tell you that I was some, like, brilliant Zen master or that it was something my counselor told me but I actually just borrowed that from a Doctor Who episode. See, I really am my mother's daughter.

Kin thought back to that afternoon months ago when Miranda tried to convince him that he might like *Doctor Who* because of the supposedly fake world he'd crafted in his journal. He dodged the question then, shutting it down as quickly as possible. But maybe she knew him better than he knew himself. Well, then, he wrote, maybe you were right when you said I might like it. I already have a list of quotes like that from your mom. So in a way, she's still with us.

Her next message appeared within seconds of sending.

From: Miranda Stewart (mirawho@messagemail.com)
To: Kin Stewart (chefkstew@messagemail.com)
Subject: RE: Brace Yourself

Geez, Dad, you're avoiding the obvious here: have you met someone you like? Because I'm pretty sure Mom would want that for you, too.

Kin scrolled back to reread Miranda's messages, burning the text into his mind until its simple logic became an instinct, an extension of his thought process.

Different people all through our lives. He squeezed his eyes shut, trying to conjure up the feeling of that dream, that party from a year ago. But all that came up was the Penny of today—the one who waited patiently for him as he recovered, the one who put her restaurant plans on hold for him, the one who told him not to worry about his radiation rehab and gray hair and wrinkles around his eyes. The one who accepted him—and their new life—for what they were, not what they had been.

He couldn't ever recover the life that would have been with Heather and Miranda, and he couldn't return to the same exact thing he had with Penny before. But thanks to wisdom from a TV show, Kin realized that he didn't always have to put up such a fight against his circumstances. He might even come to like life in 2142 if he just gave things a chance. He felt different because he *was* different. Penny was on board with that. Maybe it wasn't about trying to re-create his feelings for Penny. Maybe it was about discovering how he felt for Penny *now*.

And maybe that was okay. Different, but okay.

Her name is Penny, he wrote, I'll fill you in next time. Gotta run.

From: Miranda Stewart (mirawho@messagemail.com)
To: Kin Stewart (chefkstew@messagemail.com)
Subject: RE: Brace Yourself

Penny, that's funny. First you have that stupid lucky penny in the garage. Now you meet someone named Penny. It's like destiny or fate or something, huh?

Kin sat, reading and rereading the message for a blur of time until he flicked the comm on his wrist. "Dial Penny," he said, his foot tapping as he waited. No answer, and a glance at the clock showed that dessert was probably served ninety minutes ago.

The wind whipped against the windshield as Kin sped home, and rain flew at him parallel to the ground below. Across the bay, lightning flashed around the Golden Gate, distant sparks blending in with the stream of skycar taillights. Kin glanced at the time when he parked, and his coat trailed behind him as he ran, his shoes slipping on the growing pavement puddles. Water kicked up when he stopped by the old-fashioned flower stand next to the building entrance.

The apartment was quiet when he arrived except for the hum of the dish sanitizer. No holo shows projected, no music played, even the auto lights were on low from lack of motion detection.

Poking his head in the bedroom door, though, he saw Penny lying still but wide-awake under layers of blankets. Moonlight reflected off her open eyes, and the sound of rain pattered against the broad window. "Hey," Kin said, holding up the flowers. "I'm really sorry. I lost track of time. Work stuff. I'd explain more but, you know, it's classified."

He'd given this explanation about a half dozen times, different combinations of words and phrases but the same message. After each excuse, Penny's polite smile inched toward quiet indignation—though all in silence, the Fernandez trait of swallowing emotions while on full display.

This time, however, Penny spoke.

"You really think flowers from the stand outside will make up for this?"

Stunned, Kin set the flowers on the dresser.

"Tonight was supposed to be about us," she said, her tone flat. "Not just a dinner party, but the fact that you wanted to do it. I know work happens, I get that, but you didn't even care enough to call. Take five minutes—*one* minute— to call." Kin thought about the late nights at work. Missing dinner. Skipping out on the party. How could he explain the tug-of-war of his two lives? "Ever since the accident, you just... I'm not your priority. You're choosing something else."

He'd promised before. But those were empty, onetime offers to fix onetime mistakes. He needed her to know that something fundamental had shifted, that his own internal axis had finally tilted to *this*. To life with her and whatever it may bring. "Penny—"

She turned over under the sheets, only a swatch of her brown hair visible. "I'm going to sleep, Kin."

A handful of sentences. That was much more than he usually got when Penny was upset. This time he'd crossed a line, and each word from Penny carried a thousand in frustration.

He turned away, taking the usual way out with her, and if he continued, she'd most likely reset by the morning, all things back to normal, at least on the surface.

But that wasn't fair to Penny. And it wasn't what he would want to model for Miranda. This time would be different. He would be better.

"I'm really, really sorry," he started. The right phrases and sentences failed to materialize; he hadn't thought this through or planned it out, and instead words merely flailed. "I haven't been fair to you, and it's not your fault, it's just this...*thing*...

that's been getting in the way. And I've let it take over too much, it's like being pulled in different directions, and…"

Kin leaned into the doorway, his usual visualizations and options failing him. "I'm just really sorry. It won't happen again. I want—I need—to make it up to you. Please. Let me make it up to you. Don't just brush it aside again, don't just let me off the hook. Let's make this time *count*."

Seconds, perhaps even minutes passed, the only sounds the outside hum of skycars and Akasha's nails clicking on the kitchen tiles. Penny sat up, though in the dark, her expression remained unclear. She pushed down the covers, walked over to him and without looking him in the face, threw her arms around him.

Kin exhaled, pulling her in. He held her so tight that the rain on his cheeks made her hair damp.

"I'm sorry things happened this way," he said. "And I'm sorry I can't even get a proper apology out."

"Kin," she said, her voice strained and muffled, "you don't have to get the words right. I just want them to be there. To mean something."

Penny sank into him, and though he held her close, her words struck him in a way that left him feeling disembodied.

I just want them to be there.

All this time he'd spent searching for facts and logic about their relationship, replaying and reliving events to somehow make sense of it all. Their relationship was never about making sense. They had nothing in common (not until Kin secretly learned to cook), their personalities were total opposites, and even Markus tried to talk them out of it in the beginning. But they persisted, finding each other and staying with each other through time and space because of a gut feeling that told them it was where they should be.

Even his post-stranding analytical brain that searched for

understanding, that was its own form of gut-feeling attachment, the same way a lucky penny was more than just a coin.

He couldn't tell her about Miranda or Heather, but he could finally be honest about almost everything else. That meant being honest with himself, too. He knew Heather would want him to be happy. More importantly, she'd want him to simply try. He almost heard her telling him to stop overthinking so much and just accept things the way they were.

He gave the tiniest of nods, an affirmation to himself but also, in a way, a farewell to Heather and the life that could have been.

Finally.

"I've felt like a different person since the accident," he said, face still buried in her hair. "Like it stole years away from me. And I've spent this time thinking about that. Stuck on it. Trying to figure that out, how it relates to you and me. But I realized tonight that it doesn't matter. I'm changed, but we can change, too. We're not the same people we were at the engagement party." What was it Miranda told him? "'We're all different people all through our lives, but that's okay, as long as you remember all the people you used to be.'"

Penny pulled back and met his gaze. "That's beautiful. When did you become a sage?"

"I can't take credit for it," he said, the smirk on his mouth betraying the tears welling up in his eyes. "Someone once told it to me."

"Well, that person was pretty wise."

"Yeah," he said, his lips meeting hers. "She was." His head tilted down, and they kissed again, gentle at first before gradually becoming a full-body release, hurt and passion finally spilling over. The door shut behind them and they melted into each other, making their way to the bed.

Kin kissed her neck, bringing her into all of his senses, and though they were only a few hours removed from a catastrophic wound on their relationship, suddenly he'd never felt more connected to her.

CHAPTER 15

Tonight would truly be a fresh start with Penny.

Judging by the giant grin on her face, things began well—and he hadn't even presented a ring yet.

"I can*not* believe you got tickets for the grand opening! Look at it," Penny said, bouncing up and down in excitement. "My arteries hurt just seeing the holos!"

Fisherman's Wharf didn't quite have the hustle and bustle of its twenty-one-A counterpart. No street performers or tourist shops; those had moved about a mile down the Embarcadero, leaving the whole pier filled with museums. Kin gazed down the street, wondering if some parent down there was currently panicking like he had the first time he'd lost a young Miranda in the crowd. Penny grabbed his hand and pulled him toward the holographic sign floating above the Museum of the Modern Era entrance, its large animated letters announcing "Eating in the Time of Fast Food!" over rotating bigger-than-life hamburgers and fried chicken. It was one of the more difficult tickets to get in town, and certainly more than a sous chef and government employee should pay for a night out.

But there was no price on tonight. Tonight was about Penny.

Kin resisted offering any honest opinions regarding fast food as they strolled forward. "Markus is going to be *so* jealous." Penny's fingers crunched across his hand before yanking him forward. Of course Penny didn't know that Markus got to try the real thing; sometimes Kin wondered if the only reason he worked for the TCB was to sample dishes from another era.

Smaller holograms projected on either side of the sliding doors, showcasing other elements of the MOME, a museum dedicated to the post-digital world from the mid-twentieth century and beyond. Something about the virtual image tickled a dormant memory in Kin, a sense of déjà vu triggered by a three-dimensional holographic re-creation of a fast-food commercial. The image flashed in his mind, and a quick sting jabbed his left temple. He winced, holding the side of his head for a short second. It came and went, though not fast enough for Penny to miss it. "You all right?"

"Yeah. Sure." He felt his inner jacket pocket for the hundredth time since they'd left the cab, making sure the ring box was safe and sound. Since the night of the dinner party, everything seemed new about Penny. Her laugh, her quirks, even the way she moved; if a halo could have hovered over her, it might have. Merely catching her smile caused his heart to race with possibilities, not of the life they thought they might have before the so-called radiation accident, but those plans coupled with the wisdom and experience he'd gained in era twenty-one-A. The combination of the two created infinite ideas and dreams within him, a neverending list of where their life might lead together. It seemed like they had all the time in the world.

Funny how easily it all came about once he'd simply stopped trying to understand it. And he even had a new ring ready to present just to prove it.

He couldn't wait.

"Just thinking about how unhealthy all this replicated food is going to be." He forced out a grin despite echoes of the pain in his head.

"At uni we had a history course about this time period. Especially the early part of it. The grease! I mean, it sounds *so* bad." She fired off words at a clip even faster than her usual rate, her British accent nearly losing its crisp edge from the pace. "My old classic foods professor said that our replicators don't do it justice. He said it could take weeks to saturate ingredients so the rubs taste close to the real thing. Can you believe they used to *freeze* these things?" Penny continued rattling off all sorts of random facts about fast food as they veered off to the left at the fork in the path, bypassing the standard museum fare of popular culture, politics, and sports for the heavy aroma of grease and french fries. Off to the side, people shuffled in and out of a gift shop; farther out floated a big sign for an exhibit called *Discover Your History*, something about looking at the social media archives of ancestors.

The replicator module lifted to display two pieces of fried chicken, drawing Penny in, sniffing and staring at and around it. The aroma hit Kin, its mix of herbs and spices stronger and more accurate than anything from the past hour. Synapses fired off, and the smell no longer came from an exhibit at the MOME. The museum, the guests, even Penny disappeared in a flash; instead, he stood in a fried chicken chain somewhere in the middle of Nevada, Heather at his side. She rubbed her small five-month baby bump as Kin watched a cockroach crawl along the counter, an unaware teenager awaiting their order.

He blinked, and another memory flashed: foot traffic zooming by at Heather's law school building. Marrying Heather was a foregone conclusion at that point; their friends called it "the inevitable party," and Kin's challenge stemmed from trying to catch her off guard with a proposal. When he finally did it—by waiting in her professor's office—the quantity of her tears surprised both of them, so much so that she'd joked about it during their vows. He blinked again, snapping back into the moment. Rolling waves took over his equilibrium, turning his legs into wobbly spindles. Penny turned away from sniffing the steaming replicated chicken and grabbed him by the shoulder. "Kin? Are you okay?"

A drilling pain bored deep into his temple, taking away any ability to speak. His palms pressed against his skull, as if applying further pressure would make everything go away.

And then it did.

Kin stood up straight. He blinked away the haze, and the museum came back into focus. Yet something seemed to keep the *people* barely out of view, and he spun and angled to see who stood by or across from or behind him, cheekbones and noses and mouths lacking detail, like someone turned the focus dial on his sight. And sound, all sound became a muffled rumble.

Did the food dilate his pupils? Or tickle his allergies? He'd have to check in with Heather. "Heather, do you have any allergy meds in your purse?"

The world remained silent. Where did Heather go? Her height and red hair usually made her easy to find in a crowd, except he couldn't see any details. Something brushed his elbow, and he turned to find Miranda ignoring him while she dashed up to the MOME replicator serving station.

"Miranda? Don't spoil your dinner," he said as she took a bite of the drumstick. "The fricassee is simmering."

Miranda looked at him, her expression unchanged—did she even hear him? No, she turned and walked past him without even a nod. "It's almost done," he called out. "I only have to make the liaison." He spun to follow her, like he did years ago at Fisherman's Wharf, and like then, she seemed to dissolve in the crowd. A heavy weight pulled on his eyelids, and though he fought through it, stepping forward became an impossible task. His vision tunneled, the periphery transformed into an endless wash of muted colors.

Something fired off in his ear, but it wasn't the stinging pain that jackhammered into his temple. It roared, an indecipherable vocal mix of urgency and volume. He blinked again, and the world snapped into real time. A crowd stood around him, words buzzing from people wondering what had happened to the man on the floor.

"Kin!" A woman's voice broke through the din. "Kin!" she repeated, and he realized that the warmth on the back of his head was the woman's hand trying to prop him up.

Penny. It was Penny. Her eyes glistened with tears, anxiety pulling her expression wide. "Penny," he said.

"There you are. You blacked out for a second—"

He raised his finger to shush her as medical personnel pushed through the background crowd. "Miranda. I lost her. Dinner's almost ready."

"What?" Penny leaned in, squinting. "Dinner?"

"Chop two to three tablespoons of tarragon. Mix with softened butter and two tablespoons of fresh lemon juice, then stir gently to combine."

"Excuse me." A woman burst through and tossed her backpack on the ground, a large red cross on her shoulder patch. "This is EMT four-six, we're at the situation here. Sir—" she turned to him "—sir, how are you feeling?"

"Miranda," he said, "I lost her in the crowd." His palms pressed up against the cold tile, his muscles burning as they tried to hold him up. "We need to find her. Dinner's almost ready."

"Sir. Sir, you need to settle down." The woman turned to Penny. "Who's Miranda?"

Penny remained kneeling beside him, a tiny tremble in her lip. "I... I'm not sure."

Kin opened his eyes to the harsh lighting and endless beeping of monitors, and knew immediately that he was back in a hospital. "Where's my fast food?" he asked, his voice coming with a weakness that surprised him, and the simple act of grinning resulted in a shocking amount of muscle soreness. Penny rose from her chair, and the redness in her eyes gave away that she'd been crying. "Hey, don't worry. I'm fine. What happened?"

She knelt beside him, fingers gripped on his shoulder. "You blacked out. At the MOME." She bit down on her bottom lip with a sideways turn of her face that avoided eye contact. "What do you remember?"

Kin tried to fill his lungs with air, and although he wanted to give her hand a reassuring squeeze, even that felt like too much for him. "We passed the European section. Curries. I remember curries. And then the replicator was making the sample of fried chicken. And then here."

"That sounds about right. You collapsed, started babbling nonsense."

Nonsense? Kin hoped he didn't start lecturing anyone on

trans fats in fast food. "Well, I'm clearheaded now." He pulled the holo chart off the wall and angled the floating image closer to examine the diagnosis. "Head trauma," he read.

"The doctor said he'd never seen anything like it. I told him about your radiation accident." Penny leaned over to view the holo with him before she focused on the floor. "Kin?"

"Yeah?"

"Who's Miranda?"

During a time jump, right before the world flashed to white, fractions of a second felt like an endless pause. The world dialed down from normal to slow motion to a standstill, and a rush of cold would hit, followed by the electrical tingle that ran up and down his spine.

Penny's question created the same experience, only a dozen times over.

She kept looking at the hospital room's tile, hopefully enough that she didn't notice the stunned reaction on Kin's face. He was an agent; he was trained to think under pressure.

Delay tactics raced through his mind while shoving aside a heavy fact: he'd mentioned Miranda to Penny. Whoever Penny thought Miranda might be—an affair, a friend, a long-lost relative—that didn't matter. What mattered was taking back control of the situation.

"I don't know," he said after a few seconds. He grimaced, not because of a headache, but to buy himself some time through faking physical pain.

"You don't know? You made it sound very important. You said you were making her…" Penny hesitated and looked away, "…chicken fricassee."

The more he thought it through, the more playing dumb seemed like the path of least resistance. "What name did you say?"

"Miranda." Penny finally turned his way, and her posture became a straight line. "You kept saying her name. Who is she?"

"I don't know anyone named Miranda." Kin used the same steady voice that the TCB had trained him to employ when trying to talk down a target.

"You were so…sure that she was important."

Penny wasn't prone to jealousy. But given that he'd spent far too long of his so-called recovery being distant, perhaps it was a reasonable fear. "I promise, I don't know. Whoever this Miranda is, she probably doesn't exist. Just a hallucination or something like that. They warned me about that during the recovery period."

He watched as the words settled in, crafting a logic that eventually took hold. "You're right." Penny's chin tucked low with a small nod. "Markus said you might hallucinate even up to a year or so after the accident."

Her whole body softened, from her face to her shoulders, and they connected eye to eye with a clarity that wasn't quite there before. The ring. He originally planned to do it on the waterfront after they left the MOME. But a hospital bed would have to do. "You've been so patient with me. My recovery got in the way again. Hey," he said, "and I'm sorry I ruined another night for us. We didn't even get to the best part."

"Actually—" the small room echoed Penny's quick laugh, and she pointed to a small container on the counter "—they gave us some of the fried chicken for takeout. It's still warm. They don't allow it but they made an exception for us." Penny grinned, her cheeks blooming.

"No, not that." Kin shuffled in bed, a low groan powering his attempt to move closer. "Tonight I wanted to give you something important." Penny leaned in, close enough that her breath tickled on his cheek. "I haven't been fair to you since the accident. You've waited for me while I recovered, while I worked late and let you down. Things *are* different for me. I don't think you can go through what I did without feeling that way. But the one constant I've had through all of it is you. And it's time we got back on track." A few short moments ago, Penny had shown a blend of uncertainty and confusion and fear, though now everything melted into a welcoming glow. Despite the dull ache in his muscles, Kin reached over and took her hand.

He had Penny right here. He had Miranda across time. He had a job, his restored health, even his cat. It could all coexist together. What more could he ask for?

One thing.

"I'd reach into my jacket pocket and give you something, except I can't quite get out of bed right now. So I'll just have to say it—Penny Fernandez, will you finally marry me at our rescheduled wedding?"

She pulled the ring box out of his coat, and her face turned into a paradox of expressions, the bright eyes of joy mixed with the slanted lips of confusion. "Did you buy me a new ring?"

"You can keep either one. Or both." They locked hands, and she switched the old ring out for the new one. "Given the way things have been, it felt right."

"A fresh start." Penny's smile remained, but a softness took over, from her eyes to her shoulders to her posture. "And a take-out box," she said with a laugh. "It's perfect." She leaned in and kissed him, and though his body ached from head to toe, their shared breath freed him from any lingering pain.

How could he have ever forgotten Penny?

CHAPTER 16

The spring in Kin's step may not have been noticeable to any hallway passersby, yet on the inside, he was floating. Lights shone brighter, sounds were sharper, and everything simply felt *better*.

Despite the lingering effects of his MOME blackout—the occasional headache or memory lapse—things started falling into place. A consistent, solid relationship with Miranda. A new wedding date with Penny. And as long as he didn't jump through time anymore—not on his to-do list barring medical miracles—a life without headaches. The TCB doctors said that within a year or two they'd be history; only further time-jumping would keep them around.

Well, technically, that wasn't true. The doctors said that further time jumps wouldn't cause headaches. Rather, the pressures of one or two more jumps would most likely erode his frontal cortex, and without an immediate series of specialized stabilizers to halt brain swelling and reverse cell degradation, he'd be a babbling vegetable for the next century or so.

Thanks to his desk job, things got easier and just plain safer than chasing people across time, particularly on Mondays when he emailed with Miranda. It wasn't perfect, but it worked, and given the alternative of no relationship with Miranda and no marriage with Penny, who was he to complain?

Even though Kin's life swung forward with a weighty momentum, a lingering soreness from his blackout meant that he wouldn't be putting on cleats today. Instead, he sat at his desk reading Miranda's reply, particularly important since his last message told his daughter about Penny.

From: Miranda Stewart (mirawho@messagemail.com)
To: Kin Stewart (chefkstew@messagemail.com)
Subject: Big Decisions

Wow, Penny sounds great. A chef, how fitting, right? Somewhere, Mom is having a good laugh about that. Funny thing here is that Grandma all of a sudden seems less interested in Alister than my college options. I told her the other day that I was thinking of double-majoring in Computer Science and Comparative Literature. When she asked why, I told her I wanted to make video games. You know, program something fun with a really cool story rather than making, like, accounting software. She thinks games are children's toys still and she went on and on about so-and-so's grandson who works for Apple and makes a gazillion dollars a year. But maybe she's right. Double-majoring does sound like a lot to balance. Even though I won't have soccer practice to worry about.

Yeah, so about that.

You asked about a soccer scholarship. I'm not going to try for one. Because I want to quit.

You notice how every time you asked me about it, I just said fine and moved on? It's 'cause I didn't know how to tell you that I hate soccer. Not running and kicking a ball, but practice and tournaments and positions and stuff. I hate it, I've hated it for years. I told Mom this right before you left. Since it was midseason, she told me not to say anything yet because your PTSD symptoms were affecting you and you didn't need anything else on your mind.

Kin paused, then reread the last few sentences. His metabolizer-boosted memory pulled back another sentiment, not from Miranda, but from Penny. Back when he woke up, a bullet from Penny's list of reasons why she missed him: "Markus keeps asking me to watch soccer with him and I hate that and I do it anyway."

The things people did for family.

I stayed this season I think because I needed something familiar and stable in my life but I feel done with it. I know I might have a shot at a scholarship with the district award I got last season but I don't know if I care enough. I'd just rather be making a game with aliens and spaceships (not time travel, don't worry, I promised I wouldn't tell anyone about your journal) than kicking a ball.

I hope you're not mad. I know how much soccer means to you. Tell me your honest opinion about college, about scholarships, about everything. I could use some advice.

★ ★ ★

Kin remembered now. That final dinner with Miranda and Heather. He'd suggested they watch soccer together, so confident that his daughter would agree. And Heather had tried to steer him away. He should have known something was up. She only used that gentle tone when she knew he wouldn't take it well.

How did he never pick up on this? Even now, getting written messages from her regularly, he'd thought she'd been stronger, more settled for a while now. And yet, she'd held on to soccer because she needed something stable. And giving up soccer didn't sound like just quitting, but actively exorcising something that stole joy from her. He'd thought programming and sci-fi were passing interests, that he knew his daughter at her core.

Somehow, he'd mistaken her being good at something for really wanting to do it.

What else had he missed, not just now but for years?

The thoughts came crashing down when a single voice broke his concentration. "What the hell are you doing?" Markus's voice snapped the office silence, startling Kin into a rigid posture and rapid swiping over of mission-related windows.

"Working," he said, rapidly clicking on his keyboard. "What does it look like?"

"That's what I mean." Markus leaned against the entrance, and it took several seconds to register that he wore full workout gear. "We kick off in thirty minutes. Why aren't you getting dressed?"

"Didn't Penny tell you? I had a blackout at the MOME. Doctors say to take it easy."

"Kin, listen to me." Markus's hands gripped the metal desk in front of him, an intensity in his voice that didn't appear when jumping through time to retrieve agents and apprehend targets. "Technology Development is our main competitor for the season title. We need you out there."

"No physical exertion. Doctor's orders. Penny'd kill you if she knew you were trying to get me to play."

Markus skulked away, his audible grumbles gradually disappearing down the hall.

The four steps: log in, activate DTP, run the scripts, and contact Miranda and tell her how he felt. He owed her that. He punched away at the first step, then waited for the second step to complete when the thumps of footsteps quickly returned. "Okay, new idea," Markus said.

"Markus. Seriously." He pointed to the floating holo windows. "I'm working here."

"Penalty kicks. In case it's tied and we go into penalty kicks. Okay? No exertion. Only your aim putting us over the top."

Was this why Penny couldn't stand up to her brother? Just as Kin was about to refuse him again, his train of thought was interrupted by a here-and-gone headache. He closed his eyes at the quiet sting of these post-blackout blips, and as it faded, so did his focus on the conversation at hand.

"Kin? Come on, man. Suit up."

He felt disoriented but nodded to appease Markus. "Okay, okay. Fine. Just for penalty kicks."

"Thank you. I hope your clock is fast," he said, pointing to the displayed time on Kin's holo screen. "Game's gonna start soon. You can't time-jump in."

"Go," Kin said, pointing to the elevator. "I'll change and meet you down there."

"MVP, Kin." Markus's words were almost drowned out by the slap of his cleats against the tile. "MVP."

Kin rubbed his face, a heavy hand massaging the sting out

of his temples. He tried to focus, but his brain still felt foggy from the headache. What was Markus just saying? How long had he been sitting there staring straight ahead at his screen?

When did he pull his cleats out of the desk drawer?

One by one, answers and specifics returned. A quick glance at the clock showed that only a few minutes had passed. Markus had been here talking about penalty kicks. And Miranda's response, he had to finish that first.

Miranda was his priority. A queasy burn roiled his stomach in waves, and maintaining focus seemed to drain all of his energy and effort over the next few minutes. He pushed through, reminding himself of what he was trying to accomplish whenever his attention wavered.

From: Kin Stewart (chefkstew@messagemail.com)
To: Miranda Stewart (mirawho@messagemail.com)
Subject: RE: Big Decisions

So look, about soccer... I'm not mad. I am disappointed, though, but not for why you might think. I'm disappointed that any of my issues might have made you feel like you couldn't be honest with me. It's totally fine for you to quit soccer. I wish we could share everything, but that's not how things work. So let me just say this, both with soccer and with school. Do what you want to do. Don't do it for me, or Grandma, or friends or boys or whatever. If you want to push yourself so you can make video games, then do it. Maybe it's impractical, and it will probably be hard at times, but I know you can do it.

Kin hesitated, forefinger aimlessly tapping the surface of the keyboard. The power of the written word, transmitted electronically across a century, had helped his daughter avoid a downward spiral.

The written word saved her. Perhaps it could do even more.

Grandma is probably too practical to tell you this so I will: do it because it makes you happy. You never know when something might take that away. Just promise you won't use my journal for your games, okay? :)

If Markus ever found out he was using future knowledge to steer Miranda, he'd probably cite some company line about timeline corruption. That didn't apply here. Kin was simply nudging the universe back into balance. He sat back in his chair, indulging in daydreams of what his daughter might do with her untapped potential.

Another sting attacked his temple, one strong enough to bring a wince to his face. He shook it off and opened his bottom desk drawer to grab the rest of his soccer gear, then closed all the web portals on his system. He was needed on the field.

CHAPTER 17

Behind him, Kin heard Markus telling everyone on the line that it was *such* a good idea he got Kin down there for penalty kicks. As he said that, Kin sent a perfectly placed shot that curved a hair out of reach of the goalie from the Technology Development group. It slammed into the back of the goal, creating a ripple that flowed through the woven netting before the ball fell to the grass.

A mob of hands and arms and screaming disoriented him for several seconds. He shook his head to recover from the noise and back-thumping, and through it all, he heard his name over and over.

"Kin Stewart!"

It wasn't his imagination.

He turned, his focus returning, and something in the

words carried an urgency that didn't sync up with interdepartmental sports.

The mob around him broke apart, rowdy shouts hushing to silence, and even the other team remained quiet. "Kin Stewart," the voice called out again, and it registered that it belonged to a uniformed woman.

Dark blue jacket. Matching hat. Equipment belt.

TCB Security?

"That's me," he said, acutely aware that everyone on the field was watching. He stepped forward to assess the Security officer; she had the usual mix of weapons and restraints, though they remained holstered. "Is everything all right?"

"Kin Stewart," she repeated again, this time in a quieter yet firm tone. "You're to report to the assistant director's office immediately. I'm here to escort you."

A Security escort? "Okay. We're just about finished up here."

"Now, Agent." The unflinching cold in her eyes could only mean one thing.

She knew.

But how? He ran his code to hide Miranda. Step three of the four steps. Of course he did. He always did. He tried to picture it, the mix of swipes and keystrokes, the confirmation screen that popped up after it executed. Except those memories were of other times, days other than today. The fine points of what he'd written to Miranda this evening proved elusive, shapeless.

Searching his mind frantically, he remembered that Markus came up to bug him. He knew Miranda said something about not wanting to play soccer. He knew she asked him about choosing majors. But how did Markus convince him to play? Why didn't she want to play soccer? What school advice did he give? The details diffused into a cloudy mess, and the most important detail eluded him.

Did he run the code?

Markus leaned in, a slight tremble rippling through his words. "Just go."

Kin couldn't have forgotten step three. The very notion seemed impossible. This thing he'd created, this balance of now and then that he'd worked so hard to figure out, every waking moment was dedicated to making this work. How could he have missed such a vital cog?

Despite the denial rippling from his very bones, a quiet truth built into anxiety and grew into full-blown panic. Since the incident at the MOME, his memory and focus spotted in and out. He'd downplayed it to Penny and Markus and the doctors, but that didn't help when trying to confirm life-altering archaic computer code.

"Sure." He refused to give anything away and kept a neutral look when meeting the mix of curious and worried glances on the field. "Hold that lead, okay?" he asked, giving a nod to a clearly worried Markus.

Ten minutes and zero words later, Kin entered the assistant director's office. A second Security officer greeted them at the elevator, and they both walked him to the meeting. The door slid closed behind them, leaving them in an office with nothing other than a desk and a wall of interactive screens, some of which were pulled out into floating holos. The office din disappeared with the shut door, and the only noise came from the digital soundtrack of a faux creek trickling by.

The AD, a woman of eighty or ninety named Sierra Hammond with dark bags carved into the beige skin under her eyes and natural gray creeping into her hair, stood up behind her desk. She waved several holo screens down and motioned

Kin to the chair in front. "Agent Stewart. Our anomaly. Sit down, please."

"I can stand." In his cleats, Kin flexed his toes, curling them into tight, balled fists.

"No need to get defensive, Agent Stewart."

"I'm not an agent anymore. I'm in Research."

"All right, then. Mr. Stewart." The AD tented her fingers, a pose that made Kin think of *The Simpsons'* infamous Mr. Burns from Miranda's era.

"Kin."

"Kin. You can drop the act. I'm going to be straight with you." Her fingernails clacked against the desk as she met his stare.

"All right." Kin had never met their region's AD. Not many people had. Her name and signature had sealed a get-well message shortly after he returned, and he'd wondered if she'd even been briefed about his situation or if he was a mere name and statistic in some unread report.

There was no question now, though—she knew who he was, and the panic grew like a weed in his mind. Anxiety fought to drum his fingers at his side, but he resisted, forcing them into balled fists. He wouldn't give the AD anything she didn't already know.

"You're immediately relieved of duty. HR will transmit a severance package for you to review. I think you'll find it quite satisfactory. It's very similar to the pension plan we give retired agents. Plus a full year of active pay."

She pointed to the corner screen at the far wall and then pulled out the holo to float in front of him to review.

"For your service and the risks you've put yourself through. Take a long vacation. Relax before you look for another job. You're still welcome to play in TCB soccer matches if you'd like. All alum are. You're getting married soon, right?" The question sparked a raised eyebrow from Kin. "Penny Fernandez, born in the village of Saxony-Coburn, Exeter, England, raised in London, promoted to sous-chef at Finny Fin Catering seven months ago, sister to retriever agent Markus Fernandez. It sounds like she's been very patient with you since you returned from your extended leave in twenty-one-A. You two should enjoy yourselves for a while. Maybe help her open that restaurant she's talked about. She needs a business plan, right? Oh, don't look so surprised, Kin. A group like us, we know everything about our staff. They—" she pointed out the door, presumably at other agency bigwigs with fancy titles "—know everything about me. Checks and balances. Why do you think we have retrievers and field agents? Our organization is built with internal transparency, safety nets. It's the only way to handle temporal matters. That's why we were quite impressed by your ability to cover your tracks."

Kin couldn't tell if she leaned forward because of the nature of the conversation or if she wanted to gauge his reaction. He quelled countless internal questions, driving the noise down to a manageable fervor before selecting a careful response. "I'm not sure what you're referring to."

"We don't need to do this dance. And you can sit down. I don't bite. I'm not mad." The AD gestured again to the chair, though he remained glued to where he stood. "I understand why you did what you did. I get it. We all do. But our entire organization is based on the elimination of timeline corruption, and what you've done is just that. 'The cause of or passing of knowledge that significantly alters the timeline of any individual, group, or society.' That's what we prevent and our rules were clear—no communication. Even then, perhaps we would have let the emails slide. We understand the instinct, the *needs* of a parent. However," she said, taking in a breath, "this? That's completely over the line. Her situation needs to be addressed."

A new holo appeared, this time a mere floating image. It rotated slowly, and Kin took in the art, simple black silhouettes against a white backdrop: a woman running to the left with arms outstretched; behind her, a man falling down in midair.

Above the characters sat the title in bold blue font: *Time Flies: An Interactive Tech Demo.* And beneath it, the author's name:

Miranda Stewart.

The AD swiped the air and text floated up beside the image.

Time Flies is an interactive tech demo from programmer Miranda Stewart. This short game lasts approximately thirty minutes and features a narrative set in the Temporal Corruption Bureau, a secret agency that apprehends criminals across time. Sequences include dialogue trees, combat, puzzle-solving, and cutscenes (opening and finale). Conceived, programmed, and written by Miranda Stewart. Art by Tanya Piper and Rose Williams.

Every single muscle in Kin's body tensed, making his pounding heartbeat seem louder and more present than what seemed possible.

She'd used his journal.

Despite everything.

Or maybe because of it.

"That doesn't prove anything," Kin said, forcing each word out.

"Let's examine this," the AD said. "You wrote to her, and I quote 'if you want to push yourself so you can make video games, then do it. Maybe it's impractical, and it will probably be hard at times, but I know you can do it.' Innocent enough? Perhaps. However, we've analyzed the archival delta. Before that message was transmitted ninety-four minutes ago, Miranda Stewart earned a bachelor's in Computer Science, worked for a business software company for two years before returning to school to become a veterinarian. She never touched any type of creative storytelling. After your message, Security Overwatch detected gravitational shifts all over the world. Timeline Monitoring picked up the changes. Incremental at first, benign, almost invisible to us. It took a deeper look to see what was really unfolding."

Kin was just a field agent, the muscle of the operation. But even he knew enough about TCB's methods to recognize that something massive had happened, something significantly more powerful than time travelers attempting to create their own retirement plan.

"Since you sent that email, her timeline changed. This project was posted to a portfolio site on her birthday, 2030, just as she was about to finish her master's in Game Development. Her attempt to find a job began a domino effect that puts every single field agent in danger."

"Here she is. Her project is downloaded thirty-two times by potential employers. It is uploaded to four industry websites and lives on her portfolio as well, in addition to backups and redundant hardware. Your words of encouragement beamed every single detail about the TCB into a publicly accessible video game. The history of time travel. Technology. Mission protocols. Even the locations of worldwide branches. She's managed to include a shocking number of classified details into a mere thirty minutes. Any temporal criminal who found this would be privy to our entire history, our entire operation. Rogue agents. Organized temporal crime syndicates. Anarchists who hire mercs. Black-market time-travel traders. They all just became that much more dangerous."

If the AD could peer inside his brain, she would have seen one very specific visualization from one very specific memory.

His journal.

"First you code something fun, then you build a world around it to make people care," Miranda had said. Years later, she took his advice and combined her programming ambitions with the world described in his journal.

"I told her not to tell anyone about that."

"Perhaps she didn't feel like listening to a dad who wasn't around."

"I *am* around—"

"Through illegal means. Which we've shut down, by the way. That advice is the last thing you'll ever write to her."

Kin's fingers began drumming against his hip, a rapid-fire rhythm that was eclipsed only by the speed of his thoughts. "But that's it—that's the problem! Let me email her. Over the years. I'll remind her not to say anything. She'll make some other game. It'll never get posted."

"And while you do that—if you're even successful—our organization would be at risk the entire time you're negotiating with her. I'm not taking that bet. Consider the lives of everyone in this organization, including dozens of active field agents all across the modern age and whatever collateral damage would result from the TCB's destruction. You think I should be willing to sacrifice all of that, rather than the life of one person who shouldn't even exist?"

Heather's voice sparked in his mind, something she said to him during their last afternoon together.

The needs of the many outweigh the needs of the few.

Kin refused to apply that logic here. This was his daughter.

"She doesn't know," he said. "It's a story. She thinks it's fiction. Her favorite TV show is about a time traveler—"

"It doesn't matter. If the wrong person finds it, the entire Bureau is in danger. Anywhere and any*when*."

"So? Prevent it from happening. Reject it from the portfolio sites. Hack the source file to make it corrupt and broken."

"No, Kin. You're not getting it. Even if we remove the file, the knowledge is still in there. In her. We don't know if and when it will get out." The AD met his eyes. They didn't register as fury, frustration, or disappointment. Instead, a far more dangerous emotion was projected with shocking clarity from her face.

Fear.

"Miranda Stewart is a variable that must be controlled. The knowledge in her mind represents the greatest potential threat we have ever encountered."

Pressure returned to Kin's temples, a grip that took hold across space and time. This one was different; he knew it from the very feel. It had nothing to do with time-jump damage to the frontal cortex or memory triggers that pushed his brain too hard. No, this was the silent grind of his jaw, the increase in blood pressure, the panic-turned-anger in his heart. "What have you done to Miranda?"

The AD looked back at him, unflinching. "We don't take these decisions lightly. We don't take *any* decisions lightly."

"What have you done to her?"

"She is a variable that must be controlled." The AD's words repeated with the perfect tone and pitch of a recording.

"Answer the damn question." Kin's voice roared in a way that an office would never stand for. Behind him the doors opened, and the two Security officers stepped to either side of him. "What have you done to Miranda?"

"The question is 'what have *you* done to her?' You were

given guidelines of noninterference. *You* made this choice. Whenever you passed this information to her, whether in person or in your emails, *you* did this. Noninterference. Protocol Eleven Twenty-Three. You dismantle your equipment. You don't document any knowledge. You never, ever pass it on—in any form."

"Stop bullshitting." Security grabbed his arms. Had his fitness been at the level of a true field agent, their loose grip could have easily been torn away. Fingers dug into his shoulders, tethering him to the front end of the office. No plans came to mind. No visualizations or lists to take down everything in the room. Only white-hot fury in the form of a stare. "What have you done to her?"

"You used to be an agent. You know how we handle things. We got to work the minute after we detected the timeline change. Your damage is being undone as we speak." She sighed and nodded to Security before looking back at her holo screens, one of the most powerful people in the world calmly returning to her duties. "Go home, Kin. Get some rest. Get married. Help Penny open her restaurant. Leave the past behind."

The Security officers tugged on his body and began pulling him back. As he fought, his cleats dug into the thin office carpeting. "Damn it, tell me. What have you done to her?"

The AD offered stony silence, although her face softened when she studied him with a squint. Whether she cared or was just curious, he'd never know—he was too busy struggling against the magnetic restraints they'd placed around his wrists. The main hallway echoed with his repeated question, past the small room of offices and into the larger space where the Operations division worked. Eyes bore down on him, the weight and intensity of each one probably wondering why Security dragged the former field agent in sweaty soccer gear out of the office of the TCB's most powerful person on the West Coast.

The only person who probably understood stood right outside the elevator, a mix of regret and concern pasted on Markus's face.

CHAPTER 18

Kin stormed through the ticket booth, waving his arm to biotrigger the credit purchase. Lines had already formed to check out the fast food exhibit, though he went in the opposite direction. Signs pointed him deeper into the MOME, up stairs and down corridors until he arrived at the relatively unpopulated *Discover Your History* exhibit. "Next, please," a man's voice came from inside the room.

Outside, a view overlooking the Embarcadero showed life moving on: people walking to their destination, skycars zooming across the cityscape, and the trains throttling across in the atmotube.

None of that registered. A week or so ago, Kin had walked across Pier 39 to the MOME, hand in hand with Penny on their way to eat replicated fast food. That night they'd taken

their time, arms swinging in unison. Little jokes passed between them, the future completely ahead of them.

This afternoon, though, was about the past.

The door slid open to the so-called Discovery Chamber,
which wasn't all that different from the AD's office. Holo
screens and walls surrounded a small desk where a man sat,
his hands neatly folded as he prepared to research the digital
fossils of the customer's choice. "Hi there. I'm Edgar, and I'll
be your discovery assistant today. Your name is?"

"Kin."

"Nice to meet you, Kin," he said, taking his hand with
a suave calmness. "Back in the early twenty-first century,
the introduction of social media created a digital footprint
for many people in the world. Photos, status updates, and
videos gave us snapshots of their lives." Edgar spoke with a
banal neutrality, like this was his fiftieth introductory speech
today. "Thanks to our archive, we can now revisit the lives
of our ancestors. Who do you want to catch up with today?"

"Her name—" Kin swallowed hard "—was Miranda Elizabeth Stewart."

Edgar pulled several holo screens into the space in front
of them, all the while spouting out disclaimers about how
the subject had to be born before 2050 and there were no
refunds even if their archived social media records pulled up
very little. Kin nodded a quick affirmative to each of those
and then rattled off additional information: birth date, place
of birth, high school, even her ID number for the defunct
Social Security program.

"You sure know a lot about her," Edgar said as screens
blinked and flashed. "Grandmother?"

"Not quite. Close relative, though."

"And what is it you're looking for about her? General history? Getting to know the family story a little better?"

"Specifically—" Kin leaned forward, his hands rubbing the stubble of hair on his chin "—her adult life. What she did, who she married." He took in a sharp inhale, the next sentence needing the force of giants to push out. "When she died."

"As I said," Edgar continued, his fingers flying while information scrolled by, "the depth of our reports is really based on how much of a digital footprint this Miranda had. Most people have something, but it really varies. It's like…" Edgar's voice trailed off, and his face curled in a knot.

"What?"

"Are you sure your information is accurate?"

Of course it is—she's my daughter, he wanted to growl. He swallowed the impulse, and the urge dissolved into a few tremors that rippled through his muscles and nerves.

"I'm not getting anything with that birth date and that name. Or that region, for that matter. Here, I'll expand the search. Take the range off adulthood, expand the scope of location, and…" More screens flashed, the information whizzing by at a pace only eclipsed by Kin's heart rate. "Wait, I think I got it."

"You did?" The chair bounced as Kin sat straight up. "You found her?"

"I did." Edgar twirled his fingers, causing the holo screen to spin around and face Kin. "It's all right there. Now that we've established identity, we can look a little deeper."

Kin sat immobilized while reading and rereading the text in a whisper to himself, as if saying it would make the whole thing more real. "That's not her," he finally said at normal volume.

"Miranda *Alison* Stewart. Born January 2, 2006, in Oakland, California. Let's see how Ms. Stewart lived, shall we? She's the perfect age for the dawn of social media—"

"That's not her."

Edgar paused, his head cocked at an angle. "That's the only Miranda Stewart born in the Bay Area in that time frame."

"No, that's *not* her. Miranda *Elizabeth* Stewart. Born in San Mateo, grew up in San Francisco."

"Kin, I'm sorry but there's a good chance that whoever kept the records in your family was off by a little bit. It happens." Edgar's expression eased up, and his hands folded over. His voice adopted the tone of a school counselor rather than a digital archivist. "That was a very long time ago. People pass their records down from generation to generation, only they move or change names or lose things along the way. Even our server archives are only 99 percent accurate. They're copies of copies of copies. All signs point to this person being the Miranda you're looking for."

"That's *not* her." Kin's tone took on a fierceness that rarely, if ever, came out. "I know it. I know every last detail. That's a different Miranda. That's not *my* Miranda."

The chair squeaked as Edgar settled back. Kin sensed his eyes studying him, and it surely must have been a slightly unnerving sight: the thin layer of perspiration across his forehead, the tiny tremble in his hands. "Sir, I'm sorry, this is all I can find. You know, our policy is no refunds, but this seems very important to you, and I'm sorry we couldn't find the data you needed. Let me call my supervisor. I'm sure we can give you at least a partial refund."

"Don't worry about it." Kin stood up, the back of his boots catching the chair's leg. "Thanks for your time."

"Let me check one more thing. This usually doesn't work, but…" Edgar's hands resumed bouncing around the holo screens, their translucent glow creating a blur while his fingers poked and swiped. "Well, how about that? This doesn't make any sense."

"What's that?" Kin asked, his hands propping himself up on the desk.

Edgar turned the holo screen, and Kin blinked several times to make sure that his vision didn't cheat him. "That's her," he whispered.

"Let's get a better look." The holo in front of him fizzled, and the room's lights dimmed. The source—an archived web page from the *San Francisco Globe*—appeared on the giant wall screen. Edgar tapped the air a few more times, and the image extracted into a solid 3-D hologram of a black-and-white Miranda standing at a podium, with an apparent stuffed owl sewn onto her coat's shoulder and a long striped scarf around her neck.

Probably not a soccer scarf.

"The article was titled Local Sci-Fi Con Draws Budding Talent. 'High schooler Miranda Stewart, 17, demonstrates her work in the Junior Game Developer Contest.' Looks like your Miranda knew what she wanted from a young age."

Kin circled the hologram, walking through the foreground to get a close-up look. The holo was probably put together from some sort of algorithm that mashed together facial recognition and average sizes and heights and weights for an interpolated re-creation of whoever was in the image.

For Kin, none of that mattered. He'd never seen this Miranda before. He'd brought dozens, hundreds of digital photos with him, photos he'd taken at her soccer events or just being silly with Tanya and her friends. But this Miranda, showing something *she'd* created in public while wearing some sort of costume, might as well have been a complete stranger.

Those final days, with him insisting on watching the Arsenal match, defaulting back to the image he'd projected of her. He'd raised her. He'd parented her. He'd shown her things that seemed fun and interesting.

But maybe he'd never truly listened to her.

That had to be it. How else could the girl in the photo be a complete stranger to her own father? And with his actions, his own illegal attempts at parenting across time, everything had come undone.

Kin lost his daughter without ever finding out who she really was. And now, he never would.

"Thank you," he said.

"Unfortunately, that's all I can pull up. Technically this isn't even supposed to be here."

"What?"

"You see this?" Edgar turned a smaller screen of logistical data to him. He pointed at static digits that looked like a time stamp from an hour ago. "This is a backup cache from this morning. We keep a complete backup archive for redundancy. Everything refreshes hourly. Except this Miranda Stewart, her info doesn't exist in our live data. She's only got this one image, and it's from this morning's backup. The backup and the live data should be exactly the same, but they're not."

No headaches came. No pounding on his temples, no stinging right above his cheekbones. Inside, his chest clenched with the force of a thousand fists tightening at once. It sucked the air from his lungs, and his head dropped, neck muscles unable to prop it up.

"It's like something erased her digital footprint in the past hour." The lights came up, and Edgar organized the screens in front of him. "Like it reached into history and plucked her straight out of it. Weird, huh?" Edgar started saying something about possible hardware hiccups and opening a support ticket with the data team, only Kin had already gotten up to leave at that point. Rage welled inside him, reaching out to the very tips of his fingers and toes, creating a momentum that carried him away from Edgar's desk, out of the

MOME, and to his skycar. With each step forward, details stapled onto the plan already forming in his mind, words upon lists upon choices and options building into a matrix of possibilities and worries.

And it all started with one man.

CHAPTER 19

The startled voice echoed through the hills and into the dusk sky, sending nearby birds into flight.

"Jesus, Kin," Markus said, picking up his dropped bag. The surprise on Markus's face was replaced almost immediately with a sympathetic wrinkled brow. "You're okay?"

"Yeah," Kin replied. He knew to approach Markus with a semblance of calm, despite the rage that remained at a steady burn in his gut. Markus wasn't the enemy here. "I got a good severance package. Won't have to work for a while." After the MOME visit, a geyser of what-ifs stirred around inside Kin, building a pressure that rumbled his very core. Before he could move on in any fashion, it had to be released, and the only person in the world who might possibly understand was Markus. "Thanks for coming."

"It's rush hour. Why are we standing at the top of San Bruno Mountain? I think we're both illegally parked on the hillside."

"Miranda loves hiking here with Bamford. It's peaceful but tough terrain." Miranda had been dead for decades, regardless of whether she lived a full life or the TCB ended it. But for Kin, she lived in parallel to him, and speaking of her, even thinking about her in the past tense seemed wrong. "They got her, Markus. They've done something with her. I couldn't meet you to discuss it at the office. And I didn't want to do it around Enoch and Benjamin. Or Penny. That's why I wanted to meet here."

Markus's hands landed heavily on Kin's shoulders. He spoke slowly, every single word drawn out enough to linger far longer than it should have. "I'm really sorry, Kin. But remember, we knew this might happen. We knew that was the risk."

Kin couldn't tell if Markus was being pragmatic or sympathetic or some combination of both. "I went to the MOME," Kin said. "To check out her digital footprint. They're erasing her. They're removing her from history as we speak. In their backup archive from this morning, she was there. Somehow in their live database, she was gone. Sometime between this morning and this afternoon, they erased her. She's…" Dusk turned the sky into a burning mix of purple and pink, and in the distance, skycar headlights began to snap on, dotting the horizon with little glowing bulbs traveling by. "She's gone."

"Her footprint is being deleted." Markus turned, arms crossed and locked into each other. "Sometimes I forget that field agents probably don't know the whole protocol. You guys are too busy climbing up buildings and dodging bullets. In a case where an anomaly is created, the first step is to erase the digital footprint. That's what the Digital Security group does."

"And I thought they were just dirty players on the field."

"That, too."

"If that's the first step—" the black-and-white holo of Miranda from the MOME planted itself in his mind's eye, taking root and becoming his only focus "—what do they do next?"

Markus stood, stone-faced. The toes of his boots dug into the dirt, and his weight shifted back and forth. He looked off to the side, somewhere over Kin's shoulder and into the infinite sky. "You know what they do."

The muscles in Kin's neck stiffened, turning his posture into a wooden board ready to snap into pieces. "I'm an agent. They send me somewhere, some time. I do the job. No one tells me the how or why."

Markus's sigh projected over the mountaintop winds. "They identify the point of corruption. The assignment gets built around that."

"I chased the bad guys. Miranda isn't that. She's just a girl."

"She *is* the 'bad guy' in this case, Kin. No matter how smart or talented or *great* she is, she is the corruption. She shouldn't even exist. They're not going to give that type of person too many second chances. The longer this goes, the greater her sphere of influence becomes. They'll be monitoring her timeline continuously now." Markus hesitated, looking up as if he stood in the Mission Control war room. "She's on the big board now."

Lines and lines of emails whizzed through Kin's memory. All of those nuggets about handling classes, asking about soccer tournament scores, even supporting her during the immediate days following Heather's death—they seemed inconsequential now in the big scheme of things. The only thing that mattered was one email of encouragement, a short collection of text characters that pointed her down the path to posting her project. "They couldn't get to her before she's even developed it. This project would need to exist for them to detect the timeline ripples, even before it propagates onto other servers."

"Kin," Markus said, putting his arm around him. "We knew this was a risk. I talked with you about it."

Kin's thoughts carried too much momentum now, piecing together his personal mission experience with the possibilities created by Miranda's actions. "And they couldn't get her way earlier. That would grandfather the situation. It's gotta be right *after* she uploads it. The instant the file finishes transmitting." He turned and grabbed Markus, pulling him toward their parked cars. "I have to warn her. I need your access."

"Stop." Markus pushed away from him and held his ground. "We can't do that. These are the rules—"

"Rules? Break them for once!" Fingers curled into trembling fists. "Give me *one* email. That's all I have to do. I know you retrievers have access—"

"Kin. Stop. We shouldn't do this. This is our job. You know better."

"A single email."

"I can't."

"Fine. Give me your accelerator. I'll jump myself—"

"I'm not going to do that. Even if I wanted to give it to you, I wouldn't. One more jump could kill you. Look, the decision has been made. After next week it'll be finished. Let it go. You have to move forward. You have a life here. I'm saying this to you as a friend. Not an agent. Not as our soccer team captain. Your friend." Markus rested his arm around Kin's shoulders. "Okay?"

Kin considered the decision points that led to this moment: telling Miranda to follow her dreams, contacting her when

Heather died, his disappearance. Even before that, giving up hope of rescue and settling into 1996, approaching Heather, even all the way back to the moment the TCB recruited him with a cryptic statement at his door. Every twist and turn throughout the course of his life throttled cause-and-effect forward, events rushing and being compiled through time until culminating in one thing.

His daughter's execution.

Suddenly, Kin felt small, microscopic, and it wasn't from the vast sky of emerging dusk stars above them.

"Go home. Get some rest."

Markus's words made sense. He took them in, thinking them over and processing them, including his sentiments about Miranda. Except his mind got hung up on one thing, one particular detail that stood out.

Next week?

"How do you know it'll be over by next week?" Kin shot out in a single huff.

Sometimes Markus and Penny seemed like complete opposites. Other times their familial quirks offered a striking similarity. Markus bit down on his lip, avoiding Kin's glare and looking up and to the left. "It's, you know, standard protocol."

"Markus, we're on the side of San Bruno Mountain. No Security guards are going to sweep down and stop you. What do you know?"

"I told you, it's standard planning."

"No, it's not. Standard mission lengths are two weeks. Don't bullshit me. You're doing that thing that your sister does. The lip-bite-and-look-up thing."

The skycar sat about thirty feet away. Markus turned to it, probably contemplating sprinting to it and taking off. He faced Kin, his mouth ajar, and he took in short staccato breaths. In and out, starting and stopping; maybe his thoughts tried to form into something audible and tangible. "I'm the retriever for the assignment," he said. Kin angled to look him in the eye, though the connection couldn't be made. "I'm sorry—"

Before Markus could finish, Kin's fist flew into the jaw of his longtime friend. The sudden impact caught Markus off guard, and he dropped to the ground, lost somewhere in the weeds and grass. "How could you?" His yell echoed through the hills. "You killed her!"

Their relationship in all its forms—friends, coworkers, in-laws—was obliterated across San Bruno Mountain. A primal roar flew out, one that was meant to bend time and space itself. In reality it only caused Markus to stare up at him with wide-eyed terror.

"Kin! Stop!" Markus pushed himself up to his knees and then put his hands up. "It's me. It's Markus. I am your friend. Please, listen."

Adrenaline ramped down, leaving Kin with feet planted into the ground and shoulders heaving. He remained, glaring at Markus on the ground.

"I don't take this responsibility lightly. There's no choice here! There's no happy ending. There's no way to save her. They told you the rules, and you broke them. You broke them when you ignored Protocol Eleven Twenty-Three then, when you decided to contact her once you were back. These are the consequences. We knew this when we signed up for it. You knew this when you returned."

"I can't believe you've given up so easily." Feelings suppressed for months suddenly broke loose, faster and heavier than he could have anticipated. "You don't care about her. You've *never* cared about her. You just brush her off, like all that matters is coming home to Penny, to this life. Did it ever occur to you that my life then matters just as much as my life now?"

A different type of stunned look took over Markus's expression, one that told Kin an epiphany just went off in his friend's head. Kin exhaled, the burning rage giving way to the simpler urges of desperation. "We can still save her. Please."

"How?" The brush rustled as Markus got back on his feet and dusted himself off. "How could you possibly save her now?"

"Email her a warning."

"They're monitoring her communications."

"I'll jump back and protect her."

"Without any medical support? You'll be dead if you try—or arrive unresponsive and stranded in the past again at best."

"Then *you* jump back and save her."

Markus put his hands to his head, fingers pushing back hair to spotlight his creased mouth and squeezed eyes. "Okay. Let's play this out. Say I jump back and save her for this moment. That's a secondary detectable corruption. Then they'll send another agent back, kill me, and then kill Miranda. And we can continue this cycle indefinitely. A whole line of corpses trying to protect Miranda because *you couldn't follow the rules.*" He paced back and forth, his radius starting out small before sweeping back and forth a good five feet on either side. "We can't win. So I'm trying everything in my power to do right by her. Because you're my friend."

Despite the cold evening wind picking up to harsh speeds, beads of sweat crept down Kin's face. "Killing her is not doing right by her."

"Have you heard anything I said? She's dead. She will die. None of us can stop that. So I'm trying to save her from the worst part—the fear of dying."

In all their years together, Kin had never known Markus to lie. Even practical jokes were hard for his friend to pull off. The somber lines on his face told him that this, too, was genuine.

"They gave me this assignment a few hours ago. I almost quit on the spot. Then I read the plan."

Kin recalled the AD's words: *Miranda Stewart is a variable that must be controlled. The knowledge in her mind represents the greatest threat we have ever encountered.* "What are they going to do, send ten agents to surround her? Since it's such a big 'threat.'"

"This isn't a normal target. Most temporal criminals, they're mercs handling a job or someone with grand designs and black-market equipment or fugitives in hiding. We've even had a few former agents who went rogue for personal gain. This is unique. Her knowledge is the threat. She's a civilian. That's the difference. The mission plan doesn't have to worry about a shoot-out or physical confrontation. The job simply has to be done. So they're not sending in an army after her, they're sending an agent. And a retriever. The only difference is that the retriever, me, stays in the era and monitors the whole thing as a safety net. This isn't about apprehension or even timing. It's more about keeping it clean."

"Clean." Kin scoffed as he shook his head. "I've heard that before. Didn't quite work."

"You know what they wanted to do? Car accident. She uploads the project on August 28, 2030, then goes out to dinner. They know where she's going to be. A brutal, violent car accident that creates an easy cover-up for the Logistics department." The tension in his face released, visible even in the dim light. "If I knew Benjamin was going to die in a car accident, it would burn me forever knowing he had those few fleeting seconds of realization and terror. Those last frozen moments comprehending that that was it. I wish that on no one. No one should have to feel fear in their last seconds. So I accepted. I insisted that we alter the plan. The field agent will put a functional sedative in her drink. We'll activate it as soon as she gets in her car, and then we'll commandeer her vehicle." Markus's voice dropped, the following words coming with a fragile crackle. "At that point, she will be euthanized. Then we'll stage the car accident for clean paperwork with local authorities. She'll never have known fear or pain or violence. She'll just go to sleep before she starts the car. To take away those horrible final moments, that's doing right by her. At least if I go—" He stopped, blowing out a heavy exhale. "At least if I go," he repeated, his voice quieter, calmer, "I can oversee it. I'll know that it was done as quickly and painlessly as possible. Clean and controlled so that she doesn't suffer and it disappears into the assignment archives and *doesn't* become an asterisk in the record book or a case used for training. Okay?"

Markus's clinical description of Miranda's murder created a nauseating dizziness, and Kin had to lean on a nearby tree to steady himself. He reminded himself that Markus wasn't the bad guy here, and his twisted logic was a horrible yet somewhat sensible means to fight for the best in a worst-case situation.

But killing was still killing. "Who's the field agent?"

"Kin, I'm not telling you that. For your sake or the agent's sake."

Nervous electricity skipped up and down his body. "I can't let this happen. There has to be *something*, some other way." He grabbed Markus again and pulled, without any sort of direction or purpose in mind other than forward.

"Snap out of it!" Markus broke free and yelled with a ferocity he rarely displayed. "There's no beating this. Impossible tasks don't have happy endings, just burdens. God, I love you, but Penny's right—you can be so thick." He grabbed Kin by the shoulders and looked at him face-to-face, his voice carrying a gravelly seriousness that came out at a slow, deliberate clip. "What do you want me to do?"

"You could quit."

"If I quit, then someone else is going to do it. Is that what you really want? Someone who doesn't care about you or Miranda? Someone who sees this as yet another assignment? What good will come of that? So tell me, what do you want me to do? Think this through."

Markus was right; this was in the cards regardless of who handled it. That notion didn't sit easily. Kin wanted to fight back. He wanted to rip a tear in the universe and find a way to stop this. He needed to, if he only knew how. "Find another way."

The bright hues of dusk had started to dim, and stars began accompanying skycar headlights across the sky. "There is no other way. I'm sorry, Kin. I know that's hard to accept. I'm doing this because you're my friend. It would be easier to quit."

They stood in silence for several minutes before Kin finally gave him a silent nod. It broke the invisible barrier holding them to the small patch of dirt and weeds on San Bruno Mountain. Markus set out on his slow walk away, his drooped head bobbing with each step, and his skycar beeped before the door folded upward into its roof. "Sorry about hitting you," Kin said.

"I understand." The door sealed Markus in, and the rumble of his engine gave the ground a firm shake as he lifted toward the sky. Kin didn't watch him fly away.

CHAPTER 20

Kin's instinct was to go home.

Not the apartment he shared with Penny, but his *home* back in 2014. With Miranda, where he belonged.

He tried to find another way. He didn't infiltrate TCB headquarters with guns blazing, nor did he climb in through a ventilation shaft to bypass layers and layers of security. He'd considered it, though, visualizing each plan through its various steps. Each one ended up with a near-zero percentage of success. This wasn't some kind of spy thriller from Miranda's time.

So he reduced it to the basics. To get to her, he'd need an accelerator and the appropriate injections: a mix of standard pre-jump meds and some post-jump stabilizers for himself. Those were the essentials, but even with those supplies, any time jump for him would be risky without a partner. He'd been warned that his body was no longer equipped to make a jump—the chance of doing damage was incredibly high, and going it alone could be deadly. Ideally, he'd bring a doctor with him to inject the stabilizers, but that wasn't in the cards.

But a partner was the least of his concerns. Getting an accelerator would mean breaking into the equipment vault of the Resources division ten floors below the TCB's guarded roof, where a mix of motion and thermal sensors, eye-scanning door locks, and plain old Security guards remained.

Even if he could get past them, he'd still have to make it down ten floors and break into the vault itself. Mechanized Security bots and guards were the first layer; after that, locks upon locks stood in the way, and the individual accelerators were kept in a motion-, heat-, and sound-sensitive chamber, and the actual equipment was biometric, coded to individual field agents. Only mission planners had access to reset those codes.

If he somehow miraculously succeeded in getting an accelerator, he'd still have to go thirty-two floors down to the medical bay. Injections weren't tracked and guarded with the same ferocity as time-traveling equipment, but they still sat behind lock and key, and because recovering field agents stayed in the ward rather than at a public hospital, the entire floor was in a constant state of high alert.

Then, even with equipment and medication in hand, he'd still have to escape the bowels of the TCB high-rise and fly undetected to the jump point, all before the upcoming scheduled mission next week. Without any backup, without even time to get a blueprint of the building from public records, it truly was an impossible mission.

Kin came to that conclusion from the rooftop of a parking garage two blocks over. He'd stood, watching the unmarked TCB Security patrol skycar routes circle the roof, blending in and out of traffic. The high level of security made sense; after all, they were guarding technology that could theoretically rewrite the whole of human history.

Even at his peak field condition, there was no way he could have accomplished it. And so he took one last glance at the roof and walked back to his skycar, each step as heavy as the guilt he felt.

He could try something like a foolish frontal assault or hope to find a single hole in their security for a sneaking mission. But an instantaneous death wouldn't help anyone—not Penny and certainly not Miranda.

Instead, Kin walked with the gritted teeth of begrudging acceptance of the inevitable. One man simply couldn't break into the most highly secured building on the West Coast.

That was why he started his car and flew back to his apartment building.

The skycar hovered over the parking spot about a hundred feet below. Kin sat in the driver's seat, and his fingers grasped the wheel, the tint of his knuckles become lighter from the tension.

No sounds entered the car's interior except for the low hum of the engines and his own breathing. The display overlaid the windscreen, an endless blinking message indicating that the automated parking sequence was ready to engage. None of it registered, though; in fact, very little registered since he'd parted ways with Markus and launched his hopeless scouting mission.

And the stuff that did—well, it didn't matter.

The act of hitting the flashing orange icon seemed like surrender. It fluttered away, on and off across the lower view in the windscreen while traffic and lights and buildings remained in the distance. Behind him other skycars lined up, apartment dwellers finishing their commute home, the occasional honk urging him to park.

He couldn't do it. Parking the car, entering the apartment, returning to the home that he'd just begun to really reintegrate into, all of that represented the future. For now, all he could think of was the past, the consequences of his actions, the things he'd done.

He'd killed Miranda. Not the field agent on assignment, not Markus, not the AD. He did.

He'd broken the rules.

The driver behind finally lost his patience, horn blaring as he pulled around and lined up about twenty feet below before engaging his own parking sequence. Kin's car started repeating a warning that a vehicle in surrounding traffic engaged manual override and violated the standard traffic routes. Others gradually followed suit in breaking the rules, processing the queue until Kin was left alone, floating in the air.

The urge to fight *something* consumed every thought but even if he could snap his fingers and stop the car accident, they'd schedule another one. Unless she was shielded in a protective bubble free from the prying eyes of the TCB and history *and* unless he could convince the TCB that they no longer needed to pursue her, the same thing would eventually happen.

He couldn't do anything except wonder if Markus was possibly right.

Maybe that was the hardest part to accept. Markus's submission to the TCB was the same thing as waving the white flag instead of fighting, struggling—kicking and screaming until the bitter end. Markus may have been correct, except giving up felt so very wrong, an action so terrible that Kin wasn't sure if he could forgive him, if he could still call him a friend.

Skycars swerved around and below him, drivers confident of where they started and where they were headed regardless of traffic rules. Kin watched, envious at the way everyone else seemed to know where to go.

At some point over the next few minutes, the racing thoughts finally subsided. At some point he tapped the flashing icon. At some point the car parked, and at some point he shuffled back to the apartment. He may have even given Akasha a few scratches when he walked in.

Kin sat on the couch, his limbs stuck in Neutral. Behind him, the door slid shut and a quiet beep indicated that the automated lock had engaged. Down the hall he heard Penny's voice, a projected whisper. She popped around the corner, waving him to come in.

They walked hand in hand, Penny stepping with extra care, her feet landing with almost cartoonish silence. She motioned at the bathroom door and pointed once it slid open to reveal a small box of four sleeping kittens and a miniature vapolitter module next to them.

"I just bottle-fed them," she whispered. "Now they're in a food coma."

Kin smiled as Penny leaned into him, marveling at the way she adored the little moments, something he simply couldn't do right now. At their feet, Akasha slithered by, sniffing the air. Penny shooed the cat away, and she obliged with a hiss.

Markus had spoken about the burden of the impossible task. Perhaps in his twisted logic, he'd taken on this task because he knew that Kin faced another burden of similarly impossible odds.

He had to act like he'd simply been laid off from a government job, like someone who worked for the water district or the county clerk. Not like someone whose daughter was soon to be murdered.

Those were the rules they lived by. That was what they agreed to when they signed up.

"Paw-cific needed a foster for a few days. One of the new volunteers is a commercial Realtor who might know of a good restaurant space. Figured I'd get in good with her," Penny said. She blew a kiss at the napping felines, then motioned the door closed. Another kiss landed on Kin's cheek. "Hope you don't mind. I couldn't reach you today."

He went through the expected motions. Smile. Hug. Let her explain kitten care. Talk about going to the birthday party for Markus and Enoch's son. Reveal his job situation.

All because he was supposed to.

He joined her for dinner, played along while she gave another cooking lesson, laughed at her jokes, helped her bottle-feed four very acrobatic kittens, kissed her good-night when she turned in, leaving him alone with his thoughts.

The truth pulsed inside him, wanting to surface and unveil itself to Penny. But whenever his mind went there, flashes of Heather's panicked disbelief went through his mind. That conversation had made everything worse and left Heather worried about his mental stability. Who knew how Penny would react; she might even go to Markus with such a revelation for a whole other level of disaster.

He couldn't risk that. Not again. With Penny in bed and Akasha relaxing on a cat tree in the corner, Kin sat by himself again.

He completed the last step of the new plan: settle into the future. Because he was supposed to. Because the past was dead, and he couldn't do anything about it.

CHAPTER 21

As Kin and Penny walked up the driveway to the front door, his entire body reflexively tensed. His toes curled, his core tightened, his shoulders drew into hard knots. His fingers remained interlaced with Penny's, though within a few steps, something unexpected happened.

Her tension suddenly matched his. In fact, it may have even exceeded his, so much so that her nails dug into his knuckles.

Kin paused and looked over at her; her face drained of color, the normal gentleness of her expression erased to a straight neutral. "Oh no," she said in a barely audible whisper.

She couldn't have known the predicament with Miranda or the fact that Kin and Markus faced a friendship dangling by a mere thread, so much so that Kin bit his tongue whenever Penny brought up her brother over the past two days.

His generous severance package put her financial worries at ease, and she even talked about being ready to apply for the loan again once she figured out her restaurant angle.

He knew of only one thing that put Penny in this state, and through the open front doors of Markus and Enoch's home, he saw it.

"He didn't tell me he invited them," she said, and on cue, her mother paused in midstep across the entryway before looking directly at them.

"Penny!" she exclaimed, arms already outstretched. Edith Fernandez stormed through the open door, crossing the threshold and wrapping her daughter in her arms.

"Hi, Mum," Penny offered, her voice filled with a pep that didn't reflect how she looked.

"We're so glad you made it. You know, your father thought you might not show. Figured you'd be obsessing about that silly restaurant idea."

"I wouldn't miss Benny's birthday party—"

"That's what I told him! 'I know Penny gets carried away with her ridiculous ideas, but she wouldn't let her family down like that.' Now, if you'll excuse me, I'm decorating the cake. Sorry, sorry to come and go. You know me, attention to detail. But you can help me later. Markus said you tried the Mars spices in a dessert but got the ratios wrong."

"The ratios were actually quite—"

"Don't worry, I'll show you how to use them properly." And with that, Edith disappeared back into the house, Penny's self-confidence somewhere in tow.

They remained motionless halfway up the driveway, wind from the bay rippling through their clothes. Penny turned her back to the hillside Marin house and faced a view that would have been completely unattainable for Kin and Heather in twenty-one-A. In this era, rising sea levels and migration to off-world colonies had made this type of real estate affordable, especially for a midlevel TCB retriever agent and a hologram media designer.

"I can't go in."

"Your parents spit out noise. It means nothing."

"Easy for you to say." She took his hand and pulled him back toward the house. "You're not living in the shadow of England's most revered baking couple. Let's see how many times Mum mentions her awards today."

Kin had spent the last two days peering through archival blueprints of the TCB's building, trying to find any conceivable plan to break in and steal a time-jump accelerator as a means of contacting Miranda. For now, though, being pulled out of that anxiety and back into the passive-aggressive feuding that occupied Fernandez family events offered the strangest kind of soft landing place for his mind.

At least it was familiar.

"Right," Penny said, shaking her head and stiffening her posture. "I'm not listening to a single word they're saying." She held up the gift bag in her hand. "This day is about Benjamin, not his grandparents." Kin waited for her to take the first step, then stayed at her side as they trailed the noise of children through the home out into the backyard. "There's so many of them," she said, pointing and counting under her breath. "Thirteen kids. Nine adults."

They hadn't talked about children since Penny's awkward mention on his first night back, although her nerves about them was well documented over the course of their relationship. "Ah, it's not too bad." A girl, probably about seven or eight, ran by while dribbling a soccer ball, and he reminded himself to exhale after several frozen seconds.

"Hanging out with Markus and Enoch and Benjamin is one thing. That's easy. This looks like—" she paused at the sliding glass door and squinted "—this looks very...tiring." She nodded at her father, who sat barefoot in a lounge chair, glass of wine in hand. "Better than the alternative, I suppose."

"It'll be fine. They're great at this age," he said before realizing what he'd given away. "I mean, easier than wrangling mouthy line cooks and waitstaff, I bet." He stepped through the door without another word and avoided her confused look.

Enoch marched over, dodging the cross fire of kids chasing the ball on their small lawn. "Hey, guys," he said, trading hugs with both of them. He wiped sweat off his olive forehead and looked back at the high-pitched cacophony behind him.

"Sorry we're late." Penny pulled out two wrapped boxes from the gift bag, and Enoch nodded to the picnic table with unbalanced towers of packages.

"It's okay. Markus is still at work. He had to go in late last night. Said it was an emergency, someone else called in sick. Oh, well—figures, right?" Enoch glanced around with a look that told the opposite of his accommodating words. "He's not answering calls, though, at least since this morning."

A sympathetic smile came across Penny's face, one that was more than a mere polite gesture. "He should try to lose his job," she said, thumbing in Kin's direction. "No more long hours, and he'll get paid for a whole year."

Enoch and Penny thought that meant disappearing into the TCB building and getting stuck in meetings or whatever, only Kin knew that Markus had a retrieval scheduled. Even though the TCB had beacons to boost accuracy triangulation for agents jumping back home, the technology still wasn't perfect, and they had a return window of a few hours. Markus must have been hitting the late part of the window.

Was he returning from killing Miranda?

"The kids are getting restless for cake. And the younger ones will be hitting naps soon. And the much older relatives will stay past their welcome." Lines were etched across Enoch's face, and they stayed even as Benjamin ran over and grabbed his leg. "Hi, buddy. I know, I know, you want cake."

"Why did he invite them?" she whispered while tousling Benjamin's hair. Enoch shook his head in response.

Despite his emotional tug-of-war with Markus, things had settled down enough for Kin to engage his son. "Hey, Benjamin, having fun?" he asked, kneeling down to meet him face-to-face. The boy's bright blue eyes turned and locked in.

"I can't get the ball." He pointed to the mob roving around the yard, the ball a pendulum that swung back and forth, carrying a gaggle of children with it.

"Well, let's see." When Miranda was this age, Kin tried to instill ideas into her team about playing the sport, not just follow the ball around. His success rate at teaching that remained quite low—zero, according to feedback from irritated fellow parents—since he'd stubbornly tried to pass on visualization techniques about assessing passing options and looking for defensive holes rather than offer gentle encouragement. He met Benjamin's wide stare, and ignored any hints of young Miranda flashing through his memory. "Which side are you shooting on?" Benjamin pointed to the far left side and the glowing kid-sized holographic net. "Okay, what do you think is going on here? What do you see everyone doing?"

Benjamin squinted, exaggerated lines surfacing all around his face from his deep concentration. "They're trying to get the ball."

"Right. That's true. Look," he said, directing the boy's attention, "they're all running after it. Now, where are you going to be if you're always chasing the ball?"

"Mmm." Gears seemed to twirl and turn in his seven-year-old mind. "Behind it?"

"Yup. And you can't get the ball if you're behind it. So what does that mean?"

"Go—in front of it?"

"No, not necessarily. Left or right of it. Or in front of it. As long as it's *away* from the ball—because then it'll eventually come to you, and no one will be expecting it. Go where it's heading instead of where it's been. It's the first lesson you should learn about soccer. Try it."

Benjamin trotted across the small patio and then turned back to Kin before sending an approving nod. "Where it's heading," he called out, pointing to a patch of open grass. Benjamin moved at half speed to the empty area when the ball took a sudden bounce and landed a few feet in front of him. His legs pumped, far faster than Kin had ever seen him go before. He dribbled the ball forward, probably emulating what his father had taught him, despite looking like he might fly out of control at any second.

But he didn't. Instead, Benjamin took three strong strides forward and sent the ball through the holographic net and into the bark and succulents behind it. A smattering of cheers and whoops came up, and Benjamin ran back to the patio, a wide beam covering his whole face. "I did it, Uncle Kin!" Kin sent a high five and fist bump his way, though Benjamin finished it off with a hug. "Aunt Penny!"

"Penny," her dad called. He stood up, gait swooning from potentially too much alcohol. "Did you see your mum's cake?"

"Not yet, Dad."

"Maybe you should ask her what dessert will sell in restaurants."

"I'll keep it in mind," she yelled back. "Happy birthday,

Benjamin." The child responded by grabbing both of their hands, pulling them over to the backyard soccer field. The ball found its way to Kin, but rather than pass it back, he launched into every trick he could think of, from dribbling in midair to playing keep-away with the bunch. After a few minutes surrounded by laughter and clamor, Kin sensed eyes burning into the back of his head, and he turned to catch Penny staring his way. She blinked as they exchanged looks, a mixture of relief—probably from not having to deal with her parents—and disbelief—probably at Kin's outburst of child-rearing. Before they could speak, Markus stepped through the back door.

No one else knew that Kin recognized Markus's field attire, gray pants and a black belt used for holding equipment of various shapes and sizes. However, the standard-issue coat was missing, probably tossed into the back of his car, a simple white undershirt in its place. The outfit gave the impression that he'd come from a job spent fixing some heavy equipment. For Kin it drew a complete picture of a return jump that arrived a little later than anticipated.

A jump that may have involved eliminating Miranda.

The crowd of children dissipated with Enoch's announcement of cake and ice cream. Penny and the other adults helped guide the herd. Markus, whose messages Kin hadn't returned over the past few days, shot him a knowing look and mouthed the words, "You okay?"

Penny's arm cinched around Kin's waist, and she turned to look at the mob forming near Enoch. Kin stifled the volcanic rage inside of him, one that urged to reveal that this man, Markus, his *friend* was involved in the murder of his daughter.

He reminded himself of what had become his mantra recently: that as terrible as it was, there was a certain logic to it all. He had to repeat it, even though he didn't necessarily believe it.

There was no other way.

The line ran through his head one more time, and Kin gave a quick nod to Markus, one that seemed to spark relief in his response. "Markus," she said to her brother, "you owe him one. He kept the kids busy. And away from Mum and Dad." He replied with a laugh and a grin, and both TCB agents performed with the textbook casual demeanor used when dealing with civilians. "Just one thing," she said as they moved to join the group. "Where did you learn to handle children like that?"

Kin pretended not to notice the look Markus shot him. "Like what?"

"You were a one-man show out there. Does radiation treatment teach you how to be a crown dad or something?" Her round cheeks rose in a smile, and she bumped him, hip to hip. "You made it look easy. Even, I don't know, fun. Like it's not as scary as I thought."

Kin's mouth slipped half-open as he turned to Penny. They'd talked about children before, of course, mostly from the vague definition of eventually. Whenever the topic came up, Penny usually followed it quickly with a "but" statement: "but we have plenty of time" or "but a nephew is good enough for me now" or "but I wouldn't even know what to do," along with the occasional comment expressing gratitude for metabolizers, unlike her naturalist cousin, who had decided to have kids by thirty-five thanks to a nonmetabolizer life span. "It's not scary. It really isn't."

Penny's lips angled upward ever so slightly and then pushed out into a wider and broader grin when they looked at each other. "You sound so confident. Like you've already pulled it off."

"Penny, dear," her mother called from inside the house. "Help me with the cake."

"Daughterly duties," she said, giving him a peck.

"You could say you're busy."

"Path of least resistance." She walked to the patio door, and Kin kept a few-steps-behind pace in case she wanted a last-second bailout. Penny strode in, a confidence pasted onto her voice, even when Edith began lecturing her on all the ways her recent recipes lacked imagination. By the time Kin turned around to rejoin Enoch and the children, Edith had moved on from cooking criticisms to why volunteering with cat rescues was a waste of time. "They're survivors. They take care of themselves. You're messing with the natural order of things."

When Penny stepped back into the backyard, her hands filled by a platter displaying an immaculately decorated cake with precision piping and a detailed stadium across its miniature soccer field, all she could manage was a whisper of "mistake" to Kin. Enoch and Markus led the group in singing "Happy Birthday." Benjamin sang, too, clapping in an out-of-time rhythm while the candle glow reflected off his pupils. The song came around to its final line, everyone singing at half speed to draw out the final "happy birthday to you" before cheering. Benjamin wiggled his head around while blowing out all seven candles. The last one flickered, fighting back against the blowing air. Markus leaned over, his head right above Benjamin's, and he gave one quick puff to help his son finish.

Benjamin's movements were nearly an exact mirror of Miranda's sixth birthday. He'd watched that video on his phone yesterday morning when Penny left for work. Two children, separated by more than a century. Both shaking with laughter. Both bouncing with anticipation. Both looking to their parents. Some things must never change.

Enoch lifted Benjamin up and planted a large kiss on his son's forehead while Markus grabbed a knife for the cake.

"Look at that," Penny said, leaning into Kin. "The way they look at Benjamin. Like they'd find a way to cheat death for him if they could. I mean, can you imagine feeling something that intense? That pure? I don't think I could pull that off. I mean, when we have kids, I'll probably break them. I can't wait for Mum to comment on that one." She sighed, her weight pushing farther into him.

Penny's sentiment may have been a hint at a new path in their life. Or she may have been simply expressing admiration for her brother. Regardless, it represented the first time that the question of children was presented as a when, not if.

She didn't look up at Kin, though, which was probably a good thing. Because while the afternoon may have shifted Penny a fraction on how she felt about children, all it did for Kin was widen the gap between his present and the mystery of Miranda's life.

"Uncle Kin! Uncle Kin!" Benjamin ran over and grabbed his hand, pulling him over to Markus and Enoch. "Tell Daddy and Pappa what you showed me."

"I saw it, Benjamin. But Pappa finally got here, so maybe you can tell him."

Benjamin fired off words, his vowels and consonants running together into one semi-coherent explanation about basic soccer strategy. While he rattled things off, Penny pulled Enoch for a quick aside, and Kin took the brief opening to fire at Markus. "Did you just do it?"

"No," Markus said, his voice soft enough not to derail Benjamin's train of thought. "Tomorrow night. I'm sorry."

"I know."

"Great, right, Pappa?" Benjamin finished, looking straight up. Markus scooped the boy up, planting a kiss at the center of the unending curls on his head.

"Uncle Kin knows what he's doing, huh?"

"Yeah, Pappa. Go where the ball is heading."

"You know why that works so well?"

Benjamin nodded. "'Cause everyone else is chasing it. But you know where it's going. So you can take it!" The last sentence came with an emphatic nod.

The strategy represented the most fundamental way to transition kids from playing the game to becoming players. Except reinterpreted in its most simplistic form by a young child, the philosophy opened up a whole new realm of possibilities.

Including one idea that might save Miranda.

Kin drew in a slow, steadying breath as he surveyed the scene. Boys and girls playing. Adults talking and laughing. Penny sharing a drink with Enoch and avoiding her parents while Markus carried Benjamin around.

This was life. This was family. This was the thing he was trying to preserve, the thing he wanted to protect from the TCB's prying claws.

And he may have finally discovered a way to pull it off. Excitement bubbled through his veins, an effervescence tempered only by Penny's smiling face. She met his eyes and waved him over.

A different type of guilt flooded over him, along with the stinging realization that saving Miranda came at its own cost.

In order to do it, he'd have to break Penny's heart.

Once again his past and his future would fight for control of his present.

He walked over to her and drew her in with his arm. She looked up at him, and he offered a quick but gentle kiss.

"Well, aren't we Mr. Affectionate today?" she asked with a laugh.

"Thought you could use a boost." She leaned into him, resting her head on his shoulder, which proved to be fortunate. If she'd been looking up at him, she might have caught the split-second break in his defenses. "That's all."

CHAPTER 22

Kin stared into the camera's unblinking iris across from him. Yet again he'd reset the recording. Maybe it was because he worked off a script that was equal parts apology, explanation, and love letter. He stopped and started over and over whenever his tone sounded more like a lecturer than a partner saying farewell. Mere hours passed after Benjamin's birthday party, which didn't leave much space to come up with a perfect speech.

But this was when he had to do it. It was his only chance to get to Miranda before Markus and the TCB did.

A quick tap on the floating interface triggered recording again. Kin straightened up and looked ahead. "Hello, Penny," he said, his voice even and steady. "By the time you see this, I'll be gone. I'm very sorry to have done this to you. I hope you can forgive me someday. The truth is that I haven't been totally honest with you about—"

His notes flickered and stopped scrolling, causing him to stutter. He turned the recording off again; it didn't matter because he already knew that it came across as a half-dead reading rather than a heartfelt message, something as cold as what the TCB left for Heather and Miranda. The clock showed that it was nearly two in the morning, which meant only an hour remained before he had to leave; there simply wasn't enough time to keep messing around with this.

Not enough time—a sharp, quiet laugh escaped Kin, and he shook his head. What a concept.

The small backpack in the corner remained empty. He'd surveyed the apartment for possible gear he might need, though really there wasn't much. Everything would be at his destination. All he had to do was arrive and hope for a little something extra from his lucky penny.

Or, as he told both Miranda and Benjamin, go where the ball was heading.

He tried recording again and stopped shortly after; this time, it wasn't the holo notes that stopped him. The words simply didn't want to come out.

Head in hands, he walked over to the kitchen. After years of controlling the kitchen with Heather, the impulse to reorganize Penny's into a more cohesive and logical system, one that was arranged by function, size, and ease of use, that still arrived with a single glance—even now, on the eve of departure. Agent organizing: never a question of where equipment was under duress. He pushed that aside, going straight to the counter and pulling open a drawer. Underneath the morphing spatula and laser peeler sat something rarely used by the world anymore, something they'd only kept for emergencies: an old notepad and a pen. Technology allowed him to transmit emails across time. Yet, in the present, he had to rely on things that had been around for nearly twenty-five hundred years. The irony planted a silent grin on his face.

Penny, I'm sure you're wondering why this note is here. Since I met you, I haven't been totally honest about who I am. And since I've been back from "the accident," I haven't been totally honest about what happened.

Here's the truth: Markus and I are time travelers.

Kin went on to reveal everything to Penny—that time travel was real, that he'd used it before. He explained the TCB, his role there, and finally divulged his most recent mission and how he'd become stranded in another time. He wrote about Heather and then Miranda, knowing the truth would hurt, but that he couldn't bring himself to lie to anyone else.

Miranda is why I'm going back.

Not because I just want to be with her, though of course I do. I'm going back to save her life. It's my fault she's in this predicament, and it's my responsibility to make sure she's safe.

Please understand, I'm not choosing one life over another or Miranda over you. But because of everything that's happened, because of bad decisions I've made, the TCB intends to kill her, and I can't let that happen.

I'm going to try to jump back to save her.

Kin paused and rubbed his eyes. If the truth about his past had been difficult to admit to Penny, the reality of his future was only going to be worse. He picked up the pen and continued his letter, explaining to her the dangers involved in what lay ahead. Not only the risk he took in getting caught, but the potentially fatal gamble of the journey across time.

It doesn't matter, though. I owe this to her. I created this problem, and now I have to fix it. I'm her father, and I would give my life a hundred times if it meant she could keep hers. For the past few days,

I kept thinking there wasn't a way to save her. Tonight I found one. It may not work, but I have to try. I can't give up.

Since I've been back, you've been the one thing that helped me return to this world. You stood by my side, you were patient. You were the person I needed and the Penny that I loved. I can never repay you for that. I'm so sorry that you're the bystander in all of this. I wish I could take you with me to meet Miranda. I wish I could say that I'm definitely coming back and we'll have the wedding. But I can't. I simply don't know. All I can say is that I love you, and I want you to be happy. Have a wonderful, long, and beautiful life.

Kin's hands and arms remembered the way they felt that fateful night wrapped around Markus's neck, ready to do the vilest thing possible in desperation. The very mention of Penny's name triggered a solution, a purpose, one that brought him safely back to 2142 and into a world where things might have worked if he didn't ruin it.

And you should open that restaurant. Don't listen to Markus. Especially don't listen to your mother. Of course you'll succeed. You always do. I should have said that a long time ago. We all should have. Whatever happens, you were never "just Penny" to me. Even when I couldn't remember you, I carried you with me.

He reached into his pocket, the smooth edges of the lucky penny pressing into his fingertips.

You have been and always will be extraordinary, he wrote. *You were the reason why I came back home.*

P.S. Don't tell Markus what I've done. Please.

Kin signed his name. The point of the pen sat on the sheet where he dotted the *i*, ink pooling into a larger blotch. He wanted to say so much more about his regrets and guilt and how Penny helped him finally feel secure in this new place. Time ticked away, though, and writing even more would only increase her burden. Instead, he folded the two sheets in half and wrote her name on the outside.

Akasha stirred, probably confused by the activity at such an odd hour. She walked around him, doing figure eights between his feet. Her tail wrapped around his ankle, something that she usually saved for Penny.

Maybe cats really were smarter than dogs. Bamford would have never picked up on this.

He left the note on the bathroom counter and checked the time—still forty minutes before he planned on going. Enough to begin one last look at their living space.

Kin toured the apartment like a captain surveying his ship before a final battle. Details came crashing back, memories that had been quiet for years. In the kitchen he pictured Penny rushing about while she prepped for their first dinner party—back before he excelled at both planning and cooking. Her hair had whipped around in its ponytail as she bounced between the stove, the oven, and the counter, her frantic words the only things going faster than her movements. Finally, she put a lid on the last pot to simmer, and she looked over at Kin, totally unaware that a glob of pureed butternut squash had found a home on her forehead.

He moved on to the living room and sat on the couch they'd selected together—their first joint purchase. They went back and forth at the store, sitting on different couches and pushing down on the cushions and asking each other the same questions over and over about softness and support before Kin ultimately urged her to "go with your gut." When the delivery people finally brought it in and took off the protective coating, they settled into it, Penny sinking into Kin's arm, only to have Akasha sprint out of the bedroom and sink her claws into the bottom corner.

Kin knelt down, his finger tracing over those very same claw marks—their early reminder that with nice furniture, cutting Akasha's claws became a high priority. They'd taken that into account when Penny decided to foster three rescue kittens for several very stressful yet adorable months.

Akasha must have known he was thinking about cats; she sprang out of nowhere to land on the coffee table. Her rolling purr left a rumble in the room, and when he held his hand out, she forced her head into his palm and rubbed it back and forth.

She rolled on her back to entice him for belly rubs. However, time was limited, and the countdown crept forward far faster than he liked.

When Kin opened the bedroom door, he heard the soft rattle of Penny's snores—one of her biggest insecurities. The first night she'd stayed over at his apartment years and years ago, she even made an apologetic post-sex speech about how she sometimes snored and that it was okay to wake her up if it bugged him.

She'd moved to the center of the bed without him, her arms splayed out in an X. He sat down, and although he tried to remain careful about waking her, the mattress still squeaked and dipped. The movement must have triggered something because she rolled halfway over and blinked for a second.

"Sorry. Sorry," she said, her eyes closing again. "Did I wake you up snoring again?"

"No, Penny. You're fine." He leaned over, and her lids fluttered when he kissed her cheek. "You're more than fine," he whispered. "You're my lucky Penny."

She mumbled something incomprehensible, a half-conscious mutter that ended with the slightest of smiles before her mouth returned to the neutral half-open pose of deep sleep.

Kin wanted to turn the lights on so he could see her one more time in bright, full color rather than the dim shadows of a darkened bedroom. But he wouldn't risk waking her up.

Instead, he marched out into the hallway a few minutes earlier than planned. His back sank into the wall behind him, the *thump* causing the kittens in the bathroom to stir.

Kin took in a deep breath and reminded himself that in order to get this done, he had to shut everything down—any worries about getting to Miranda, any guilt about leaving Penny, any hesitation about what he'd committed to doing.

Sheer will stilled the turmoil, and Kin moved with swift efficiency, just as they'd trained him at the academy. He grabbed his backpack, gave Akasha one last scratch behind the ears, and stepped toward uncertainty, ready to go to where the proverbial ball was heading.

CHAPTER 23

Knees bent. Head down. Arms tucked. Left foot. Right foot.

Kin crept through the darkness, moving by muscle memory more than anything else. The wind kicked up from time to time, blowing bits of leaves and dirt around, and for the most part, that was the only noise that broke the silence. A sliver of moon provided some visibility, along with the city lights across the bay from the Marin hills. The TCB rotated jump points every week—usually middle-of-the-night ventures to remote wilderness spots inaccessible by general public flight paths and ground roads—and Kin's calculations for this time were correct.

After a good forty-five minutes spent contemplating in the dark, a skycar flew overhead following standard TCB jump protocol: lights off and running on low-power batteries for minimal audio-visual disturbance. It touched down in a patch and shut off about a half mile from where he waited, the only sound coming from the opening and closing of doors and moving of cargo.

Kin had done that very same drop-off dozens of times. Each sound ticked off a vintage checklist in his mind, echoing his own memories of unloading gear and confirming that the tech was ready to go.

The skycar powered up and hovered for a few minutes before flying away, presumably back to the dispatch dock on the main TCB building's fourteenth floor. In most cases that meant that the field agent and retriever were the only people in a several-mile radius, allowing them to initiate a jump across time safely ignored by the rest of the sleeping Bay Area.

Except this wasn't most nights. And this wasn't most cases. This time the pair was being tracked.

Not all of Kin's agent training had faded away. Clad in all black with only a small backpack, he remembered basics about staying low, moving when the wind picked up, and other details that helped him remain stealthy while he crept up to the target. Except unlike the old days, he didn't stalk a criminal tonight.

While tomorrow's scheduled jump would see Markus and his partner depart to eliminate Miranda, this target was a different TCB agent-and-retriever pair waiting right in front of him.

If he couldn't break into the equipment repository to steal an accelerator, he'd simply have to be at the exact time and place an agent brought one.

The two TCB operatives moved up to a small clearing, a patch of about fifteen square feet that the TCB kept clear of weeds and debris to minimize any field interference. Kin moved in a low crouch to the edge of the clearing, the arches of his feet burning as he steadied himself, and watched the field agent go through the motions—an equipment check, a radio check-in with home base, and a review of mission notes.

Agent and retriever. They always traveled together, the retriever the pilot for the accelerator and the agent the payload for the journey across time. He'd have to take them both out. Most likely, he'd target the agent first, as agents were the ones trained in aggressive combat techniques. It would have to be quick, and the cover of darkness certainly helped. From there, he hoped the element of surprise was enough to get a jump on the retriever.

Once accelerators were out in the field, they became locked by a retriever's individual biometrics. Kin let beads of sweat roll down the side of his face while looking for the telltale sign that the lock had been bypassed and the system powered up. The retriever knelt down and put a hand on the top panel until a tiny voice announced identity confirmation. First a hum kicked in, low-frequency buzzing undetectable to those who weren't used to it. Then a small light activated, bright enough to illuminate the pair's respective faces, followed by the appearance of several floating holo screens.

That was the signal Kin needed. His plan visualized, projecting the path to target.

The retriever began punching in coordinates on the holographic interface, pausing only to look down at the tablet in his hand. The agent had already gripped the proxy handles, kneeling in the prep position.

He was prone. A silent takedown was possible. Maybe the retriever wouldn't even notice.

Kin sidestepped quietly to the right, one leg crossing over the other until he remained undetected directly behind him. The holo changed from blue to green, indicating that the jump coordinates had been set. The retriever crouched low and gripped the accelerator handles in textbook fashion—head tucked in, elbows set against the knees to minimize the impact of any dizzy spells that might occur upon landing.

This was it. This was his moment—*the* moment to knock out the TCB operatives, grab their equipment, reprogram it to Miranda's time, and see what fate had in store for him. Each muscle tensed up, burning with anticipation as they locked together into a tightly wound machine, ready to pounce.

Kin leaped up and took a step toward his only hope.

He got one step farther before crashing back down to earth.

The ground slammed against his back, causing shock waves up and down his vertebrae. He blinked and focused from the light of the moon, only to have the silhouette of a head block his vision. Cold steel pressed against his forehead, and as the accelerator's hum ramped up to a palpable buzz, the figure leaned over and whispered.

"Don't move."

Before he could say anything, a bright light flashed through the field. It came and went fast enough that the uninitiated probably thought it to be lightning, nothing more. But Kin knew better than that. He inched up, only to have the distinct weight of a knee land on his throat and the metal barrel guide him back down to the ground.

It didn't matter, though. The flash meant only one thing: the agent and retriever had jumped through time.

CHAPTER 24

The steel held hard against Kin's forehead, enough for him to identify the rough size and shape: a charge pistol with plasma rounds—TCB standard issue, although local law enforcement used them, too. "Just stay there," the voice whispered again, followed by indecipherable mumbling.

The TCB operatives—and their equipment—were gone, somewhere in time. His captor leaned back to look at the now-empty field, enough for Kin to feel the weight shift off his throat. In a split second, Kin pictured four quick moves capable of taking the man down.

"Stay there and listen to—"

First, with his left arm, Kin pushed the gun off angle and pulled the man's wrist down hard. He jerked forward, the gun landing somewhere in the field. Second, Kin met him with a head butt. The man staggered, arms flailing in the moonlight. Third, Kin propped himself up on his hands and then ran his legs with a sweep through the man's calves. The man fell to his knees, which was all the time Kin needed to do the fourth move: grab the man's arms and bend them back into submission.

Maybe he didn't have all the nuances of his agent training, though basic survival skills combined with being in athletic shape proved to be successful enough. Was he really that good, or did this guy not get rough-and-tumble that often?

Kin looked into the blackness of the empty hillside. Empty. No accelerator to hijack. His vision adjusted; the vague dark of the night slowly coming into focus, and indeed, the only movement came from a slight tremble of weeds and plants blowing in the wind.

It was definitely gone. Kin's lip curled at the thought, and the tension in his body returned tenfold. It was *gone*.

"That was my ride," Kin said through gritted teeth. He yanked down on the restrained arm again, causing the man to yelp out. His only way to Miranda, now gone thanks to some overzealous Security guard or would-be vigilante. A new list ramped up in Kin's mind, sending his brain into a highway of questions on overdrive. If his old self, the man living in a suburban home with a nuclear family, if that person could see the list, the deterioration of his own mind into dark and violent places would have shaken him to the core.

Interrogate him. Break his arm. Hold him for ransom. Torture him for information.

Kill him.

"Kin, stop!" This plea didn't come from the man locked in his grip, but from a woman nearby.

Penny.

"Stop, Kin. Please. It's me, Penny." She rushed out of the

black night and knelt down next to him, her breath against his cheek. "That's Markus. Please, let him go."

"Markus. Markus put a gun to my head?" Kin pulled the crossed arms again, eliciting a cry from Markus. "What happened to all that stuff about friendship?"

"Stop, please. The gun's not loaded," Penny said, arms on Kin's shoulder. "It's a prop."

A moment of quiet, broken with the sound of Markus hitting the ground. Kin felt with his hands in the dirt, stopping to grip the cold metal of Markus's gun.

From the weight and shape, he knew it was a real gun. The charge indicator on the back of the grip showed a dull red: empty.

The earlier rage dialed down into something lesser, a palpable anger that at least released control of his mind enough so that he could begin to think clearly. "That was stupid, Markus. I could have killed you."

"I didn't think your close-quarters combat skills were still so sharp. My mistake." Markus teetered back up, finding his balance. The moonlight created shadowed lines across his face with each wince.

"Kin, let's just talk about this. We'll figure something out," Penny said. Her words sounded comforting yet cursory, a default to show empathy while she digested this strange new world where time travel existed. There would be no denying what she saw, and after the letter he'd left her, she had all the proof she needed.

"Penny. Why are you here?" In another context, such a question might be seen as accusatory or threatening. But here, he asked it with outstretched arms, and she sank into his chest.

"The kittens were stirring Akasha up. She woke me clawing at the bedroom door. You weren't there, and I saw your note."

"I hated to leave you like that, but it was the only way." They stayed in the embrace as he explained what he'd planned—to hijack another jump, steal the equipment, and then make a jump of his own—and though he couldn't see her face, she wasn't panicking or pushing him away at these revelations.

"So, what you wrote… Time travel is actually real? Markus has been trying to convince me this whole time. Explaining that you two travel through time to arrest people, like some sort of time cops."

In the back of his mind, a memory flashed by, one where Heather showed Miranda a movie called *Timecop*. With a name like that, he remembered being unable to hide his smirk at the time. But now, it was just a reminder of what needed to be done.

And who stopped him.

Kin's head tilted as he looked at Penny. "You called him?"

"If all of this is true, it sounds like I already lost you once before. I didn't want to give up without a fight."

"That's what your brother wants me to do."

Markus let out an exasperated sigh, hands in the air. "Look, your plan is ridiculous! You're just going to get yourself killed. Even if you survived the jump, the TCB would send someone after you immediately. Tonight's jump was targeted for 2062, not Miranda's time. The TCB would've detected the time discrepancy in the accelerator's jump signature. Kin, it's pointless. That's what I mean when I say there's no way around this. You have to give up. You know what?" The steely resolve dissolved in Markus's face, leaving him weary. "It's not even giving up. It's giving in."

Markus was right—Kin hadn't thought of those logistics.

Scientific details were generally left to mission planners and the retriever agents who helped them; field agents like himself merely executed the job. But that nugget from Markus triggered a memory, a fact dug up from a lesson or lecture somewhere across another lifetime: time jumps left residual signatures detectable by TCB monitors, and those signatures created echoes in the arrival era for up to five days. The only way to muddy the TCB's ability for detection would be if a second jump landed in the same geographic area within that short time window.

That was a risk he'd be willing to take.

"Give in and let you kill Miranda?"

Markus groaned in frustration. "Come on, Kin. I am not just killing her. I'm trying to do right by her, you know—"

"Wait, wait," Penny said. She broke free of Kin and faced her brother, hands on hips. "What's Kin talking about?"

"Penny, I'm not revealing how our mission protocols work. We're breaking enough rules here tonight."

"Are you or are you not going to kill Kin's daughter?"

Markus remained silent, so Kin faced Penny and explained Markus's role as a retriever, both from a procedural perspective and the specific instance of this case, including his push to change the mission parameters. With each classified revelation, Markus squirmed further and further, though Kin was far past caring. Penny, on the other hand, didn't react at all. She took in the information with a blank stare, perhaps a result of having the curtain removed from two very significant aspects of her life.

"You never said *you* were going to kill her," Penny said.

"What difference does that make?"

"The difference is that if you're going there, you could come up with *something*." Penny crossed her arms and glared at her brother.

"I *can't*. I don't know how many times I have to repeat this. It doesn't matter what I do, what anyone does. No one can save her." He looked skyward in frustration and sighed. "Do you think I want to do this?"

"Can't you bring her here?"

"She was born about a hundred fifty years ago. Her temporal frequency is different. She'd be detected immediately by the underground transponders, identified as an anomaly. They'd be on her in a day, maybe less."

"Okay then. Theoretically how do you rescue her?" Penny's question came across as more of a demand than an inquiry.

Various scenarios played out in Kin's head; he bit down on his lip, filtering through the list until it was whittled down into the most plausible option. "Convince the AD to remove her from the assignment list."

"No, see, there you go again," Markus cut in. "That's impossible."

"Think outside the rules," Penny urged. "Kin, if we could do anything, what would it be?"

"Well..." An alternative future projected out, one where things went their way and somehow covered all of their tracks and ensured a clean debriefing report. "First, we'd convince the TCB that the mission was a success. All traces would confirm that the subject was eliminated. Then someone hacks the era's official county records to match so no one asks questions. Then the field agent has to successfully jump home without any problems, and Miranda has to escape somewhere with a new identity. No connection to her old life. And she has to agree to even do that." Kin stopped, pausing to gaze up at the stars sprinkled above him. "You see the problem here? She can't escape if the TCB ever discovers that the job isn't complete. We can travel through time, but we can't perform magic."

Penny had her nervous tics, the ones that surfaced when she was unsure or anxious. Yet she also had another familiar movement, the one that only came about when deep in thought—usually when trying to figure out the missing piece to a recipe, one that might mean the difference between disaster and brilliance. Her eyes looked up and to the right, and the forefinger of her left hand tapped against the tip of her chin. It sped up and slowed down and sped back up again. Whenever Kin saw this, he pictured synapses firing off in her head to the rhythm of her tapping finger.

If that was the case, then after a lull of twenty or thirty seconds broke, her mind went into overdrive, finger tapping at a breakneck pace. "What if," she said, words coming out at a measured rhythm that belied her excited gestures, "we substituted the ingredients?"

Kin shot a look over at Markus, who was already looking back. "Substitute what?"

"The main ingredient. When we need to make our customer happy with a special request, like a food intolerance or something, we substitute the ingredient for something else, something that doesn't change the recipe and still gets the job done. Can we do that here? Can we do something to fake her death? Convince your bosses that the mission was finished? I mean, look, we have a person on the inside," she said, pointing at Markus. "And we have someone who's done this, what, dozens of times?" She pointed at Kin. "That's gotta get us somewhere."

Kin expected Markus to do his usual spiel about regulations and rules. But maybe the challenge from his sister—or more accurately having his younger sister one-up him at his own game—got him to think a little differently for once. "You know," he said, "there might be a way to make this work. We falsify records all the time. Maybe even get a medical cadaver for show. Messy car accident, lots of fire. Then plant the falsified records so no one actually looks any closer." Kin often wondered what Markus and other retrievers did when they brainstormed missions before passing the intel to field agents. This was probably as close as he'd get. "Only I can't do it myself. I'll need someone else to jump. No, Kin—" he put his hand up "—don't even volunteer. I'm not sending you to your death."

"Too late. I volunteer. There's no guarantee that we'll get someone to agree before your jump tomorrow night."

"This plan won't work if you're having seizures upon arrival. Unless you know how to give yourself stabilizers while you're unconscious. And even then, that's no guarantee. There's a reason why the medical staff doesn't want you jumping anymore."

"It's the best we got."

"He needs someone to go with him? Hello—" Penny put up her arm "—right here." She stood straight up, a tangible clarity in her expression despite only the light of the stars overhead. Pride surged through Kin, a warmth that melted through the chill air. If Markus hadn't been there, he'd have hugged her and not let go for at least an hour.

"No, Penny. You're a chef. You're a civilian. It's far too risky."

"You think I really care about that risk when it comes to my family?"

"I am trying to keep you *safe*. That's what I do. You're my little sister. There's stuff that you have to do to physically and mentally prepare for this sort of thing. Classes, training, certifications and qualifications and all kinds of stuff," he said, counting off his fingers.

"Markus, stop telling me what to do—"

"No, Penny, you're not ready."

The tone shifted into sibling rivalry; Kin and Markus literally traveled through time, but this hillside argument might as well have been a portal to Markus and Penny's life as children. Nostrils flared, feet stomped, they both pushed their voices to higher and higher pitches.

If so much hadn't been at stake, Kin would have been endlessly amused.

"Penny, this is extremely reckless. Listen to me—"

"No, Markus. You're always trying to shut me down."

"There is a *huge* difference between running a kitchen and traveling through time."

"I'm doing it."

"No, you're not."

"I'm telling you, *I'm* doing it."

"You're only saying that out of spite. Think of the risks—"

Finally, Penny threw her hand up to stop Markus in mid-sentence. *"Stop!"* she said to her brother, with a forcefulness in tone if not volume that seemed thirty-some years in the making. "I am not doing this out of spite. We take risks out of love. You're just too afraid to see that. You've always been." She turned to Kin. "What would I need to know to be ready?"

"Honestly," Kin said, running the procedure through his head, "close your eyes, hold on, and then take a deep breath when you get to the other side."

"Close eyes. Hold on. Deep breath. Got it." Penny nodded at Kin before reaching over to take his hand. They turned together, a united front attacking Markus's by-the-book logic. They stood alone in the clearing, only wind and dirt at their sides, though Penny's words made Kin feel taller, stronger, brighter, as if anyone in the Bay Area could look over and see the bold decision Penny made. She didn't pick up on the surge in his emotions, though; instead, she stood stone-faced, not out of apathy, but out of determination. "What else do we need? We've got a daughter to save."

CHAPTER 25

Penny's bravado disappeared once they were alone, as if her furious confidence only surfaced when powered by the bubbling cauldron of sibling rivalry.

But with Markus gone, the new reality of their lives settled in, seemingly stealing all of her words. In the morning, they'd dropped the kittens at the rescue and bought supplies, including stops at antiques stores to purchase whatever twenty-one-A era cash they could find. In the afternoon, they reviewed time-travel logistics and the massive amount of noninterference guidelines provided by Markus.

In between, Kin cracked open the topic of Heather, just so Penny might be able to release whatever pressure built up in her mind. Per her family style, she gave a stoic tight-lipped smile and said, "I'm fine," when she was clearly not.

Kin brought tonight's final drop-off from Markus to the bedroom. He opened the large composite case and spread the items out on the bed: an unlocked accelerator with two sets of proxy handles, the right amount of pre- and post-jump injections despite Kin asking for a few backups. Next to them sat an era-specific gun, more era-specific cash from Markus's personal antiques collection, fake IDs, communication earpieces, and a small notebook with a handwritten outline of the plan they'd discussed for the fourth time mere minutes ago. This didn't include the additional ration packs, disguise for Miranda, or era-specific clothes that Markus said he'd leave at a storage facility for them. "Come check it out."

"I thought Markus said you couldn't explain classified equipment to me."

"Well, you *are* risking life and limb to do me a favor. And helping me not die in the process." He motioned for Penny to come closer. "That probably squares things up." They went through the gear, item by item, Kin explaining the how and why behind them. Penny absorbed all the information, her expression fixed in deep concentration like she was building a recipe. "And we'll have to bundle up. Pre—climate change weather. The Bay Area's about five degrees cooler."

He then broke down the plan he'd conceived with Markus: the night prior to Miranda's assassination, Markus planned to lace the field agent's food with some of Penny's Mars colony spices. At the right dosage, that would give the agent flu-like symptoms for a good seventy-two hours, so Markus would transmit back to TCB headquarters and suggest the monitoring/active roles be swapped because of apparent illness. Since the mission involved faking a car accident rather than chasing criminals and dodging gunfire, he was certain they would approve, particularly because he'd helped plan it. In that era, Kin and Penny would land, with Penny giving the additional injections to him for stabilization. Kin left out the part about feeling unsure whether that would necessarily be enough; the TCB doctors were vague when they told him about the risks, and he didn't have anyone to consult now. Assuming he did survive, they'd use the cash to get a rental car and drive up to the city of Davis, where Miranda was finishing grad school, and then stake out the parking garage where history recorded her car's location. As long as they got to her before 8:20 p.m., they'd be able to whisk her away when Markus took her empty car and staged the false execution and car accident. They'd drop Miranda off at the airport to start her new life while Markus hacked records to confirm Miranda's official death. And they'd time-jump back to the same night they left, landing safely within the range of avoiding detectability.

Best-case scenario, anyway.

Penny picked up the lone unopened box in the equipment case, one that Kin had purposefully passed over. "What about this one?"

"That," he said, holding his hand up to keep her from opening it, "needs to stay secret. Even to me." He guided her hand to lay it back down in the case. "Especially to me. That's Miranda's new identity."

Her new identity—falsified passport and birth records, along with cash in both American dollars and euros. "When I knew I was stranded, I paid people to build a new identity for me. In that era, it's not that hard to do. There were how-to guides posted on the internet. It's a pre-DNA/retinal world, so once you get two or three official records established, everything else propagates. A passport, a driver's license, a Social Security number. Any of those. Having Markus to hack records and fake documentation makes it easier. She'll be this new person. Only I can't know anything about it," he said over the lump in his throat. "All I get is the chance to make it right. After that I can never know where she goes or who she becomes."

"I don't get it." Penny straightened up, hands on hips. "You're not a time traveler after this. Why can't you look her up to see how her life played out?"

To almost anyone else, Penny would have made perfect sense. Yet Kin knew—he *knew*—that being both a parent and a former agent would create a level of irresistible temptation should he ever have access to a DTP portal or an accelerator or any possible means of reaching Miranda under her new identity. If he found her, if he connected with her, then so could the TCB. And that wasn't a risk he was willing to take. "I just can't. It's my promise to her. She's suffered enough because of my choices. I can *save* her but I'll never get to know who she truly becomes."

Penny sat on the bed, examining the spread of top secret equipment in front of her. "There's something you haven't told me about Miranda," Penny said. "What's she like?"

The question seemed so simple, so generic. Yet the answer itself was somewhere far-off and elusive, and its distance only amplified the guilt that lingered whenever Kin thought of Miranda. "I'm, uh," he replied with a sigh, "actually, not sure. She'll be an adult when we find her. I'll have missed half her life."

"What about the Miranda you knew? What was she like?"

Kin considered the question while opening the other small bag to bring, the one that held his items from the past. Not that anything in there could really help, but if he didn't return, the last thing he wanted was to leave Penny with incriminating evidence.

His old smartphone came to life with its archaic bright screen, and he tapped away at it to load his photos of her. "She was smart. Very sharp. But guarded. She knew how to read people. She had empathy, especially for her parents. Perhaps too much. She bore a lot of burdens herself. She thought my time traveler's brain was PTSD."

"PTSD?"

"Sorry, they called it post-traumatic stress disorder. What our doctors call the trauma recovery period. They didn't know how to handle it back then." He handed the phone over to Penny. "She called her ability to read people her 'bullshit detector.' I didn't approve of the language." He slid his finger across the screen to load another photo and nodded at her to do the same. "See there. That was a few weeks before I left. High school soccer. Turns out she hated it the whole time and I was oblivious to it. Feels like I never really knew her. I don't know if I ever will."

It took several seconds for Kin to realize that Penny stared at him. Not a wide-eyed look of shock, but rather a piercing inquiry, an unblinking commitment to dig past layers down to the truth at Kin's core. "You love her very much," she said as they locked eyes. "I can see it in your face."

"She's my daughter."

Penny nodded, the edges of her expression softening enough to project a sincere but subtle sympathy. "And this, this is her as a baby?" she asked, holding up the phone.

"Yeah."

Penny continued to swipe through the baby photos, though he heard her take a sharp inhale and linger at one particular picture: Heather in the hospital holding an hours-old Miranda. Heather's long red locks were matted and sweaty, joy and fatigue both on her face. Though he pretended not to notice, Penny glanced up at him and swiped through the photos at a rapid-fire pace to snapshots of Miranda's life— not Heather's.

"Parenting," she said after a pause. "Did it come naturally?"

"Well, it's different from being a secret agent." Kin held up the accelerator and visualized the start-up sequence in his mind. Even though Markus unlocked it, he still had a tiny fear that powering it up would send TCB Security forces down on them. Or maybe he'd mess up the start-up configuration; agents knew the ins and outs of accelerators only as a precaution—retrievers handled it in all but extreme circumstances.

Or maybe it wouldn't even work. This was, after all, the same hardware that made Markus late for his son's party. He'd reported that this unit had a malfunction in its chrono sensors and requested a replacement, then conveniently forgot to return the problem hardware. Markus made Kin swear that he'd return it without a scratch because he'd promised Resources that they'd get it back tomorrow after they landed back home. "Or a computer guy. That was my job in that era. Computer networks for a video game company." Penny's eyes softened, and she put down the smartphone, leaning her shoulder into his. "The first year of parenting, you hold on for dear life. Nothing can prepare you for it. It's like entering a different world. And then you adapt. It's the hardest thing I've ever done, especially the beginning. And it's also probably the best. You know what's funny," he said, picking up and examining the injections, "we have it so much better here because of these. As parents, I mean. Living to two hundred. Back then you really had to choose between career and family. Even if you balance both, usually there was always one side asking for more." Bedroom light bounced off the syringe's chrome casing, and the reflection of Kin's eye came through surprisingly clear. "Heather always joked about 'if only we lived twice as long.' We didn't plan on Miranda. It just happened when Heather was in law school. We improvised. If she had had metabolizers, all that stress would have gone away. So we're lucky, you know? You can choose kids and your career or your second career or whatever. You can open your restaurant, then have a baby or vice versa. Or do them at the same time. Heather didn't have that choice."

It took several seconds for Kin to realize that Penny's entire posture had gradually stiffened into a tight wire. She looked away from him, either at Akasha lying on the carpet or the three-tiered cat tree in the corner or maybe out the window at the twinkling skycar lights.

"I'm sorry," Kin said, "it's awkward bringing up Heather, isn't it? This whole thing is—"

"No, no, it's all right." Penny's words picked up their pace, which usually meant that things weren't all right. "I mean, it makes perfect sense. It's, you know, logical considering how long you were there, your memory, everything."

"It's still gotta be strange for you—"

"It's fine. It really is." Penny's tone didn't change from its sudden flatness. "We have to leave in, what, four hours? I'm going to freshen up and get some sleep." She stood up without a word and walked to the bathroom. The door shut, followed soon by the sound of rushing water.

Kin remained, standing in the bedroom with only Akasha and the gravity of the situation as company. While he battled the paradox of past and future, Penny must have fought something else. Despite the brave face put forth to Markus in the name of love and justice, the weight of the past twenty-four hours crushed her enough that Kin heard muffled crying from the shower.

He didn't need anything else to understand the seismic shift Penny wrestled: there really was another life with another family, one that existed in the not very distant past for her fiancé.

Kin knew what he was fighting for. With only hours remaining, he hoped Penny felt as sure.

CHAPTER 26

One of the first lessons during agent training involved the psychological approach to missions: keeping a clear mind to avoid any potentially fatal distractions.

Despite Markus's crash course in protocol, Penny didn't seem to abide by this one. Her pensive face still barely hid a lurking uncertainty. "I've got to catch my breath," she said, kneeling down against the shrubs. At three in the morning, they'd almost finished the steep climb up to a remote spot in the Santa Cruz mountains, a familiar walk fueled by muscle memory, probably because Kin had taken Miranda on this hike several times. Back then he never understood how he navigated the terrain so easily, only that it felt like instinct. Now he recognized it as another hidden memory from his agent life, the journey up to the Santa Cruz jump point.

"Another ten minutes or so. We're close."

"Right," she said, taking a drink of water. "If you'd asked me earlier what I had planned for the week, this isn't what I had in mind."

"I know it's a bit much to take in." He crouched next to her, a hand on her knee. "Do you need a few minutes? Any last-minute questions?" He cleared his throat and paused, opening the opportunity for her. "Anything on your mind?"

Penny huffed in and out, nervous tic after nervous tic unrolling before him. He was about to brush it aside, move forward, when she spoke. "We should talk about Heather."

He'd held out hope that maybe she'd simply accepted that his relationship with Heather was part of his warped situation, that maybe she wouldn't let it affect her. Looking at her slumped silhouette in the shadows of trees and shrubs, he knew it had, and he owed her anything she might need to help her cope. She'd made the extraordinary leap, not him. "I know it's been strange. We have some time. What do you want to know?"

"How did you meet her?" She retied her ponytail, pulled her backpack over her shoulder, and then motioned upward to move on.

"College," he said, beginning the final ascent. He responded quickly, not giving in to anxious hesitation. "She was a student at UC Berkeley. I worked there."

"Were you two happy?"

Sticks and brush snapped underneath their feet with each step. Kin tried to form a response, though nothing definitive wanted to come out. "I think so."

"You think so? Like you can't remember, like how you couldn't remember me?"

"No, it's just hard to sum up your time with someone that simply. We were together for sixteen years. The last six months were rough, actually. I was losing parts of my memory. Fainting. Dizzy spells. I was pretty sure that it had something to do with my time traveling, but I couldn't tell her that. I didn't even absolutely know. So I played it off as PTSD. To protect my past, I resisted getting help. And we fought about it." Kin pulled himself up a steep ledge, his heel digging into half-soft dirt for traction. He turned and held his hand out to Penny. "She's a lawyer. She can be brash at times. She's quick. Very practical. Sometimes takes herself too seriously. Sometimes has the biggest laugh in the room." Kin stopped when he realized he used the present tense. "She's dead now. I mean, not dead because we're in the future. She got cancer a few months after I left. They didn't have the technology to save her back then."

The path ahead proved to be less strenuous, allowing Kin and Penny to walk side by side through redwood trees that reached upward forever. Whether it was the shadows and moonlight or how she actually felt, her face revealed nothing. She remained silent over the next few minutes, and only when Kin stated that the jump point was close did she stop them.

"I've been thinking this over," she finally said, her eyes clear as the moon above despite the lack of light.

"Don't think about it too much. These jumps can mess with your mind. Hold on and—"

"No, not that. Accepting time travel actually came easy. It's kind of reduced to a footnote when you find out the man you love has a secret family," she said with a quiet laugh, though the tone behind it was indecipherable. "Your...wife. Heather. That's the hard part. I've been thinking about it all day."

The cool air carried voices from around the bend, presumably of Markus and the field agent doing their pre-jump check-in. Kin reminded himself to not look at the agent's face when they got closer. Nothing could ruin a soccer team's chemistry more than knowing a teammate tried to kill your daughter. "She's not my wife anymore."

"I get it, though. This situation's not fair to anyone. Not you, not me, not Heather or Miranda. Not even Markus. The guilt that he's feeling. The burden of his decision. He'll never let you know, but I can tell. The colder he seems, the worse he feels. We Fernandezes excel at stifling guilt—thank you, Mum and Dad." She stood up at the peak of the mountain. To her left, bits of the ocean were visible in the distance. To her right, remnants of the city blinked. And below, about a hundred feet or so down a slope, was their launch point. "We can't change what happened—"

"Technically, that's what we're trying to do."

"Okay," Penny said with a grin and slap to his shoulder before returning to a more serious posture. "You know what I mean." She angled back, her ponytail dipping downward as her chin turned up. Above them stars burst through the blackness of the night sky, so bright that any twinkle seemed like a direct message from the universe. "I know that Heather is dead but that doesn't mean you owe me anything. I mean, you loved her. You had a family with her," she said. "Just because she's gone doesn't mean you have to go back to the default. And I—" she let out a tiny exhale, a puff of air rolling out and illuminated by the moonlight "—wouldn't want you to. For either of us."

"Penny—"

"No, listen. You say she's not your wife anymore. Technically, sure, but what about in your mind? In your heart?" Her finger tapped him in the chest before she spun away.

"You're not a default."

She turned back to face him, gaze locked in with a wide intensity he'd rarely seen. "We'll never know, though, will we? *I* will never know." She spoke quietly, barely audible over the sound of the wind whipping through the mountains. But it was enough. "And I don't know if I can live with that."

The truth of her insecurity crawled out from behind the bravado she'd displayed since last night, probably because he'd wondered the same thing about himself. If he *could* have chosen between Penny and Heather, who would he have picked?

She deserved to know where she fit in.

The question should have whirlpooled doubt and debate. Somehow, Kin's mind remained surprisingly calm and clear. Despite Markus getting extra injections from Resources, Kin knew there was a chance he might not survive the jump, and even slimmer odds on the jump back. That didn't quite matter in this moment, the present snapshot of intersecting lifetimes. Worries and fears disappeared for a fraction of moving time, enough for Kin to see clearly that the future he wanted stood on the hillside beside him.

"I want to show you something, something I couldn't have before you knew about…this." He took her hand, and though they both wore gloves to handle the terrain up the hills, her touch remained soft. "When I was stuck in the past, I couldn't remember you after a few months. My brain lost the details closest to me as a survival mechanism. Only…you were always with me," he said, releasing her grip to pull off his backpack. Out came a smaller bag, one with his items from the past, and his fingers felt in it until they came across a weathered old coin. "They still used physical currency back then. This is called," he started as he beamed at her, "a penny. I took it everywhere. Protected it from everything. I didn't know *why* because I couldn't remember—I only knew that I had to keep it safe. Whenever I looked at it or touched it, everything felt right. And I know it's because if I was with my lucky penny, then I was home."

"Lucky penny." She took the coin from him, holding it up so that it caught the light of the moon.

"You stayed with me. Every day for eighteen years in the past. Even when I didn't know it."

"God, now you're going to make me cry," she said, still looking at the stars. "Are you sure this isn't a really elaborate practical joke to impress me? That there's no such thing as time travel, and you're not some sort of secret agent—"

"*Former* secret agent," Kin said with a laugh.

"Right. You're not a former secret agent. There's no daughter to save. You're just a really sweet fellow with a romantic side, trying to make up for missing our wedding, right?"

Penny's wide eyes glistened over, and as they locked on to his, a flutter rippled through his chest.

Like how he used to feel when he touched the lucky penny. Like how they looked at each other on that engagement night.

"My life is stranger than fiction."

"Well, then." Penny handed the coin back to him, took in a heavy breath, and wiped the corners of her eyes. She rolled her hand and motioned him onward. "Let's go rescue Miranda. Isn't it time we both get to find out what she's really like?"

They marched downhill in short, silent steps toward the small grove the TCB used as a jump point. Kin's legs locked with tension as they crouch-walked to blend in with the brush, every muscle in his body tingling with anticipation.

So many things could go wrong, yet a certain calm resonated in the face of potential disaster. Perhaps underneath all the years of office work and child raising, his agent instincts had remained intact, even hardened. Or perhaps the real difference came from knowing he went into this trying to do the right thing while being honest with Penny. And if he was going to fail, at least this let him fail heading in the right direction instead of running away.

"Why here?" Penny asked while Kin unpacked the accelerator equipment. She turned and surveyed the sprinkling of city lights far beneath them. "Besides the nice view."

"The TCB has transponders planted in the ground at all jump points," Kin said, motioning to the brush and trees surrounding the grove. "They boost the accuracy of the jump, at least when coming back here. Going to the past is a little trickier." The accelerator hummed to life, bypassing the usual identification step thanks to Markus's override settings. "It's not the most accurate process, so standard jumps usually target three days before the mission executes. The unit we're using has had more accuracy problems than usual—it's why Markus was so late for Benjamin's birthday. Still, it's the only one we've got."

If it deviated Markus's return by several hours, who knew how it might affect them? Markus's warning about the signature from accelerators tickled Kin's anxieties regarding the TCB possibly detecting unauthorized landings outside the safe range. His matter-of-fact explanation projected something steadier to Penny. "We have to land within five days of the other field agent to avoid detection. Miranda uploads the project on August 28. On her thirtieth birthday. So we'll set it for the twenty-third and hope for the best. If we're lucky we'll get some sightseeing time before the plan kicks in."

"Sightseeing in the past." Penny's eyes lit up. "I'd love to try the food. Compare the MOME to the real thing."

"Your brother thinks the same way." The navigational holo lit up in front of them. Kin punched in the coordinates and sanity checked the equipment in his backpack:

accelerator, Miranda's new identity, paper cash, gun ("only for emergencies," he promised Penny), and communication earpieces. Behind them the far echoes of an unintelligible voice rattled the air.

That wasn't the same voice they'd heard before, was it? Didn't Markus and the field agent already come and go?

"What's that?" Penny grabbed his shoulder, fingers digging in.

"Not sure," Kin said, punching a chrome syringe for the pre-jump booster into his neck. Penny craned her neck out and winced as he did the same to her. "So we better hurry." He handed her the post-jump stabilizers, which she shoved in her jacket pocket. "Once we arrive, you're going to feel disoriented. Close your eyes until you feel like you're not spinning anymore. Then inject this. Remove the cap, stick the needle in four finger widths below the ear, and press the plunger. You'll have to do me next. If I don't make it—"

"Don't say that."

"I have to." Kin's mission sensibilities took over with a rhythmic reflex that made spouting out instructions and preparations easy, even when discussing his own possible demise. "If I don't make it, I have a detailed plan in my left jacket pocket. Markus can contact you based on that to get you home. Okay?"

Penny responded with several seconds of silence. "You better come home. I haven't gotten to see you cook yet."

"Things will be fine. We'll land, coordinate with Markus, eat some historic food, and save Miranda."

The voice rang out again, and even though it came through muffled, it almost sounded like it was calling Kin's name. He glanced at the coordinates one last time, and then met Penny's wide-eyed stare. They gripped the proxy handles connected to the main unit, and the accelerator began audibly counting down from sixty. A quick check on Penny showed that she had a textbook time-jump posture. "Ready?"

"Not really, but it's okay." The countdown continued, a steady, nearly hypnotic march to the unknown.

"You'll be fine. Penny, just rem—" Behind them, the voice became clearer and closer. It *did* call his name. A quick scan told him nothing. Did TCB Security stalk the jump zones? Would that pose a risk on any jump back? Maybe it was random hikers? Kin reminded himself to project something soft, something reassuring. "We'll be fine. Just remember. You and me."

Four. Three. Two. Kin looked at Penny, who huddled tightly beneath the hair and nervous shoulders. "You and me," he called out again. "Till death do us part."

Even from the hunched-over angle of the ready position, he could see Penny smile. The final second ticked off, and the accelerator began rumbling, causing the dirt at their feet to dance. "I love—" she started before the world froze and bled into an overwhelming brightness.

CHAPTER 27

White. A blinding white, an all-encompassing lack of color in an endless web around and through all points. It came with the totality of silence, something that, had Kin been conscious, would have lit all his nerves on fire.

But he wasn't conscious. Aware, perhaps. He was aware of a lack of form or sound, though details remained elusive, only arriving in flashes of silhouettes against the white and a stinging pressure closing in on him.

The flashes grew more and more frequent, enough that he saw the white bleed into a bright sun and a cloudless sky for a sliver of a moment. Other details gradually melted into the images: arms waving over him, a brown swish of hair, wide eyes surrounded by concerned creases. The pictures blinked at a rapid rate until they formed rough movement, and although Kin couldn't feel his arms or legs, he became increasingly certain of what unfolded before him.

They made it. Daytime, no less. So much for accuracy and landings. Was this the vegetative state the doctors talked about? Aware, able to see and think, but lacking the ability to talk or merely blink? He wasn't even sure if oxygen pumped into his body or if he was slowly suffocating via organ shutdown. Though no one could hear him, he screamed for Penny to hurry up and inject the stabilizers.

Penny scrambled, seemingly moving in slow motion. The precision with which she operated in the kitchen disappeared. Her fingers fumbled and dropped the injection case, and despite a lack of hearing, he clearly read the series of curse words that escaped from her lips. She looked over her shoulder and then began waving her arms.

Was she calling for help?

So much for Markus's rules.

Two new faces entered the frame, a sunburned man with cutoff sleeves and orange stubble and a woman with olive skin and black hair. Penny launched into her rapid-fire speech, the kind that rattled off words faster than thoughts. She tilted her head, the sun catching it barely enough to reflect the glisten of tears on her cheek.

The other woman knelt down beside him, hands searching the area. Penny's hands concealed her face as the wind kicked her hair in all directions. A mouth covered his, blocking out what little he saw, though it pulled back, and flashes of hands and faces came through. His body stayed numb, though he saw the woman take the syringe and place her hands on his neck while Penny leaned over, repeating the phrase "four fingers" over and over.

In an instant the world went to black, and as sound faded in, Kin realized that the darkness didn't come from any neu-

ral or ocular dysfunction but from his eyes reflexively closing with the booster flowing through his body. His lungs
ate up the hillside air—shallow at first, then gasps out of his
control. The post-jump scent, a burn similar to a day-old
barbecue pit, tickled his nose and his memory, though Kin
was simply happy that *anything* tickled. "Look," the woman
said, "he's breathing. Come on, here you go."

"Kin?" Penny kneeled down, face-to-face. "Kin, come on.
Say something. The injection went in four fingers below the
ear. Like you said. Come on, come on, come on."

The very tips of his fingers came alive with the brush of
dried grass and the cool kick of the wind. Movement worked
its way up from the extremities, leaving him capable of a
gentle flex of hands and feet. Tactile sensations returned,
most notably with Penny's tears dripping on his cheek. "We
made it," he croaked out as laughter stuttered out of Penny.

"Sir. Sir, we think you had a seizure or a stroke," the
woman said. Her companion came closer, kneeling word-
less next to her, and Kin detected a strange crunching sound
with his movement. "We should get you to a hospital. I don't
know what that injection is, but it doesn't mean you shouldn't
get checked out."

"Kin," Penny said, cradling his head in her arms. "These
hikers were passing by. She's a doctor."

Kin could feel the air coming in and pushing out, the rise
and fall of his chest. And yet, something was missing...

"EMT, actually. You're pretty lucky. We didn't even see
you guys over here. It's like you popped up out of nowhere."

"Right. Thanks." He turned to Penny. "What time is it?"

"I..." Penny looked around, her eyes blank while she pro-
cessed the question. Given the circumstances, the urgency
of time and deadlines must have slipped her mind. "Afternoon? I think?"

The plan. They needed to get to the plan. "Wait." Kin propped himself up by his elbows and looked directly at the hiker couple. "What day is it?"

The man's brow furrowed into three dark lines as he glanced at the woman. "Saturday the twenty-eighth. It's about four in the afternoon."

Saturday. The twenty-eighth. Four in the afternoon. The afternoon of Miranda's thirtieth birthday.

The afternoon before she uploaded her project.

They were late. Not just a little late, but later than Kin or Markus predicted even in a worst-case scenario. Kin stood up, mind crunching numbers and options, only to collapse down to his knees, Penny offering a steadying hand. They'd barely arrived within the range of sneaking past TCB detection.

Miranda had mere hours.

"We need to go. We're late."

"Kin, you can't even walk."

"Look, let's get you checked out," the man said. "Your name's Kin? I'm Alex, and this is Briana. Whatever you're late for, I'm sure it can wait. We'll drive you to the hospital. We're parked right down the path."

The world—a sprawling landscape of trees and brush over-looking the Santa Cruz mountains—spun around, creating a dizzying effect that nearly stole Kin's dinner straight out of his stomach. Landing from a time jump was never quite like this. He pressed his feet into the heels of his boots, searching for definitive ground beneath him before he tried his first stride forward. "We need to go. Miranda." They had to travel north about a hundred fifty miles. But how?

"Listen to me." Penny grabbed him, arm matching arm. "You can't help Miranda if you keel over on some mountain-top. Let them take you to a hospital. Then we'll do what we need to do."

Markus was set to commandeer Miranda's car at twenty past eight. If they hadn't intercepted her by then, Markus would be forced to carry out the original mission. A car. They needed a car, though they didn't even have a spare hour to get the rental Markus reserved for them. Percentages jumped through Kin's mind with possibilities and consequences leaping in and out so quickly that he had to remind himself to take a breath to sort it out.

At least that was what he tried to do before another dizzy spell sent him face-first into the dirt.

"Kin!" Penny rolled him over and sat him up. His equilibrium swirled about until finally settling into something normal. "Please. We need to get you to a hospital. Then we'll get to Miranda."

The dizziness subsided, leaving only a trace of the familiar stinging temple in its wake. Kin looked over his shoulder; their gear—complete with the accelerator, proxy handles, and bags, all safely untouched—remained out in the field. That provided a starting point. If Alex and Briana thought that it seemed out of the ordinary, both hid it well. Perhaps the specter of a near-death collapse put those suspicions on the back burner.

"You're right," he exhaled. "I'll pack up our stuff. Our camping gear," he said, nodding to the dormant accelerator.

"We can help," Briana said, only Kin waved them off.

"No, no. I took a lot of this equipment from work. If anyone gets in trouble for breaking it, it should be me." He powered out a wry grin and a chuckle, motivated equally to buy time and assure Penny. "Gimme a minute."

The case for the injections lay open at his feet, probably from Penny fumbling it when they landed. Kin kept a straight face while scanning despite only seeing two syringes in the case.

There should have been three.

The two in the case were the booster injections they would take prior to jumping back to their native era. Where was the extra stabilizer, the post-jump injection that only he needed?

Panic fluttered through Kin's body, pricking his throat and lungs in the form of stuck air. He maintained his stoic face while searching through the brush and dirt when his fingers came across something cold and metallic.

Cold. Metallic. And cracked across the middle with drops of liquid oozing out.

That noise. That strange crunching noise when Alex moved next to Briana, right after his hearing returned.

Kin didn't have the strength to hide the emotions bubbling inside him. He turned his face away from Penny's view and vowed that if he survived this, he'd tell Markus that the TCB needed to invest in stronger materials.

Now they were *really* off the plan. And running out of time.

"Everything all right?" Penny called out.

For now, though, broken syringes didn't matter. He was a field agent. His training dictated that if something went wrong, he'd simply execute the mission until he had to face it. Anxiety and a thousand what-ifs shut down.

Miranda. The rest could wait.

Penny stood at an awkward distance between her time-traveling fiancé and a pair of hikers who were born about a century before her. Reality sank in as Kin gingerly checked the different pockets and packs and assessed the situation.

The path down. The couple's car. The distance to Miranda. Time, time ticking away.

They seemed like reasonable, friendly people. He calculated a high percentage of being able to convince them to at least take them partly there, and then they might get another vehicle...

Assess and execute. Even with that, no options came with a certainty that identified the best choice.

He pictured their equipment again, visualizing everything they'd brought before lingering on one item, his instinct screaming to forget the percentages and go with the one sure thing he could do.

Regardless of what he promised Penny.

The last time he chose instinct over percentages on a mission, it got him stranded, stuck, failed. It also led to Miranda ultimately being born, which brought him here.

His instinct would save Miranda. In order to go with his gut, he still needed a plan. He gave a reassuring nod to Penny and waited until she stepped ahead before pulling the gun out of his bag and sticking it in the back of his waistband. "Ready to go. We should hurry."

Alex and Briana led Kin and Penny down the nearest hiking trail, one markedly different from the agents' route up the rock-and-tree-laden steep side. During the journey Kin stayed quiet—he claimed a headache from the would-be seizure—but his mind was more alive and awake than it ever had been. Years of agent training and experience compounded with an urgency that only a parent-child bond could create, his mind a mixture of calculated risks and dangerous impulses.

Another five minutes from the trailhead sat a small parking lot and a lone muddied SUV, one that had logged probably at least six or seven years of adventure.

Time for one more. "I forgot to ask," Alex said, "what insurance do you have? I can look up the nearest—"

He stopped, mouth caught open, and no further words

arrived. Briana turned, too, only to freeze and slowly put her hands up.

Penny finally spun around. Unlike the couple next to her, her expression didn't change. Instead, it remained stone-faced, like she didn't understand what she saw. "What are you doing?" she quietly said.

"We need to go." Kin continued holding the gun on Alex, though he motioned Briana to stand by him. "We don't have much time."

"Kin, let's take it easy." Penny spoke with a hesitant cadence. "You're not thinking straight. Remember how we got here. Remember the warnings from the doctor. You're just a little off right now."

"Penny, I promise you I am 100 percent here. I've thought this through. Keys," he said to Briana. "I need your keys. Toss them here."

Briana looked at Alex and then at Penny, who gave an anxious nod. The keys flew through the air and landed at Kin's feet with a jingle. "Briana. Alex. I'm very grateful for what you've done. Now I have to borrow your car for one day. Borrow, not steal. One day only. Twenty-four hours. Come back to this parking lot. Same time tomorrow. Your car will be waiting for you. I'll hide the keys under a rock behind that sign. Got it?"

The couple bobbed their heads in unison without looking at each other.

"I know this doesn't make much sense. And it probably won't after I return your car. Understand that we're doing something good here. We're not harming anyone. In fact, it's the opposite. Problem is, we need to go now. It's that important. Twenty-four hours. Right here. And don't even think about calling the cops before then. Otherwise, you'll never see your car again," he said, his tone rising with a snarl.

Penny turned to him, but he knew that if he saw her reaction to his empty threat, he'd break character. "Do the smart thing and wait. It'll be like nothing ever happened. I'll even leave it with a full tank and this," he said, reaching into the bag and holding up a wad of era-specific cash. "Consider it a rental fee. Got it?" They nodded again, and without losing eye contact, Kin knelt down and picked up the keys. He thumbed through to the car key with the large unlock fob. The car beeped as he pressed it down, and the driver door's autohydraulics sprung it open. "Penny, put the gear in the back. We've got to catch Miranda."

Penny remained petrified, her mouth stuck open and breathing deep.

"Penny," he said, maintaining eye contact with his targets. "Trust me on this. We're not hurting anyone. We're giving them their car back. This is the only way we can get to Miranda."

"But...but... Markus—"

"We don't have time to coordinate with him. We have to leave. The plan has changed."

If someone had driven into the parking lot in the precious seconds that ticked by before Penny responded, things might have crumbled into dust. But instead she quietly agreed and gathered their things. Gun still trained on the couple, he handed the key to Penny.

"What do I do with this?"

"There's a slot next to the steering wheel. Put it in there and turn."

The couple exchanged confused glances while they waited for Penny to start the car. It came to life with a low hum, the product of supercharged hydrogen battery technology that became popular several years after he'd left the era.

Penny stepped out of the car and dashed to the passenger

side, her legs nearly tangling into a spilled mess. Kin waited for her to get settled and buckled in before taking the driver's seat. "Twenty-four hours. I promise."

The back tires tossed up clouds of dust that filled the rear-view mirror. When it finally started to dissipate, Kin realized that neither Alex nor Briana had moved. They got smaller and smaller until Kin made a hard left turn onto the front-age road leading to civilization.

CHAPTER 28

Every few minutes Kin caught Penny glancing at him—a quick twitch of the eye before abruptly snapping away. Over forty-five minutes into their journey up Highway 17, only the sounds of classical radio kept the car from being totally silent.

"It's really too bad we landed late," Kin finally said. He glanced at the bags of gear in the back seat—gear that they brought, not the things that Markus stowed away for them. They simply didn't have time to coordinate with Penny's brother. Instead, things fell into their backup-backup plan, hashed out on the fly for this worst-case scenario. "I know how curious you are about this era. I'm sorry."

Penny nodded, an almost reflexive gesture without eye contact.

"I don't know how things will play out. Or what kind of time we'll have after...everything. Maybe a few hours will open up before we have to jump back." He adjusted the rearview, although rather than look at the mirror, he peeked to gauge Penny's reaction.

The car rumbled along, bouncing over uneven pavement.

"So maybe we will get to eat somewhere good. It's not like we've got time to get Markus's ration packs. I mean, you have to eat, right?"

Penny continued to stare at the road, elbow propped up against the window. "Have you done that sort of thing before?"

"Eat before a jump home? Yeah. Sometimes it makes you nauseated when you land, but—"

"No." Finally Penny straightened up and turned to engage him directly. "What you did to those people. Have you done that sort of thing before?"

Kin's teeth pressed against his bottom lip while considering his answer. Part of the reason agents kept their job secret stemmed from the practical nature of denying time travel's existence. However, secrecy also relieved agents from the burden of the job's nastier elements, and while his response stewed, a new list formulated in his Kin's head: the things he'd tried to forget, the nights when the dirt and sweat and blood didn't seem to wash off no matter how justified. "Not like that, exactly. No."

"Worse things?"

Seconds ticked by before he could answer. "Yes."

"I..." Penny rubbed her face, fingers pressed against her brow. "You're so gentle. How can you do something like that? I mean, I can't imagine you running across Victorian England to assassinate someone. That's not you."

"Actually, I couldn't do that. Time jumps max out at a

hundred fifty years. Go any further and the energy needed literally implodes you." Kin gave his explanation with a joking tone, one that he hoped would restore levity to the conversation.

But Penny didn't reciprocate. "You know what I mean," she said, her voice as dry as her blank stare.

He'd prepared himself for this. He knew Penny would react with some mix of shock, fear, accusation, or other jumbled harshness. Even then, even with his feelings compartmentalized, the question bored an ache in his chest. "This job. Sometimes you have to do things you don't want to do in order to set things right. That's the life of an agent."

"And Markus. Does he do these things, too?"

"Not as often. He's more involved in planning and support. He's had to get involved before. You can't chase criminals across time without getting your hands dirty eventually."

"It's just…a lot to swallow. I could accept the existence of time travel. I could handle the fact that you had another life, a daughter. Even a wife. But violence? That's not the man I know." Penny tilted her head back, angling into the curved rest above the seat. "Have you ever killed anyone?"

The question came with equal parts hesitation and confusion. Her hands rested on her knees, though a visible tremor still rumbled through her fingers, and if he found a way to peer inside her mind, he was sure that her usual rapid-fire questioning occupied her inner monologue.

"I'm not a killer," Kin said after several moments of silence. "There's a difference."

"That's not an answer." The reluctance left Penny's face, and in its place stood a chiseled determination. "Have you killed anyone?"

"In my line of work—"

"Yes or no, Kin. Have you killed anyone?"

"Yes."

The highway remained a straight line to the horizon and beyond, large patches of farmland zooming by on either side. "How many?"

"Four." Penny's eyes continued to elude him. "I completed twenty-eight cases as an active field agent across eight years, including my last one. Twenty apprehensions. Four eliminations. Three instances where backup was needed and another agent finished the case."

"Killing is killing." Her voice barely crept above the rumble of the car.

"Look, I know it's not exactly what you want to hear. I suppose there's always going to be a question about whether or not it was justified. At the time, in the moment, there was no other way. The people I killed, it came down to them or me. They were criminals hired to alter history. These are professionals. During those cases, I was shot at, hit with a crowbar, and stabbed. You know the scar on my left shoulder blade?"

She turned to him with a nod and an uncertain posture. Almost reactively the scar tissue on that wound began to ache. "You're probably wondering if killing someone changes you. And it does. The first time I did it, the TCB sent a psychologist with the retriever agent to talk me through it. It was my seventh case. We stayed an extra week in the past. I'm sure police officers or soldiers feel the same way."

"What did the psychologist tell you?"

"He said everyone reacts differently. I felt like everything became more immediate. Heightened. Life seemed more real, more important. Miranda would call it PTSD." Kin took his focus off the road for a second to meet her gaze. "I don't know if I believe in fate. Probably not. Not after the things that I've seen. But a few days after I returned from that case,

Markus invited me out for a pickup soccer game to try to get my mind off it. For some reason you decided to show up."

The car's navigation system told them to veer off onto Highway 680 toward the Sacramento area. The *click-clack* of the turn signal filled the car, ten times louder than it normally was thanks to the absence of words. Several minutes later, after going up and over the merge, they sped on the highway toward Miranda.

"Markus told me it was a barbecue," Penny finally said.

"I think he wanted people to bring food. We didn't, though. We only wanted to play soccer. At least until I met you." Kin took in a sharp breath. All the time spent worrying about Miranda, trying to figure out how to maintain a relationship with her, how to break the rules of time to stay in touch, and yet he never considered the impact on Penny if she ever found out. "For weeks, Markus tried to talk me out of it. He kept saying that we were too different, too opposite. He wrote me a list of why we shouldn't go out."

The harsh air between them broke. "He gave me one of those, too," she said softly.

"I didn't listen to him. I trusted my gut, and it told me that we had something beyond what your brother, my partner could see. And it was all because of that mission. And now you know. There's nothing else that I'm hiding. Do you regret that afternoon?"

The question lingered, and Kin didn't know if it did because of the stakes or if Penny really needed a while to gather her thoughts. "No," she finally said.

Relief trickled down from top to bottom and let him exhale the breath he'd unknowingly held in. He indulged in these few seconds before reminding himself to focus on the mission.

"I'm glad I went. I'm glad I met you. I'm glad we didn't

listen to Markus." A smile still seemed elusive for her, but her shoulders relaxed as she looked at him. "I'm glad we're here with no more secrets."

"I can't imagine what it's like to be blindsided by this all," Kin said. "I'm asking you to take a leap of faith despite all *this*." Penny nodded and turned to the road ahead. "Sometimes when nothing makes sense, it's the only thing you can trust."

On the opposite lane of the highway, cars zoomed past, coming and going at a dizzying pace. On their own side, they remained alone, rolling along at a steady yet urgent clip. Miles passed, and the landscape changed from flat dirt to rolling green hills. Over the horizon hints of civilization peeked through.

"Well," Penny said, breaking the silence. Her voice rang out a hair brighter than a few minutes ago, "it's like I said earlier. I can't wait to meet Miranda."

CHAPTER 29

Kin peered through the window, first seeing his own weathered reflection before his vision adjusted to the depth and lighting before him. There she was, grown past the lanky gawkiness of her teens into a woman on the cusp of thirty. Her black hair fell to her shoulders, and her cheekbones seemed more defined beneath her brown skin, with even a few small creases framing either side.

Miranda sat in the restaurant, oblivious to the fact that her father stood some twenty feet away after traveling across more than a century, stealing a car, and driving a hundred or so miles. Kin glanced behind him and squinted, focusing to look past the dusk sky's purple-and-orange hues. Beside him Penny stood, face hidden behind big sunglasses and the tall collar of a coat they'd hastily purchased at a department store along the way.

He wore similar garb, perhaps not in style but at least with the purpose of obscuring his features from facial recognition. It got the job done and kept them warm in the era's late-summer evening weather, although standing side by side, Penny's expression clearly stood out. She turned to him, pupils dimly visible behind the sunglasses, and he knew that she read through him the same way.

Kin didn't realize his hand had gone to his chest until Penny covered it with her own. "You all right?"

He wanted to speak an affirmative, except the lump in his throat blocked any sound from coming through. His eyes welled up, despite his effort to will the tears away.

"She looks like you. I don't even have to ask which one is her."

The sentiment made Kin want to hug Penny into a million pieces. The surge of affection made no sense—Penny had no connection with Miranda—but he'd stopped trying to rationalize things at this point. He just took it as a sign that this really was the right thing to do. "I'm really glad—"

Before he could finish, Kin's entire body jerked backward. It took a second to realize that something had collided with his shoulder. He turned, only to see the back of a man brushing himself off. "Sorry," a muffled voice came before a piece of folded sheet slipped out of his hand and fell to the ground. The toe of his boot tapped the pavement next to the paper, then he strode away without a second glance.

"People are clumsy in this era, yeah?" Penny said, linking her arm with his.

"No, that's not it." Kin knelt down to pick up the folded sheet. "That was Markus. He must be monitoring us. The fact that he didn't say anything means he's wearing a communicator for the mission. Standard protocol when agents and retrievers are actively teaming up." Penny leaned over to read the note scrawled in Markus's handwriting.

Be careful. Stay out of surveillance. The FA is at the safe house monitoring audio only. I can falsify tracking her to the parked car but not much else if she actually makes it there. Grab her before that happens. Go now. If she shows up at her car, I won't be able to fake it and I'll have go through with the TCB's plan. Don't be conspicuous, they're listening.

A handwritten note. No digital footprint for the TCB to trace.

"FA?" Penny asked.

"Field agent." The person tasked with drugging Miranda, killing her, and covering things up. The agent must have succumbed to Markus's food poisoning plan enough to stay in the safe house yet not enough to be incapacitated. "This accelerates things. If they're monitoring Markus's movements, we can't coordinate with him. We have to get her out ourselves. Quietly." He glanced at the window again. "And soon."

"How do you know?"

"The waiter is clearing the plates. Look at the bar." He pointed to the silhouette of a lone man taking a seat. "Markus. He's probably already placed the sedative. It won't affect her until he activates it. Which he won't once we get her out of here. They're monitoring for time. They expect Markus to intercept her at eight twenty. If we don't act fast, their plan will kick into action."

"Okay. Well, I'm sure once she sees her unaged dad, she'll come along—"

"No. It has to be you." Kin turned, hands placed square on Penny's shoulders. "Who knows how she might react if she sees me? If we cause a scene, the FA will hear it over the monitor. You need to convince her to come with you. Discreetly. I think even mentioning me would be a bad idea."

"Me?" Penny took off the sunglasses, her eyes wide. "I'm not a secret agent. I mean, I'm not even a head chef. I'm just—"

"Don't." Kin put his finger against her lips. "Don't say you're 'just Penny.' Because you're not. You're smart, capable, and strong, so much more than what Markus or your parents tell you, more than what you let yourself believe. You can do this. Listen," he said, pulling her in for a hug, one that carried weight far greater than mere adoration. "I know you can do this. I know this so much that I'm trusting you with my daughter's life."

They remained in the embrace, and Kin felt Penny shift from tensed to relaxed. She pulled back, focus locked with his, yet something seemed different. They'd stood face-to-face countless times, even battled trivial matters like buying sofas and quitting jobs. During those personal moments Penny usually gave away her nervousness—a finger flutter here, an upward glance there.

However, this time, with dusk melting into evening blue behind them, she straightened up and took a calm, even breath. "Right. Okay. Any ideas where to start?"

He peered into the restaurant, distance measurements and foot traffic patterns superimposing over what he saw. A bar. A waiting area. Rows of tables. Ideas came to life, quicker than his racing pulse.

Assess and execute indeed.

"Well," Kin said, a smirk crawling onto his lips, "I *do* have a thing for planning these days."

Kin stared at the lamppost in front of his parked car. The earpiece proved to be an awkward fit, and his finger pressed up to keep it snug, though his attention veered off to the lamppost a few feet from where he sat. Was this lamppost there in his era? Could Penny go visit it when she returned and commemorate where they parked on their voyage to the past?

The mental questioning and endless possibilities of time travel crept in like rookie mistakes. Instead, he focused solely on Miranda's voice on the earpiece. Her words remained unclear, yet her pitch and inflection were so familiar that picking it out of the din was almost as easy as if she stood right next to him.

When she gave a yelp, it made it even easier. "Oh no," Penny said, her voice trembling in a way that probably meant something different to Miranda. "I'm so sorry. Let me help you clean that up."

He couldn't see it, but the exchange—from Penny's fumbled apology to Miranda's understanding response—visualized in his mind, bending space and time to connect two people in his life who should have never, ever met and somehow did because of a secret plan and spilled drink.

"It's fine. I'm all right. I'm okay."

"I feel so bad—it's in your hair. On your shirt."

"I'll be fine. Accidents happen. I'll run to the bathroom for a minute."

"I'll help. My fault—it's the least I can do."

The din of the restaurant changed, shifting tone and volume until it became a silent space where footsteps echoed against linoleum.

Then Penny dropped the bomb.

"Listen," she said, her voice taking on a quiet urgency. "I need to talk to you."

"Really, it's okay about the drink. It happens."

"No, wait. This is going to sound very, very absurd, so

bear with me. You need to leave with me right now. You're in danger."

Kin couldn't see the two women, but from the pause he pictured Miranda's reaction. Eyes widened. Mouth slightly agape. One hand perched on her chest in surprise. "Excuse me?"

"Okay then…" Penny's words picked up their pace and fired off at an increasingly rapid tempo. Kin hoped she wouldn't start doing that thing where all of her syllables mashed together. "Sounds ridiculous. I get it. Give me five minutes. Look, we don't have much time, but I promise I can prove it to you."

The sound of running water came through, then the hum of the era's hand dryers. "I'm sorry—I really have to go. My friends are waiting."

"I know how insane this sounds. I mean, I know you have no reason to believe me." Penny's voice came clearly over the earpiece, a strength of conviction creating a steadiness to her words. They built layers upon layers of pride in Kin's chest. After so many battles with guilt and regret and frustration, he could definitely get used to this. "I'm asking you to take a leap of faith. Sometimes when nothing makes sense, it's the only thing you can trust."

Empty seconds ticked by, and even the occasional static blip over the headset amped up Kin's nerves.

"Tell me here."

"What?"

"Tell me here. Why am I in danger? There's no one else in the bathroom. Just say it, okay?"

Penny's sigh blunted the comm's details for a minute, and he sensed from her quickening huffs that her mind was in full-on race mode before blurting out everything she'd learned about Miranda. "Here's proof you can believe me.

You played soccer a lot growing up. Something you did with your father. But you always hated it." Kin cringed as Penny fired the sentiment out. "You wanted to create instead."

"You're starting to creep me out. I think I should go."

"No, listen to me. God, how else do I prove that I'm not lying? We're running out of time."

It took Kin a second to realize that that question was meant for him, not Miranda.

"I'm going to do it. I have to." More words meant for him. Air caught in his lungs, and his fingers pulled into a tense grip against the static steering wheel. "We're in a closed room. No one will know."

"Okay," Miranda said, "now you're really not making sense. I think it'd be better if—"

"I'm a friend of your father, and something awful is going to happen if you stay in this restaurant."

A sharp inhale came; it might have been from either woman. "My...dad?"

"Yes. Your dad. Kin. In fact, he's listening right now." A muffled sound came over the comm, probably from Penny tapping the equipment to show it to Miranda.

"My dad is a bullshit artist. Or dead, maybe. I haven't heard from him in more than a decade—if that was even him. I don't know. I don't care. He should stick to what he's good at—leaving me alone."

Miranda's words stabbed through the electronic signals that carried her voice.

He'd told Penny not to mention him. And the logic behind it—not creating a confused scene in public, one that TCB might pick up on—was sound. But behind it all, bubbling beneath the surface lay a hidden fear, something that silently lingered in Kin's mind since their correspondence got cut off.

What if she hated him for disappearing again? He never

intended to, never wanted to, only when the AD cut him off, their correspondence fell off a cliff.

"I learned a long time ago that he'll tell you anything to get you to believe him. Did he say he was some sort of special forces hero? Something stupid like that? He's playing you. I don't know why, but he is." Miranda stopped, though her words had already torn into him, leaving emotional incisions up and down his chest. "Wait a minute."

"I know you must have a lot of questions. Believe me—"

"Look at how *young* you are."

"It will all make sense—"

"I can't believe this. He's been lying left and right. Listen, I don't know who you are, but my dad is a master con artist. I mean, you must be, what, half his age? You look younger than me! I'm guessing there's a whole string of women who've been sold a bill of goods by him." Miranda huffed, the force of the air blowing into the tiny microphone clipped to Penny's collar. "A word of advice. He had some sort of midlife crisis and left his family behind. One day, just gone. He'll do the same to you someday. Just forget whoever this person is. Go find someone your own age, and don't let him in."

Footsteps echoed across the comm, along with the clicks of door handles. "Stop. Please."

"Let go of me—"

"Miranda, I can't explain this to you. But he can. Just stay here for one minute with me. Kin? You there?"

"Yeah." Kin gulped in some air. "I'm right here."

"I'm giving the comm to Miranda. Here." Shuffling and static pops came over the earpiece, and with each sound, pressure caved in on Kin's chest and throat. He was going to talk with Miranda. "Your father wants to talk to you."

"Are you serious? I can't believe this." Miranda's voice

punched through. "What do you want? You left me twice already. What, do you think you get three strikes?"

There was no time to prepare for this. His daughter, separated across time, was now on the line with him. He hadn't thought this through or prepared a speech. No lists visualized to save him. This situation didn't even seem like a possibility—everything they'd planned went exactly the opposite of this path. Still, something, *anything*, needed to be said to prevent the absolute worst. "Miranda. It's me. It's Dad."

"I don't have time for this. If that was you on those emails—"

"That was me. I promise. Listen to me, right now your life is in danger. I'm breaking a lot of rules to come here and tell you that. We both are. So please, come with us and let me explain." Kin's breath stuttered with each passing second, accompanied by the cannon fire of his own pulse under his skin. "Please. If you need to, ask me anything right now. All I need is five minutes. Five minutes for you to hear me out."

"You were gone," Miranda finally said. "Or maybe you left. There's a difference. But it doesn't matter."

"I had to leave."

"You know the only good thing you ever did for me? Tell me to accept counseling. Because after what you pulled, I sure as hell needed it."

"Please. Remember what I told you about my job before you were born? Special forces—more like a secret agent actually. Except now, the people I work for, they're after you. You're in danger."

"I'm a grad student. I have nothing to do with you anymore. Why would they come for me?"

"Because…" It suddenly hit Kin that he was actually talking to Miranda. The conversation arrived so quickly and came so filled with venom that the very miracle of the exchange had failed to register until now. Despite danger being on his heels each step of the way, he couldn't help but relish it, and even the most difficult things began to release. "Because of something I did."

"So they're doing this out of spite."

"No. Not spite. I created something that shouldn't exist." The tension that choked out his air earlier gradually loosened. With each revelation, the world felt a little easier, a little lighter. He only needed Miranda to acknowledge it. "Just follow Penny to our car," he said, a calm agent dryness taking over his voice. "Quietly and discreetly. Please."

"Wait a minute," Miranda said after a short silence. "Penny?"

"Yes. Penny. That woman there."

"*The* Penny? You mentioned a Penny right before you disappeared. Oh, god, Dad, how old was she when you ran off with her? This is sick. She's younger than me!"

Kin had initially approached this whole thing with some commitment to respecting TCB guidelines on corruption—telling Penny only what she needed to know, hiding away from Miranda until they could be alone. Except at this point, he knew that if he didn't say something definitive, Miranda would walk away from them toward certain death. "Miranda," he said at an even tempo, "it's not like that at all. I met Penny before I met your mother. She had just graduated the culinary academy in San Francisco when we met."

"That's impossible. She's younger than me."

"This is reality. It's like…" Kin gulped in air, his mind racing to find *something* to bridge her understanding. Lists visualized in his mind, running through anything and everything he knew about Miranda until landing on something so obvious he grinned in the empty car. "It's like that show you like. *Doctor Who*."

"But that..." Miranda's voice lowered enough that it nearly matched Kin's. "That show..." Her voice trailed off, creating a vacuum long enough to make Kin check the comm.

"Miranda?"

"That show is about time travel."

Father and daughter remained silent, and buried somewhere in between came an unspoken acknowledgment, one that was finally broken by a realization from Miranda.

"Dad. Your journal."

"You need to go now. Tell your friends that—"

"It was so detailed. I wondered *how* it was so detailed if you'd never written anything before. You couldn't make that stuff up." She paused, taking in a sharp breath loud enough for him to hear. "You didn't make that stuff up."

A quick look at the time prompted Kin's agent sensibilities to resume control, despite Miranda's giant epiphany. "Miranda, listen. Tell your friends that you're going home to get cleaned up, and then follow Penny's lead. Don't make eye contact with the lone guy sitting at the bar."

"Is that... I mean, is he here to—"

"Yes and no. He's on our side. You still need to go. Now. Act casual. If someone asks if anything's bothering you, tell them that the spilled drink broke your phone, and you lost your photos." It was all reflex, finding logical excuses and projecting forward like an agent. It didn't matter that this was his daughter or that he was trying to save her; the thoughts and ideas sparked with an effervescence that always made his superiors happy. "Use that excuse, meet Penny outside the restaurant, and she'll take you to where I am. Then you'll get the full story. You need to be discreet."

"Okay," Miranda said. "Okay."

"Stay calm, and you'll be fine."

"Okay," she repeated again. The comm earpiece flooded with muffled noise and scratches as she presumably returned it to Penny. "Dad?" she called out again, her voice tinier and more distant.

"Yes?"

Penny spoke as the intermediary. "He can hear you."

"I used your journal. I'm sorry."

"Tell her," Kin said with one eye on the car's dashboard clock, "tell her that I can't wait to see her."

With that, Kin removed the mic from his collar. Giving her instructions as an agent was easy. Emailing the teenager he'd just left wasn't that different from talking with her in her bedroom. For now, a good fifteen or so years had passed for Miranda—half her life—and as he sat in the car, the path ahead seemed foggier than ever.

All that time planning, pining, focusing on trying to make things right. With the finish line in sight, he realized that after getting so far, he had no plan, no list, no idea about what to say to the adult he was going to meet.

CHAPTER 30

Two silhouettes appeared in the rearview mirror. They walked with hurried steps past the parking structure entrance: Penny, her face tensed with a surprising determination, and Miranda, who moved with a youthful uncertainty despite the new adult contours on her cheekbones.

New to Kin, anyway.

The engine fired up as Kin tracked their approach. He rolled the window down, and the doors clicked as he unlocked them. "Get in," he called out.

From the side mirror, he saw Penny's expression break into a puzzled frown. "What?"

"We need to move," he said, staying locked on to the RPM gauge on the dashboard. "We have seventeen minutes until Markus takes her car. We should be out of the area before then."

Not that he wasn't happy to see Miranda—his heart had sprinted at the mere notion for minutes now—but he was fully immersed in the mission at this moment. Saving her being the top priority.

The only priority. Deep down, an agent reflex kicked in, his emotions shutting down to focus on the task.

At least until Penny chimed in.

"Kin," Penny said, leaning into the window, "this is your daughter. She hasn't seen you in years. You've jumped across time to save her. Don't you want to say hello?"

"We can do that when we're safely away from here." The engine ramped up from a hum to a low roar, and it took Kin a moment to realize that the weight of his foot had caused it. He eased up and exhaled, although nothing cleared the tightness in his shoulders. "We can't take any risks."

"Don't you trust Markus?"

"Of course."

"And if they sent someone else after us, wouldn't they have gotten to us by now?"

"Yes, but the security cameras. The TCB has facial recognition technology—"

"You've got a hat on. Look down, and you'll be fine. You said it yourself, seventeen minutes. Come on." Penny turned around and nodded to Miranda.

The drone of the car died to silence, only an echo through the concrete structure remaining. Words dried up in his mouth, unable to take shape or form. He should have *planned* for this moment. It was inevitable, but the uncertainty of her reaction petrified him, and for all the mission prep he'd done, anxiety kept pushing his thoughts out of reach. "I don't know what to say," he finally let out.

"Dad?" Miranda's voice trembled through the short burst of a single syllable, and Kin felt his fingers loosen. The voice sounded like her, more so than the one over the comm. Except even in the nervous timbre of one word, a richness and confidence came through, something that didn't exist in the Miranda he once knew. "I'm right here."

Penny stepped away from the door and craned her neck to look around. "I'll keep an eye out." As he nodded, his hand pushed the door open and he got out. "You two take your time."

He'd seen Miranda through the distorted view of a restaurant window earlier, with reflections and smudges and mood lighting obscuring the details.

Now she stood in front of him, clear as day for the first time. Gone were the rounded nuances of childhood, replaced by stronger angles and a depth of maturity in her face that only came from experience and time. Her hair fell shorter than before, neatly cropped at the shoulder line, and tiny hints of age had crept onto her face, from the delicate crease between her brows to the faint lines that framed her mouth.

They stood together in the shadows, harsh industrial lighting and stale air filling the few feet of space, although it may as well have been a vacuum between them. Neither inhaled or moved a muscle; Kin's brain was too busy processing that the woman before him was Miranda—his Miranda—at twice the age he'd known her last. He was pretty sure her mind ran through something similar.

She broke first.

"I... I can't believe it," she said. Her eyes welled with tears that reflected the fluorescent lighting. "It's so good to see you."

Kin wanted to say something, though no words came out. Instead, he pulled Miranda in, hugging her with all the strength he could muster. The top of her head rested against his cheek—an unfamiliar feeling thanks to a growth spurt that had occurred after he left. They'd always figured she'd be tall, given that both he and Heather stood about six feet. Now he knew.

A flood of memories whirled through Kin's mind. Her first bath. Her first bike. Her first day of school. And now everything fast-forwarded, all the years between then and now lost to hope and the imagination.

He'd missed much more than growth spurts.

"I'm so sorry I left you," he whispered into her ear.

"You came back." A quick laugh escaped, brightening the thick concrete of the parking structure. "This is really real. I can't quite believe—" She pulled back, nose wrinkled as she studied him. "Wait a minute. You haven't aged at all. You look *younger* than I remember."

"Like I said—" Kin placed his hands on her shoulders and nodded for Penny to come over. "It's like that TV show you used to watch."

"Still watch, Dad." Her cheeks rose and eyes crinkled with an overwhelming smile. "It's still on. But it's not quite as good as what I found in your journal."

"Which you're turning into a video game."

"How did you know?"

"Let's just say," he said, opening the car door for her, "that in about a hundred years, some very powerful people will be upset about that."

Over the next thirty minutes, Kin gave his daughter the complicated zigs and zags of his own personal journey. In doing so he realized that he'd never told her about himself in this much detail before. His cover story had worked well enough years ago, leaving it so that his daughter didn't really know him. She only knew of him.

Life in 2142. The TCB academy. How time jumps feel. The lucky penny and the real Penny. Getting stuck and meeting Heather. Metabolizers and the human life span. Missing memory and the headaches. Classical music, cooking, planning, how it all was a reaction to his old life in some way. Why he wrote the journal, and why the TCB faked his disappearing act. Information spilled out of him, some textbook and some personal anecdotes, it all colored the details in a way that made Miranda stare wide-eyed in the rearview mirror while he drove and talked.

"And that's why I got pulled back. That guy you saw in the backyard that one time, that's Markus. I actually play soccer with him every week."

"I thought you couldn't run."

"The metabolizers, they healed my knees."

"Please don't get him started on soccer," Penny said from the passenger side. "That's all he and Markus talk about. If I never have to hear about Arsenal again..." She leaned over to look in the back seat, and from the corner of his eye, Kin saw the two women grin at each other.

"So, Dad, I gotta ask."

"Yeah?" Kin braced himself for some sort of difficult, squirm-inducing question.

"Why haven't you killed Hitler?" Miranda asked.

Penny faced Kin, leaning in with the most curiosity she'd shown since they'd started this whole thing.

"We can't go that far back," he said with a laugh. "But even if we could, the TCB protects tentpole historical events and figures, good and evil. The sphere of influence for those events is too catastrophic."

Miranda nodded in the rearview mirror, and she suddenly

lit up with a beaming grin. "I remember those terms in your journal. You know, I'd sneak down late at night to look at it. I'd write down details so I could have my own copy of them. Then it just disappeared one day, along with you." Her energetic expression quickly dropped, and a seriousness took over. "In terms of life-changing discoveries, I think I can handle this whole time-travel thing. But you still haven't explained why you're here *now*. And where we're going."

She was right. Maybe it was the sudden urge to reconnect with his daughter. Or maybe he'd just been avoiding the whole life-or-death topic.

Whatever the reason, that particular spot on Highway 80 marked the turning point in all of their lives.

"I came to save you," Kin quietly said.

Opposing headlights flashed on Miranda's face in the rear-view mirror. Even in those brief images, the mix of confusion and worry stood out. Kin's pulse quickened, even as he tried breathing techniques to steady himself. "Save me?"

"If we hadn't come, a TCB agent would have drugged and killed you tonight, then covered it up as a car crash." Kin selectively omitted Markus's involvement, and from Penny's solemn nod, she seemed to agree with the decision.

"But...why me? What did I do?"

"It's not what you did. It's what I gave you." Kin told himself to focus on the road, on the strict lines and lights in front of him. If he hadn't, the admission might have been too much for him.

"After I returned, the TCB recognized you—your existence—as a timeline corruption. You didn't originally exist in this era. You're only here because I got stranded, because I met your mother when I never should have and... Even though they pulled me back, they agreed to let you be. But I couldn't just leave you here alone. I was never supposed to contact you, but I found a way and set up a system to cover my tracks. It was perfect, almost. I got sloppy. They found our emails. The last one you got from me—the one that encouraged you to quit soccer and focus on what you love—that moment is apparently what propagated you into creating a video game for your portfolio. It doesn't matter who sees it or how big it gets. The information in that game—the information in *you*—is a threat to TCB Security."

The back seat squeaked as Miranda sank into it. "I just uploaded it. Like, an hour ago. You're here today because of my game? What if I just delete it?"

"That's not good enough, unfortunately. They were willing to ignore your existence when they saw you as harmless to them and to the timeline. But now that they know you've read my journal, that you have knowledge of the future and of the TCB—they refuse to take any risks. That's why they're coming for you. To make sure that knowledge never gets out."

"Why not prevent me from getting that knowledge in the first place? Couldn't they go back to when I was fourteen and steal the journal from the garage before I saw it?"

"Point of detection. The TCB reacts to the point of detection to avoid grandfathering the situation. Um," Kin said, realizing he was using company lingo among the uninitiated, "what I mean is that it creates a thing called—"

"The grandfather paradox," Miranda said.

She knew. Of course she knew. This was the girl who would rather go to a science fiction convention than a school dance. "What does your grandfather have to do with this?" Penny asked.

"The grandfather paradox goes like this," Miranda offered without skipping a beat. "If I went back in time and killed my grandfather, it creates a paradox. Because how could I—the grandchild—exist without my grandfather? A paradox exists when you remove the thing that caused the event or the event happens before you caused it. It's very—" she paused to let out a quick chuckle "—timey-wimey."

Penny frowned, a rugged crinkle taking over her mouth. "This time travel stuff gives me a headache."

"Yeah," Kin said. "It does that."

As the car rumbled down the highway in silence, Kin glanced at both of the passengers. Each held the same pensive look: lips pursed, eyes narrowed and unblinking. He probably wore it, too. "What about the people that download my game?"

"The TCB will corrupt the source file so that it can never be opened. They may have done that already. You are the concern because you've created it." Kin's bottom lip stung from his teeth digging into it. "You know it. That's what scares them."

In the rearview, Kin watched Miranda start to respond and then hesitate. She closed her eyes and inhaled sharply, like she always did when forming big definitive statements.

"Pull over," she finally said. "Pull the car over, please. Before we get any further, I need the whole truth." Kin glanced at Penny, who gave a simple affirmative nod. The car swerved to the shoulder, kicking up dust and gravel until it slowed to a halt. "Dad, where are we going?"

The answer to Miranda's question was simple, probably one of the simplest answers he'd give during this whole journey. Yet the battle to transform air and sound into words caused Kin to grip the steering wheel until his palms stung. "San Francisco airport."

"Why?"

"Because you have to disappear," he said, his voice dry and low. Regret knocked him off balance despite being seated.

"You have to fly to somewhere, *anywhere*, under a new identity and go." He pulled out the passport with Miranda's new identity and a large wad of cash. "And I can't know where. Or who you become. No one can. You have to start over in order to live."

"This is wrong. I have friends, a life. A boyfriend. Family." The last word jabbed at Kin, causing him to wince. "You're telling me to get on a plane, erase all of that, and...reset somewhere? Like it's moving apartments? I'm not doing that."

"You have to."

"You don't know that."

Blood rushed to Kin's face, although the veil of night hid it from the darkened vehicle's passengers. His hand trembled as it rested on the gearshift, and he squeezed the knob to steady himself. "Miranda, I *do* know that."

"I'll fight back."

"It wouldn't work. Even though you've escaped this particular attempt, they'll just reorganize and come back for you. They know who you are and where you live, so staying here—being *you*—they'll find you. If not today, tomorrow, or next week, next month. The only way this stops is if they believe you're dead. Then the mission is accomplished and archived as a success." The seat belt dug into his neck as he twisted to face Miranda. "You can't stop this. You can't fight it. The only thing you can do is to sneak away, undetected, and begin again."

"My life!" she said with a ferocity that eclipsed any teenage meltdown he'd witnessed before. "Daniel. We wanted to get married. We wanted to have kids. I'm finishing grad school. I'm trying to get a job. I have friends. This is my life. These things, these people, they *are* my life. I refuse to give it up. I am not disappearing on Daniel. Or anyone else. I'm just not. Because *I* know how terrible that is."

"But you will, Miranda. You have to see that it's inevitable. All of those people? Tomorrow they'll get the news that you are dead. Because, really, you're dead to them either way. There's no alternative where you get to stay here with them. If you don't leave with us, the TCB will kill you." Kin nearly choked while swallowing hard at the next thought. "It's what they do. It's what I used to do. It's the same reason I had to leave you all those years ago." Despite the gravity of the situation, Miranda's tenacity caused a blip of satisfaction. He supposed if she simply rolled over and took this life-shattering event without any kicking, he would have been a tiny bit disappointed.

"Listen," he started again, "things aren't—"

"Wait." Penny, of all people, grabbed control of the conversation. "Let me say something. Two days ago, I was just a chef in San Francisco. My fiancé had a government job. We had a cat. I was going to try to open a restaurant. We lived a normal life. And then I found out that time travel is real, that the person who knows me best in the world lived eighteen years in another life with a wife who wasn't me and daughter who wasn't mine, that he's fought and killed fugitives in different eras as a profession. My life is different now. It's the same, yet different. It's scarier because all these unknowns are now part of it." She smiled, passing over soft encouragement while looking solely at Miranda. "It's a lot to take in."

Miranda matched her expression and nodded. "You could say that."

"The one thing that can't change is the fact that it's real. My fiancé and my brother travel through time. I mean, I'm right here, in an era I've only learned about in school. *You're* real. And I think my old life, the one from two days ago, it was a lot simpler. Easier. But I can't go back to that now. We can't go back. We can only move forward."

"You have to understand," Kin jumped back in, "there are only these two options—stay here and die tonight, or take this opportunity for a second chance at life. You don't get to pack. You don't get to stew on it or talk it over. You don't get to say goodbye. I know that's unfair, to force you into a decision when you don't have time to think. But at least we can give you the choice. Not everyone gets that." The dim lights of the car's dashboard and controls reflected across Miranda's inscrutable face. He stared back, searching for any clues about what she was thinking. "Look, it's possible to start over. Completely over. You survive, you adapt. You can find love and be happy and live. You can do that while still honoring your past—even when your past is taken from you. The only thing you can do is run with it and turn it into something good." A warm weight came over his hand; he looked down to find both of Penny's covering his. "I've done it twice."

"This is impossible." The darkness of the back seat enveloped Miranda as she sat back, obscuring any clues to what she might be thinking. "This situation. This decision. It's all impossible."

Silence continued to fill the car, the only noise coming from the *whoosh* of passing vehicles. Miranda adjusted in her seat a few times, though she took no further action, and the entire car felt like it might implode under the mounting tension.

"You know what?" Kin turned the key and roared the engine back to life. "Ignore us. This is up to you, not me. We can turn around, and I can drop you off, and you can live like this never happened. I may travel through time, but the future is never 100 percent, that much I can tell you. Maybe you're the exception that finally wins out. Maybe you delete the file fast enough, the info never gets out, and TCB lets this go. I can't say. I can only tell you their plan, but the decision is up to you. This is your life. You decide. We can go back, or we can keep going west toward San Francisco. Toward the airport. Where to?"

Car after car sped past them. First one, then another one, then a dozen had passed, and then so many that Kin lost count. He turned to Penny, who waited with openmouthed anticipation. Seconds turned to minutes, or perhaps it only felt that way. The anxiety he'd held off began crawling through his body, first tingling from the toes up until it gripped his chest with a silent tension, waiting for his daughter to release them all from this paralysis.

At some point, Miranda finally reached forward and placed her hand on Kin's shoulder.

"I'll go," she said in a slow, even cadence. "But there's one person I need to say goodbye to."

Many different responses played out in Kin's mind, and he ultimately went with the safest bet. "Seeing Daniel or your friends is out of the question. Anyone you talk to might break the cover that we've worked so hard to set up for you. It might even put them in danger."

"Believe me," Miranda said. She turned to look out the window, her face cloaked in shadow. "It won't matter."

Over the next hour, they sped down Highway 80 toward Oakland, and during the drive, it was Miranda's turn to fill in the blanks. Kin heard his daughter's story through the lens of maturity, a wistfulness coloring in the details of her teenage and young adult years. They laughed together, as if no time had passed—as if the shadow of heavier decisions didn't linger over every passing second.

"Poor Bammy," she said. "When I was seventeen, she broke her femur. Osteosarcoma. They amputated her leg.

Such a strong girl, she learned to tri-paw in only a week. She made it one more year before liver failure took her. Those days after her surgery, I cleaned her bandages, gave her medication. Helped her stand. It taught me to appreciate all the little moments, how you could capture beauty in the smallest things. I skipped class so I could be with her at the end. The last thing she felt was me rubbing her ears." Miranda's tone dropped, and she released a slow sigh.

"I miss that dog."

"Yeah. Me, too."

Kin let the moment breathe before digging deeper. "So you're in grad school now?"

"Yeah. Well, *was*, I suppose. I don't know if I'll get another shot."

"Anything is possible," Kin said. "Your life is still your own."

They veered off the highway onto city streets, quiet taking over for the first time since getting back on the road. Kin wanted to say something more, anything to cushion the blow for her, but nothing came. Even if he could impart some wisdom, their situations were still totally different. Was it better to hit the reset button on life before things were settled or after?

"Mom missed you," Miranda said, breaking the silence. "She tried to play it off. Told me we could only control *our* lives. But I'd catch her sometimes, staring off into space. Or I'd wake up in the middle of the night and hear her watching *Star Trek* for hours. She wouldn't let me see her trying to cope, but I knew." She leaned forward, and her voice cracked with the next words. "She thought her headaches were just stress. We found out too late. You traveled through time to get here. Can you… I mean…" She gulped loud enough for Kin to hear, but nothing else came out.

It took several seconds to realize why Miranda couldn't finish her questions. "No," he offered gently. His chest tightened, like everything in him imploded, and Penny's hand landed on his knee. "I can't do that."

"Right. Paradoxes." She sank back into the back seat, her silhouette deflating in the rearview. "I had to ask."

"Please don't hate me for it. I wish I could."

"I would never hate you." Passing headlights flashed on Miranda's sullen face in the rearview. "That's a lie. I did. I hated you for the longest time. You couldn't see my emails anymore, so you missed a bunch of them where I asked where you went or why you'd left. Then a bunch of them calling you a liar or worse things. I thought you gave me a tall tale to cover your ass. I got mad. I questioned my bullshit detector. I wondered if I was stupid for ever believing you." Her words struck with a power that only unbottled honesty could carry. "I pretty much hated you until about two hours ago. All those times I promised not to blow your cover, to keep you as part of the family, to not use your stupid journal. I went back to counseling a few years ago and I knew I had all this *rage* piling up inside me and it had to go somewhere. So I broke my promise. I took your journal notes and I channeled everything into this idea, of stealing your story and making it my own. I took your world and built something out of it, something to show how angry I was at you for everything. For not addressing your PTSD. For pushing soccer on me. For wanting me to be something else for the longest time. For disappearing on me when it felt like you *finally* understood me." Miranda swallowed hard and took in a breath, one that wasn't released for a good ten or fifteen seconds. "So yes, I did hate you. And I'm sorry I did that."

"I understand," Kin said, almost too reflexively. He had rage of his own, a seething fury that he wouldn't let anyone see—not Penny, not Markus, and not Miranda now that they were here. It burned underneath the surface, a venom directed straight at the TCB for making this decision for him, for all of them, despite his protests. He understood *why* from an objective perspective, but that didn't absolve them—just like how Miranda's feelings were justified.

And yet, the juxtaposition of the two somehow balanced each other out. It wasn't right, but at least it made sense. "I get it."

"Do you hear me, Dad? I'm sorry." A warm grip landed on his shoulder; it squeezed down and held itself steady over the bumps and grooves of the road.

Kin had wished for many moments with Miranda, to share life milestones and little victories and the ups and downs. But since the TCB built a wall between them, the thing he wanted most, even more than getting to know her, was her forgiveness. His defenses broke, and though he remained focused on the road, streetlights and passing traffic appeared through glistened eyes and rapid blinks. "Thank you. And I'm sorry, too. But I'm glad we can finally be honest with each other. About everything." He nodded to himself, and the weight of Miranda's hand seemed to counterbalance the emotional release that lifted a burden from both of them.

"We're almost there. Next right. Go up the hill, at the light."

The car angled around the bend, then twisted and turned up a steep hill for a quarter mile or so. On the horizon, a brick wall stood next to the entrance path. "It's okay," Miranda said, "they're open till midnight." As they approached the threshold, Kin's eyes adjusted to read the signage in the dark.

Oakland Memorial District and Cemetery.

CHAPTER 31

Kin and Penny kept their distance, huddling for warmth some ten feet back while Miranda knelt at Heather's grave. The wind carried only fragments of her muffled voice, and it wasn't clear if she was saying goodbye or explaining the situation.

Or both.

"I know I keep asking you if you're all right," Penny said. Her eyes peeked out beneath the brim of her hat. They'd remained incognito to avoid giving themselves away on any security cameras: hats, bulky coats, looking at the ground anytime a camera might be nearby. Her expression was strong enough to burn through all of that. "But are you all right? It's okay if you're not. This was…" Penny opened her mouth, though nothing came out for a good minute or so. "I mean, you were married. I'd think it's only natural to feel something. Don't hold back on my account. You're allowed to be human."

Miranda stood up, her shoulders bobbing in rhythm with the unintelligible words coming out of her mouth. She turned and gestured them to approach. "I only come here once a year. On her birthday," she said when they'd reached her side. "Before she died, she told me not to be one of those people who talks to tombstones. Said she'd be dust and bones at that point, to save my breath. So I never said much when I came. I just brought flowers." Even though Kin had told her repeatedly to look down as much as possible, she tilted her face up, lips locked in a wistful smile. "We don't have any flowers this time. So I finally talked. You should, too. Since you never had a chance to say goodbye."

"You think she's listening?"

"I think she's right about dust and bones. But the fact that we're together again might be enough for her to come out of hiding for a few minutes."

"She was defiant like that." Kin couldn't stop a grin from taking over. "She's probably standing here right now asking why I haven't seen *Star Trek II* yet."

"You haven't? Come on, Dad. It's the best one. Promise me you'll watch it someday."

Kin let out a short laugh. Breaking the most serious of moments to talk about some sci-fi show—truly her mother's daughter.

"I promise."

Penny leaned in for a reassuring squeeze. "Let's give you some space. I should get to know your daughter anyway, right?" She led Miranda away, their quiet murmurs carrying on the wind as they strolled the nearby paths.

Nerves had gotten the better of Kin plenty of times with

Heather, all across the spectrum, but never quite like this. With only dim cemetery lights around, Heather's tombstone was the same as the countless others around it. Some were plain, some were curved, and others came in more symbolic shapes. It took Kin kneeling down until the details became clear enough to see, though he could have guessed.

This was Heather, after all. Simple and square, he traced the carved letters with his fingers. Flashes of that last evening together came back to him, the fear in Heather's eyes as he'd tried to convince her that she must blindly trust him. After all they'd been through, that wild, terrifying moment was how it ended.

Now he got a chance to be honest with her.

Finally.

"Hi, babe," he said with a sigh. Back when she knew him, kneeling in this position would have burned his knees and caused him to stand up within thirty seconds. But here, he remained static, as if staying as still as possible would help broadcast the words to wherever she was now. "I probably don't have to explain anything now, huh? I mean, I hope that when you die, the truth about your deadbeat husband is revealed. Pretty harsh if it's not."

A breeze tickled the grass at his feet. Kin continued, sometimes rambling, and sometimes focused. His mind suddenly exploding with all of the things that he'd always wanted to say but couldn't. Somehow, of all the lists and visualizations he'd done across his life, "things to tell Heather after she died" had never been one of them; anything and everything came out, in no particular coherent order, a stream of consciousness that was part guilt and part excitement. Minutes passed, and the watch on Kin's wrist vibrated.

Time was up.

"I need to leave. Duty calls, and it still feels like there's so much more to say." He stared at the tombstone, the characters etched in stone failing to give him a proper response. Heather's voice rang out in his head, a loud room-filling laugh followed by the words he'd heard so much over the past eighteen years or so.

Stop overthinking things.

"I guess I just wanted to say that I'm sorry for all of it. For never being fully honest with you about who I was, where I came from. Only now can I see just how unfair every single decision was for you. We didn't know it then, but it was. It's funny, but the TCB was right after all about that. I changed things for you, without giving you a choice. That wasn't fair." He scrubbed a hand down his face and sighed. All of these things facing Kin and Heather and Miranda, stealing their choices and forcing them down new paths, often with a wake of rage and sorrow. But this one, the very first one, it was different.

Fair or unfair didn't matter. Only the result did.

"It might not have been fair, but look at her. Look at Miranda." He glanced over his shoulder, stealing a peek at Miranda and Penny locked in conversation, totally unaware he spied on them. "She's smart and strong and perfect. Like you, she's a survivor. I think we can agree—it was worth it, fair or not.

"I have to escort Miranda to safety now. I have no idea what her new identity will be but I know 100 percent that she'll be okay. Because she's your daughter. And I trust in that completely." He sucked in a breath, his mind searching for the final words. He drew a blank, not because of a chaotic whirl of last-minute ideas, but from the strange warmth that flushed him.

Was that peace?

Kin stood up, only a slight tickle in his knees compared to the familiar burn that had plagued him for years.

Nothing else was necessary. He knew Heather would have agreed.

Penny and Miranda were sharing a laugh when they noticed that Kin had returned. "I'm ready," he said, "and we should go." Miranda nodded, giving a long look back at her mother's tombstone.

"Actually," Penny said, "can I have a minute with Heather?" Her eyes darted back and forth between Kin and Miranda as she awaited an answer.

"Dad? I think Mom would want that."

Father and daughter watched as Penny approached the grave, her fingers fluttering in an awkward wave. In some other world with impossible circumstances, Penny and Heather probably would have chatted away, possibly bonding over all the ways Kin could be an annoying partner.

But here, while Miranda and Kin wanted to say goodbye to Heather, Penny simply took a minute to say hello. Somehow, that all felt right, at least until the shattered stabilizer injection came front and center into his mind. He blinked reflexively, as if that would make it go away, leaving only the miracle of this journey for the moment. Miranda glanced at him, her eyes sharp enough to betray that she understood something bigger was on his mind.

CHAPTER 32

In theory, things ended well. They'd traveled across time to find Miranda, but it was Heather who ultimately brought them all together. And after they each made their peace with that, they hit the road.

Which made the current mood seem a bit out of place. Tension ran through the car, freezing each of its passengers. They drove in silence toward the airport, making only a short pit stop to buy a burner phone for Miranda.

Was it the anticipation of the future? Regret for the past? Coming down from an emotionally charged and bizarre day in this present? Everyone in the car probably felt some mixture of all of the above.

Except the time for inner contemplation had ended.

The car motored down the off-ramp, one exit before the

airport. No particular destination came to mind as long as it was a quiet and safe street. Kin veered through the industrial section until he got to an area of empty business parks neatly lined up against one another. He pulled into a brightly lit but empty parking lot and settled the car to a halt.

"The next part is up to you." Kin reached into the glove box and pulled out the package of materials Markus had prepared for Miranda. Things that were impossible to accurately replicate in twenty-one-A—security seals, hologram patches—could simply be printed in the modern era. Markus, who falsified records as part of his job, often joked about how easy it was to create people, and now he had proof. "Passport. New identity. Birth certificate. Cash. Prepaid credit card. Basic paperwork and life history. Penny's brother has hacked official records to match. You exist, or at least this person does. Oh, and we bought a wig for you on our way to Davis." He handed the stack over. "Wherever you want to start a new life, you can. And when you get there, lay low for at least a few months. No social media, cover your face with sunglasses and hats as much as possible. After that, time and distance should keep you safe as long as you don't give them a reason to believe you're not you."

Miranda put aside the bob wig and flipped open the passport. "So now I'm—"

"No." The seat belt stretched as he turned to the back seat, palm up. "I can't know your name. I can't know your destination. I can't know anything. It's safer that way. Use that phone to call a cab for the airport. Buy your ticket, and go anywhere you want. It's a little past nine. You'll still have plenty of flights to pick from."

"My first step into a larger world," Miranda said while thumbing through her new life story. "Nice." Her face finally broke from its stoic mask, her mannerisms betraying a wistful melancholy over the smile on her lips. "Part of me still wonders if this is all a dream. Or maybe I got my drink spiked at dinner. I'm tripping right now, right?"

"I've felt that way for a few days," Penny said.

"It's just…" Miranda had maintained her tough shell, only allowing brief bursts of emotion to bleed through. With a new identity in her hand and the airport mere minutes away, the weight of reality must have applied too much pressure for her shields. "I've spent my whole life trying to figure out who you are. My project was like a therapy session wrapped in code. I finally have a chance." Her eyelids dropped, and then her brow squeezed, forcing little cracks to appear on either side. "Can't we, like, go get coffee together or something? Or you guys come wait at the airport with me? I mean, I just got you back," she said, her voice fighting through the words.

"I think that's a good idea," Penny offered quietly.

Life-or-death situations weren't anything new to Kin. Nor were permanent decisions. He knew how they felt, the wavering, the wanting more—the things training prepared someone for, only solidified through experience. This day, this mission, was about saving Miranda. His feelings didn't matter. "We can't take the risk. The TCB might spot us anywhere. Especially at the airport. If there's one place we'd get seen, it'd be there. They're not all-powerful, but they're smart. They don't have the resources to process everything all the time, so they'll scan for identity recognition in the geographic and temporal vicinity of an anomaly. They say there are at least seven people in the world at any time who look like you. Facial recognition is only one of the flags. That's why the airport is the finish line. Once you're away with your new identity and Markus falsifies your death records, there's no reason for them to keep looking. If everyone believes you're dead, they'll move on." Kin sighed, palms rubbing his face. "Then you can, too. You've got to be inconspicuous here, though, and having us with you only heightens the risk. Wear the wig, wear your sunglasses whenever possible, don't look up at any security cameras. One wrong move before we get there, and this is all for nothing."

"All for nothing," Miranda said. She held up the passport. "What if *I* want to assume that risk? So I can do something with my dad one last time?"

"I…" Kin's seat belt snagged as he turned back around. He pulled on it over and over until it finally loosened and sprang back taut. For Miranda that last meal together was more than a decade ago. It probably existed in flashes and smells, vague shapes and sounds. In Kin's memory things were a little more vivid, the details sharper and the volume louder.

For him it had only been a year ago, the gravity of everything capable of pulling the moon out of orbit. So what did it possibly mean for Miranda? "I—"

"I don't think this is your call," Penny interrupted. "This is your daughter's life. Like you said, she has a choice."

"I'd rather take a chance for this moment than spend the rest of my next life regretting it." Miranda's uncertainty gave way to something different now, a maturity mixed with the defiance that powered her words. She stared into the rearview mirror, the reflection of her eyes meeting his. "I need a chance to get to know you."

Kin wasn't like Markus. He didn't toe the company line with precision. He found rules to be guidelines, not unbreakable barriers. Still, this decision came with the highest risk.

And it was a risk that Miranda wanted to take.

After all they'd been through, he no longer steered this ship. His daughter did. "Well, then," he said, turning the key, "where should we go?"

"Actually—" Miranda pointed toward the passenger side "—it sounds like there's something Penny wants to try."

Kin had originally planned on being safely at the jump point with Penny by midnight. That would set them well within the window of when the TCB couldn't detect their jump; Penny would get safely home and he, well, he'd be a fifty-fifty shot at best without any immediate medical assistance.

Instead, they found themselves at an all-night fried chicken hut, picked bones and side dishes spread out on the table before them. The conversation didn't dwell on impossible futures or woeful pasts; instead, it might have been any family dinner, all happening with an ease that seemed like Kin had been there for Miranda's full life, not only half, and Penny was a permanent fixture, not a mere flash in the night sky.

They sat in the corner booth, faces covered by hats and high collars to minimize security risks. Despite the garb, Penny's smile was unmistakable. "I can't believe this food is legal."

"Dad hardly ever let us get it. He always insisted he could cook something better." Her voice dropped in pitch and she waved a mocking finger. "'Do you think the people on *Home Chef Challenge* eat this stuff?'"

"*Home Chef Challenge?*"

"A TV show I wanted to try out for." The gentle mocking led to laughter around the table, an impossible moment in time that couldn't be captured again except in memories. "And it's true. I doubt *Home Chef Challenge* contestants eat this. It's terrible for you."

"It feels so bad for you, but it's *so* good. The MOME exhibit doesn't even come close."

Miranda and Kin carried the same bemused expression

as Penny excused herself to look at the desserts. "So you go back to September eighteenth? Two thousand, one hundred, and forty-two," she said, her voice changing to a deep tone for each part of the future year before shifting back to normal. "It sounds so ridiculous to say that. I love it. So, what happens then?"

The return date. Classified knowledge. Kin's eyes went wide despite his best efforts to stay cool. "How did you know that?"

"Penny told me."

Kin could almost hear Markus freaking out about rules and corruption and guidelines. What was done was done, and Penny was lucky that her brother had to create a fiery fake-death-by-car accident rather than see her stomping over space-time boundaries. "She shouldn't have. Timeline corruption."

"Okay, what happens when you two go home to—" her fingers formed quotation marks "—'the future'? Resume life? Wedding plans? God, you must be good at that. Penny's restaurant? She mentioned getting a loan for that."

"Yeah," Kin said, after a long silence. "Something like that."

Miranda squinted, thoughts in motion as she bit down on her lip. "No." Her fingernail began a small rhythmic tap against the table. "No. Something's off."

"It's fine—"

"One of the first things you taught me about soccer was how to scan the other players. Their body might go one way even if they're looking another. There's always a little tell to figure out when they try to head-fake you, you said. Their posture or looking at their teammate or whatever. That's what you taught me when I was little, and I learned to use it my whole life, even after I quit soccer." She leaned forward, meeting him nearly eye to eye. "My bullshit detector. It's strong. And you're bullshitting me right now. You always either respond right away, like you've prepared a speech. Or you take too long, like you're drawing a blank. Either way you're hiding something. I sensed it when Penny was talking to Mom."

Bullshit detector. Everything about Miranda caused him to beam with admiration; if she had flaws, he certainly couldn't figure them out now. "The thing is," he said, glancing behind him, "I may not make it back alive."

Miranda sat, quiet and unblinking, the only sound coming from across the room as Penny inquired about the different desserts. "Are they coming for you?" she finally asked. "Will they be waiting to kill you, too?"

"Maybe. But that's not it. The human body's not meant to time travel. We support it with a bunch of different medications. My body's worse off than most because I was stuck here for so long. There's an injection I need after I jump back." His posture, which remained rigid and taut like an agent taking the field, began to slump as he explained the smashed syringe.

Miranda gradually sank in her seat before she shot back up with bright eyes. "Penny. Can't she help you? Like call an ambulance when you get there?"

"Penny is many things, but she's not a doctor. And an ambulance is all sorts of rule-breaking. But hey," he said, forcing out a smile, "you never know, right? Maybe my body decides it's got enough juice for one last go. We land, we're safe, we get married, and no one is the wiser."

A sway took over Miranda's shoulders, the smallest rocking to an unheard rhythm back and forth. He couldn't see it, though he knew she'd begun tapping her foot beneath the table. "Does she know?"

"No." The word came out with force.

Penny returned, bringing a silence over father and daughter. "You two sure you don't want anything?"

Miranda's snappy response covered up their grim discussion. "Trust me, the desserts are never good at fast food places."

"That might be," she said, "but a good historian researches her subject." Penny flashed a wide beam before returning to the counter. She leaned over, pointing to various items on the glowing display.

"Dad, you should tell her."

"I can't do that. I can't burden her with that. Not after everything we've been through. She has to have faith to get through this. I have years of training—this is all new to her."

"This isn't about faith." Miranda shook her head and gave him an unblinking stare. "This is about honesty. Knowing what you're getting into."

Penny returned with tray in hand, three small cardboard boxes subtly moving with each step. "I know, I know," she said as she set it on the table. "It's a might excessive. I figured, when else am I going to get the chance to try the real thing, right?" She slid back into the booth, planting a quick kiss on Kin's cheek and handing over plastic forks. "And I got a chocolate chip cookie for you. Come on, we'll share. Family style."

Miranda sent a knowing look his way, one that came and went so quickly it might have been a figment of his imagination. The glint of regret disappeared, replaced with a rosy grin sent Penny's way, and maybe that was Miranda's way of shielding her father from the inevitable.

They waited in silence. Ten minutes had passed since Miranda called a cab and gathered the few things they'd packed for her to take into her new life. They watched while she stood on the corner, counting down to the cab's imminent arrival.

Kin thought those final moments would be filled with heart-wrenching torment, a scratching and clawing to get one more second together. Yet while the emotions ran deep and the words came out a little blubbery, it lacked the drama of a Hollywood film.

Instead, he'd given her one final hug, a hold that lasted a good fifteen or twenty seconds, then dug into his bag to pull out an old copper coin. "For luck."

Miranda held it up, examining it under the harsh brightness of streetlamps. "This isn't going to cause timeline corruption?"

"No," Kin said with a laugh, "it's just a penny." They hugged again and a different kind of instinct surfaced, a parenting reflex reaching out. "You said you spent your whole life trying to figure out who I am. I'm sorry I can't give you more of me."

"You know what?" A clarity shone through Miranda's eyes, a deep and tangible focus tempered with the confidence that only wisdom could bring. "I know you're the type of person that will do anything to save the people he loves." She glanced at Penny, then returned to him. "In the end, that's all I need."

Kin nodded, his legs weak despite the ground solidly beneath his feet. "It doesn't go both ways, though. Whoever you become, whoever is in those papers, I can never know. I feel like I should ask you the four questions," he said as she blinked back tears. "But that, *that* would be all sorts of timeline corruption."

"What are the four questions?" Penny asked.

"When she was old enough to go places on her own, we

came up with a list of things we needed to know before she left."

"The questions." Miranda leaned in to give Penny a hug. "I'm having flashbacks now. Well, if I can't tell you, then you tell me. First question—where are you going?"

"We shouldn't say anything," Kin said. "Timeline corr—"

"That place in Santa Cruz," Penny blurted out, her voice muffled with her head still buried in Miranda's shoulder. She let go of her stepdaughter-to-be, then hooked her arm around Kin's waist. "You said you used to go hiking there."

"Point Davies?" Miranda asked.

Kin's fingers squeezed into fists, every word exchanged working opposite his agent directives. "Turns out, the reason I knew it so well is because it's a TCB jump point. I'd just forgotten."

"Who's going to be there?" The questions were directed to Kin, despite Miranda watching Penny's reaction the whole time.

"No one." The answer seemed neutral enough. "Just us."

"What time will you be home?"

"We can't say. And really, we wouldn't know."

A gust of wind blew past; Penny shivered and hugged herself before locking on to Kin's arm. "I'd like to see a sunrise from there. Wouldn't that be nice?"

Miranda opened her mouth for the fourth and final question and stopped midway. In the cold night breeze, he watched her huff air out to form small clouds that dissolved away. "In case," she started. Her lips pursed, and she turned away for a moment before recentering herself. "In case of emergency, is there anything I need to know?"

"No," he said. He met Miranda's eyes, his stoic surface covering up the creeping fear that he refused to acknowledge. "We'll be fine." His fingers drummed for a moment before taking Penny's hand and giving it a reassuring squeeze. "And you, you shouldn't give up on your dream. A new identity doesn't change who you are."

They had their final goodbyes and another round of embraces before Kin and Penny sat back in the car so Miranda could catch her ride without any threat of time travelers captured on the cab's security camera. The taxi pulled into the parking lot, and Kin's breath stopped as he scanned the situation before him for possible threats.

What if they'd been caught? What if Markus let things slip or they'd been tailed or somehow someone found out? The questions repeated over and over.

Then Miranda stood up straight, looked their way and gave a wave, and then got in the back seat. The cab pulled away, and as it passed, he could see she tracked them in return, her hands flattened against the window.

Not that long ago, he'd left his daughter for her own safety. This time he sent her away.

"Hey," Penny said. She leaned over and, despite the cramped quarters of the car, enveloped him in her arms. "You all right?"

"Yeah. I'm fine." And he was, at least in regard to Miranda. He'd never know what happened to her, never know the name she assumed or the life that she'd led. He only knew that he was there for her when it mattered. He'd swerved her away from certain doom and toward a second chance.

That was enough.

"Okay, then. Let's go home."

"Right," Kin said, starting the car. He stared straight ahead while the engine revved to its full power. "Let's go home."

CHAPTER 33

Miranda's words weighed heavily on him, reinforcing his urge to tell Penny what happened with the stabilizer injection. The truth was inevitable. The only issue was how and when.

"I've got it," Penny yelled as they'd reached the grove that doubled as the launch point. Her voice echoed up and down, all around through the cool night air. She grabbed Kin, her hands gripping his arms. "I've got it. I've figured it out."

Kin and Penny had hiked back through the Santa Cruz mountains, Penny's steps taking on nearly a victory-lap gallop. Other than a brief nap on the car ride, she'd chattered at a breakneck pace: Miranda was so great; time travel—wow!— and Markus had concerns, but they showed him; what kind of excitement they had, what a *crown* adventure, something that could bond them in a way no other couple might experience, and who needed a honeymoon after that!

As promised they left the car with a full tank of gas and remaining wad of cash stowed in the glove box and placed the keys under the large rock behind the sign. An hour up and around and through the brush and trees led them to the grove where they'd landed.

Where an EMT had helped stabilize Kin less than twenty-four hours ago.

If only he could take her with them.

"Figured what out?"

"The angle for the restaurant. The bank wanted something unique for the business plan. Mum and Dad have given me so much grief about that. I know Markus says it, too, I've overheard him. But now I've got it. I've been thinking about it since we dropped Miranda off. The food we ate, it was all savory and oily, but there was a very subtle hint of sweetness to it. Something you couldn't even detect if you didn't think about it."

"You're right," Kin said, reaching back into his memory. "I think I'd read something about how most fast-food places incorporated sugar into their foods."

"So, trans fats are illegal. Deep-frying is a dead cooking language. We know that the old ways are terrible for you. Modern methods have pushed it all out. It's never tasted the same as the old ways. Every cooking historian says that. The retro places, they're just not that good. Until now."

Penny looked up, the brightness in her eyes nearly uncontainable. "The Mars spices."

Kin thought back to Penny's dessert, all those nights ago. A rare balance of sweet and savory, something that required precision to truly bring it out. "The Mars spices," he repeated.

"Everyone's using it for desserts, for baking. Like my

mum." The words flowed out of Penny at a nearly incomprehensible pace. "But no, you could use it for entrées, too. The timing has to be perfect, but that blend, that flavor, it finishes the recipe. That's what I'm gonna sell. That's what will convince the bank. One taste and I *know* they'll approve the loan." Despite carrying a backpack on her shoulders, Penny threw herself at Kin, rapid-firing kisses at him until they lingered in one, her side filled with celebratory passion and his absorbing the sweetness before the great unknown. He held her, balancing the two of them on a dark path overlooking the Bay Area. Her laughter was broadcast out, head tilted back and hair swishing with the breeze. "We did it. We really did it. We saved Miranda and found my angle." She let out a holler, one so pure and direct it might have been detected in 2142. "Let's get home. I have a business plan to write."

Kin's metabolizer-healed body was capable of swirling Penny around, her laughter providing them with a triumphant soundtrack. Except there was still one thing she needed to know.

"Same deal as before, right?" Penny pulled out the equipment piece by piece while Kin programmed the accelerator for the time jump. "Kneel down, grab the handles, and don't let go?"

Kin punched in the arrival coordinates and leaned back to take in the view. This era was outside his jurisdiction of twenty-one-A, somewhere between his old life's near future and his new life's ancient past. Funny, then, that an out-of-time era for both of his lives would reunite him with Miranda, reconcile him with Heather, and probably be the cause of his death.

The zip pouch opened on the bag, and Kin pulled out the small case of remaining syringes—only two pre-jump boosters. Like before, he would administer the boosters, one to himself and one to Penny. Unlike before, though, he didn't have any post-jump instructions for her. "That's basically it."

"Wait a minute. Don't we need some shots after we land?"

"You don't. The transponders that the TCB planted in the ground make the jump back faster, more accurate. It puts less pressure on your body. You'll be fine. Healthy agents don't need stabilizers upon returning to the present."

Penny stepped forward. For the first time since they'd left Miranda, her face soured, moonlight casting harsh shadows across it. "But you're not healthy."

Kin nodded without looking back at her.

"So, what, did Markus not give us the right tools? I thought you went over this with him. Your plan."

"I did. And he did. He gave us the exact right amount." Kin jabbed the booster shot on his neck. Penny angled her neck, and he did the same to her. "No backup if one breaks."

The wind picked up, the rustling brush and dancing leaves the only sound between them. Penny knelt down, wrists propped on her knees and fingers folded together. "When did you know?"

"Right after we left the grove with that couple. I saw it on the ground when I was packing the gear. It must have fallen out of the case during the commotion. I think Alex stepped on it."

Penny's breathing was visible in the cool night air; it puffed out, first heavy and deep before coming in short bursts. "You didn't tell me."

"What good would it have done? It didn't change the mission. It would have only robbed you of this experience. All you would have done was dwell on it."

"Markus. We could have called Markus—"

"We didn't have time. We arrived too late."

"I'll call an ambulance right away when we land."

"No. If the TCB discovers you, then who knows what they'll do?"

"There has to be *something* we can do." Penny looked up, her hands slapping her legs to accentuate her point.

The rough skin on Kin's palms pressed against his face, dragging across the prickly stubble on his chin and jawline. "I don't think there is. Other than hope."

Penny stood and turned. In the darkness, Kin heard the heel of her boot grinding into the ground. "No," she said, and although her face remained hidden, the break in her voice made it clear that tears accompanied it. "It can't end this way. We've come too far."

"You know what Markus always told me. These are the rules. This is the job. We signed up for it." He walked up behind her, wrapping his arms around her and pulling her in tight. He half expected resistance, a show of defiance, but she gave in right away and sank into him.

"Fuck Markus," she said through a teary cough. "He's an idiot."

"Yeah."

They remained in silence for some time, two people folded into each other. Finally, Penny straightened up and faced him. "I'm not saying goodbye to you."

"This could be it."

"I know. Believe me, I know. Saying goodbye to you, that means I'm giving up. If this is the end, then this is how we do it. With hope." She nodded to herself, her hair swishing around as she repeated the gesture skyward. "We take risks out of love. My risk this time is holding on to hope. And I'm not letting go of that. We are going to go home. You are going to be fine. We are *doing* this."

Once again, Kin pulled her in with both arms. Their lips

met, and they shared the same air, taking the oxygen in with the urgency of a lifeline across space and time. Kin absorbed everything: the scent of her hair, the feeling of her fingers on his shoulders, the way she leaned into him when they embraced—it was all imprinted on his thoughts and memories. If this was it, it was the right way to go out.

"Okay," Kin said after they finally separated. He looked Penny in the eye, and she returned it, the moonlight revealing a piercing clarity from her hazel irises.

"Let's go."

CHAPTER 34

This time was different.

There was no blinding white light, no flashing of silent, disconnected images—no confusion.

Kin knew where he was. He knew when he was, or at least what they'd targeted and the way things looked. The night sky had begun its gradual transition to purple, pulling up the first bits of dusk color.

He remained horizontal, his head crooked against the brush and dirt of the hillside. He couldn't feel the details—no weeds pricked into his cheeks, no rocks dug into his hands—except a total sense of cold enveloping him. The sky blinked with the passing traffic lights of skycars, and the corner of his eye picked up the modern skyscrapers of the twenty-second century.

He was home.

A quiet groan emerged alongside him, its tone clearly feminine. He couldn't see her, but he knew Penny grunted and pushed her way to her feet somewhere out of sight. She made it, too. If he never regained feeling, if everything simply slowed down and faded to black, he at least knew that Penny made it back.

"Okay," Penny said. "We're here. We're here, and…" She came into view, kneeling in front of him. Her hands pushed her hanging brown hair repeatedly back over her ears, though it refused to stay up. "Kin? Kin, can you hear me? Oh, god— oh, god, you're not blinking."

Kin's view became a jumbled mess of clothing and shrubbery as, he presumed, Penny checked his vitals. "Breathing. I can't tell if you're breathing. Okay, first aid." The sound of cloth and fabric rustling muffled everything. He couldn't feel it, but he knew Penny tugged at his coat from the back and forth jolting of his field of view. "CPR, CPR, CPR," she whispered to herself, her hands scrambling left and right. "Okay. Okay. Here we go."

A slight pressure came and went, flashing through his body. It refused to stay, and despite wanting to claw, scream, and will anything out of himself, he remained silent and static on the ground. Even pain would be welcome at this point.

"Come on, come on." The pressure came and went again, its fleeting impact fading quicker than the last time. "You're not here. No breath. Come on. What do I do? What do I do? Markus, why couldn't you have come back with us?" She stood up, only her boots visible to him, and she paced in and out of his view. "Markus and his stupid rules." The feet spun toward him, and based on her tone, he knew the following words were directed his way. "After everything we've done, you're afraid of me calling an ambulance? For what? We need help." She came back into view. Her hands reached out; he couldn't feel her cold palms against his skin, despite knowing she held his head. "Okay. I don't know if you can hear me or not, but there's something I have to do. Bollocks to Markus's rules." Her voice maintained a steady cool, something that didn't exist even a few days ago in the same situation. "Bollocks to *your* rules. I'm going to—" She stopped suddenly, her neck craned over her shoulder. "Hey! Over here!" she called out, her voice echoing through the hills and down the canyons below. "Help, please! Help!"

She stood up, silent and tense with her head turned away. "Am I imagining…" she mumbled to herself. "Help," she yelled again, "over here!"

"Kin Stewart," a voice came in return—the same voice they'd heard before the jump. "I'm looking for Kin Stewart."

"He's here." Her voice wobbled as she jumped up and down, arms in full waving motion. "He's here, and he needs help! Hurry!"

Kin wanted to yell his objections, to tell her to stay quiet, remain hidden from a sure TCB trap. Who else would know it was him, here, now? His voice echoed in his own mind, filling the space with a silent scream.

Footsteps cut through the brush, going from a thin *pat-pat-pat* to a full-on stomp that crushed the foliage and kicked up dust clouds. The man knelt down beside him, his face out of view. "I'm a doctor. I was told to find Kin Stewart here."

"By who? Did Markus send you?"

"Markus?" His words flew out at breakneck speed, only eclipsed by his hands opening pouches from his backpack. "I don't know anyone named Markus." A small device beeped in his hand as he waved it over Kin's fallen body. "Brain swelling. Minimal respiration and circulation. Barely detectable by the scanner. Probably can't even see it," he said, snapping his fingers in front of his vision. "No reflexive motion. Come on, prognosis." The device beeped again, and the man focused in on the holographic text it projected. "Okay. That's it. A few more things. We can do this. Stabilize." More pouches and pockets opened from his bag, and Kin's whole world shook as the man jabbed him in the neck. He heard a hissing sound. "Eight…nine…ten. Okay, now this one." Another hissing sound came by, and within seconds a familiar pounding hammered Kin's temples.

It was the best headache he'd ever had in his life.

Pins and needles soon came to his fingers, and he remained horizontal. He could feel—feel!—a massive weight on his chest, a tension that turned his whole musculoskeletal system into a closed fist. "Pen…ny," he squeezed out. He couldn't tell if she heard him or not.

The man rolled him onto his back, and the star field above him consumed his view. The man waved the device again, its blue-and-yellow lights illuminating his face. "Right. Right. Respiration and circulation are back to normal. Inflammation is decreasing. We're halfway there. We only have to bring down the brain swelling. Just a few more…"

His voice trailed off as he dug into his backpack and pulled out a palm-sized device. A small cord popped out from its side, and Kin felt the man tug on his wrist. He pressed the cord up against Kin's wrist, and a high-pitched noise cut through the air, followed by a sharp piercing pain. "All right, Kin. Hang in there. Let this do its thing." Penny crept into view, hovering over the kneeling man. Her face stared at the glowing lights of the device while it pumped some sort of chemical combination into his system.

Color dripped back into his vision. Not that he'd gone color-blind during the last few minutes, just that everything seemed brighter and more vibrant, like the stars and blinking skycar lights might burn into his retinas if he lingered on them long enough.

Kin stayed on his back, breaths slow yet regulated. He looked at the man, finally able to see his face. Something about it seemed familiar. He was a little older than Kin, perhaps sixty or so in metabolizer-based years, and Kin was sure that if he had his full faculties, he'd be able to place this man.

Who was he? TCB medical staff? That meant that someone must have leaked their mission. Only if the TCB was monitoring for elimination, why did they have him stabilized?

Unless this was about Penny.

"Penny," he said, pressing his palms against the cold dirt and flexing his arms. His neck muscles burned, rusted gears barely cranking up for a better view to scan for threats. "Run."

"What?" Penny said, catching herself from looking skyward. "Kin, don't get up. You need to rest."

"She's right," the man said. He gently pushed Kin's shoulders to guide him down, but Kin resisted with what little strength he summoned. "Give yourself some time. The pain and stiffness will go away in ten or fifteen minutes."

"No," Kin said through gritted teeth. "Penny, run." The muscles in his shoulders felt seared as he pushed the man off, a burn flaring under his skin and down to the bone. "Run," he huffed out, "this man's here to kill us. The AD sent him." Penny's mouth dropped, and Kin mustered all his strength to throw the man down and lock his arm behind him.

At least he tried to.

In reality they both fell to the ground with Kin's hand clumsily gripping the man's wrist. "I'm not going to hurt you," he said, his voice muffled against the dirt.

"Bullshit. Penny, go."

Instead of listening to Kin, Penny came over with a tentative step. "Who are you?" she asked. "Why are you here? Is this a direct order from the AD?"

"Who is the AD?" The man coughed into the ground. "I'm here to help, I swear."

Kin readjusted his weight, his strength returning enough to try to hold the man down with meaningful purpose instead of dumb luck. "Who sent you?"

"My..." The man turned his head, dirt peppered on his cheek. "My grandmother. I made a promise to my grandmother."

Kin's grip on the man's wrist loosened, and he looked over at Penny, whose expression changed from determination to shocked curiosity. "Your...grandmother?" she asked.

"I promised her. When I graduated med school, she asked me to do the strangest thing, but I promised her. She told me to remember four answers to four question. Kin Stewart. Point Davies. After sunset but before sunrise. Come alone but with emergency medical treatments."

"Four questions..." Penny said, her voice barely audible. *The* four questions.

"That was forty-two years ago," the man said. Kin let him go and stumbled back onto his heels, only to have Penny catch him. The man pushed himself up to his feet and dusted himself off before kneeling back down to meet him face-to-face. "You are Kin Stewart?"

"Yeah."

"She wanted to give you this." He reached into his pocket, and it took several seconds for Kin's eyes to adjust enough to clearly see what the man held up between his thumb and finger.

A coin.

Even in the dim light, he could see it. The bit of oxidation on Abraham Lincoln's hair. The etched "1978" by Lincoln's lapels. The scratch across the top half of the dull surface. "Her—"

"Lucky penny," they all said in unison. Kin took the coin, reflexively giving it a quick kiss, then handed it to Penny.

"She recorded a message for you about six months before she died. The holo is a little old. I kept it in a safe for years." The man reached into his backpack and produced a small black rectangle. "I changed the battery this morning, and I swore to her I wouldn't play it until it got to you." He laughed to himself and shook his head. "I thought I'd probably be camping tonight—I can't believe you're actually here. What she asked was so...*specific*."

The man pressed several buttons on the bottom of the device and then set it down in front of them. A beam of light flashed out before a light blue oval flickered to life, resolution lines trailing up and down.

Old holo tech, probably from the turn of the millennium or before, back when it was more of a 3-D projection than a hologram. Despite the occasional visual hiccup or distortion, the woman before them was clear.

It was Miranda.

Not the Miranda he knew. Not the wily teen or the confident woman they'd saved. This was a Miranda with decades of life etched into the wrinkles of her face, her once-black hair withered into short gray waves. She smiled, her mouth pushing into well-worn crevices that only years and years of use could produce.

She looked happy.

No, it wasn't happy. He'd seen her happy countless times, and her expressions repeated themselves throughout her life, despite age and maturity. This was more than happiness. He leaned in, allowing the image to burn into his mind until everything clicked.

This Miranda, the elder version of the girl he once knew, was content.

"Hello, Dad. When I left you and Penny, you saved my life. If you're seeing this, then I've finally been able to return the favor." She paused, taking a breath and looking off center. "I hope Penny is with you right now. Hi, Penny."

The awestruck stare on Penny's face broke into something softer, something that matched the little wave she offered the glowing holo. "Hello, Miranda," she said softly.

"Miranda?" the man said.

"Name change. Long story," Kin offered while lingering on his daughter's image.

"And so here we are," she said. The image talked straight into the camera, and although she barely moved, every syllable felt full of life. "It's a Saturday. January 2, 2103. I lived to see the millennium. I'm in a little village outside Bath. This is where I lived after a few stops in London, Paris, Manchester, and London again. I even learned to like coffee with honey. Oh, and I want you to know my name. I know you said you couldn't know it. Well, I've lived a full, good life. Ask the young man—well, I suppose he's not that young anymore, but ask the man who brought this. My grandson, Julius, the doctor. He's going to graduate from med school in a few months. Ever since he told me he wanted to be a doctor, I thought about this. I thought about you. I suppose I'll never know if this actually gets to you. It'd be nice to get a simple yes or no answer. Guess you have to leave some things to mystery, right?

"So now we meet again. The most important thing for you to know is that I was happy, I am happy, and I owe that to you. And any messages or money or whatever you might send my way might alter that, so please don't do it. I don't want to change a single thing. I only want you to know what I did with my life. You understand, Dad? I'm giving you a chance to learn who I was as long as you don't try to rescue me. Not anymore. I don't need it. And I think—I hope—that's good enough for you. Deal?"

The image of Miranda lingered, and it took several seconds for Kin to realize that the visual was on a short loop of her waiting. "Oh," Julius said, "her note said that you had to make a decision. It's programmed to detect your answer."

Everything taken from them, everything risked in a literal race against time, all of that was now on the table. Kin could learn her identity, and if fate somehow gave him the opportunity to jump *one more time*, he might see her again. Maybe even more than that.

Except that wasn't what she wanted. In fact, the very temptation might jeopardize the life she had lived. Her question pleaded to control her own path for once, to finally free herself from the external forces imposing their will on her fate. And it meant that by agreeing to her terms, he would let his daughter go.

But in a way, he'd finally be letting her in.

Wasn't that the point all along?

Kin let out a quiet "yes," as if the projection was a portal across time rather than a recording.

The holo resumed, Miranda offering a warm smile. "Thank you. I'm so glad. When I left you, I became Veronica Bamford. Bamford. I miss that dog."

Bamford. Of course—Markus picked the name.

"I bought a ticket to London with nothing but a passport and cash. I'd always wanted to go to London, you know. That night I started fresh. I lived to see a cure for cancer, but unfortunately not those wonderful metabolizers you talked about. So you can't win them all." She gave a short laugh and looked off for a moment, perhaps wondering what those metabolizers might have done for her if she'd held on for another decade. "That day I began my second life, and here is how it unfolded…"

They stayed for the next hour, Kin, Penny, and Julius sitting around the glowing holo like an electronic campfire. "There's one more thing," Miranda said. "There's only so much I can fit in this recording. But since we parted, I've wondered how I could tell you everything. Then it dawned on me. All those years ago, when I used your journal, I thought I did it out of spite. It wasn't that. I realized that deep down, under all the hurt and anger, I just wanted to have a piece of you with me. Now it's your turn. Julius, the box."

Julius stood up and motioned Kin over, then flipped open his bag before pulling out a small black cube, something that neatly sat in the palm of his hand.

"I've worked on sixteen video games in my career. Taught programming for eight years at two different schools. Yet I think this is my greatest accomplishment. Not just to hear me tell it or to see holograms, but an interactive experience so that you can live it. My life *after* my life ended, that is. Almost like being there." Miranda smiled, the creases in her face seemingly lightening with the gesture, then faded out of existence, leaving them only with the pinks and blues creeping into the light above them.

Kin took the cube from Julius. A single button sat at the base of one side, and when he pressed it, a floating image illuminated the space around them.

An airport terminal.

Near the bottom of the holo sat glowing blue characters: *11:59 p.m. August 28, 2030.* An arrow appeared on the image, and Kin tapped it with his finger, setting forth a virtual walk toward the gate. The holo moved through Miranda's virtual eyes, and Kin angled the view around, pausing on the sign next to the window.

Departure for London, England / HEATHROW.

Penny crouched down next to him, one arm wrapped around his shoulders. Her cheek brushed against his, and he could hear her suck in a breath as she looked.

"We went through all of this to give her a chance to live," Kin said. He hit the cube's power button again, dismissing the hologram before clutching the black box against his chest with the delicate tightness of holding a newborn baby. "And because of it, I'll finally discover who she really is."

They remained in silence, sinking into the moment: a quiet morning on a hillside, the culmination of moments that spanned a century and a half. But now, finally, it was finished.

Julius turned to Kin, his voice dry. "That was her story. But that doesn't explain you. She called you 'Dad.' You're younger than me. And how did she know to send me here?"

"This is where Markus usually says something about the rules," Penny said, her head still on Kin's shoulder.

"I think we can throw the rules out this time."

"The rules." Penny's nose wrinkled as she looked Kin's way. "We heard Julius's voice before we made the jump. So he was already *here* before we went *there*. Isn't that some sort of paradox? The grandfather thing?"

Kin scanned the scene before them: a clear view of sky-car traffic in the distance. The last gasps of darkness before dusk. City lights twinkling away below them. No giant holes ripping open the space-time continuum, no implosion of the universe or the destruction of everything they knew, no sudden appearances from TCB's Paradox Prevention squad. "Well, either the space-time continuum is about to collapse or things are going to be okay. Who knows?" A breeze ruffled through the air, causing the blades of grass and thin weeds to sway around them. "Either way, don't tell Markus." From the wisps of light over the horizon, Kin guessed it was coming up around six o'clock. "Sorry I tried to choke you out."

"He did that to my brother, too," Penny said with a smirk. "Welcome to the family."

CHAPTER 35

Kin used to be a time-traveling secret agent.

That was easy compared to the task he had to complete tonight.

Veronica's eyes opened with an intensity that belied the far-too-early time. She'd squirmed for a few minutes, rolling left and right with limbs doing everything except staying still. When Kin tried to get one leg down, the other kicked up; when both settled down, arms flailed up. The act of putting pajamas back on after changing a diaper proved to be as tough as chasing criminals across time. And no amount of planning or visual scanning would help.

This little one had some fight in her. And a grimace to match.

Kin knew the expression well. She'd only been around

for five weeks, though he and Penny had learned Veronica's cues and tics, and the big, bright stare meant that the newborn was mere seconds away from a hunger cry.

Above her bassinet, an image of Miranda watched over Veronica—her half sister, technically. The old-fashioned picture frame reflected the moonlight creeping in from the angled window blinds—vintage, they called it these days, with physical prints trendy again. Two images of Miranda greeted him; the left frame holding her high school portrait, the Miranda that he'd left; and in the right frame was an old woman, life aged into her wrinkles and smile, the image captured off the holo she'd made during her final days. In between the two sat a weathered old coin. The sight of it relaxed him, and on instinct, he kissed two fingers and planted them on the penny, just for luck.

Some things hadn't changed since the first time he became a father. For him, only about sixteen years had passed since he first gave bottles to Miranda as a baby, but from the perspective of the world, a century had come and gone. Kin tested the bottle's temperature on the underside of his wrist before setting it on the dresser and peering into the crib.

Veronica wriggled on her back, gurgling noises swapping in and out with the heaving of infant cries. "I know, I know," he said, picking her up and giving her a little bounce. "I'm not Mom. But it's my turn, and bottles are almost as good as the real thing." His words didn't seem to satisfy Veronica, and the volume turned up on the tears. "Shh, come on. This move worked all the time on Miranda."

Bounces and sweet talk didn't offer any consolation to the crying baby, so Kin went straight for the good stuff and grabbed the bottle off the dresser. "I don't take offense. I cry when I'm hungry, too." Thirty minutes passed, the only noise coming from the baby swallowing each gulp. "You think that's good," he said halfway through, "wait till you start eating solid foods. There's this restaurant that books tables weeks in advance but I know the chef. I can get you a good spot." Before the bottle was empty, Veronica passed out, mouth half-open and hand clasped around Kin's pinky finger.

Penny appeared, or at least her pajama-wearing holo did in the nursery's communication panel. She pointed to Kin and offered an inquisitive yet silent check-in, eyebrows raised with a hopeful thumbs-up. Kin nodded and mouthed "go back to sleep." Penny smiled and mouthed the words "love you" before disappearing.

He could put her back down in her crib; Veronica was thankfully a sound sleeper, unlike Miranda at the same age. But Kin had learned to appreciate these little moments in time, even middle-of-the-night bottle-feedings. The baby moved in his arms, shifting her weight and turning up over Kin's shoulder as if she wanted to see the lucky penny. Her eyes opened and shut in a flash before she returned to sleep, though he felt wide-awake despite the hour.

Perhaps he'd finally watch *Star Trek II.*

Yes, perhaps he would.

He chuckled to himself, just loud enough for the infant's eyes to flutter. With the past and future surrounding him, Kin leaned back in the chair, Bartók's *Rhapsody No. 1* playing softly. A smile emerged as he rocked back and forth with Veronica.

After all, the here and now was a fine place to be.

★ ★ ★ ★ ★

ACKNOWLEDGMENTS

First off, thank you for reading!

Books aren't created in a vacuum, and that's doubly true for debuts. It's a long road from idea to agented to published with many people to thank on this journey...

To Mandy, my companion in the TARDIS, thank you for putting up with me in so many ways, including the strange solitude required for writing and editing. Also, thank you for being awesome. You are truly an N7-class partner.

To Amelia, thank you for simply being you. I hope you inspire stories forever.

To my nonwriter friends and family, I know I hardly talk about book stuff but thank you for your support during our awkward conversations about it. Guess I'm gonna have to get used to it.

This book would not exist without two great publishing professionals: my agent, Eric Smith, who believed in this book even when I didn't (and who sends me coupons for video games), and my editor, Michelle Meade, who had an infectious enthusiasm for this story from day one while pushing the manuscript further (and rightly having me cut subplots).

Thank you to my writing support team: to Sierra Godfrey, who has been there since the beginning and suffered through some truly terrible manuscripts. To TeamRocks past and present in all our waterfall glory—laughs, venting, advice, Seinfeld gifs, and Canadian candy (the last two courtesy of Rebecca Phillips). Also, extra thanks to Diana Urban, Sangu Mandanna, Laurel Amberdine, Dave Connis, Rebecca Enzor, and Samira Ahmed for fast reading and feedback. To my gripe-and-write pals, thank you so much for listening and supporting, particularly Jessica Sinsheimer, Kristen Lippert-Martin, and Randy Ribay (and our weekly In-N-Out cheeseburgers).

Extra special thanks to Kat Howard, whose impeccable insight really unearthed the heart of this story.

To Idris Elba, Jenna Coleman, Karen Gillan, Arthur Darvill, River the Dog, and Akasha the Cat, thanks for starring in the movie of this, at least the one in my mind.

To everyone behind the sci-fi stories that have powered my thoughts and dreams my entire life, thank you. *Allons-y!*

Finally, years ago in Olson Hall at UC Davis, my creative writing teacher Wendy Sheanin encouraged me to switch majors from Mechanical Engineering to English after the quarter. I didn't, but she still offered one more nugget: "Keep writing."

Thanks Wendy, I took your advice. Hope you've enjoyed the result. (Go Ags.)